"An extraordinary novel, which makes a long-vanished culture seem urgent, contemporary, and alive. Wishnia gets the nuances just right: The Yiddish is used perfectly, and the religion, politics, and prejudices of the old German empire are as real and believable as if they were behind our television screens."

—Sara Paretsky, author of *Hardball*

"The author's breathtaking scholarship clearly delineates the many religious and political factions of the day, the arguing and infighting within each one, and the deep-seated and rabid anti-Semitism of the time. There is also considerable wit in the telling and an engaging breeziness to Benyamin's portion of the narrative." —*Denver Post*

"Whatever you are currently reading, I promise you it is not nearly as intelligent, witty, compelling, or entertaining as *The Fifth Servant* by Kenneth Wishnia. A great protagonist, a vivid set of supporting characters, a winning voice, a gripping plot, and a lively historical context—this book is the total package. Too many historical novels try to make textbooks come alive. Wishnia makes *history* come alive."

—David Liss, author of *The Devil's Company* and *The Whiskey Rebels*

"Well-developed characters and detailed portrayals of life at the time help make this historical crime thriller a gripping page-turner."

—*Publishers Weekly* (starred review)

"In his fiercely intelligent and entrancing novel, *The Fifth Servant*, Kenneth Wishnia gives us a sixteenth-century Prague that is rich, labyrinthine, and utterly compelling. Drawn in first by its soft wit, we soon find ourselves swept into a tale both intricate and haunting, its twists and turns carrying us breathlessly to the very last page."

—Megan Abbott, Edgar Award–winning author of *Bury Me Deep* and *Queenpin*

Bob Hall

About the Author

KENNETH WISHNIA has a Ph.D. in comparative literature, and has been widely published in various academic forums. His crime fiction has been nominated for the Edgar and Anthony awards. He teaches composition, literature, and creative writing at Suffolk Community College. He lives with his wife and children on Long Island.

www.kennethwishnia.com

The Fifth Servant

KENNETH WISHNIA

HARPER

NEW YORK · LONDON · TORONTO · SYDNEY

HARPER

A hardcover edition of this book was published in 2010 by Willam Morrow, an imprint of HarperCollins Publishers.

HarperCollins books may be purchased for educational, business, or sales promotional use. For information please write: Special Markets Department, HarperCollins Publishers, 10 East 53rd Street, New York, NY 10022.

FIRST HARPER PAPERBACK PUBLISHED 2011.

Designed by Lisa Stokes
Map by Nick Springer, Springer Cartographics LLC

The Library of Congress has catalogued the hardcover edition as follows:

Wishnia, K. J. A.
   The fifth servant / Kenneth Wishnia. — 1st ed.
      p. cm.
    ISBN: 978-0-06-172537-1
  1. Jews—Czech Republic—Prague—Fiction. 2. Inquisition—Fiction. 3. Murder—Investigation—Fiction. 4. Prague (Czech Republic)—Fiction. I. Title. II. Title: 5th servant.
   PS3573.I875F54 2009
    813'.54—dc22   2009013166

ISBN 978-0-06-172538-8 (pbk.)

11   12   13   14   15   WBC/BVG   10   9   8   7   6   5   4   3   2   1

For a thousand unknown ancestors
whose names have come down to us as
Fink, Greenberg, Passoff, and Wishnia

shammes—*n* [Yiddish *shames*, fr. MHeb *shammash*, fr. Aram *shemmash* to serve] 1: the sexton of a synagogue

shamus—*n* [prob. fr. Yiddish *shames;* prob. fr. a jocular comparison of the duties of a sexton and those of a store detective] (1929) 1 *slang:* policeman 2 *slang:* a private detective

—*Webster's Third New International Dictionary*

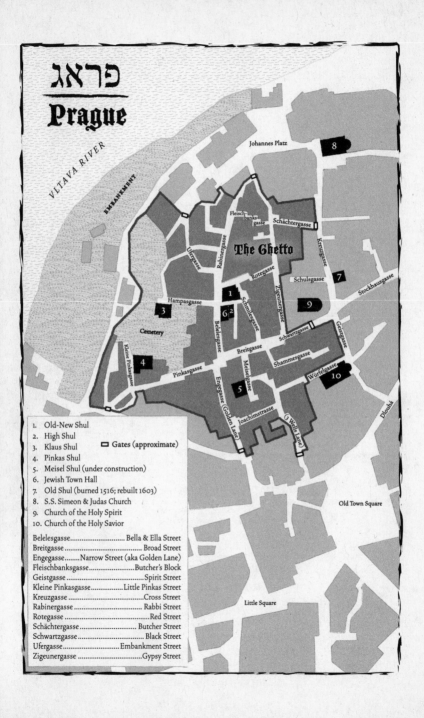

פראג

Prague

VLTAVA RIVER

EMBANKMENT

Johannes Platz

8

Fleisch-
banks-
gasse

Schächtergasse

Kreuzgasse

Ufergasse

Rabinergasse

The Ghetto

Rotegasse

Schulsgasse

7

Stockhausgasse

Zigeunergasse

1

3

Hampasgasse

6 2

Schmiesgasse

9

Belelesgasse

Schwartzgasse

Cemetery

Breitgasse

Schwartzgasse

Shammesgasse

Geistgasse

Kleine Pinkasgasse

4

Meiselgasse

Würfelgasse

10

Pinkasgasse

5

Engegasse (Golden Lane)

Joachimstrasse

(6 Wells Lane)

Old Town Square

1. Old-New Shul
2. High Shul
3. Klaus Shul   ☐ Gates (approximate)
4. Pinkas Shul
5. Meisel Shul (under construction)
6. Jewish Town Hall
7. Old Shul (burned 1516; rebuilt 1603)
8. S.S. Simeon & Judas Church
9. Church of the Holy Spirit
10. Church of the Holy Savior

Belelesgasse............................Bella & Ella Street
Breitgasse..Broad Street
Engegasse........Narrow Street (aka Golden Lane)
Fleischbanksgasse........................Butcher's Block
Geistgasse..Spirit Street
Kleine Pinkasgasse.................Little Pinkas Street
Kreuzgasse......................................Cross Street
Rabinergasse.....................................Rabbi Street
Rotegasse...Red Street
Schächtergasse............................Butcher Street
Schwartzgasse....................................Black Street
Ufergasse....................................Embankment Street
Zigeunergasse.................................Gypsy Street

Little Square

AUTHOR'S NOTE

ONE OF THE MANY PROBLEMS facing me as I wrote this book was how to present the dialogue, which represents conversations in Yiddish, Czech, and German.

I found the answer while reading a Yiddish translation of the Book of Jonah. You know the story: God calls on Jonah to tell the people of Nineveh to stop their wickedness, but Jonah flees from his duty to God and boards a ship. God raises a storm, and all the sailors start praying to their various gods and tossing cargo overboard, but the storm doesn't subside. Then the ship's captain discovers Jonah asleep in the hold. At this portentous moment, instead of giving a high-minded warning about the wrath of God, the captain says, *"Vos iz mit dir?"*

I couldn't help laughing when I read that passage because it seemed like an incongruously informal statement under the circumstances—literally, "What's with you?" So I checked with Professor Robert Hoberman, a linguist at SUNY Stony Brook, who confirmed that the phrase in the original Hebrew was quite common, colloquial, and very modern sounding.

That served as my guiding principle: the idea that these late sixteenth-century people were speaking a language that sounded perfectly ordinary to them, although I still needed to find a compromise between the excessively archaic and the jarringly modern. (And if some readers feel that phrases such as "Somebody must have blabbed" sound too modern, I would point out that Chaucer used *blabbe* in the 1370s. Other examples include "protection" money in several sixteenth-century sources, legal "cases" from the fourteenth century, and "witness," which dates to the tenth century.)

This solution can also be found in contemporary foreign-language translations of Shakespeare, which deal with the same problem by modernizing obscure, archaic, and obsolete words in the source language (Elizabethan English), rather than by supplying an equally obscure word in the target language, such as an "equivalent" medieval French word in a modern French translation.

So there you have it. If I can cite translations of the Bible and Shakespeare as supporting examples, what more do you want from me? Now *geyt gezunterheyt*. Translation: enjoy.

—K.W.

I form the light, and create darkness:
I make peace, and create evil:
I, the Lord, do all these things.

—ISAIAH 45:7

פרײטיק

Freitag

Pátek

Friday

CHAPTER 1

A DISTANT CRY WOKE ME.

I sat up and looked out the attic window over the sloping rooftops on the north side of Broad Street, which the German-speaking Jews called the Breitgasse. It was too early to see the horizon. The city and sky were an inseparable mass of darkness, and the scream's dying echoes evaporated into the air, like the breath I could see coming out of my mouth.

I was in bed with two strange men—the *mikveh* attendant and the street cleaner—and the room was damn near freezing. It was spring by the calendar, but it was still winter at heart, and I could feel in my bones that it was going to rain, like it did every year on the Christian holiday of Good Friday. I'd have bet five gold pieces on it, but there weren't any takers, and I didn't have five gold pieces. If you turned out my pockets, all you'd get for your troubles would be a few lonely coppers and some mighty fine lint imported all the way from the Kingdom of Poland.

But something had jarred me awake. Like it says in the *Megillas Esther*, the king found no rest, so I listened intently, the fog of sleep still swirling around in my head.

Muffled and ghostly, a distant cry floated over the narrow streets of the Jewish Town:

"Gertaaaaaah—!"

Goose bumps rose on my arms, as if the spirit of God had blown right past me and withdrawn from the room. If a Christian child was missing from its bed we were sure to be accused, and all of a sudden I was reduced to being just another Jew in a city that tolerated us, surrounded by an empire full of people who hated us.

Did I come all the way from the quiet town of Slonim just to get butchered by a bunch of latter-day Crusaders? And if the Jews got scattered, or worse, I might never see my wife Reyzl again.

Acosta's shadow filled the doorway. "Hey, newcomer, *shlof gikher, me darf di betgevant.*" Sleep faster, I need the sheets, said the night watchman, his rough-edged Yiddish softened by the rolling *R*'s and open vowels of his Sephardic accent.

"Did you hear that shouting?" I asked, planting my feet on the cold floor. "Any trouble out there?"

"You just stick to your morning rounds and let the watchmen handle it, all right?"

My knees cracked as I stood up and groped around in the darkness for the pitcher and basin.

Seven people crammed into two beds. Three men in one, a family of peasants in the other, part of the yearly crush of country folk visiting the imperial city for the week from Shabbes Hagodl to Pesach. The country folk had washed their bodies for the Great Sabbath the week before, but their clothes still had the overripe tang of a barnful of animals.

The night watchman took it all in and said, "What, there wasn't room for the goat?"

I had to cover my mouth to keep from laughing. It wasn't good to joke around until I chased away the evil spirits that had settled on my hands during the night, and said the first prayers of the new day. Fortunately, the rabbi in Slonim had taught me how to get rid of the invisible demons by washing them off my hands in a basin of standing water.

Every year on Shabbes Hagodl, we listen to the Lord's words to His servant Malakhi: "Behold, I will send you Elijah the Prophet before the coming of the great and dreadful day of the Lord." Then we watch and wait for a mysterious stranger who appears around this time of year and asks to be seated at the

Seder. And woe to the family that turns the stranger away from their door! Because he just might be the herald of the Messiah himself.

Such is the faith that has guided us through so many narrow scrapes. When the Romans destroyed the temple in Jerusalem, we rebuilt the temple out of words and called it the Talmud—a temple of ideas that we can carry around with us wherever we go.

And so we outlasted the Roman Empire, and we'll outlast this empire, too.

The watchman pulled off his boots, grabbed his share of the blanket, and was snoring by the time I faced the eastern wall and said my morning *Sh'ma*. I paid special attention to the part about teaching your children the word of God in order to prolong your days and the days of your children.

Halfway down the crooked stairs to the kitchen, I could hear Perl the rabbi's wife issuing orders to the servants to scour the house for *khumets*, the last traces of leavened bread. So there were no oats or porridge or kasha to keep my stomach from growling, only a mugful of chicken broth and some stringy dried prunes. Hanneh the cook shouldn't waste a piece of good meat on the new assistant shammes.

I warmed my fingers on the tin mug, while pots clattered and doors slammed all around me. Despite the noise, I overheard Avrom Khayim the old shammes telling the cook, "What do we need a fifth *shulklaper* for? Like a wagon needs a fifth wheel."

But—wonder of wonders—Hanneh actually stood up for me and told the old man that the great Rabbi Judah Loew knew what he was doing. She had heard that the new man from Poland was a scholar and a scribe who had only been in Prague a few days, without a right of residency, when the great Rabbi Loew had seen a spark of promise in him and made him the *unter*-shammes at the Klaus Shul, the smallest of the four shuls that served the ghetto's faithful.

Maybe Hanneh was thinking of her own husband, dead these many years, because she ended up stirring the ladle around the big pot and giving me a boiled chicken neck. I thanked her for this, one of the first signs of kindness anyone in this strange new place had shown me.

I sucked the bones dry, then went to the mirror to clean the *shmaltz* off my beard, and noticed with some resignation a few prematurely gray hairs curling around my temples. But I thought of the disembodied screams that had roused me from my bed, and suddenly a few gray hairs didn't seem like such a bad thing.

I found the master putting on his short *tallis*.

"What should we do, Rabbi? Should we prepare for an assault?"

"Just attend to your duties, Benyamin Ben-Akiva," he answered. "God will show us the way in due time."

So I grabbed the big wooden club and went to chase the spirits out of the shul.

THE KLAUS SHUL STOOD in the elbow of a disreputable side street between the Embankment Street and the cemetery. I listened for the sound of spirits rustling about, then I raised the club and pounded three times on the narrow double doors and told the spirits worshipping inside to return to their eternal rest. I dug out the big iron keys, which jingled coldly in my fingers, found the right one, and opened the shul for *shakhres* services.

I traded my thick wool hat for a linen yarmulke, and stood on the platform in the empty shul and chanted a Psalm that was supposed to keep the restless spirits at bay. The melody wavered in the chilly air. I never claimed to be a cantor.

Back outside, I listened to the silence and prayed that it wouldn't be shattered by the sound of boots and breaking glass. Then I doubled back and headed east along the Schwarzengasse to the far-flung Jewish houses outside the ghetto on Geist and Würfel Streets in the Christian part of Prague.

When the limits of the ghetto were established after the Papal decree of 1555, several Jewish households fell outside the line of demarcation, including what was left of the original Old Shul, and the rebellious Bohemians were content to ignore the shrill voices demanding that every single Jew in the city be relocated within the gates. But none of the Jews were more than a minute's dash from the main gate, just in case they had to retreat inside the ghetto to seek shelter from the gathering storm.

Maybe it was fine for the Jews of Prague, but I wasn't used to being cooped up like this, behind a wall.

The watchmen were still changing shifts. The night men looked beaten and tired, but their tightly drawn faces betrayed their agitation. And yet somehow I was still hoping to finish up early and go see Reyzl before she got too busy helping her family prepare for Pesach, which fell on Shabbes eve this year, when all work had to stop a half-hour before sunset.

Women carrying heavy tubs for spring cleaning sloshed soapy water on the steps of their homes and onto the newly laid cobblestones. I had to dodge a butcher's apprentice holding a big basket of meat on his head and step around the masons chiseling away at the paving stones. Then I nodded to another shammes, who was out collecting "wheat money" so the poor visitors would have matzoh tonight. Two Jews were handing sacks of flour to a couple of Christians to store the forbidden *khumets* for the next eight days.

The big eastern gate rose up in front of me. Penned-in with no place to go, the Jews had built one house on top of another along the narrow streets of the Jewish Town. After a few years away from city life, I'd gotten used to the grassy paths and open pastures outside Slonim, which calmed my spirit and helped me talk to God. How could a man talk to God on a street like this? I mean, besides a cry for help.

"Stop right there!"

The gatekeeper laid a hand on my chest.

"Where's your Jew badge?"

"My what?"

"Listen, stranger, you've got to wear the Jew badge whenever you leave the ghetto. You got that?"

"Yes, sir."

I hurried back to the house with the stone Lion of Judah over the doorway and persuaded one of the Christian servant girls to take a moment out of her busy morning to sew a bright yellow ring on my cloak.

We don't have such things in Slonim.

I rushed back to the gatekeeper, who let me through this time, now that I was wearing the *gelber flek*, the yellow stain required by an imperial decree— the *Reichspolizeiordnung*.

The street outside the ghetto was quiet compared to the Schwarzengasse, with only a few whores and drunken soldiers refusing to call it a night, crossing paths with clear-eyed kitchen maids and shopkeepers with pink cheeks as round as apple dumplings. They all looked harmless enough, but I knew very well how the sunniest Christian faces could turn mean in an instant once an accusation is made.

I avoided eye contact as I walked down the Geistgasse, crunching over a thin layer of frost that had settled on the old stones. And I almost jumped out of my boots when a couple of rats scurried around my ankles, joining a slithering mass of rodents swarming over a piece of fallen meat. I've seen plenty of field mice in my time, but these city rats were *huge*.

Hoofbeats rang off the pavement, and suddenly the rats scattered as a horse-drawn cart clattered over them and came barreling right toward me. I jumped to the side and the cart thundered past, nearly crushing me beneath its wheels, the driver violently whipping his horses while his big-boned helper held on for dear life. They just missed flattening a tiny Christian servant girl as the heavy cart swung east onto Stockhausgasse and rattled away.

My heart was pounding, and I hoped that no one had seen the panic in my eyes.

Bohemia was relatively safe for the Jews these days, certainly safer than the other parts of the German Empire, where Protestants and Catholics had been furiously fighting for control of the soul of Europe ever since the reformists broke from the Roman Church a few decades back. And for a while it seemed like a good plan to just step back and let them fight each other, but we have a saying in Yiddish: A cat and a mouse will make peace over a carcass.

And spring is open season on Jews. Holy Week and Eastertide were especially risky, and a gambling man would say that we were long overdue for some old-fashioned Jew-hatred. Every year the Jews got thrown out of *somewhere*. The lucky ones merely got beaten up, had their property stolen, and escaped with their books and the clothes they happened to be wearing at the time. But one Easter a while back, a mob of enraged Christians had practically burned down the entire Jewish Town, leaving only the blackened stone shul and a few crummy houses that refused to fall over. Three thousand people murdered in one weekend, all because some idiot said that a Jewish boy had thrown a handful of mud at a passing priest.

Some say it was worse than just mud, but I don't believe that for a minute. What Jew in his right mind, outnumbered by hostile and well-armed outsiders, would invite such trouble?

When my ancestors first set foot in the land of Babylonia, they didn't rush around smashing the idols, they made the place their home and wrote the monumental Babylonian Talmud there.

The Bohemian capital was as alien as pagan Babylon in many ways, but I knew enough to move closer to the wall and yield to a couple of footmen in red-and-gold livery walking a pair of sleek black dogs. Despite my good faith effort to get out of the way, the dogs' ears flew back and they lunged for my groin. I stepped back once again and found myself pressed to the wall with nowhere to go, and before I knew what I was doing I had taken a fighting stance, with the big wooden *kleperl* raised and ready to clobber the first dog that came at me.

The footmen laughed.

"Don't worry, they don't like Jewish meat. Isn't that right, girl?"

The dog snapped at my privates.

"I don't know," said the other one. "She seems to like the smell of kosher salami."

Reflex had gotten me into this. What was going to get me out? *Think, man, think.*

"Go ahead, Jew. I'd like to see you try."

I didn't understand Czech very well yet, but I got the general idea.

The dogs strained against their leashes, but the footmen were well mannered enough to hold them back. It sounded like one of them called the dog Miata, but I might have heard wrong.

I slowly lowered the club, searching for the right combination of words to placate these lackeys.

Finally, I said, "Forgive me for startling your master's dogs."

My *poylishe* Yiddish was close enough to the local dialect of German for the footmen to understand me, and they seemed satisfied. They nodded curtly and strolled away, patting the dog and saying "good girl."

So that's how it was. A couple of spoiled livery servants could taunt me like that and I couldn't respond. I could have broken the two of them in half if they didn't have those dogs with them. And some rich man's coat of arms on their sleeves. And every Christian in the kingdom watching their backs.

I was still considering this when I heard the cry again:

"Gertaaaaaah—!"

Closer this time.

I pounded on the doors and windows of all the houses and shops with mezuzahs on the doorposts, calling *"In shul arayn!"* and asking if anyone knew anything about the missing girl. Was Gerta a woman or a child? But nobody had any answers for me. Some of the shop doors rattled loosely, their locks clearly worthless.

I turned into the Würfelgasse. In the middle of the narrow lane, two children four or five years old, a boy and a girl, took turns shooting marbles into a chalk circle.

As I called on all the Jews to come and serve the Creator, a pair of women's voices answered from opposite sides of the street. The children obediently got up from their game and went in to their mothers, the boy through a doorway marked by a mezuzah, the girl through a doorway with a cross nailed squarely in the middle of the upper frame.

So young and compliant, I thought, smiling to myself. They haven't learned to be difficult yet.

They haven't learned to think of all human relations in terms of what language you pray in or how much gold your family has to buy friends in high places.

Because you can only buy fair-weather friends.

That's why Rabbi Shemaiah says, "Love work, hate authority, and don't get friendly with the ruling powers," because no matter who's sitting on the throne, all those petty lords and nobles just use your friendship when it serves their needs, but they do not stand by you in the hour of your need.

Just look at Emperor Rudolf II's grandfather Ferdinand, who expelled the Jews from Bohemia, even though he *gave his word as king* that he would never do so.

Back on the lower Geistgasse, a middle-aged Christian woman with a dark blue headkerchief was banging on the door of one of the Jewish shops I'd just called to shul. She looked up at the second-floor window, then went back to rattling the flimsy door. Another woman, who must have been the proprietress, stuck her head out of the upstairs window.

"What can I do for you, *pani*?"

"Are you open today?"

"Sure, sure. Until noon. I'll be down in a minute."

I was halfway back to the East Gate when a bleary-eyed Jew and a pair of Christians beckoned to me.

"Come join us," said the Jew. He was trying to open his door with a key that was far too large for the narrow lock.

I didn't budge. "Join you doing what?"

"Is there something wrong with your eyes? Can't you see that we're celebrating Purim?"

"Purim was over a month ago."

"Can I help it if I celebrate Purim a little more often than other Jews?"

I turned to go, but the Jew spread his cape wide and blocked my path.

"We, sir, are entertainers to the lords and burghers, and only a gawking newcomer from the provinces would fail to recognize the great Shlomo Zinger and his associates. Professional merrymakers, *a su servicio*."

"We also do weddings," said one of the Christians.

"And when we see a man looking troubled"—Zinger patted my cheek with sloppy familiarity—"it is our sworn duty to cheer him up."

"Taanis, folio twenty-two A," I said, reflexively citing the Talmudic passage in which Elijah the Prophet announces that two humble jesters will have a share in the World-to-Come because they are helping people to forget their troubles.

"Ah yes, I heard you were a scholar," said Zinger.

"You did?"

"The *Yidnshtot* is big, my friend, but word gets around just like in a small town. A promising disciple of the great Isserles and some other Polish rabbi, who tossed it all to come after a woman. That's the stuff of romantic ballads, mate."

"No, it isn't. She hasn't spoken to me yet."

"Don't worry, she will." He leaned in closer. "We also heard that one time you fought off six men at once. Six big, drunken Cossacks."

The other Christian said, "Is that true?"

"Well, no," I said. Actually, I had *talked* my way out of that one, but as a newcomer to this town, I figured I could use the reputation.

"It was only *five* Cossacks. And two of them were kind of scrawny."

The two Christians looked genuinely disappointed.

"Listen," I said. "Do you know anything about—"

Zinger nudged me as a young woman with long black tresses and broad Slavonic features walked up to the East Gate carrying a basket.

"That's the little mouse's *Shabbes goye*."

"The who—?"

"Mordecai Meisel's sabbath maid. The big *makher* who built the hospital, the orphanage, the *mikveh*. He paved the streets. Pretty much owns your ass, too, Mr. Benyamin from Slonim."

"Oh. Listen—"

"You want to come in and see our costumes for Sunday's feast at the Rožmberks?"

"No, I need to get back in time for the *Amidah* prayer—"

And just at the moment when I should have been somewhere else, a woman's scream pierced the morning air.

CHAPTER 2

ANYA HATED KILLING PIGS, especially when it took a couple of tries to hit the main artery. Cows and sheep were finished in a moment, if you did it right. But pigs *knew*. They knew you were trying to slit their throats and they didn't understand what they'd done wrong, or why they deserved it. She felt their animal incomprehension when they struggled to get away from the glistening knife, and heard it in their plaintive squeals. Sometimes she swore she could even see it in their faces.

She hated it even more when her father asked her to help do it when it was still dark outside.

"Let me finish doing my braids first," she said.

"No time now. Do it after."

So she tied her hair back with a kerchief and ran downstairs. The pig was tied up in the courtyard, and her father Benesh was sharpening the long knife. She pushed up her sleeves, and tied a butcher's apron around her waist.

When he was ready, she gently wrapped her arms around the animal's shoulders, took hold of its front legs and hugged it tightly, bracing herself.

"Why so early?" she asked.

"The cart came through early."

He closed his fist around the pig's ears and prepared to cut its throat. The animal bucked and squealed, but Anya held tight.

She couldn't help thinking of the *shoykhet's* blessing before the *sh'khiteh*— the swift cut to the neck meant to minimize the animal's suffering.

Borukh atoh Adinoy, eloyheynu melekh ha-oylem . . .

When it was over, Benesh wiped the bloody knife with a rag. Not like the crude men who wiped the blood on their sleeves and spent the day surrounded by swarms of buzzing flies. He took some pride in his appearance.

Anya wiped her hands with the rag, and helped her father lift the carcass onto a slotted table so he could gut it. But first they had to carry a fresh side of beef into the shop. Benesh grunted from the effort.

He said, "We need you to marry someone quick. I'm getting too old to haul a side of beef onto the slab by myself."

He was half-joking, but the joke had been going on for a few months now. Still, she tolerated it.

She said, "Yes, father," tossed the bloody apron into the washtub, and went into the kitchen to wash her hands before they got too sticky.

Her mother Jirzhina was rolling out the dough for *knedlíky*, special Easter dumplings.

"Anya, I need you to hang this up for me," she said, nodding toward a bun with a cross baked into it.

Anya washed and dried her hands. She took a knife, got up on a stool, and cut down last year's Good Friday bun. Then she hung the new one from the ceiling to protect their home from fire for another year.

Her mother told her to open the shop and sweep it out.

Anya said, "I'm supposed to be at the Meisels' place as early as possible."

"Why do they need you? It's Friday."

"It's Pesach. It's their Easter."

"Their Easter starts on Friday?"

"At sundown. They asked me to help out today."

Her mother considered this. "They pay you the same?"

"Yes."

Jirzhina shrugged. The Jews paid well. But still.

Anya said, "What?"

"Nothing. Janoshik said he might be coming by."

Anya said nothing.

"You don't like him?"

"He's all right, Mama. But sometimes he can be such a *balvan*, like he's got rocks in his head."

"Better a boring man who stays with you than a thrilling horseman who leaves you with a baby."

"Don't worry, Mama."

"I'm not worried about you. It's them."

Jirzhina aimed her rolling pin at the street, where drunken mercenaries were passing by, singing dirty songs.

Legions of foot soldiers, *Reiters*, and musketeers from the Turkish front had swarmed into Prague on Holy Thursday, and hadn't wasted any time tearing the town up. Fortunately, the town was big enough to absorb the shock, Anya thought. She told her mother that she would be careful.

She went upstairs to finish braiding her hair, but there wasn't time for that now. So she gathered her long black hair and tied it back with a lace ribbon. She had to look good for the rich folks. Back downstairs, she put on a clean apron and opened the shutters and the heavy wooden door to the shop.

The neighbors were already yelling at each other, Ivana Kromy's shrill voice cutting through whatever protests her husband Josef barked at her.

Anya wondered how people could be so angry with each other before they even had their morning porridge. It took most people a good part of the day to build up to a fury like that.

She swept out the rear of the shop, keeping an eye out for the beggars who relied on true believers like Benesh Cervenka for a bit of Good Friday generosity. She also watched out for thieves and other lowlifes who thought that the best cure for warts was to steal a slice of beef, rub it on the afflicted area, then toss the beef down a privy hole, so that when it rotted, all their scabby warts would fall off.

Why couldn't the recipe start out with *buying* a piece of beef? No, it had to be stolen for the magic to work properly.

She felt the floor shift under a man's weight, and she turned around. Janoshik was leaning on the counter, a toothy smile on his round peasant face.

"Hey, cutie. Want to go see the pageant in the Old Town Square?"

Anya said, "Sorry, the Meisels need me today."

He was disappointed. "You're always working for those *Zhids*."

"They're not so bad. And it's only one day a week."

"Right. And that's supposed to be Saturday. Today is Friday."

She explained for the second time this morning that today was a special day for the Jews.

"Seems like everything's special if it's about them," he said. "So what kind of spells do they use to clean their meat?"

He meant the koshering process.

"No spells. They just soak the meat in water, drain it, sprinkle it with coarse salt to remove the blood, then wash it a couple of times. That's it."

"There's no way that that's it. They've got secret magical words for everything."

"They just praise God before they do anything."

"So now you know Jewish prayers? Who's teaching you?"

"Janoshik, please—"

"No, really. I want to know where you're learning all this Jewish magic."

"They say the same ten words about fifty times a day, that's all. I'm used to hearing it."

He glared at her.

She said, "They kill a cow, they praise God. They cover its blood with dirt, they praise God. They wash their hands, they praise God. They cut a slice of bread, they praise God. They take a wizz—they praise God. Get it?"

"I get it. You're turning into a secret Jew."

Her reply got sucked right down her throat. He might as well have accused her of killing cattle with sorcery. The Church moved swiftly against anyone accused of "Judaizing" beliefs, and the punishment was death by public burning. How could he say such a thing so carelessly?

She swept the floor with renewed furor, thinking about the way the Catholics had been sweeping through Bohemia, reclaiming the land for the one true faith. One powerful sweep sent the pile of dust swirling into the gutter.

She was putting the broom away when a fragment of a faraway plea floated past her ears:

". . . ertaaaaah . . . !"

Anya stopped what she was doing.

"Anya, let me—"

She shushed him, but the cry was not repeated.

"Anya, I didn't mean . . ."

To what? Accuse her of heresy?

Her father brought in a tray of meat from the newly killed pig.

She said, "Excuse me, I have a customer."

She had several customers. An old woman bought a slice of beef liver so thin you could almost see through it. A kitchen maid named Erika, on her way back from the fish market with a basket full of eels, selected the best cuts of pork for her master, Janoš Kopecky, one of the richest burghers in the neighborhood. A couple of old beggars came for a handout while Janoshik stood and watched silently. A tipsy cavalryman picked out a couple of eggs and counted the coins into her hand so slowly Anya thought he was going to pass out on the street, until she realized that he was taking his time so he could look her over with an expert eye. Fine. Let him look.

She even gave a coquettish swish of her behind as she walked to the back of the shop to get some fresh pork.

A Jesuit priest in a long black cassock stopped and stared.

When she came back carrying a side of ribs, the priest raised an accusing finger. "Aren't you supposed to be closed today?"

"Protestants buy meat, too, Father."

The priest stepped up to the counter. He was relatively young, but Anya saw that he was as stone-faced and humorless as any fossilized Church elder.

"I suppose you have a dispensation to sell to Hussites and Utraquists?"

What did he want? Money?

"What is it, Anya?" Her father stepped into the shop, wiping more pig's blood on a rag.

"I'd like to know why you are open for business on the most somber day of the year."

"People like to buy for the next day, Father."

"That's not what she just said."

Anya lowered her eyes from her father's sideways glance.

Janoshik cleared his throat. "Say, father, isn't there a law that says Jews can't have Christian servants working for them?"

Anya felt a cold needle prick her heart.

The priest looked at Janoshik.

"Yes, my son. The Holy Fathers have issued more than one decree condemning that absurd practice. But we all know it still goes on," he said, looking around the shop with renewed suspicion.

Benesh tried to assure the priest. "Father, we are simple Christians. We close at midday, then we'll go to Mass, do the stations of the Cross, and have fish *knedlícky* after sundown."

The neighbor's door burst open. Josef Kromy was still yelling at his wife. Something about his breakfast not being hot enough. Then he slammed the door and stormed off.

Anya used this momentary distraction to step into the back and slip off her butcher's apron.

Benesh poked his head in the back room.

He said, "If there's any of that meat the Jews want to get rid of because the animals aren't quite kosher enough . . ."

"Yes, father. I know."

She hurried down Haštalská Street toward the Jewish Town, thinking about the mess she had left behind and how much of it would still be waiting for her when she got back at the end of the day. Then she heard it again, a howling like a trapped animal:

"Gertaaaaaah—!"

CHAPTER 3

AND SHE KEPT ON SCREAMING, whoever she was, shrill screams rippling through the air, shredding the brief moment of peace on this gray morning. My feet sprang to life, carrying me toward the disturbance.

Zinger grabbed my sleeve. "Don't go, mate. It's bad stuff."

But I had to go. The uproar was at a Jewish shop, and as the only shammes at the scene, it was my duty to respond, preferably before too many Christians got there.

I just wished I had some beeswax to stuff in my ears, because that woman was screaming like one of Homer's own high-pitched sirens. I sprinted back down the block, dodging all the whores and mercenaries who turned to gape at the wide-open doorway. She kept screaming as a swarm of rats spilled over the stone lip of the doorsill, fleeing discovery. She kept screaming, drawing the night-weary street people and the early morning housewives together in a strange consortium of people not usually associated with one another, thanks to their common enemy in the form of a tall Jew running freely through their territory.

The woman must have paused for breath, then she started screaming again, only this time transforming her inarticulate shrieks into hateful words that cursed the Jews for their eternal evil. Faces—bleary, wide-eyed, and curious—filled the windows on both sides of the street.

The rats scattered in my path, leaving thin traces of blood with their tails. I kicked some of the vile creatures out of the way, stepped over the melting footprints in the frost, and pushed past a couple of onlookers standing frozen to the spot at the threshold to the store.

I recognized the hysterical woman as the same one from before with the dark blue kerchief on her head. She must have been in the middle of doing her morning errands. Carrots and flowered herbs spilled from her basket as she flailed her arms like a broken windmill, threatening red-hot irons and worse for the perpetrators of this crime against Christendom, while the terrified proprietress begged her to stop her infernal wailing.

On the floor between them lay the body of a blond girl, maybe seven years old, her shift torn and bloody, her face waxing pale in death. I checked the impulse to kneel close and touch her, just to make sure, to see if there was any warmth left in the poor creature. But I couldn't do it in front of an hysterical Christian witness. No point in making a move like that.

I've seen a lot of people get hurt in my time, so I noticed that most of the blood on the girl's nightshirt was drying to a rusty brown, but some splotches of dull red looked quite a bit fresher. It looked like she had lost a lot of blood, but there wasn't that much on the floor around her, as if she had bled out somewhere else before being deposited here.

Ill-tempered foot soldiers pushed me aside to get a look.

"What's all the f—?"

"Oh, good God—!"

"Christ!"

I looked around the shop. The stock was mixed. Bolts of coarse linen filled the lower shelves, fine fabrics sat safely on the shelves near the ceiling, and jars of apothecary's herbs and powders stood behind the central counter. Crates of exotic feathers left little room to move around.

The women of the night joined the outcry.

"Let us have a look, you slobs."

"Yeah, shove over."

"Sweet Jesus—!"

Now the walls were quaking. I almost expected to see them split open to the sky, but it was only two sets of hurried footsteps tramping down the stairs outside.

A couple of the mercenaries roughed up a worried-looking Jew as he squeezed between them into the store, then they groped and cursed at a young woman who must have been his daughter as she passed between their burly shoulders.

The man had well-trimmed fingernails and streaks of gray in his hair and beard.

He said, "What's going on, Freyde?" But one look at what was on the floor and he turned a sickly shade of gray.

His daughter's hand flew to her mouth, and it looked like she was going to puke, but she held it back.

"What took you so long?" his wife said.

"I was in the middle of the *Sh'ma*. And Julie was—"

"You're the owner?" I asked.

"Yes."

"Jacob, *do something*," his wife said.

He was going to need more than a *Sh'ma* to get out of this. Jacob took a step forward.

"Keep away from the girl!" the Christian woman screamed.

Jacob held out his hands and begged her to calm down. A mercenary with dark circles under his eyes told him to keep his filthy hands off good Christian women.

I had to alert the rabbinical authorities, but I couldn't leave the shopkeeper's family alone with these trained killers. They may have been tired and hungover, but they were waking up fast, and I'd need more miracles than the Maccabees to take them on by myself. There wasn't enough room, for one thing.

Jacob looked at me for support. "Any prayer for this kind of situation?"

Now everyone was looking at me.

All eyes fell on my Jew badge.

The soldier with the dark circles unsheathed his sword. Two more brawny fighters followed his prompt. The bald one drew a short stabbing sword out of his belt, the one with a scar over his left eye, a spiked mace. They spoke as if acting out a scene they had rehearsed and played out many times over the years.

"You'll pay for this, Jew."

"I'll cut off your horns for a trophy."

"Let's start with the old fart."

They might as well have been wearing carnival masks and reading lines from the crudest anti-Jewish folksplay, like the *Judenspiels* of Endigen or Oberammergau—except that I was sure that none of them could read.

That was a possible way out, if I could manage it.

The killers advanced on Jacob, taunting him with their swords. The third one raised his mace and splintered off a chunk of countertop, just in case Jacob had misinterpreted their intentions.

It was time to cast in my lot. I stepped between the sword points and their target.

"You gentlemen had better hold your peace, unless you want to face the consequences of breaking the emperor's laws."

The men slowed, puzzled.

"Don't tell me you haven't read the emperor's laws!" I said, amazed at their lack of preparedness. "Then it's a good thing I got here in time to keep you from getting in trouble with the law, because the statutes clearly state that the Jews are granted permission to live in these lands as vassals of the emperor. That means we are his servants. We belong to him. And the imperial code dictates severe penalties for anyone who willfully damages the emperor's property."

They weren't sure what to do about this. The pikemen looked at each other for assurance, clearly not used to feeling doubt about their actions.

Jacob's daughter Julie finally said something. "Yes, yes, it's true. We belong to Kaiser Rudolf II."

Whisperings rippled through the crowd. Could it be? Was it possible? They weren't going to listen to some smart-mouthed Jews, were they? Hell no! Kill them all, God will know his own.

A woman standing at the periphery yelped as a gruff stranger elbowed her aside. The man shoved some more gawkers out of the way and planted his boots on the threshold. I had never seen the badge on the man's left pectoral, but I had no problem recognizing the unmistakable attitude of a member of the municipal guards.

"Uh-oh, Kromy's here," said one of the whores.

"Come to collect your Good Friday freebie, Josef?" said another.

Josef Kromy looked at her. "Better keep it warm till Monday."

The women tittered.

Kromy glanced at the remains of the lifeless girl. The rodents had left teeth marks on her arms, and tiny paw prints in the dark stains on the floor around her. He displayed no shock, no revulsion.

I wondered how many depraved crimes the man had seen for him to have no visible reaction to such a scene.

Kromy said, "Somebody want to tell me what happened here?"

The woman with the blue kerchief said, "I found her. Oh, it was horrible. I made that woman come down and open the door, and there—"

Freyde Federn said, "I've never seen this child before. When I came downstairs to open the door, the lock was broken."

"Which stairs did you use?"

"There's only one set of stairs, Mr. Kromy, the ones outside the house."

Kromy said, "Let's see this broken lock." He waved a couple of dumbfounded observers aside, and examined the main lock.

"Doesn't look broken to me," he declared.

Freyde fumbled for the words. "I mean that the door was unlocked, and I'm sure I locked it when I closed up last night."

"Then why did you say the lock was broken?"

"Because they're all liars," said a woman with bright red lips.

"Hang the bloody lot of them."

Jacob spoke up. "I opened the shop later on to get something. I might not have closed the latch properly."

"*Ach!* What Jew wouldn't make sure his gold was safely locked up for the night?" said the woman with the kerchief.

Kromy's lip slowly curled into a lopsided smile. "Trouble always seems to find you, Federn," he said.

"He knows something about this," said the woman.

"Anybody know who the girl is?" said Kromy.

One of the housewives crept in close enough to get a good look at the victim's face. "*Pane bože!* It's Gerta Janek!"

"Who's that?"

"Viktor Janek's little girl."

"Oh my God, they've been looking for her all morning," said one of the women.

"Janek the apothecary?"

"Yes."

The housewife said, "I saw Janek and the Jew arguing the day before yesterday in front of this very shop. But I never thought—"

"What were they arguing about?"

"What do all businessmen argue about?"

Kromy nodded. He looked around the shop, taking stock and fingering the fine goods.

"Getting back at the competition, Federn?"

"It wasn't me, I swear," said Jacob.

"You just said you were the last one in here, Federn," said Kromy.

"Enough talk. My dagger's hungry for blood." The dark-eyed mercenary evidently had a flair for the poetic. The other two raised their weapons again.

I said, "Remember what I told you about the Jews being under the direct protection of the emperor?"

"Oh, yeah," said the dark-eyed one. It had slipped his mind.

"Who's this fellow?" said Kromy.

"The new shammes," said Jacob.

"Nobody's asking you."

"Come on, Kromy," said the woman with the red lips. "Everybody knows the Jews kill a Christian every year so they can mix the blood with their filthy Passover bread. All we want's a good hanging out of it."

"Upside down, with dogs," said the one with the mace. An ugly laugh escaped from his throat.

Kromy said, "My orders are that all criminals are to be arrested and held until a proper trial. Don't worry about the ladies while you're in the stocks, Federn. I'll keep a close watch on them for you."

He eyed the women hungrily.

I said, "This is a matter for the imperial guards, not the municipal guards."

"That's for the sheriff to decide, Jew."

"Then, by all means fetch the sheriff."

CHAPTER 4

Janoš Kopecky's lowest kitchen maid, Erika Lämmel, was washing her hands when the soap slipped from her fingers and dropped into the basin.

"Oh, no. That means death," she said.

"Silly girl," said one of the older maids. "How could something that happens all the time mean death?"

Erika muttered under her breath, "People are dying all the time."

Two cavalrymen came in by the kitchen entrance. The maids rushed to get food and drink ready for them, but they demanded bread and salt first. Erika served it to them on a wooden tray.

"So how's about a kiss for a couple of gallant heroes heading back to the front?"

She blushed. They were such dashing knights, defenders of the land and faith. Exciting, and just a little scary, like all the *Reiters*.

The cook interrupted with the master's orders. Erika was to buy fresh eels at the fish market, the choicest meat from the butcher shop, and stop off at the apothecary's for a packet of medicinal herbs.

Erika was confused. Why the eels? Only the Papists had to obey the restriction against meat today.

"Nobody asked for your opinion. He feels like having eels today," the cook said.

The other maids snickered. The fish market was the lowliest duty imaginable at this hour of the morning.

Erika hurried through the dim streets, sidestepping boisterous soldiers with uniforms still stained from the battlefield, who laughed about how skittish she was. She passed the day laborers from the countryside gathering at Haštal Square without a word, and headed up Kozí Street to the waterfront. She could already hear the ferrymen hawking driftwood for heating and cooking fires, and smell the river.

The Jews sold fish cheaper, since the Christian merchants always raised the price on Good Friday. But despite her mistress's kind feelings toward the Jews, Erika wasn't about to brave the foul streets of the Jewish ghetto to save a few pfennigs. Her master could afford it.

The river was high with the early spring flood, and the waterfront was busy. She worked her way past a barge unloading cattle and barrels of wine, gave a wide berth to the longshoremen hauling crates of Italian figs, and paused for a moment at bins of Flemish brocade and cheap gray cloth from Poland. At the fish dock, heaps of carp wriggled hopelessly, mouths agape, still alive after many hours out of water.

The big man unloading a crate of eels looked her over. His eyes were cold, emotionless, like an eel himself. He could see that there was a female body under those gray skirts as she walked toward him. Erika was nearly seventeen, but she looked about twelve. Thin and mousy, with stringy brown hair as dull and coarse as a straw broom. His thick lips curled up into that half-smile that some paintings are famous for. He'd have whistled at her, but the seamen would have blackened his eye for raising ill winds.

Erika asked about the eels.

The man said, "I've got a big, slippery eel for you, honey. Come into the shed and I'll show it to you."

Eww. She found another merchant to buy eels from. Men were such . . .

The sound of iron-rimmed wheels ringing on stone caught her attention. A gilded carriage clattered across the square, a coat of arms ennobling its polished doors, accompanied by four mounted escorts, two in front, two behind. No doubt about the position and privilege of the person inside *that* vehicle. She pictured him as young and handsome, naturally. Unmarried. Rich. Clever.

Able to see the true value of a woman despite her outward appearance as a lowly kitchen maid.

In a moment the carriage was gone.

Her basket got much heavier at Cervenka's butcher shop. She struggled to carry it, and counted the steps to the apothecary's shop and back to Master Kopecky's townhouse on the Langergasse.

A traveling preacher who called himself Brother Volkmar stood on a corner near the Old Town Square preaching in plain German, instead of the stupid old Latin the priests used, which nobody understood. Erika put down her basket and rested her arms.

The preacher earnestly berated the passersby. He said the correct reading of Scripture showed that Jesus stood with the powerless against the oppressive lords, the rack-renters who loaded poor peasants and bondsmen with bridge tolls, highway tolls, tithes, clerk's fees, city taxes, imperial taxes, war taxes— in return for what?

His hair was long and dark, his speech fiery and passionate. Don't believe what the Papists say about the Jews, either, he said. Every Easter they remind us how the fiendish Jews killed our Savior, to keep us angry and afraid, to keep us divided, so we won't join with the Jews against our common oppressor, the Roman Church. We must reach out and enlist the Jews in our battle. Dr. Martin Luther said that Christ Himself was born a Jew, so we must deal kindly with them and instruct them in Scripture. (He was beginning to sound like her mistress.)

Of course the Jews refuse to embrace a Church wallowing in the filth and stink of corruption, from the selling of offices and indulgences, to the slanderous blood libels against the Jews, and the arrogance and obstinacy of its clergy, when any common Bohemian peasant woman knows her Bible better than the most pompous Papist priest.

He spoke with such conviction that Erika almost forgot how evil the Jews were, but she had to lift up her heavy basket and trudge back to work before she got another scolding. Which is how she happened to be walking past the Geistgasse when the screaming started.

CHAPTER 5

THE MUNICIPAL GUARDS PRESSED the unruly crowd back, and none of them were happy about it. Sheriff Vratislav Zizka ordered one of the guards to light a lantern as he stooped to enter the gloomy shop. Once inside, he straightened up. He was a tall Slav with a broad forehead and prominent nose passed down through generations of Hussite warriors. The flickering oil flame chased the shadows from the splayed-out corpse in the middle of the floor. The city guard who should have been standing watch over the victim was fumbling with something behind the counter.

"Got something to report, Kromy?" said Zizka.

"I thought I might have to impound the cash box as evidence, sir," said Kromy.

"There'll be plenty of time for that later."

"Yes, sir."

"It's empty anyway," said Julie. She got a sharp stare from her father Jacob.

"Is that so? Where's the money?" asked Zizka.

I watched the family closely. They were accused criminals now, and it was best for them to say as little as possible under the circumstances.

"We just opened up," said Freyde. "I didn't sell anything yet."

"Do you always open so early?"

"She was pounding on the door—"

"Besides, it's a *mitsveh* to get up early on Friday to get ready for Shabbes," said Julie.

"What the hell is that? Some kind of Jewish magic?" said Zizka.

"No, it's a good deed," said Jacob.

"Black magic is a good deed?"

"No, no, no. It's not black magic—"

"They've been making contradictory statements like that all morning, sir," said Kromy.

"She means that it's a religious obligation to serve God on the Sabbath," I said.

"Well, what do you know? I thought you were made of clay," said Zizka, turning the lantern on me. "Who's he?"

Kromy said, "The new shammes of Jew Town. A newcomer."

"Newcomer, huh? You picked a hell of a day to start work. Think you can get your friends out of this?"

"They're not my friends yet. But they are my people," I said.

Someone outside swore at us, but I couldn't make out the thick Moravian accent.

Julie said, "How long do we have to sit here? We have a lot to do today."

"Really?" said Zizka, his eyes fixed on the dried bloodstains on the floor. "What's so damn urgent, if you don't mind telling me?"

"We have to rid the house of *khumets* before midday."

My stomach tightened. Julie was such an innocent, she didn't realize what trouble her plain speech was causing.

"You have to rid the house of *what*?"

I said, "All traces of leavened bread."

"And why is that? Because you don't want us to find all the evidence of blood in your Passover bread?"

"We don't cook with blood. The Torah forbids—"

"Kromy, have you searched the house yet?"

"Not yet, sir. I was waiting for more men, and I didn't want to take my eyes off these Jewish swine for an instant."

Zizka nodded. "You two, go upstairs with Kromy and search the place."

"Yes, sir."

"What are we looking for?" said one of the guards.

"Evidence of illicit wealth," said Kromy.

Zizka said, "Bottles, jugs, vials, basins—anything that might contain blood. And not just in the obvious places. The Jews are extremely clever about these things."

"Yeah, sometimes we hide it in our veins," I said.

Zizka glared at me as if he'd never heard a Jew talk that way before. Maybe he hadn't. Kromy and the two guards left the shop and clomped up the outside stairs.

Their first reaction to this crime is to seek vengeance, not justice. I had to do something to prevent a disaster. That such a mission was probably doomed to fail did not excuse me from trying. As Rabbi Tarfon says, "It's not your job to finish the work, but you are not free to walk away from it."

Looking at the girl, I tried to imagine who could have done such a thing. Certainly not Jacob Federn. Nobody kills a harmless child and leaves the body in his shop to be discovered by an angry Christian mob the next morning. The only way out of this mess was to discover what was gained from this girl's death. But how could I do that? They'd never let me openly question any Christian witnesses. They might not even let me walk around the Christian streets of Prague. I had to confer with the great Rabbi Loew about this. He'd know what to do.

A great crash shook the ceiling as Kromy and his goons started tossing things around upstairs.

I told the sheriff, "Somebody ought to tell the girl's parents. They've been searching for her all morning, calling her name from one end of town to the other."

"I don't need any advice from you, shammes," said Zizka. But he dispatched a guard to Janek's apothecary shop, then he ordered the three remaining guards to transport the victim's body to the Town Hall.

The guards knelt beside the girl's body. Just as they began to lift, one of them gasped, dropped the girl and pointed. Her neck wound had begun to flow with fresh blood. They all knew that such a thing only happens in the presence of the victim's killer. The guards crossed themselves and swore at the cowering family.

Zizka brought the lantern closer. He stuck his finger in the victim's blood, and pointed it at the Federns. They pulled away from his finger as if it oozed with the great pox.

"So, you shrink from the sign of your own guilt!"

"It's not guilt, it's a commandment from the highest authority," I said. "Any contact with human blood makes us unclean for a week. Are you unclean from contact with blood, Reb Federn?"

"No, I'm not."

"Are you, *fraylin* Federn?"

The women cried and denied it.

I turned to Sheriff Zizka. "With your indulgence, my good sir, I don't believe that a Jew would ever lie about such a thing."

"And I didn't believe Jews really did such things till I saw it with my own eyes," said Zizka. "Put them in irons."

"Yes, sir."

The guards closed in around the three accused criminals, the women emptying their eyes of tears and begging for God's intercession.

I played the one card I had left in my slim hand. "I know that the evidence implicates this humble family, but according to the Carolinian Code, the Jews are the emperor's concern, and are subject to his benevolent protection."

Zizka said, "Is that so? Well, I didn't bring my copy of the Carolina with me, but somehow it stuck in my mind that it also calls for the burning of unbelievers and sorcerers, and if you ask me, these Jews are both."

"Then you're supposed to summon the royal guards. Jews are under their jurisdiction."

"Not for murder, they aren't."

"In all matters—"

"This is a matter for the city. Come on, you—"

The municipal guards seized Freyde and Julie. A couple of them struggled to force the irons around their wrists, knocking over boxes of feathers, which flew around as the women cried out in despair.

Another crash came from upstairs.

Seeing his stock damaged and his women manhandled so harshly, Jacob finally stood up and took responsibility.

"They had absolutely nothing to do with this. It's all my fault."

"Jacob, no—!"

"Silence, woman! Now we're getting somewhere," said Zizka. "You swear that your wife and daughter are innocent?"

"I swear."

Zizka was clearly pleased with this statement. He probably figured that eliminating the women made things simpler, since women are much more difficult to prosecute in these matters. They have a much higher threshold for pain, for one thing.

"Then who were your accomplices?" he asked.

Jacob hesitated. There was no right answer to this one.

"Answer the question, Jew."

I said, "He doesn't have to answer. This line of questioning is reserved for the formal inquest at the emperor's court."

"Well, aren't you the little Jewish lawyer. Go ahead. Try to use your clever words to get past me."

"You don't have to be a lawyer to know a frivolous murder charge when you see one," I said, meeting the sheriff's gaze.

The sheriff was only a couple of inches taller than me, but he had more than enough clout to back up his threats. Feathers drifted in the air between us. Zizka seemed to be suppressing a smile.

"Don't listen to his lies," said the woman with the blue kerchief, standing just outside the doorway.

"Just let us do our jobs, ma'am."

The sheriff spoke to the whole room, but he was looking at me. "Now here's how it's going to be. Either the accused, Jacob Federn, tells us who his accomplices were, or you personally deliver them to us, shammes."

"The imperial law code forbids the application of collective guilt—"

"You better shut up before I take you in as well, Jew. You know very well how to force the murderers to come forward."

I opened my mouth to protest, and found that a feather had planted itself in my beard.

Zizka delivered his ultimatum. "You've got three days. And if we don't get the truth out of this fellow, we'll hold the whole community responsible. I wouldn't want to be in your shoes when Monday morning comes around and you're empty-handed."

A few of the bystanders snickered.

"We're going to seal up Jew Town, effective immediately. If anyone tries to escape, it'll be taken as proof of guilt, and we'll burn the whole damn ghetto down to the ground."

CHAPTER 6

EVERY NOW AND THEN the Christians go a little crazy.

Did any of them stop to think about who might profit from this crime? Or consider the possibility that someone might have wanted to stir up hatred and mayhem for unknown reasons? No, all they can see is bloodthirsty Jews everywhere they look. They see what isn't there and don't see what *is* there. And they think that whatever they can't explain must be inherently evil. This is only partly true.

The rabbi in Slonim says that we spend every hour of the day surrounded by evil spirits who press in on us from all sides like an invisible army, and that the only reason we *don't* go crazy is because most of the time we simply don't realize that they're there.

But there are other unseen forces that hover around the edges of our experience. The *Slonimer Rebbe* will also tell you of the *tsadek nister*, the hidden wise man who labors among us, perhaps as a humble shoemaker, whose inner wisdom and strength remain invisible to the outside world. The Jews say that at any given time, there are thirty-six such men in the world, who are known as *lamed-vovniks*, and that for their sake alone, God keeps the universe in one piece. Their true value is so carefully hidden that even *they* may not realize who they are.

For this reason, the great *ReMo*, Rabbi Moyshe Isserles of Kraków, always

encouraged us to read the *khokhmes khitsoyniyes*, the "external wisdoms," because he believed that all forms of wisdom were ultimately derived from the
Torah. So we read Pomponazzi, who was excommunicated for claiming there
is no way to prove that the soul is immortal, and Kopernikus, who dislodged
mankind from his privileged location at the center of the universe, and Friar
Bruno, who was excommunicated *three times* (which I believe is a record of some
kind) because he didn't believe in the power of miracles, prayer, or divine intervention in our daily lives. And what did it get us? Did the Christians really
care if we read their heretics?

No, but the other rabbis did. They tried to silence Rabbi Isserles and shut his
yeshiva down, denouncing us as *fraydenkers*. Freethinkers. The label stuck.

Then Rabbi Isserles, may his memory be a blessing, passed on too soon,
and I woke up to find out that the Freethinkers weren't welcome at the other
yeshivas.

So I had to prove myself all over again by toiling among the bookshelves,
and never venturing beyond the Jewish Quarter, past the Corpus Christi
Church, or across the Vistula to the main market square.

But I was never mystical enough to suit the mystics, or rational enough to
suit the rationalists, or compliant enough to become a follower of any of the
established schools of thought. So they made me deliver firewood to the study
rooms and haul buckets of heavy tiles up to the roof in the middle of winter
to help chop off the ice and patch up the holes.

They assigned me to classrooms with no heat and more than forty children, in direct violation of the Talmud, which states that a teacher shall have
no more than twenty-five pupils at one time (Bava Basra, 21a). When I pointed
this out to my new masters, they told me to comb through three centuries of
rabbinical *responsa* to find supporting citations, and to present my case to the
board of rabbis for review if I wanted them to take my petition seriously. I took
up the challenge, and I labored with such determination that I attracted the
support of Rabbi Ariyeh Lindermeyer, called Ari *der royter* because of his flaming red beard, and the way his face flushed when he was making a particularly
impassioned argument.

Under his direction, this project took on a life of its own, and from the way
people reacted, you'd think we were trying to undermine the thousand-year-
old tradition of publicly funded education.

Finally, the day came. I stood before the chief rabbis of Kraków and defended my outrageous proposal for providing smaller classes, with bread and milk for the children of laborers, and putting an end to the preferential system that placed mediocre students from well-to-do families in the best positions while superior scholars from poor families got stuck teaching seven-year-old girls how to read the Torah in Yiddish in overcrowded classrooms. I had done everything they asked. I found support in the *responsa*. I documented what every other yeshiva in the city was doing. I cited Abbaye, who says that "only he who lacks knowledge is poor" (Nedarim 14a), and the *Mishlei* of Solomon, wherein it is written that wisdom is more valuable than silver and gold (Proverbs 3:13–14).

The result? They told me to write down my entire argument, along with all the supporting documents, and make enough copies to be circulated among the heads of the rabbinical court and the community council for their consideration.

So I spent six months researching and writing a book that eight people read and promptly dismissed.

But that's not why I came to Prague.

The Talmud says that many things in life depend not on merit, but on *mazl*. Luck. Sheer chance.

And believe me, it's true. Because soon after we started working together, Rabbi Ari *der royter* died, and once again I was left without a rabbi to support my cause. He also left an office full of books that he had instructed me to distribute to the neediest students. So after sitting *shiva* for a week, I carted the books over to the yeshiva, carried them up the stairs, and left them on a table for the students to go through and take what they wanted. But Rabbi Ben-Roymish, the acting head of the yeshiva, complained that the dusty old books were cluttering up the hallway, and told me to remove them immediately. I asked him to let the books remain for a few days to give the poor students time to go through them. But he said that he didn't want students "picking at the carcass" of old book collections, and that in the past such "remains" had been left for months. I gave him my word that I would remove them after a couple of days and sweep up the hall besides, but it meant nothing to him. He made me pack the books up that very day and sell them for practically nothing to a traveling book peddler.

I guess that was just the last straw. How could I stay there after that? How could I stay in a place where my solemn word of honor had no value?

The Talmud asks, "Why are scholars compared to a nut?" The answer given is that even though the outside may be dirty and scuffed, the inside is still valuable. But I could think of other reasons for the comparison.

But that's not why I came to Prague.

I stayed away from Kraków for many years, but when I returned, I discovered what had been missing from my life. Rabbi Simeon ben Eleazar says that the Holy One, blessed is He, endowed women with more understanding than men. And my Reyzl was living proof of this. She was strong and beautiful and endowed with a natural talent for running a trade.

And I couldn't get enough of her. I loved her very essence, and how it lingered on my lips for hours as a sign of our love, and how I would cling to her, trying to get closer to her than is physically possible in this world, as if I were trying to annihilate the distance between us. Maybe she tasted of the womb, and fed some deep, forgotten desire to return to it, floating in warmth, protected on all sides, cared for, loved. I'd make her want me, need me, and desire me completely before she took me in. All I ever wanted was to be as essential to her as she was to me, in that moment when the rest of the world disappears and one woman becomes all women for you.

But all the years of study with sharp minds in dusty rooms hadn't taught me what to *say* to her. All the Torah, the prophets, and the endless pursuit of Talmudic logic couldn't guide me to the words I needed to set things right between us. Only the mystical *Zohar* had offered a hint: "The ideal man has the strength of a man and the compassion of a woman." A tricky proposition, but I was working on it. Just not fast enough for some people, apparently.

Perhaps I should mention that it's perfectly normal among Jews for a woman like Reyzl, whose family had some standing, to marry a poor scholar and live on her parents' charity for a few years. But then the husband is supposed to get a prestigious position as a respected rabbi, and start building a house of his own with cooks and servants and lines of students going out the door, and well-connected people seeking his advice about money and other important matters. He's not supposed to turn and head the other way, beyond the borders of the empire to a snow-covered wasteland near the Pripet Marshes just to study with *one* obscure rabbi.

It didn't occur to me to talk it over with her first.

Not that I would have listened.

And that's why I came to Prague.

It was time for me to listen.

THE RAMPARTS OF THE CITY were eerily silent, as the town criers held their tongues while the dreadful edict was formalized, written out, and copied by municipal scribes. And so my beloved people made their last-minute preparations to welcome Pesach in blissful ignorance of the cauldron of trouble simmering outside the walls. Tablecloths and *kittels* blossomed in doorways and windows along the Breitgasse as housewives shook out the special white garments, and checked the dull gray clouds for signs of rain.

Servants hired by the Jewish Town Council prowled the streets collecting for the matzoh fund, hawking the World-to-Come with their steady refrain and promising us that "Charity saves from death, charity saves from death."

"Have you given yet?" said one of them, thrusting a tin box at my chest. The box was shaped like a house with a peaked roof, with a coin slot where the chimney should be. Hebrew letters on the front panel spelled out צדקה, *tseduke*, charity, though the hawkers pronounced it *tsedoke*.

I tried to step around the little man, but he had the legs of a spider, and quickly blocked the way again with the *tseduke* box.

"Listen, friend, anyone who isn't *getting* from the fund has to *give* to it. That's how it works. Now, you look like a fellow who could spare a few kreuzers so the poor and destitute can have matzoh on Pesach. Maybe even a couple dalers."

I reached into my pockets. A merchant of furs and pelts had leaned out of his shop to watch, and it wouldn't look good for the new shammes to brush off the matzoh fund on *Erev Pesach*. I held out a pair of copper coins that seemed to get lost in my suddenly huge hands.

"I only have a couple of *groshn*."

"A couple of what?" said the little man, staring at the strange Polish coins.

"I don't have any Bohemian money yet."

"Not even a few pfennigs? What kind of cheapskate are you, anyway?"

"It's all I have. You want it or not?"

"Listen, *Reb Ployne*, Mr. Whoever-You-Are, you're in Prague now, and we use pfennigs, kreuzers, and dalers—"

A voice from the street called out, "Hey, Meyer, take it easy. He's with us. He's new to the job."

My rescuer came toward us and greeted the little man with a slap on the shoulder. He had wavy reddish-brown hair, an easy smile, and a nose that had been flattened in a couple of close encounters with the flying fist of fate.

"He's with you, huh?" said Meyer, appraising me from head to foot. "Where you from?"

"Slonim."

"Where the hell is that?"

"East Poland."

"Never heard of it."

"Well, it's pretty far from here. It used to be part of Lithuania."

"So you're a Litvak! No wonder."

"No wonder what?"

"A Litvak is so clever he repents *before* he sins," said Meyer, repeating a bit of folk wisdom. "Fine, keep your groschen, smart boy."

Before I could reply, Meyer skittered away on his spidery legs, drawn to prey with heavier pockets, rattling the *tseduke* box and chanting, "Charity saves from death, charity saves from death."

I said, "Thanks for rescuing me from the valley of She'ol."

"Who, Meyer? More like a bump in the road. Besides, we've got to stick together, right, brother?"

The red-haired man said his name was Markas Kral, shammes at the Pinkas Shul.

"I should know where that is," I said.

"Kleine Pinkasgasse, on the other side of the cemetery from the Klaus Shul."

I nodded. I had seen the Pinkas Shul's peaked roof looming like the prow of a ship over a sea of crooked headstones.

"How's the rabbi on your watch?"

"Rabbi Epstein? He's all right. Maybe a little too by-the-book sometimes, but what do you want? That's the job."

"I know what you mean. Who are the three other shammeses besides us?"

"Well, there's Avrom Khayim, who handles the Klaus Shul and splits the shift at the Old-New Shul with Abraham Ben-Zakhariah, and there's Saul Ungar, who covers the High Shul."

"How reliable are they in a crisis?"

"*Vi a toytn bankes.* Avrom Khayim's too old to do any of the heavy work, Ben-Zakhariah acts like he's too much of a scholar to get down on his knees and scrub the floor, and the Hungarian's all mouth and no action. He'll talk your ear off for a week before getting off his butt to help out. Looks like I'm your only hope, brother."

"I'd say you're right. It would really help me out if you could show me around. You know these streets better than I do, and if I have to learn it all from scratch we're going to be completely *farkakt*—"

"Wait a minute, there's my master," said Kral, stepping away and greeting Rabbi Epstein with all due reverence.

Rabbi Epstein told Kral to stop gabbing and get busy responding to a woman's complaint that her husband was being cruel to her.

"Oh, crap. I hate domestic quarrels," Kral confided to me.

"Hang on a minute—"

"Sorry, I've got to go now. Don't forget to tell everyone to burn their *khumets*. See you later," said Kral, falling in line behind the rabbi as he turned toward the Pinkasgasse.

I watched them go, balling my fists for no reason except that I had finally met someone who could help me navigate the twisted streets of the ghetto, only to have him weave his way right back into the masses of men that made up the vast tapestry of the neighborhood.

The hell with my regular duties. I had to alert Rabbi Loew that the Jews were facing exile, annihilation, or both.

At the sign of the stone lion, I waited for one of the maids to sweep a pile of crumbs into the street, so that I wouldn't track any forbidden *khumets* into the newly swept hallway. The Christian girls in the front hall swirled around me in a perfumy maelstrom, and for a moment it felt like my heavy boots were the only things anchoring me to the surface of the globe as I marched between them. If they only knew what was hanging over their heads, I thought— except it wasn't their heads that would roll, was it? They were all *shiksehs*.

Just then a man stepped away from the shadows behind a row of long winter cloaks hanging on their pegs. I recognized him as one of the young mystics in Rabbi Loew's inner circle. His name was Yankev ben Khayim, and he wore the plain black robes of a student.

"Aha, you enter without knocking," he said. "That shows you are more interested in the World-to-Come than in this world."

I had gone in and out several times that morning, and had kissed the mezuzah each time. But I didn't think it mattered if I knocked on the open door.

"Are you like the *tsadek* who was so pious that he never noticed that his wife was missing a thumb? Unaware of the mystical meaning of your gesture?"

"Yes, that must be it," I said.

"Ah, you admit your ignorance. That is a good start. Teach your tongue to say 'I do not know' instead of inventing some falsehood."

I said, "Brukhes, folio four A. I'm glad to meet another Talmud scholar, but right now I need to talk to the rabbi."

"*Brukhes*? Oh, you mean *Brokhes*. It's hard to understand you with that *poylish* accent. Your lack of intellectual conviction tells me that you need to study the wisdom of the *Khokhmas Hanister* with us."

He meant the Kabbalah. I needed to start forging some alliances against the forces gathering around us, so I chose my words carefully.

"You're right about that, my friend. I don't always get the answers I want from the Talmud, and it's also true that I mustn't miss out on this rare opportunity to study the hidden wisdom with the great Maharal. But right now I've got to talk to the rabbi about a completely different situation."

"Something more important than the healing of God's creation through mystical communion with His endless spirit?"

"This is more in the realm of the *practical* Kabbalah."

"All the more reason why you should never act without thinking."

"Right. Sometimes I act without thinking. That's why I need to talk to the rabbi."

I was about to push open the door to the rabbi's study when I remembered how different these city folk are from the *shtetl* Jews. In Slonim, the tiny cottages huddled together under the big, empty sky in a valiant effort to keep their dreadful loneliness at bay. In Prague, five families might share a two-room apartment, but each family's property lines were rigidly delineated. If that's what it took for the highest concentration of Jews in the European Diaspora to live together without trampling on each other, so be it. Space had a different meaning here.

So I knocked.

"Who is it?" a voice said, stiffly.

"Benyamin Ben-Akiva."

"Who?" Still no softening of tone.

"I'm the assistant shammes at the Klaus Shul."

"What do you want?"

I pressed down on the curved iron handle and opened the door.

Three men sat around the rabbi's table, scrutinizing the same passage in a set of Hebrew books bound in plain brown leather. I recognized Isaac

Ha-Kohen, the rabbi's son-in-law, but I didn't know the other two, a roly-poly man who was clearly another rabbi, and a young student who appeared to be about thirteen. Two more chairs sat empty.

"Where's Rabbi Loew?"

"Close the door," said Isaac Ha-Kohen.

"Yes, the women are dusting and it's quite a mess," said Yankev ben Khayim, slipping past me to take his place at the table.

I stepped inside the study room and closed the door.

Two rooms away, Hanneh the cook demanded water from the well. Girlish footsteps clattered down the back hall to the courtyard.

Isaac Ha-Kohen reached for a cup of water and struck it sharply with his fingernail to frighten away the invisible spirits gathered on the rim so he wouldn't swallow them as he took a drink, God forbid. I waited for him to take a sip and wipe his mouth with a fine white napkin before I spoke again.

"Pardon me, O esteemed Rabbi Ha-Kohen. Can you please tell me where I can find our teacher Rabbi Loew?"

"The High Rabbi cannot be interrupted," said Isaac Ha-Kohen.

Two non-answers in a row. I took one more stab at being polite.

"How soon can I speak with him?"

"Rabbi Loew does not give audience during the morning study session."

"Maybe we'd better let him decide that."

Isaac Ha-Kohen looked up from his book as if I had burst into the study room with a team of filthy and incontinent mules. He looked me over, weighed my worth and value in an instant, and went back to the text before his eyes.

I stepped closer and peered at the pages the young teen was studying. It was the *Gvuroys Hashem*, The Powers of the Holy Name, Rabbi Loew's commentary on the Haggadah, published anonymously in Poland to avoid reprisals from the old-shul rabbis for his biting attacks on their rank and privileges. The copies were already battered and frayed, as if they had been smuggled into the country in a barrel of chestnuts.

I skimmed over the discussion of *Shmoys*, Names, the Book of Moses that the Christians call Exodus, until my eyes fell on the rabbi's analysis of two key Biblical phrases. According to the Maharal, the first phrase, "they *worked* Israel with rigorous labor," refers only to physical enslavement, but the second, "they *embittered* their lives," suggests a different level of meaning entirely—that slavery ate at their souls, until the Israelites ended up internalizing their condition and believing that they *deserved* to be slaves, a much more insidious form of servility that was passed from one generation to the next like a bad case of smallpox.

The words struck a chord deep within me, as if Rabbi Loew had looked directly into my soul and plucked it like a string. Somehow I had always known the truth of this observation, because the lesson applied to me as well. I, too, had once believed in the inevitability of my place on the bottom rung of the social ladder in this world, but no one had ever explained it so succinctly. And it played a central role in the festival of Pesach—the idea that every Jew in every generation must regard himself as having *personally* made the exodus out of Egypt. The hardest part was shedding that inbred slave-like mentality.

Right. Then comes the "easy" part: wandering in the wilderness for forty years, looking for a place to call home.

In any case, a rabbi capable of such insight clearly deserved every bit of his storied reputation.

And I sure felt like a fool when it finally dawned on me why no one would tell me where the rabbi was. He was, you should pardon the expression, in the *beys ha-kises*. The house of thrones.

I wondered how long I'd have to wait for the great rabbi. The sages in the Talmud say, "Who prolongs his stay in a privy lengthens his days and years." But Rabbi Loew wasn't the staunchest Talmudist, and I wasn't sure where the Kabbalists stood on the issue.

I asked the boy, "Can you tell me something? What exactly is a daler?"

"You mean a Reichsthaler? It's a huge piece of silver. Worth a week's pay to a skilled craftsman."

"Or a month's pay to a *shleper* like you," said Isaac Ha-Kohen, without looking up.

The rabbi next to Ha-Kohen shook his head and *tsk-tsk*ed his neighbor's unnecessary comment, and told us that the leading artists and scientists in *keyser* Rudolf's court made as much as three thousand dalers a year. I looked into the other man's face and held on it, until I remembered the face thinner, the beard shorter and darker.

"Rabbi Dovid Gans?"

"You know each other?" said Rabbi Ha-Kohen.

I said, "We studied under Rabbi Moyshe Isserles, may his name be a light unto nations."

Rabbi Gans laid down his book and squinted at me. Then his eyes brightened. "My God, it *is* you. I see you've gone a little gray since your days with the *fraydenkers*."

And you've put on about fifty pounds, I thought. "What can I say? We were just kids back then."

"Like our young prodigy, master Yontef Lipmann here."

I looked at the thirteen-year-old boy.

"No, I was more like his age," I said, indicating Yankev ben Khayim, who sat before an open book, absently stroking his wispy teenage beard.

"If you were a student of Isserles, you must have showed promise," said Isaac Ha-Kohen. "How come I haven't heard of you?"

"Because the angels who sing my praises do it beyond the range of normal hearing."

Ha-Kohen sat frozen a moment, as the back door creaked open, and measured footsteps trod the length of the back corridor. Blue-veined fingers drew back the curtain and the great Rabbi Loew entered the room rattling a jar of almonds in his left hand. He was in his late seventies (some say his early eighties), with a full white beard. He wore two layers of heavy black robes under an academic gown with a black rabbit's fur collar, and a soft octagonal hat with thick silver threads radiating from the center, dividing it into eight slices like a velvet pie. His shaky hands displayed all the frailties of age, but his eagle's glare declared to all within range that his eyes were still sharp and his mind was still quick. All the Jews in the city knew of his commanding presence, his *yikhes*, his stature. Even his enemies respected his opinions, feared his tongue, and called him the *MaHaRal mi-Prag*, Our Teacher and Master Rabbi Loew of Prague. He was said to be descended from King David.

I spoke: "Most venerated High Rabbi Yehudah ben Betzalel—"

"Just call me 'Rabbi,' " said the master.

"Yes, of course, Rabbi—"

"Where were you during the *Amidah*, Benyamin Ben-Akiva? Poor Avrom Khayim had to cover both services, running between the Klaus and the Old-New Shuls. He's getting too old for that."

I did my best to explain the situation without running out of breath.

Dishes clattered in the kitchen as the everyday plates were put away and the special kosher-for-Pesach set was brought out.

Rabbi Gans groaned *"Oy, gvalt!"* and covered his ears and rocked from side to side as if he were hearing of an earthquake, a flood, a punishing deluge of fire and hailstones.

Rabbi Isaac's shoulders slumped forward as if a piece of the heavens had just landed on them.

Rabbi Loew grabbed a fistful of his robe and yanked at it until he split the seam and ripped out a good six inches.

Yankev ben Khayim clutched at his own robe and worked at it till he tore a piece loose.

Rabbi Loew lowered his head and said, *"Borukh dayan ha-emes."* Blessed is the true Judge.

Yankev ben Khayim did the same, imitating his master in every detail like a true disciple.

Rabbi Loew said, "Listen to me, Rabbi Gans. I need you to gather sheets of parchment, take up your quill, and begin a chronicle of these events."

"Why is that so important now, Rabbi?" asked young Lipmann.

Rabbi Loew said, "Who do you want to write this story—the Christians?"

Gans sharpened his nib with a short knife.

Yankev ben Khayim lit a couple of candles, and sat next to Isaac Ha-Kohen. The two of them began rocking rhythmically back and forth, murmuring ancient prayers as they set out on the long, slow voyage toward a state of near-ecstasy that would allow them to receive the energy flowing from the divine emanations of righteousness and mercy.

"Yes, you men begin the *tfiles*," said Rabbi Loew. "If we assail the gates of heaven with our tears, God willing, they may open for us. In the meantime, perhaps we can buy the *goyim* off before this turns into another dreadful blood—"

Rabbi Loew stopped suddenly. I followed his gaze. The rabbi's granddaughter Eva was standing in the doorway, holding a long feather. She was about twelve years old. Not much older than the victim.

She said, "I'm here to dust the books, *zeyde.*"

Rabbi Loew said, "You're a big girl, Havele, but you still need help dusting all these books."

"I can do it myself, Grandaddy."

Eva Kohen had dark curly hair and bright eyes, and something passed across young Lipmann's face when she came into the room, though she may not have been aware of it.

"Very well, my little jewel," said Rabbi Loew. He resumed his discourse, leaving out the references to blood. "As I was saying, we are dealing with people who don't just tell lies, they tell so many lies that they build a parallel world out of their lies, and in *that* world, those lies are true. For such people, it's not what is, it's what they happen to believe. For surely we have learned that even if all the words of slander directed against us are not accepted as true, half of them *are* accepted."

He turned and quizzed his grandchild: "Eva, can you tell me where that citation is from?"

Eva repeated the words to herself, and said, "Is it the *Breyshis Raboh*?" The great commentary on *Breyshis*, In the Beginning, which the Christians call Genesis.

"That's my girl," he said, giving her a loving squeeze.

She was a smart girl, all right.

Rabbi Gans opened the pot of ink, dipped in the nib, and began to anoint the blank pages with the majestic block letters of the Hebrew *alef-beys*.

Isaac Ha-Kohen and Yankev ben Khayim kept up their soft chanting, but they needed more voices, more prayers pounding on the unyielding gates of heaven.

Rabbi Loew stroked his beard and considered a moment. Finally, he asked a question: "Benyamin Ben-Akiva, are you schooled in the Kabbalah?"

"My knowledge of Kabbalah is like a page that has fallen out of an old book. But I know something of the Law."

"Good. Come with me, then. We need to build a legal case that will convince the emperor to intervene on our behalf before Federn confesses."

"Confesses? He hasn't done anything."

Isaac Ha-Kohen shook his head and gave me a *shows-what-you-know* look without losing his place in the prayers.

Rabbi Loew said, "A man will admit to anything after three days of torture."

I shuddered at the thought. I'd been made to stand thigh-deep in snow until icy needles pierced my thickest flesh; I'd been slapped with a switch, a stick, a calloused hand; I'd been forced to sleep in the stables without food or a blanket; I'd been called a fool and a slob and a thousand other useless names. But my legs eventually went numb, my bruises healed, I learned to withstand hunger and cold and harsh accusations, and I never confessed to something I didn't do.

Eva was going through each book on the shelf with a feather in a largely symbolic search for wayward crumbs that might have fallen into the cracks between the pages. Rabbi Loew gave her a pat on the shoulder as I followed him toward the door.

We stopped to look at what Rabbi Gans had written. After the first few words, he had switched from ornate Hebrew capitals to cursive Yiddish:

> On Friday, the 14th of Nisan, 5352, or March 27 of the Christian year 1592, in the sixteenth year of the reign of Emperor Rudolf II, may his glory be elevated, there arose a new persecution based on the ancient lie, the dreaded blood libel.

"Good start," said the rabbi. "Now write that the first thing Rabbi Loew and his assistant shammes did was go to the *kehileh* to secure a formal request for the transfer of the accused, Jacob Federn, from the municipal to the imperial prison. He'll be safer there."

I asked, "Why are we wasting time going to the Town Council? Why not go directly to the *keyser*?"

"We've got a better chance of getting the emperor's ear if the request comes from the whole community."

I nodded.

"All right," said the rabbi. "Then *kum aseh*." Get up and do.

I helped Rabbi Loew put on his winter cloak, and together we went out to the street armed with nothing but the will to perform a *mitsveh*, a positive act, almost a holy deed, since it is written that whoever saves a single life is looked upon as if he had saved the entire world.

CHAPTER 7

WHEN THE INQUISITOR'S CARRIAGE and retinue crossed the Vltava River into Prague, the waters were churning so violently that it spooked the horses. The driver said the river was riding high with early runoff from the highlands, but the Inquisitor knew this was surely the Devil's work. And so was the slow fire eating through his guts. His backside also hurt from the long, hard ride down through the Brenner Pass, another sign of the Devil's torment, but he took courage from the protective shield of the true faith that hung around his neck like a mantle of steel. Bishop Heinrich Stempfel had spent a lifetime sniffing out unbelievers and heretics, and was ready to confront the enemy in any form. He challenged the wicked ones to reveal their ugliness and try to keep him from exposing their sinful acts to the pure, bright light of truth.

He winced as their hellfire clawed at his tender places, but he was damned if they were going to keep him from seeing this mission through to the end. His cause was just.

Bishop Stempfel had his own priorities, but the new pope had given him his orders: Catholic Prague had been without a leader for two years since Archbishop Medek's death, may God rest his soul, and that empty seat had to be filled by someone who was prepared to crush the gathering forces of Protestant heresy and reclaim the fractious Bohemian territory for Rome. As his caravan pulled into the courtyard of Our Lady of Terezín, with its Italian-style parish house, all arches and orange roofing tiles, Bishop Stempfel thought, "And here come a couple of the contenders."

Archpriests Hermann Popel and Andyel Zeman were positioning themselves at the head of a long red carpet, jabbing each other with their elbows while waiting to receive the Pope's envoy with all the drums and colors and pomp and protocol appropriate to his station.

A pair of liveried footmen opened the carriage door and placed a velvet stool on the flagstones for the bishop, who waited for them to lay an embroidered handkerchief on the cushion before he stepped down. He was followed by his closest aide, Grünpickl, and his scribe, Stuck.

Popel and Zeman led a procession of choirboys holding pure white candles to greet Bishop Stempfel, who took a gilded casket from Grünpickl and presented it to the two archpriests as a gift from His Eminence in Rome to the faithful of Prague. It contained a holy relic, the bones of a child killed by King Herod of Judea during the slaughter of the innocents. Popel and Zeman opened the casket to gaze upon the objects of such long-term veneration. The bones were extremely well preserved. They looked only a few years old, clear proof of their miraculous powers.

"Thank heaven you're here, my lord," said Popel. "The *verfluchte Juden* have spat in our faces for the last time."

"Can it wait till after breakfast?"

"My lord, this sacrifice calls for swift vengeance."

"What form of sacrifice do you mean?" he said, looking over the faces of the innocent Christian boys whose well-being he had sworn to protect.

Popel was surprised by Bishop Stempfel's ambivalence. The Inquisitor was supposed to swoop into this sluttish city, which had opened its gates to every possible heretical belief, with the glowing cross of the True Faith emblazoned on his chest and a flaming sword in his outstretched hand. He put great emphasis on his next words:

"My lord, I speak of the dreaded *Blutbeschuldigungen*—"

"Not another bloodcrime, Popel." The bishop turned and began the majestic walk down the bright red carpet toward the marble steps. The two priests followed alongside. "I keep telling the legions of the faithful that the Jews don't use blood. It's against their Law. Even the Poles know that. King

Boleslaw the Pious and His Eminence Innocent IV settled the matter quite some time ago."

Zeman was content to keep quiet and let Popel dig himself deeper into this hole.

"Rome may have spoken, but the matter is far from settled," said Popel. "Just last Easter a Jew from Löwenstein tried to buy a four-year-old child for his blood."

"Well, God knows you can't believe anything from that bunch of lunatics in Löwenstein. Aren't they the ones who are convinced that a Jewish woman once gave birth to a sow?"

"Those events are well documented, my lord. The Jews have broken into our churches, desecrated holy images, and even mocked the Savior's crucifixion by wounding the Body of Christ with their daggers."

"They did all this in front of a hostile congregation, and nobody tried to stop them? Surely there is some exaggeration here."

Popel didn't answer. He was beginning to understand what it meant when people said that when the mighty arm of the Lord takes human form, the vessel is sometimes too weak to stand the strain.

As they passed through the main archway and climbed the stairs to the private dining chambers, Zeman asked Bishop Stempfel if he enjoyed the trip from Rome, and if he found the weather to his liking.

The table was laid out with a variety of Bohemian fare, but Bishop Stempfel filled his plate with German sausages smothered with pepper, cumin, and other costly spices. The Bishop of Bishops, Pope Clement VIII, had personally declared that Stempfel could dispense with fasting during this expedition because he needed to keep up his strength for the fight against demons.

The bishop sat in the finest chair, with a red velvet cushion and a high back crawling with gilded curlicues in the latest fashion. He took a moment to admire the floral patterns on the high ceiling, which were endlessly reflected by the full-length mirrors.

Popel tried again: "My lord, give me license to use all available means to deal with the Jews for their detestable crimes."

"Leave them to the judgment of God for a moment," said Stempfel, slopping hot mustard on a steaming pile of sausages. "Rome has established a clear policy. Our first order of business is to rid the country of heretics, and purge their ranks of those arch-heretics, the witches. We'll have plenty of time for the Jews later."

Popel drummed his fingers on the table while breathing rapidly through his nostrils.

"Don't worry, my friend," said the bishop. "Our sacred mission is to restore the unity of mankind under the banner of the universal Church. First it was the Hussites, with their nasty habit of tossing people out of windows. But we learned to tolerate them. Then came the Utraquists and the Picardians and the Unitarians, and we tolerated *them*. And now the place is crawling with followers of every persuasion, who act like we still roll into a town, set up a table, and charge people a daler a head minimum to buy off their sins. Heaven is not for sale, they say. Bah! As if we haven't progressed beyond the wholesale merchandising of dispensations and indulgences."

Popel watched the bishop spread a thick blob of liverwurst on a slice of toasted bread. Then he said, "My lord, His Eminence Pope Julius wisely saw fit to ban the blasphemous, anti-Christian Talmud nearly forty years ago, but if you look around today, you see Jews everywhere reading the hateful book. If we would just gather all the books of Jewish sorcery in a pile and burn them in a holy fire in the town square—"

Zeman said, "How could a bunch of backward letters exert any effect on God's will? Witchcraft spread through our land when the Protestant heresy arrived."

The bishop was inclined to agree, but Popel barreled on, "How can we keep wayward Christians in line when we allow Jews from the four corners of Europe to gather under our noses? Their very existence proves that unbelievers can prosper in our midst. I say we drive out all the Jews with burning faggots!"

"We could exile them all to the Holy Land," said the bishop. "But the truth is that we *need* the Jews."

Both priests stared at him.

They were such provincials, thought the bishop. Especially Popel. But he was useful, in the way that a trained hunting dog is useful.

"Come, brothers, even a fresh-faced novice knows that the Apostle Paul has written that the conversion of the seed of Abraham is one of the key events preceding the Second Coming of Christ."

Both priests nodded.

"The Jews will come around eventually. At least we can force them to listen to a true Christian sermon three times a year in church," said the bishop.

"Even if they stop their ears with wax," said Popel.

"They use cotton," Zeman said. "And we have trained guards on duty to control for that."

"We keep the Jews apart," said the bishop, "distinct and recognizable. But how are we supposed to root out the Sabbatarians, or the Czech Brethren? Are we supposed to let those sex-crazed Adamites into our Church? Or those subversive Anabaptists who wander about the countryside convincing gullible peasants that only freely choosing adults can be baptized?"

Zeman shook his head. "It would never have happened if you had been in charge of the local Inquisition, my lord."

"I'll have to go along with you on that," said the Inquisitor, spearing a piece of sausage with his knife. "And that's why I'm here. Rome feels that the locals have been far too lenient in prosecuting the unbelievers, and it's time for the Holy Inquisition to re-open its Prague offices."

"The move is long overdue, my lord."

"Yes," said the bishop, glad to see that somebody was finally agreeing with him. "It's time for a little housecleaning, boys. It may take us twenty to thirty years or so, but eventually we'll sweep all these heretics aside, and the Roman Church will take back its rightful place as the one true religion in all of Bohemia, Europe, and the New World."

Zeman felt like kneeling and kissing the bishop's ring.

Popel said, "That is why we must deal with the Jews right away, my lord, since they are siding with the Protestant cults against us."

Bishop Stempfel reluctantly set down his fork, returning a fatty slice of sausage to his plate. "And where is the supporting evidence for that?"

"They openly traffic with the burghers in this city."

"That only means the burghers of Prague are mostly Protestant." He patiently explained the problem again. "That's not the Jews' fault. It's our job to bring the wayward sects back into the fold."

"*All* of them?"

"Yes, all of them."

Without warning, the bishop cringed beneath the folds of his robe. It felt like some kind of acid was snaking angrily through his lower intestines, inflaming that already shameful excretory place until it was red and raw. He poured some wine down his throat to cool the fires.

No one said anything for a while.

It was a strain for him to speak: "Except, of course, for the *maleficae*." Evildoers.

"Witchcraft," he said through clenched teeth, "must be uprooted like an evil weed before it can spread any further."

"Evil weeds frequently grow back, my lord," said Popel.

"That's why our work is never done. It's up to us to toil in the vineyards of the Lord, uprooting the weeds, and above all, saving the sinners' souls from the torments of hell."

"But the Inquisition is also charged with handling matters of Jewish blasphemy—"

"Save your breath, Popel." Bishop Stempfel held out his greasy fingers, and Grünpickl handed him a folded parchment bearing the words, *Pascere Populum Suum* in an elaborate hand, and a red wax seal.

"His Eminence Clement VIII happens to agree with you. Issued just four weeks ago. It calls for maintaining a strict separation between Jews and Christians in business and personal matters."

Popel was pleased, but Zeman looked worried. He asked, "Will we be able to keep using Jewish treasurers, my lord?"

"Relax. Nobody's going to take away your precious Jewish bankers. You don't expect good Christians to get their hands dirty handling Jewish gold, do you?"

"Certainly not, sir."

"Good. You'd be surprised what you can learn just by keeping your ears open. You sure you don't want something to eat?"

"No, thank you, sir."

"You can't get good German sausages in Rome," he said. "How does Count Rožmberk feel about all this?"

"Oh, you know him, my lord. Always calling for moderation and fair treatment for the Jews."

Popel sniffed hard enough to inhale a cherrystone. The Bishop turned to face him. "You have something to say on the matter of the Jews?"

Popel said, "My lord, you've got to divert resources to prosecuting them for this unspeakable crime. A young girl was ritually murdered sometime early this morning and several pints of blood were drawn from her body. We're holding a Jewish suspect in the city jail."

"Fine. Then he isn't going anywhere. Because we've got divisions within the enemy camp, gentlemen, and now's the time to strike. You don't seem to realize that the Jews think of the Catholic emperors as their protectors. That makes them loyal supporters of the Hapsburgs, who happen to be our benefactors."

Illumination slowly flooded the faces of the two priests, who now understood why the Bishop had been chosen to be the Pope's envoy.

Bishop Stempfel reached for his cup of wine, and drew his hand back in horror. A fly was buzzing around it. He quickly made the sign of the cross and dumped the wine out on the floor. The Devil is exceedingly clever, but no match for a man of faith with a quick eye and a nose for sin.

A servant quickly filled his cup again while another mopped up the spill.

"Is something the matter, my lord?" asked Zeman.

Bishop Stempfel stared at a spot in the sky through the arched windows over Zeman's shoulder. Something foul was gnawing away at his guts, and he knew of only one way to stop it.

The archpriests were still waiting for an answer. The bishop fumbled with his fork, pushing the last half-eaten piece of sausage around his plate. He considered the two men on either side of the table. Popel was an attack dog, but he was focused on the wrong target. Zeman didn't seem to understand that the Catholics were a decided minority in Prague.

It was his job to mold them, and test them, and determine which one was a worthy successor to Archbishop Medek, capable of leading the flock into the next century. Prague was a mighty city, a bustling center of commerce and trade. But the Catholic population was so small that the two archpriests were strangely isolated from the reality of the streets beyond the walls of the seminary. Not like the worldly courtiers at the Vatican, where the popes had included a pair of Medicis and a Borgia.

A spasm of fire gripped his insides, and he began to sweat. He closed his eyes till the attack passed, then spoke to the archpriests. "Every day, I fight off the tortures visited upon me by those who are determined to attack my body in the hopes of breaking my spirit."

"That only proves that you're closing in on them, my lord," said Zeman.

"Yes, but their attacks are growing stronger."

"Can you describe these attacks?"

His enemies were everywhere. The loyal guardians of the faith were surrounded and outnumbered. But the Church was the only true road to salvation, as confirmed by God himself.

The archpriests waited.

"It's . . ."

"Yes, my lord?"

They waited some more.

Finally, he told them about his problem.

The priests exchanged glances and told him not to worry, that their special healer could work miraculous cures.

"Bring him immediately," said the bishop, rising from the table.

"As you wish—" Zeman began.

"Immediately, sir," said Popel, jumping up and beating his rival to the door, leaving Zeman to survey the damage left behind by the bishop's breakfast. The puddle of red wine had stained the edge of the carpet, and the tabletop was spattered with mustard and pork fat. He was directing the servants to clean it up when Popel returned.

With a swish of his satin robes, the bishop set up court with his aide and scribe in attendance, and explained the broader situation to the two priests. The Catholic Armada of Spain had recently been decimated by the renegade nation of England, turning Amsterdam and the rest of the United Provinces into a haven for Protestant refugees. While this might be seen as a setback, they had to remember that England's newfound wealth came from plundering Spanish ships laden with treasures from the New World. So it was perfectly clear to the truly faithful that the speedy conquests of Mexico and Peru were proof that God supported the Catholic cause, and that the hateful English would never permanently plant their flag in the Americas. The Inquisition had exposed heretics and "secret Jews" hiding out as far away as Lima and Quito, so now was the time to gear up for the final confrontation here at home, and cut the Protestant population of Europe in half within a generation. And if anyone doubted the reasoning or the purpose, let him visit the barbaric city of London, and stand by and watch as God-fearing Jesuits were torn to pieces for public entertainment.

The doctor arrived, a pale and shrunken man, with a few wisps of hair clinging to his head like the whitish mold on a walnut. He told the servants to set up a screen.

The bishop asked the priests what Emperor Rudolf II was like personally. The Catholic Church enjoyed imperial protection, but was he fully committed to the cause?

Zeman hesistated. "My lord, the emperor is a deeply Christian man—"

Popel jumped in: "But there is no better place than his court to be a Jew. His Highness has collected quite a menagerie of Jewish magicians, astronomers, and counselors, who prance around the royal galleries like a bunch of perfumed monkeys dressed in men's clothing."

"Good use of animal imagery," said the bishop. He instructed his scribe to make a note of the phrase, since it would play well with the country folk.

The doctor laid out his bloodletting instruments and collection bowl, and gestured for the patient to approach.

Bishop Stempfel was a big man who had been eating well. The doctor asked the bishop to describe his symptoms, then said that he needed to examine the patient more closely in order to palpate his abdomen, since fire in a bodily organ was the most likely cause of his ailment.

The bishop stripped to the waist, while on the other side of the screen, Popel condemned the casual social proximity of Christians and Jews in Rudolf II's court and in the well-to-do houses in the ghetto, which resulted in all kinds of opportunities for illicit and unnatural couplings.

"Why would they want to invite their own destruction?" asked the bishop, getting gooseflesh as the doctor probed his gut with cold hands.

"Jews are more lustful than our people," Zeman explained.

"You'd think they'd keep it in check, considering what we did to the last Jew who took a turn at the grindstone with a Christian maiden," said Popel.

The bishop felt a sickly tugging in the scrotum as he was prodded in sensitive areas. His fingers fidgeted for a moment, then found comfort fondling his special set of rosary beads carved from human bone.

The doctor said, "My lord, I need to perform a *complete* examination of the digestive tract."

The bishop stood dumbly for a moment before he realized what this meant. The room was quite cold by Roman standards, but he removed the last layer of linen covering his shameful places. The doctor directed him to bend forward slightly.

The probe was a hollow metal tube, with a flat projection at one end with a hole cut in it for viewing the exposed tissue.

Popel continued: "My informants tell me that in the *Judenstadt* the Jewish beadles have been in the streets all morning commanding them to burn something, but it's all in some dreadful Hebrew code. So the Jews live among us, and repay our generosity by conspiring to burn the city to the ground, just as they once did in the Kleinseite district across the river."

"Conspiring? With who—?" The bishop let out a yelp. The probing was much more painful than he thought it would be. The doctor kept turning the lead instrument roughly to view the damaged area.

"They have allied themselves with the Turkish menace, my lord."

The bishop gasped for breath. He was sweating, which made his exposed skin turn clammy.

"I know, I didn't want to believe it myself," said Popel. "But honest mercenaries returning from the Hungarian front speak of a terrifying horde of Jewish cutthroats hiding somewhere to the east, waiting for the chance to descend upon us and feast on our flesh."

The bishop felt as if a hot poker was searing his entrails.

"We know the Jews have gained insight into the black arts with their forbidden learning," said Popel. "And their perfidious Talmud mocks the virtue of celibacy, saying that a man who has no wife cannot be called a man."

The bishop begged, "Please—stop."

"I won't stop until the Talmud is forbidden once and for all," said Popel.

"I'll have it placed on the *Index Librorum Prohibitorum* as soon as I get back to Rome," said the bishop.

"That could take months. You have your secretary and scribe here at hand. You must do it now, my lord."

The clock on the table rang the hour for mid-morning prayer. It was a *memento mori* device, with a jeweled skull that popped out to remind the viewer that the moment of his death could come at any time.

"All right! Stuck—"

"Yes, my lord?" said the scribe.

The doctor removed the probe. The bishop gave a cry of relief, and stayed bent over, breathing heavily.

The scribe repeated his query.

The bishop said, "Draft a missive—PUFF PUFF—to His Eminence—PUFF PUFF—requesting that he ban the study of the Talmud—PUFF—in manuscript or any printed form."

"Yes, sir."

The doctor explained to Bishop Stempfel that he had a fissure in an embarrassing location.

"What's the cure? Surgery?"

"The Jews may practice such quackery, my lord, because they have no recourse to our miracle cures," said the doctor, reaching into his bag for a bottle of Saint Anthony's water and a small wooden box.

"They'd poison us all if they could," said Popel, "so thoroughly have they mastered the secret art of killing. And that is why we must avenge the blood-crime."

"Enough speeches," said Zeman. "We all know how you feel about the Jews."

Popel glared at him but said nothing more.

The doctor opened the box and removed a small object wrapped in faded golden cloth. He gently unraveled the blood-stiffened cloth and held up the withered finger of a long-dead saint. He sprinkled the relic with holy water and touched it to the bishop's wound, then the ordeal was finally over.

Greatly relieved, the bishop pulled his underclothes back on.

Zeman said, "My lord, grant me the authority to prosecute the heretical unbelievers in the neighborhood of Bethlehem Chapel."

A Protestant stronghold. Yes, that made sense, thought the bishop.

"Consider it done," he said.

"And sites of Christian martyrdom draw pilgrims as well," said Popel. And pilgrims spend money.

The bishop didn't take much stock in the bloodcrime story since the Laws of Moses forbid the shedding of innocent blood, but he felt obliged to draw up a report.

He finished dressing, and ordered the two priests to begin a campaign of general intimidation to ferret out and round up the leaders of the heretical sects. He was sure he'd find some witches among them.

CHAPTER 8

THE WIND SHIFTED, BLOWING DUST into my eyes and making me feel that I was fighting the wind no matter which way I was going. It didn't help that most of the Jewish Town was laid out in a labyrinth of dark and unfamiliar streets.

Rabbi Loew steadied himself, and we trudged toward the main street.

"Do we have a moment so I can go see my wife?" I asked.

"No, we need to prepare our case for the *kehileh*."

"What do you mean, 'our case'? We're making a simple request to remand a prisoner to the emperor's custody."

Rabbi Loew stopped and fixed one of his eagle eyes on me, his long cloak flapping in the breeze. "Tell me, Ben-Akiva, what happened to the Israelites after they crossed the Sea of Reeds into the wilderness?"

"They came to a place called Marah where the water was too bitter to drink."

"And—?"

"And they thought they were all going to die of thirst."

"But God said—?"

I searched my memory for the correct verse of Torah: *Vayoymer ... lekoyl*

*Adinoy... veha'azantoh lemitsvoysov veshomartoh kol khukoysovkol hamakhaloh
asher samti...*

"He said, 'Study Torah and you will live.'"

"Before He actually gave them the Torah."

True. The Lord had told them to keep His commandments before He gave
them the list of commandments.

"How is that possible?" asked the rabbi.

I focused on the deep furrows in my teacher's brow, with his white hair
blowing around like wild wheat along the edge of a lovingly plowed field that
had yielded harvest after harvest of wisdom.

I said, "Because the seven laws of Noah are so basic that they even apply
to the other nations that have not received the Torah, like the prohibitions
against incest, robbery, and murder."

"A good, straightforward answer, and ethically valid," said the rabbi. "But
only on one level. What is the deeper *d'rashic* meaning?"

Right. There was always a deeper meaning.

The narrow street was full of people who, despite their physical separation
and sparring elbows, shared a common thread stitching their lives together. It
was good to be among Jews, but I was not a part of their world yet—the world
of the Jews of Prague. I needed allies, contacts, connections. Hell, I'd welcome
an old enemy just to see a familiar face.

I floundered for a moment until the holy spirit of the *sh'khineh* came to me
and revealed the words I needed to fill the silence: *Eyn mukdem u-me'ukher ba-
toyreh.* There is no before and after in the Torah. "The Lord told them to follow
the Torah before they possessed the written text because the true Torah has
no beginning or end."

Rabbi Loew smiled the way other men do when a bet pays off. But there
was more. "You say that the Noahide laws are so basic that even idolators
should follow them."

"Well, except for the laws against idolatry."

"Don't joke with me."

"I wasn't joking—"

"And yet there are people who break God's most basic commandments
every day of the week. So what makes you think they will follow our little man-
made rules?"

A group of street boys ran past us toward the Fleyshbanksgasse, where the butchers were making a show of giving away their weight in meat to the poor.

I was getting used to the rabbi's humorless manner and elliptical logic, so I waited for the lesson to circle around to the point where it would reveal its relevance.

After a moment, the rabbi said, "The Sages warned us many times about the dangers of official corruption, but from what I have seen here, I would take their argument further and say that anyone who takes a rabbinical post in order to profit materially from it might as well be committing adultery."

His disillusion over petty corruption sounded awfully familiar, I'm afraid.

And I realized that I had allowed myself to nurture the hope that the magical city of Prague would somehow be different from other places.

But I recovered quickly. "That's probably why the Sages say that if all Israel were to observe two Sabbaths properly, we would immediately be redeemed."

"Amen to that," said Rabbi Loew. And he proceeded to fill me in on the local politics, telling me how the wealthy burghers get elected to public office because of their high standing in the community. But their standing is largely determined by their wealth, so the evil twins of money and power feed off each other in an endless cycle, while everybody else gets left out in the cold.

"I didn't know things had gotten that bad."

Rabbi Loew's eyes glowed with satisfaction, as if I had made the most remarkable statement. "I see that you are like the great Rabbi Hiyya bar Abba, who was never ashamed to admit when he had not learned something from his teachers. I think we are going to work very well together, Ben-Akiva."

This was my first taste of meaningful praise from Rabbi Loew, and my eyes dropped to the pavement. It was still cold out, but the temperature had climbed past freezing and the frost had long since melted with the passing of so many feet. I studied the wet footprints on the paving stones.

"What is it, my shammes?" asked the rabbi, following my gaze.

A faded mental picture was forming. "There were footprints in the frost outside of Federn's shop. When I first got there, before the crowds came."

After a moment, I added, "They were definitely men's boots. Much bigger than Federn's feet."

"Which way were they pointing?"

"They were entering the shop."

"Are you sure?"

I tried to bring the picture out of the watery fog.

"No," I said. "I'm not sure." But I had a pretty strong impression. As if *that* would sway the magistrates.

"The frost will be long gone by now," said Rabbi Loew. "We'll have to re-examine that from a more intuitive perspective later. Right now we need to be strictly logical."

The rabbi filled me in on the essentials of our strategy, while the breeze carried the tantalizing aroma of driftwood fires and the yearly ritual of matzoh preparation. The bakery's sooty windowpanes blurred the combined motions of the meal-master measuring out guarded flour, the *vasser-gisser* adding cold water for the kneader, and the *redler* making holes with a matzoh roller three-and-a-half-feet wide—really a huge rolling pin embedded with hundreds of iron spikes. It would make a formidable weapon, if such a use were permitted.

I shook off the thought.

The rabbi sensed that I had something important to say.

"Yes? What is it?"

I hesitated, my feet tingling with cold. I didn't know why it was so hard to speak about this. "Early this morning . . . I let myself get into a situation where I almost defiled the *kleperl* by using it to defend myself. First against dogs, then with rats."

"Well, in these exceptional times, we may be called upon to do exceptional things. It's just a piece of wood, after all. It's not worth losing your life to preserve its *kashres*," said the rabbi.

My breathing came back to me as if I had stepped away from the edge of an abyss. A different rabbi might have condemned me on the spot, depending on his inclination. Whenever a Jew seeks answers, he will find that Rabbi So-and-So says *this*, but Rabbi Such-and-Such says *that*. We are constantly introducing other interpretations of the passage under discussion. Even on the subject of resurrection, the Talmud refuses to provide a definitive answer, saying, "We will consider the subject when the dead come to life again."

In other words, we'll believe it when we see it.

Rabbi Loew said, "But that's not really what's bothering you, is it?"

"I thought you said we didn't have time for this."

"Don't dodge the question. It's not the law, but the situation you got yourself into, correct?"

The rabbi stopped and stood there, clearly expecting an answer.

So I took a deep breath and told him that the Cossacks had raided my village when I was barely old enough to go off to *kheyder* to learn to read and write.

"The whole *Yidngas* was looted and burned. Most of my *mishpokhe* were killed and the survivors scattered along with the ashes."

The rabbi nodded knowingly. "And yet you were not abandoned in the wilderness, or devoured by wild beasts."

We turned northward and walked past the busy storefronts. But I barely registered the sturdy women unfurling bolts of cloth and lifting crates for the customers while the men sat in the back rooms drinking tea with sugar and debating Midrash because women have no head for such things.

I told the rabbi that a Polish family had taken me in. It was heavy work, so they had to feed me. But they were cruel as only peasants can be cruel, and their children were sometimes worse.

"So I was just learning the *alef-beys* when most boys my age already knew whole tractates of the Talmud by heart."

"You didn't miss much. Germany is full of overpriced schools for rich kids who study Torah with Rashi's commentary before they are ready for it, with no Prophets or Holy Writings, then skip the Mishnah and go straight to the Talmud, which they learn by mindless repetition. I ask you, what nine-year-old can understand the Talmud?"

"What about young Lipmann?"

"That boy is a true prodigy, and he's following the regimen laid out in the Pirkey Avos. Torah at five, Mishnah at ten, Talmud at fifteen. But these days anyone looking for true insight has to leave the yeshivas and find his own pathway, as you are doing."

He added that he'd like to see my book of essays on education reform. I was stunned that he had heard of it, but I suppose I shouldn't have been.

"I don't have a copy with me," I said, very much aware of the sound of the words coming out of my mouth. "They might have one back at the old yeshiva in Kraków."

"I'm sure they do—in spite of whatever else you might think."

The Jewish Town Hall stood on the corner where Beleles Street widened into Rabbi Street, opposite the legendary Old-New Shul. I stopped to take in the sight of the miraculous stones that had come from the ruins of the Great

Temple in Jerusalem, or so people said. The shul's high-peaked roof soared over the sunken roofs of the ghetto. In the rarefied world of the Talmud, the shul is supposed to stand taller than all the other buildings in town. But in the nearby world of the Christians, its spire could not rise above any church within the fortified walls of the city. When they built it three hundred years ago, the Jews of Prague called it the New Shul. It followed the same twin nave layout as the shuls in Vienna and Regensburg, but those two bright pearls were destroyed during the expulsions of 1420 and 1519, leaving only this one and its older sister in Worms as the last Ashkenazic shuls standing in the two-pillar style of the ancient temples. Over the years, newer shuls had risen from the floodplain of the Vltava River, and the great synagogue was given its distinctive Old-New name, embodying within its very walls the mystical principle of the union of opposites.

Altneuschul in German, and *Staranová skola* in Czech.

It was the only freestanding building in the *Yidnshtot*, the only structure that did not seem to be squeezed against a sooty tenement with a couple of broken windows.

"So how did a Polish farmboy like you end up meeting a big city girl like Reyzl Rozansky?" the rabbi asked.

I woke up as if from a bad dream. We were still standing across the street from the Jewish Town Hall.

"At the fair in Kraków," I said. "I was collecting books for the poor students, and the Rozanskys were shopping around for a suitable match for their daughter. Rich or poor, it didn't matter, as long as the young man had some *yikhes*."

"And you had some *yikhes*? How did you manage that?"

"They saw one of Rabbi Lindermeyer's disciples speaking to me in the open market, and that was enough to satisfy them."

Rabbi Loew nodded solemnly.

I would always remember my old master, the great philosopher of Kraków, as a logical and forceful teacher who was brave enough to stand up in a crowded room and tell the authorities precisely what they didn't want to hear. And I suddenly found myself wishing that I could summon the spirit of my old master to help us argue this case before the Town Council.

"And then?"

"And then Reyzl came with me to Slonim and we shared the holy fire that holds the material of creation together."

It seemed to be taking forever to cross the street.

The Jewish Town Council met in a cavernous room with a high-vaulted ceiling and rows of white benches for the plaintiffs, their supporters, and anybody else who happened to wander in from the cold. Three judges with gray beards sat on a raised platform, listening to an old woman plead for public assistance while the community secretary transcribed everything with a silver pen. She had no family left, her eyes were weak and her hands too gnarled from decades of piecework to continue supporting herself as a seamstress.

The community secretary sat at his little desk, waiting for the woman to say something he hadn't heard a hundred times before.

She asked for a few kreuzers a week from the community fund to keep her out of the *hekdesh*.

The secretary shook his head wearily. Nobody wanted to go to the poorhouse.

The judges brought the proceedings to a close, and Rabbis Joseph, Aaron, and Hayyot were about to vote two-to-one against the old woman, when several of the spectators rose to their feet in a customary show of respect when they realized that Rabbi Loew had entered the hall. Rabbi Joseph took a good look at Rabbi Loew and switched his vote. The decision stood two-to-one in the old woman's favor.

Rabbi Hayyot called for the next case. His eyes were gray and watery, his face drained. As the outgoing Chief Rabbi of Prague, he looked like he was counting the days till he could retire from all this.

The court secretary consulted the docket and called out the name of Reb Bernstein, a jewelry merchant specializing in Bohemian amber.

Rabbi Loew nudged me, and I stepped forward and addressed the bench.

"Your honors, forgive the disruption, but we have an urgent matter to bring before the *kehileh*—"

"Really? Well you can wait your turn. I'm next," said Reb Bernstein.

"Submit your names and they will be put at the end of the docket," said the secretary.

"Your honors, we can't wait until the end of the day—"

Reb Bernstein said, "Neither can I, mister. Who do you think you are, anyway?"

Someone answered back: "Hey, Bernstein, he's the fifth shammes."

Rabbi Aaron said, "Why are we hearing from this servant?"

In ancient Hebrew, *shammash* literally means *servant*.

"Your honors, this man has no standing in the community," said Bernstein. "He has no right to address the council ahead of me."

Rabbi Loew cleared his throat. "Your honors, I have authorized Reb Ben-Akiva to speak on my behalf," he said, deliberately using my Hebrew name to evoke the fallen heroes of the second-century uprising against the Roman Empire.

"Are you making a formal request that we take your case out of the prescribed order?" said Rabbi Aaron.

Rabbi Loew said, "Yes, we are, your honors."

"The court secretary will note that Rabbi Loew has made a request for his case to be taken out of order. Reb Bernstein, do you object to this request?"

Reb Bernstein shifted uncomfortably. Rabbi Loew held no official position in Prague's Jewish community, but he was a distinguished scholar and a known firebrand who was respected well beyond the borders of the empire. Reb Bernstein chose not to object.

"Very well," said Rabbi Aaron. "The council will hear the case of Rabbi Judah Loew. Rabbi Loew?"

Rabbi Loew weighed his words carefully. "We are facing a grave and immediate threat to the whole community which must be given priority."

Rabbi Loew now turned to me.

He was leaving it up to *me* to make the case?

I quickly explained, "The Christian authorities have arrested Jacob Federn and taken him to the city jail on a false bloodcrime charge."

A great commotion rattled the benches and churned up the hall.

"And what action do you expect the court to take in this matter?" said Rabbi Aaron, shouting over the noise.

"The Jewish community needs to ask *keyser* Rudolf to transfer Reb Federn from the stockhouse to the royal prison, or else we'll have to bail him out ourselves."

"Look who's talking like he's part of the community," said Reb Bernstein.

Rabbi Aaron said, "How much is that going to cost us?"

I had no idea. The monetary disputes in Slonim were pretty small by comparison.

Rabbi Loew came to my aid. "In capital cases of this kind, bail is usually set around ten thousand gulden."

A collective gasp escaped from the spectators' lips, as if they had all been slapped in the face at the same time. The *gildn* is a small gold coin worth about ten dalers.

"That is a great deal of money to spend on one man," said Rabbi Hayyot.

"A merchant of feathers, no less," someone said, bringing smiles to the round faces in the first few rows of benches.

I told them, "This is not about one man. They're going to seal off the whole ghetto. And if the city authorities torture him, by Sunday night he'll be telling them the Jews drink blood, and by Monday morning we'll all be in deep *tsures.*"

"Then why hasn't it been announced by the city criers?" Rabbi Aaron said, and cautioned me to be mindful of how I addressed this distinguished body. I had forgotten to use their titles.

I said, "Forgive me, your honors. Sometimes I have the manners of a Polish peasant. I don't always knock on doors, either."

Rabbi Joseph ignored my unseemly remarks and said, "There is a reasonable precedent in a case like this. The last time the *goyim* tried to expel us from Silesia, we bought them off with a couple of thousand gold pieces."

"And we only had to put up one-fifth of the total amount," said Rabbi Aaron. "The rest was collected from the communities in Moravia and the three lands—"

"We only have three days, your honors," I insisted.

There were so many ways to make the case, but I needed time to prepare *and* the respect of my listeners, and I didn't have much of either.

"Too bad you can't pummel your way out of this one," someone said, turning my hard-earned reputation against me.

"Yeah, we're not a bunch of drunken Cossacks," someone else agreed.

I searched the book-lined corridors of my mind for the best place to start the discussion. Always begin with a joke, urged a Babylonian sage cited in the tractate on Shabbes, but that wasn't appropriate to every situation. So I appealed to the Sanhedrin, the council of seventy wise men convened to pronounce judgment on the weightiest issues.

Somehow my tongue turned my scattered thoughts into a reasonably coherent argument. "Your honors, esteemed burghers of Prague, and members of the Jewish community: the Rabbis taught us that no one member of our tribe may be sacrificed for the good of the many. If a group of Jews in a strange land is surrounded by a heathen mob who say, 'Give us one of your number, or we will kill you all,' they all must be killed, for no Israelite may be deliberately delivered to the heathen."

The room grew tense as each of the spectators imagined his own death. They saw themselves run through with pikes and steel swords, felt the rough brown hemp tighten around their throats, the horses' hooves crushing their bones, the Inquisitional flames consuming their clothes, hair, and flesh.

"Your logic is certainly to the point, except for one problem," Rabbi Aaron replied. "The Christians aren't heathen. And the rabbis also ruled that if the mob specifies an individual by name, we must surrender him and save our own lives."

The benches exhaled with collective relief.

I was ready for that one. "But in what circumstances does this apply? Rabbi Karo teaches that ransoming captives is the most supreme act of charity, more than building a shul or feeding the poor—"

Rabbi Aaron dismissed Rabbi Karo's modern interpretation of ancient law. "The Talmud clearly states that captives should not be ransomed at excessively high prices, or else our enemies will learn to profit from it."

"But that ruling doesn't apply in this case," I said. "Reb Federn hasn't been kidnapped. He's been arrested."

"Big difference," said one of the merchants, a spice trader in the fourth row.

Rabbi Aaron countered with a Midrash: "Rabbi Joshua once stopped at a roadside inn, where a woman prepared lentils for his meal—"

"Some say it was beans," Rabbi Joseph interjected.

The judges took a moment to discuss this discrepancy among themselves, nodding their heads as they debated the issue.

I looked to Rabbi Loew for direction. He gestured for me to be patient. So I stood there watching a drowsy merchant in the second row whose eyelids were fluttering on the edge of sleep.

Rabbi Aaron resumed his homily. "We have decided that the question as to whether it was lentils or beans must be left for Elijah the Prophet to resolve when he returns to bring peace to the world. The point is that after the meal, Rabbi Joshua overheard one of the other travelers talking about the dark days of the Empire, when the Romans surrounded the holy city of Jerusalem, and a group of hot-headed radicals urged the Jews to fight to the death."

He paused to make sure that everyone was listening closely. They were.

"Rabban Yohanan ben Zakkai, may his name be exalted, didn't want to see his beloved people die in a pointless standoff. So after careful deliberation, he decided that the best possible action was to accept that the Romans had won, and to try to negotiate with them. However, he was well aware of the fact that if the Jews saw him approaching the enemy camp, the gossip might spread that he was betraying them. What could he do? I'll tell you. He had himself smuggled out of the city in a coffin, risking his own life in order to save many."

I told the court, "So what's your solution? Sneak everyone out of the ghetto and hope the Christians don't notice? Any idea where we can get three thousand coffins on such short notice?"

The astonished burghers rose up like waves in a storm, and Rabbi Hayyot called for order.

Someone shouted, "Yeah, why don't we just dig a tunnel under the wall all the way to Jerusalem while we're at it?" and I sensed a shifting of the tide as bits of laughter cascaded down from the galleries.

Rabbi Aaron's eyebrows collapsed into an angry V. "We can't risk provoking the Christians in such a manner. That would only inflame their anger and make things worse."

I couldn't help saying, "How could it get any worse? They already think we cook with blood."

Rabbi Loew stepped in. "Your honors, and my longtime friends in the community, in difficult times we must remember the words of Rabbi Akiva, may his light shine in Paradise, who taught us to attend to God first, then to our own needs. He taught us that if a Jew in the desert has only enough water left to drink or to wash, but not enough for both, it is better to die of thirst than to eat without purifying the hands."

Good strategy. Hold a mirror up to their own mortality. Nobody wants to look death in the face unless God is by their side.

"We must act together to save Jacob Federn," said Rabbi Loew. "As it is written, *Loy samed al dam reyekhoh.*" Thou shalt not stand idly by the blood of thy neighbor.

Yes, a commandment. That'll shame them into action.

"I agree that this is definitely a test of our worthiness," said Rabbi Joseph. "We need to enter into a state of purity and concentration in order to find a way out of this dilemma. Normally, the first step in the process would be fasting, but since we cannot fast during the festival of Pesach, we must first purify our bodies by immersion in the *mikvehs* and by staying away from women and other unclean things for several days."

I said, "We don't *have* days."

Reb Bernstein threw up his hands in disgust. "Your honors, when are we going to discuss *my* situation?"

Rabbi Joseph said, "In a moment, Reb Bernstein. Don't you realize that the cause of this terrible problem could very well be that one of our mezuzahs is written incorrectly? I have heard of cases where a single misspelled word—*even a single letter*—can bring about such tragedies. It is therefore my opinion that we must organize a committee to inspect all the mezuzahs in the *Yidnshtot*. We'll need some volunteers."

Several voices from the floor answered the call.

The sleeping merchant's head jerked up.

"What are we discussing?" he asked, confused about the flurry of activity.

I said, "Your honors, we still need an official request from the Jewish community for *keyser* Rudolf to transfer the accused, Jacob Federn, from the city jail to the royal prison in the castle."

The spice trader spoke up again. "Your honors, am I the only one who remembers that another Hapsburg *keyser* named Rudolf ordered the confiscation of Jewish property in Speyer, and Mainz, and the rest of the lower Rhineland? So why should we trust a second Rudolf?"

Talk about a long memory. That was a hundred years *before* the big Easter pogrom, but it might as well have been yesterday.

Rabbi Hayyot nodded in agreement. "Without proof of Federn's innocence, such a request would only anger the gentiles. It's too risky."

Rabbi Loew said, "Fine, fine, we'll get proof. But we will need a small allotment of funds in order to proceed effectively."

Rabbi Aaron said, "What do you need money for?"

Reb Bernstein said, "Your honors, *please*—"

Rabbi Loew cut him off: "Since the alleged bloodcrime took place in the Christian part of the city, we're going to need to speak to Christian witnesses. And that's going to take a little *gelt*."

Rabbi Aaron was outraged. "Are you suggesting that the *kehileh* support the deplorable practice of *bribery* when it is written that a bribe corrupts the mind and perverts justice?"

I objected. "Your honor, those passages of Scripture specifically refer to taking a bribe as payment for finding an innocent person guilty of a crime they did not commit."

But Rabbi Aaron overruled me. "You should stick to studying the Talmud instead of that heretic Rambam and other books which ought to be burned in the fire. Haven't we learned from Rabbi Eliezer that whoever teaches his daughter Torah teaches her to be a whore?"

Even though I was a newcomer, I knew that was a personal attack on Rabbi Loew's family.

"Bring us proof of Federn's innocence, and we'll take up the matter in a special session on Sunday."

Rabbi Hayyot said, "Call the next case."

The secretary announced Reb Bernstein's case.

"Finally," said Reb Bernstein.

I said, "Your honors, just give us a few dalers to finance the investigation."

But they refused even that.

"We'll meet again on Sunday."

CHAPTER 9

"WELL, THAT CERTAINLY SUCCEEDED," I said. "It succeeded in making things *worse*."

"It only appears that way," said Rabbi Loew. "But the hand of God is working behind the curtain."

"Must be a mighty thick curtain."

"Don't take it personally. They do that to everybody who's not from the community."

"Well, I'm not everybody. You must have really annoyed Rabbi Aaron with your last book."

"Just be thankful that the Lord in His wisdom created only a few wise men, because if every man were as wise as those judges are, the human race would die of starvation in a few weeks."

We had to step around the piles of rough-hewn stones where masons and their harried apprentices were paving the side street. The sound of their chisels rang through the air. Then the Breitgasse abruptly narrowed and we found ourselves sharing the street with a group of country folk driving their livestock to the Butchers' Block to be slaughtered for their holiday dinner. A couple of high-class Jews wearing doublets of Bohemian brocade with silk highlights raised the hems of their cloaks and stepped gingerly over the clogged gutters.

But there was trouble at the East Gate. A pair of stiff-necked burghers insisted that they had urgent business to attend to in the Old Town, but the guards weren't letting anybody in or out. Sheriff's orders, they said.

"Let me see the written order," I said, trying to bluff my way past them.

But the guards laughed in my face. "Written order? That's a good one!"

"Then let me hear it from the sheriff himself, not his underlings."

The guards must have had some doubts, because they actually called the sheriff over.

"What is it now, Jews?" said Sheriff Zizka.

"We need to speak to His Majesty's consuls," said the rabbi.

"No one is allowed to leave the Jewish Town," said Zizka.

"Not even to appeal to the emperor?"

"What did I just say?"

"May we at least speak to the accused's wife?"

"Take the wax out of your ears, grandpa."

I pushed forward. "Pardon me, Sheriff, but you're the one who ordered us to hand over the killer, and now you won't let us visit the shop where the crime was discovered, ask the neighbors what they saw, or examine the area for signs of what actually occurred. So maybe you can tell me how we're supposed to solve a crime that took place outside the ghetto when we're trapped on the inside of it?"

One of the burghers said, "Killer? What do you mean, killer?"

But when Zizka didn't tell me to drop dead right away, I knew we had a chance.

"Oh, hell," said Zizka. "All right, come on. I'll have to escort you. Just the two of you," he said, while his men forced the outraged burghers back onto their side of the gate with the blunt ends of their pikestaffs.

"You've got one hour," said Zizka.

I started to protest.

"He said you got one hour, Jews," a burly city guard breathed in my face.

"With four guards on you at all times," said Zizka.

"Yes, sir." The guards took up positions, two in front and two behind us, forming the official escort for a couple of unwilling ambassadors from the *Yidnshtot*.

Confused voices in the crowd asked:

"Where are you taking them?"

"What's going on?"

The sheriff reached inside his tunic and pulled out a handwritten proclamation about the bloodcrime offense.

"As soon as the final copies of this proclamation receive the official seal of the city, it will be read in every public square on both sides of the river. And for those of you who can't read Christian writing, it says that no one gets in or out till one of you produces the criminal or comes forward and confesses to the crime himself."

"How soon before the announcement is made?" I asked.

"The criers are getting their boots on right now, Jew."

"Then we'd better get moving."

Zizka cocked his eyebrow at me, trying to figure out what kind of hand I was playing. But we set out on our mission.

Rabbi Loew said, "Now, let's talk about the matter at hand. If we presume that Federn is not guilty, the question then becomes—"

Zizka said, "I understand your Jewish jargon, you know."

"*To je v pořádku, pane Žižko,*" said the rabbi. Very well. So he began replacing the Germanic words in his speech with Hebrew wherever possible, because it was true that many of the Czech officials understood spoken Yiddish.

"So if Jacob Federn didn't *hargeh* Gerta Janek, the *shayleh* is, Who did *hargeh* her? What do the *tsadikim* say? What is the one thing that makes people risk everything that really matters?"

"That's an easy one. *Kesef. Gelt.* The almighty daler. And the *tsadikim* say that a man 'will not commit a sin unless he is going to profit from it,'" I said, quoting the Bava Metziah tractate in the original Aramaic, which was also the language of Jesus.

"Yes. The love of money can poison people's souls and drive them to commit horrifying acts. Only one other thing makes people go so completely *meshuge.*"

I knew that one, too: "*Yodah.*"

To know intimately, as in *Breyshis* 4.1: "Adam *yodah*'d his wife Eve."

"Was there any sign of it?"

"I couldn't tell. Not in front of all those Christians, Rabbi."

"So we may be dealing with the crime of *yodah*, and the innocent *nareh* was left in a Jewish shop to make the proprietor look like the guilty one."

"It's possible, but if I needed to get rid of a body quickly in this town, you'll excuse me for saying so, I'd just dump it in the river. This was too well planned for that. The girl had to be concealed, the lock had to be picked— somebody went to a lot of trouble, and it's more likely that it was a business rival with an old grudge or someone else who'd profit from ruining Federn by implicating him in the bloodcrime."

"Maybe, maybe not. We don't have any evidence yet."

The sky was grim and gray.

Freyde Federn sat in her family's shop, under heavy guard, staring blankly out at the world like a soldier after a long day on the battlefield. She hadn't bothered to relight the lantern, even though the wick had burnt down. But at least she hadn't been arrested yet.

Zizka led the way into the store. I inspected the threshold, but of course heavy foot traffic and rising temperatures had erased all traces of the outsized boot prints I had seen before.

The floor was still covered with bloodstains, plainly visible to all, and dried to a rusty brown.

Rabbi Loew tried to console her. "Have faith, Freyde, we'll get you out of this."

"How?" she asked. "I'm surrounded by armed guards who keep glaring at me and stroking their weapons."

I said, "They may have the advantage of weapons and superior numbers, but you have something better than that—a pair of professional Midrash scholars on your side."

I wasn't just kidding around, since the root word of *midrash* means to inquire or investigate.

I asked about Federn's business rivals. Was anyone jealous of him? Greedy? Did some partnership go sour? Was he—I stopped myself from asking about their marital relations. It was too early in the investigation to put her through that.

She said no to everything. Federn wasn't a scholar like we were. He had little time for Torah studies because he spent most of his time running the shop, and she didn't know anything about his possible dealings on the side.

"Did your husband leave your home at any time before I knocked on the shutters this morning and called you to shul?"

"No, he hadn't stepped out yet."

"You're sure?"

"He was still in his nightshirt, Mr. Shammes. Believe me. He was in no hurry to face the day."

I wondered if there was another reason that Federn was in no mood to face the day besides the cold winter morning, but I believed her. So those boot prints going into the shop must have belonged to the men who brought the girl's body here. The prints were fresh, which meant that just before I made my early morning rounds, someone carrying the lifeless corpse, evidently still warm and bleeding, waited for his accomplice to open the lock, then tossed the child's body inside. Since my own desire to bring a child into the world had ended with the premature expulsion from Reyzl's womb of a couple of blood-soaked kidney beans on a twisted cord, I couldn't imagine the heart cold and unfeeling enough to do that to someone's little girl. They must have had a dark reason indeed, and I was determined to bring it to light, no matter whose reputation was shattered or what damage followed in its wake.

"Courage, Freyde," said Rabbi Loew. "God will show us the way."

The municipal guards stood on the pavement outside the shop, their round metal helmets aligned in a series of distorted reflections of Freyde's moment of agony. My eyes dropped to the dark bloodstains on the floor.

I needed to sound calm and reassuring, but my voice seemed a bit out of practice. "Listen to me, Mrs. Federn. Whoever did this thinks he's got us beaten. He's probably out there right now, laughing at us."

Freyde cast a quick glance outside, as if she might spot a pair of red-rimmed eyes floating in a cloud of foul-smelling smoke.

I leaned in closer. "But if we can light a fire under him and make him sweat a little, maybe he'll get nervous and make a mistake."

"That sounds wonderful, Mr. Shammes. But how does a bearded Jew make a *goy* nervous?"

"A wise old rabbi once told me that for certain people *it's not what is, it's what they happen to believe*. They already think we're powerful magicians. We might as well use it against them," I said, straightening up and walking over to the spot where the girl's body had lain, clearly outlined in her own blood.

The guards turned around to watch. Zizka warned me not to touch the bloodstains.

I said, "I have no intention of touching any of your precious blood, since there's a much easier way to solve this riddle."

I planted myself with my legs apart and announced in my most authoritative call-to-prayer voice, "The man who left the girl's body here was about six feet tall, and strong enough to lift ninety pounds with one arm. He wore eleven-inch-long boots with pointed metal toes, one of which was slightly dented at the left instep. His accomplice was about the same size and strength, but despite their well-developed muscles, they can't hide the fact that they were both yellow-bellied cowards."

I let that sink in a moment.

"Such big men going after a little girl," I said, shaking my head disgustedly. "But their ignorance will be their undoing, because such appalling and unmanly behavior leaves unmistakable traces that will betray them just as surely as I am standing here."

I took a pouch from my cloak and said, "All I have to do is gather some of the dust from this spot, which contains tiny traces of the murderers' essences, bind it with a cloth and bury it in a shallow grave. And just as the dust cannot leave the place where it is buried, so will the assassins be unable to escape the confines of the city until the knot is untied and the dust is scattered once again by the winds."

The Christians watched wide-eyed as I knelt next to the dried blood, gathered some dirt and grit from the floor, and sprinkled it into the pouch.

Rabbi Loew drew in a sharp breath, but I kept going, waving my hand back and forth over the pouch while reciting a litany of oaths in Hebrew and Yiddish. Then I slipped the pouch under my cloak and followed the great rabbi into the street.

"Where to now?"

"The offices of *keyser* Rudolf's consulate in Old Town Square," said the rabbi.

"Don't get used to leading us around like this, Jew," said Zizka.

"Don't worry, we won't," I said.

The sheriff looked me in the eye. "Keep talking like that and I'll lead you both straight to the gallows."

"Really, Ben-Akiva," cautioned the rabbi under his breath. "You have to be careful not to incite the *goyim* with that kind of *abracadabra* talk."

"They're the ones who made up the rules to this dirty game, Rabbi. I'm just bluffing my way through it. Maybe it'll throw a scare into their thick hides. It worked all the time on Polish peasants."

"Well, these are *not* Polish peasants. They're sophisticated burghers."

We marched down the Geistgasse, guarded in front and behind, looking every bit like prisoners being taken to the stockhouse. Tradesmen and housewives stopped and stared as we waded through a stream of lambs being driven to market to be slaughtered and roasted for Easter. A group of street kids started tagging along, pelting us with clods of dirt and laughing and chanting their nasal *nyah-nyahs*.

"*Barook anooka hakh anakha laka haka shmaka!*"

"What are they saying?"

The rabbi said, "I believe they are trying to make fun of the Holy Tongue."

A wet clump of mud struck my shoulder and spattered on Zizka's tunic.

Zizka said, "All right, knock it off, kids. You're not helping me any."

Some of the boys made crude farting noises with their mouths and ran off, the streets echoing with their laughter.

We turned onto Dlouhá Street and caught a strong whiff from a big pile of rotting vegetable and animal matter. It was much bigger than the small-town dunghills, but it didn't smell any different.

Suddenly the street opened up into the big square and a bumpkinish "Oh my God" came out of my mouth.

The Old Town Hall's square bell tower was three or four times taller than the Old-New Shul. It must have been two hundred feet high. Bigger than anything had a right to be. Huge. Talk about having more power than you knew what to do with. It was an overwhelming display of Christian dominance. What chance did we have against such power?

The square was jammed with merchants and carpenters setting up for the Easter festivities, the men whistling springtime airs and nailing their display booths together while the women stirred steaming pots of vegetable dye and prepared colorful strips of cloth for Sunday's decorations. A solemn procession snaked through the middle of the square to the entrance of Our Lady of Týn, bearing tall crosses draped with purple-and-black cloth. The pious processionists took little notice of the sheriff and his quartet of armed guards leading a pair of convicts to the imperial consulate.

Some of the whistling stopped as the craftsmen spied the yellow rings on our cloaks that clearly marked us as Jews. But they kept right on working.

On the far side of the dunghill stood the public pillories, overflowing with the sagging limbs of thieves, swindlers, and other petty criminals whose crimes did not approach the level of blasphemy. Two women stood off to the side of the raised platform with their hands shackled behind them and leather masks covering their mouths. I wondered what their crime was. Licentiousness? Infidelity? Cursing in public?

"Disobedience," the sheriff explained. "They must wear the Mask of Shame for three days for talking back to their husbands."

Imagine if we had that law, I thought. My wife talked back to me three times a day. Or, she used to, when she was talking to me.

We kept walking. The streets were full of statues of Christian heroes. We passed a tall pedestal bearing a moss-covered statue of some bearded saint with a starry halo, a flowing robe, and two fat cherubs at his feet. *Where are the statues of our heroes?* I wondered. If the Christians were going to ignore the broad prohibition against making graven images of the holy ones, why couldn't we? Where is the statue of Moses, who led the people out of slavery? Or Joshua, who made the sun stand still in Giveon? Or Samson, who brought the whole damn building down in Gaza?

At this point, I'd settle for Jonah, I thought.

A gargoyle frozen in mid-scream greeted us over the double doors to the consulate's office.

In the darkened vestibule, a bone-white ghost of a man in long black robes materialized and told us to wait. The man's skin was pale to the point of translucency, and his face seemed to hang in the air above his body.

Rabbi Loew lowered himself onto a wooden bench and let out the long sigh of a tired old man. He had been full of fire when we left the community council chamber, but the flame was starting to wane. I took a seat next to him, and the guards leaned on their pikestaffs and waited.

I heard the tentative pitter-patter of rain on the roof, then it started coming down in sheets as it did every Good Friday. Of course, early springtime was the rainy season, so the odds of getting rain on any given Friday were pretty good. But it sure seemed like a pattern, a definite sign of the divine presence.

For a moment, I almost envied the Christians for their simple relationship with God. They were so assured, so certain that God in the form of a man called Jesus had walked among them, that he had stood at such-and-such a place and said all you have to do is believe in me and you'll go straight to heaven, guaranteed. Then he broke the matzoh in pieces, passed around the wine cup, and said let's drink to it. Meanwhile the Jews had to contend with a God who had withdrawn into Himself in order to create the world, dooming His creatures to eternal separation from His endlessness, leaving nothing but the faintest golden pathways of mysticism as the only way to bridge this great gap, even for a fleeting instant.

Rabbi Loew looked at the thick raindrops hitting the diamond-shaped panes of glass and said, "See how God always reminds us of the more powerful forces that exist outside of ourselves."

"As if I needed reminding," I said.

If Abraham, who had *direct* contact with God, couldn't always fathom the ways of the Judge of all the Earth, what hope did we have? Every tractate of the Talmud began by skipping page *alef* and starting on page *beys*, the second page, just to remind us that our knowledge will *never* be complete.

"Let's get back to business," I said. "Maybe somebody owed Federn money. We should go talk to this Janek fellow. One of the witnesses saw them arguing a couple of days ago."

"A Christian witness? *Vey iz mir.* Use your head. Why would anyone kill a child to get out of a debt to a Jew when it's so easy to stir up hatred against us?"

"It's been done before."

"You need to ask yourself what larger benefit is gained by sealing off the whole ghetto."

"You mean, aside from canceling all the debts, chasing the Jews out of town, seizing all their property, and dividing it up among themselves?"

"There are always larger forces at work," said Rabbi Loew. "But you're right. After we're through here, I think it would be a good idea to speak to the girl's father."

The double doors opened soundlessly, and the ghostly apparition reappeared. Not a board had creaked. I checked to make sure that the man's feet were touching the ground.

The spectral figure said, "Go home, Jews. The emperor remains secluded in his Hall of Wonders high up on the hill, and he won't be able to see you until tomorrow, in his chambers in the castle."

The Hapsburg courtier spoke High German, so I had no problem understanding this royal brush-off.

Rabbi Loew said, "Very well, but could you at least convey a message to the emperor, humbly asking His Majesty to consider authorizing the transfer of Jacob Federn to the imperial prison?"

"Is this a formal request from the community council?"

"It's an exceptional case," said the rabbi, avoiding an outright lie.

"What is so exceptional about it?"

"The emperor has always behaved like one of the righteous Gentiles toward my people. It is not pleasing to God for a wise and just ruler to stand aside and allow one man's sins to lead to the destruction of an entire community."

"Oh, I suppose we can look into it," the man conceded.

Eloquent praise for the emperor and his consuls poured forth from Rabbi Loew's lips.

Good thing one of us is skilled at this kind of carnival act, I thought. Thank God for small victories.

Because that's the only kind we ever get.

We were preparing to leave when the emperor's representatives called Zizka into the inner chamber. Alone. The sheriff agreed, but his face was a tight mask as he disappeared through the double doors, which clicked shut behind him.

"What kind of man is the *meylekh*?" I said, using Hebrew words again so the guards wouldn't follow our conversation.

"*Der meylekh* Rudolf is a better friend to the Jews than most German monarchs, but he carries in his veins some of the bilious humors of the Spanish Hapsburgs. His mother, the Empress María, went utterly *meshuge* at the end."

I nodded. So even the emperor wasn't at peace with himself.

INSIDE THE CHAMBER, AN ICY voice instructed Sheriff Zizka to step forward onto the silver-threaded carpet. One of the emperor's councilors had come down from the castle on the hill to talk to the restless locals. The man had so much precious metal on his chest he might as well have been wearing a service for twelve of the emperor's own silverware.

"The monarch has just welcomed the Holy Inquisitor to the imperial city," said the councilor. "And we need to show Pope Clement's emissary that the Bohemians are not a tribe of wild men who just learned to eat with a knife and spoon. Now what's all this I hear about a bloodcrime charge? This isn't the Dark Ages. We don't want any riots, Zizka. It would look bad. *Rosumíte mi?*"

"Yes, I understand. But it won't be easy. The city is crawling with soldiers on leave from the Turkish front—imperial soldiers, I might add—and all the farm girls coming to the city to work as maids for the rich burghers are getting fleeced by robbers, rapists, *banditi*, you name it. Hand-held pistols are starting to get more popular with the cutpurses and highwaymen, too, and I don't like it one bit."

"Sounds like you could use a little help from the imperial guards, maybe with cracking down on dissident religious sects?"

"We can keep order among the regular citizens just fine. Most of the religious hatred comes from outsiders."

Like you, the sheriff's tone implied.

"See that no atrocities occur, Zizka. Keep a lid on this madness, or it's your head."

And that wasn't just a figure of speech.

BACK ON THE STREET, Rabbi Loew said, "We need to visit one more place. Viktor Janek's house."

"In this rain?" said a guard.

"Why should I allow you to disturb the family in their time of grief?" said Zizka.

"It's on our way."

"Don't push your luck, Jew."

I said, "Yeah, I was wondering when this fabulous streak of luck was going to end."

"What is the matter with you, you smart-mouthed Jew? Have you got a damned death wish or something?" Zizka seized the hilt of his weapon. And before he knew it, every eye in the square was upon him. Some of the devotees even stopped reciting their Good Friday prayers, and for a moment, the only sound I heard was the bleating of Paschal Lambs.

I saw the sheriff vacillating, trying to decide whether to issue a stern reprimand or simply run me through. I had never seen such hesitation from an authority figure determined to save face.

A man tugging on a couple of stubborn sheep mocked us by asking, "Tell me, Jews, if you're so smart, what is this sheep saying?"

I listened to the animal's drawn-out bleating and said, "Help, I'm being pulled along by an idiot."

Some of the women hid their faces and giggled. Even the sheriff shook his head and chuckled.

And the whole thing was defused by laughter. The craftsmen went back to work, and the pious citizens who had stepped out of line rejoined the procession.

It is better to be ridiculed than shamed, the saying goes. But I was starting to wonder when the luck would run out.

Rabbi Loew laid a hand on my shoulder. "The next time we're surrounded by hostile Christians, we won't be able to break it up with a laugh."

A cold wetness was seeping into my cloak as we plodded through the rain to Janek's apothecary shop on Kozí Street.

The shop was closed and shuttered, but smoke was rising from the chimney.

"You sure you know what you're doing?" asked Zizka.

"I'm afraid that I have a great deal of experience consoling the grieving parents of murdered children," Rabbi Loew said, stepping under the eaves out of the rain.

Zizka said nothing as he pounded on the door with a chain-mailed fist.

But when Marie Janek opened the door, her eyes grew wide and she screamed at us, calling us shameless murderers for daring to show our faces. Then Viktor Janek came toward us with a heavy iron poker straight from the fire.

Rabbi Loew spoke quickly. "I realize that you can't help hating the people you believe are responsible for the death of your child, but you must understand that we are trying to find the guilty one because your loss is being turned into a rallying cry for more blood. May God punish us for our sins, but violence always begets more violence, and no amount of bloodshed will bring her back."

I waited to see what effect the rabbi's words would have.

Then Viktor Janek swung the poker at our heads. I threw myself between the rabbi and the impaler's edge, as the guards deflected the blow with their pikes. Rain sizzled on the hot metal tip of the weapon as they grappled with Janek and kept him from branding any Jews with it.

"I ought to shove this down your throats!" Janek shouted. Some of the neighbors egged him on.

"Take it easy, big fellow," said Zizka, restraining the vengeful man with both hands.

"Thanks for protecting us in the name of your city," I said.

"Stuff it, Jew," said one of the guards.

"I told you this was a lousy idea. Let's get out of here," Zizka complained.

"No, let them stay."

The men stopped struggling. Marie Janek stood in the doorway, her face streaked with tears.

"Marie—"

"Why have you come here? What do you want from us?"

Rabbi Loew said, "We are here because we are your cousins and brothers in blood. And we grieve for you, as we would grieve for any parent who has lost a son or daughter. But you should take comfort in the fact that the soul of this innocent will shine a light upon the darkness."

"How can that be?" she asked, desperate to find comfort anywhere in the wide, empty world.

Janek said, "Don't listen to this garbage—"

But she stepped inside, and left the door open for her rain-soaked visitors.

We followed her in, and were greeted by the faint aroma of exotic herbs and spices. I removed my hat in deference to the Christian custom. Rabbi Loew faltered, then did the same. He must have felt naked without his fine velvet hat, but at the moment the Janeks did not need to be reminded how different we Jews were.

We sat near the fire, waiting for the mourners to speak first, even though this was not a place of *shiva*.

I got a glimpse of the barrels stacked inside Janek's shop, and noted the jars of herbs and oils and powders before Janek slammed the connecting door shut.

Eventually, Marie Janek said, "One of you took my little girl away. They tell me she's in a better place, but I will never stop seeing the emptiness all around me, her empty clothes, her empty bed. What can you possibly do about *that*?"

Rabbi Loew nodded, and let a moment of silence pass before saying, "Children are supposed to carry our memories with them into the future. We never really die, as long as someone is alive to remember us. For even when a mighty cedar is felled, there is always hope that if God sends the rain, fresh shoots will sprout up from the roots."

"And now we have nothing."

"You have more than you think," I said.

"What do you mean?"

"They say that the less you have in this world, the more you shall have in the next."

Marie nodded dully.

I spoke in Germanic Yiddish now, reversing my earlier emphasis on Hebrew words. "Doesn't the Gospel of Saint Mark say that whoever is like a little child shall enter the kingdom of God? So you should take comfort in the knowledge that Gerta's spotless and innocent soul is up there in heaven praying for you."

"And for all of us," said one of the guards, crossing himself.

Marie was shedding tears of thanks.

Rabbi Loew seemed surprised by my knowledge of Christian Scripture, but he must have felt compelled to complete the eulogy because he said, "The Lord gives, and the Lord takes away. Blessed is the name of the Lord. Amen."

"Amen." They all said it reflexively.

I let the echo of their words drift down and settle around our ankles like the ashes of a fire gone cold. Then I said I had to ask a few questions. Marie agreed.

"When did you notice she was missing?"

"Early this morning."

"Didn't you hear us calling her name all over town?" said Janek.

"As a matter of fact, I did," I said. "How early?"

"Before sunrise."

I didn't want to press her, but I had to ask for specifics. "How much before sunrise?"

"She doesn't have to answer that," said Janek.

"No, she doesn't. In fact, you can throw us out anytime you want. But we'll get to the bottom of this one way or another, and it would go a lot quicker if you'd help us."

"It's all right, Viktor," she said. "It was about an hour before sunrise. I got up to check on her and . . ."

"Had her bed been slept in?"

"Yes."

"Where is it?"

Marie Janek glanced at her husband before answering. "She sleeps in our bedroom. We draw a curtain between us at night."

Someone stole your child from your own bedroom and *neither of you woke up*? I couldn't quite picture a pair of burly cutthroats tiptoeing up the stairs without making a sound. It was possible, of course, but something about it didn't smell right.

"Did you leave her bed exactly the way you found it?"

I saw the pain in her face as she pictured her child's empty bed.

"Yes, I did."

"May we examine it?"

"All right, that's enough." Janek bristled. "I want you both out of here. Now!"

"Were any of your locks tampered with? Any windows broken?"

Marie looked like she was seriously considering the question, when Zizka said, "Let's go, Jews."

I asked Janek what he and Federn had been arguing about on Wednesday, just before Janek threw us out into the street.

"Nice work, Jew. We could have had another ten minutes in front of that nice warm fire," one of the guards complained.

We tried to question Janek's neighbors, but it was a waste of time, and we came away with nothing, the doors closing behind us with a heavy thud.

"Time's up. Back to the ghetto, Jews," said Zizka.

We trudged over the cobblestones toward the East Gate, and it seemed like Rabbi Loew questioned me the whole way.

"What did we learn from that experience?"

"I'd say that we need to look at the father's motives more closely," I said, keeping my voice low.

"How are we supposed to do that?"

"I know it sounds crazy, but we need to find a Christian who is willing to help us."

"And how likely is that under the current conditions, Ben-Akiva?"

"What about one of the Rožmberks?"

"Hiring Jewish musicians to play at your cousin's wedding is not the same as granting us equal rights before the law, but I'll make some inquiries."

He sighed with frustration.

"What is it, Rabbi?" I asked.

Rabbi Loew said, "How can we expect to solve the riddle of the universe if we can't even solve this petty crime? The answer should be right in front of us, but we have to open our eyes to it. And unless we read the signs before the ultimatum comes due—"

"What kind of signs?"

"I already told you that every act leaves a trace. Just go and look among Federn's circle of friends and acquaintances, and see if they can help you find a willing Christian, and when you come back, tell me everything that you have seen and I will tell you what is a sign and what isn't a sign. I will know them when you describe them to me."

"All right, but if I'm going to be your legs, Rabbi, there's one thing you've got to do."

"What?"

"Hire me."

"We've already hired you. You're a public servant."

"That just means everyone in the *Yidnshtot* gets to boss me around. You know how people are. If they know I'm working for *you*, and you alone, they'll show me some respect. It'll be a lot easier to get them to talk to me if I'm acting as the High Rabbi Loew's personal investigator."

"Personal *what*?"

"Like an Inquisitor of sorts—only for our side."

"You're certainly not afraid to ask the hard questions, which may be just what we need in a case like this."

"We can draw up a contract of some kind stating that I'm authorized to act on your behalf. A formal-looking parchment with your signature on it would open a lot of doors."

"Very well. But we haven't discussed your fee."

"Have you got a kreuzer?"

"Yes, but—"

"Give it to me."

Rabbi Loew smiled wearily. He plucked a coin from his purse, and placed it in my open hand.

"Here's a daler. Keep the change," the rabbi said. "You're hired."

We shook hands on it.

"Nice to be working for you, Rabbi Loew."

"Save it for after we catch the killer."

The Kreuzgasse was temporarily blocked off by a gang of Jesuits in long black cassocks filing out of the Church of the Holy Spirit. They gave us a few dirty looks as they marched toward the rebellious neighborhood of Bethlehem Chapel, but most of them concentrated on just looking menacing.

Then the distant voices of the town criers announcing the edict sealing off the ghetto came drifting toward us, carried by the wind through the streets and alleys of the city.

Rabbi Loew said, "All right, Mr. Investigator. What's your next move?"

Besides getting the hell out of town?

I said, "The Talmud tells us that a corpse is like a Torah scroll that has been damaged beyond repair. If we could examine the child's body as closely as we examine the *seyfer Toyreh*, wouldn't it tell us things? Think what we could learn from it, what hidden meanings it would reveal."

"Do you actually think the authorities will honor such a request?"

"No. This bunch of tight-lipped dandies would never allow it," I said, as the last of the swishing black cassocks vanished around the corner. "So we appeal to the emperor. Another thing to ask him when you see him tomorrow."

"Let's hope. We don't have a firm appointment with him yet, and Rudolf can be very moody and withdrawn at times. He once refused to grant an audience with a special envoy from the College of Cardinals in Rome. Unless Mordecai Meisel is willing to help. After our failure with the *kehileh* and the imperial consulate, Meisel's our best connection to the *keyser's* court at this point."

"I keep hearing that name. Who is he?"

"Time to start earning that daler, shammes. He's the mayor of the Jewish Town."

CHAPTER 10

THE BAND OF JESUITS MARCHED through the Little Square like a column of black ants chewing a path through the jungle. Seasoned ironmongers stepped back to watch the black cassocks swishing from side-to-side in unison.

The bladelike movement sliced fear into the heart of a clockmaker's apprentice, and he ran off to warn Father Jiří that the men in black were on their way.

The precise tramping of their boots made a servant girl's heartbeat quicken in admiration for the selfless bravery of these soldiers of Christ who were spreading the word and stamping out heresy. All that shiny black leather sent shivers down her back and between her thighs.

To Janoš Kopecky, they were the worst kind of thugs—arrogant Papists willing to use any weapon against honest Christians in their fight to regain control of the imperial city and its environs.

A town crier stood in front of the Gothic portals of Old Town Hall, loudly proclaiming the anti-Jewish edict while the rain loosened the mud clinging to his boots. A couple of beer-bellied merchants stood listening to the crier with their mouths hanging open. Kopecky strode past them to a quiet street behind Our Lady of Týn and ducked inside the columned walkways of Granovsky's house.

Six capitular members of the Greater Bohemian Mercantilist Alliance sat around a long oak table. The wood was polished to a lacquered finish, reflecting the men's faces like a dark, smoky mirror.

"You're late," said Masaryk. "Where were you?"

"Sorry. I had to wait for a parade of whipping boys to pass by."

"Sit down, and let's get started."

"Wait a minute," said Kunkel. "Where are Hürwitz and Goldschmied?"

Kopecky said, "Haven't you heard? The ghetto's been sealed off. No Jews can get in or out."

"Really? Then what's this Jew doing here?" said Kunkel, pointing at a pale stranger with long dark hair and a neatly trimmed beard. The stranger's striped vest glistened with tiny pearls.

Masaryk laughed. "They haven't had Jews where he comes from in three hundred years."

"Yeah, well he could pass for a Jew in those clothes."

"So who is this fellow? What's he doing here?" Kopecky demanded.

"This *gentleman* is Bobby Johnson, and he comes from the court of Elizabeth of England with an offer of material support for her Protestant allies in Central Europe."

The men around the table showed great interest in cultivating such a profitable alliance.

"Since this is being such a delicate matter, I am not an official envoy," said Johnson in tolerable German. "So I also have some leisure time."

"He wants to talk business with you," said Masaryk.

"He wants to trade with the butcher's guild?"

"No, Janoš. Your other business."

Johnson had a glimmer in his eye.

"Oh. Well, that's nice. Too bad the ghetto's going to go up in flames sometime in the next three days."

"Oh, crap," said Hrbeck. "Do you know how much money I'm going to lose if that happens?"

"Then maybe you shouldn't be doing business with the damn Jews," said Tausendmark, a recent arrival from Bavaria.

"I was about to collect the Easter tribute, you *dummer Esel*. What am I supposed to tell my customers?"

"What are we going to do about this?" said Kunkel.

"What's to do?" said a wine and beer merchant named Švec. "They'll break a few windows, burn a few shops, then everything will go back to normal."

"Easy for you to say," said Hrbeck. "You don't own any houses in the ghetto. Business will probably pick up for you. There's nothing like a bunch of *Judenschläger* running riot for selling cartloads of booze."

"Not this time," said Kopecky. His wife was always telling him to go easy on the Jews, but this was serious business.

"Don't be a woman, Janoš. The Jews will find a way to weasel out of it, like they always do."

"Are they really being that clever?" said Johnson. "I've heard a lot of stories about how smart the Jews are, but I always thought they were a little exaggerated."

"They're not exaggerated, Englishman," said Hrbeck. "The Jews are confined to the ghetto and forbidden from owning property, right? So that ought to make it easy for us to charge them whatever we want for rent, you'd figure."

"I am expecting so."

"Yes, but you don't know the Jews. They've got second sight when it comes to money. The rabbis saw it coming a mile away, so they got together and prohibited their people from competing with each other for lodging. They're not allowed to pay more than the established rent, or do anything to get another Jew evicted, no matter how crowded the *Židovské Město* gets."

"And if we try playing them off against each other, the whole community stands together and refuses to pay us anything," said Masaryk.

"They'll live twelve to a room if it means keeping a three-story building vacant until we meet their terms."

"Can't you be taking it up with the emperor?" asked Johnson.

"Right. And you know what he'll do? Establish a commission to study the problem," said Hrbeck.

"How can you continue to let the Jews live among you?" Tausendmark said.

"Because the Turks are less than a hundred miles from Vienna, and Meisel gives Emperor Rudolf all the gold he needs to run the war," said Masaryk.

"Let me get this straight. You can't get rid of them because *one Jew* is financing Emperor Rudolf's army?"

"There are plenty of others, but Meisel's the emperor's favorite. He doesn't even have to wear the Jew badge when he leaves the ghetto on business."

"And yet somehow, we've managed to expel the Jews from almost every city in Germany," Tausendmark said.

"I guess we're just not as efficient at expulsion as you Germans are," said Masaryk.

"And *der Kaiser* always lets them come back, anyway," said Kopecky.

"Perhaps I should remind you that it is not proper to criticize one's rulers when we are at war with infidels," said Tausendmark.

Johnson was still curious. "With all their wealth, is there no Jewish gold left for you?"

"Each Jewish household pays the city fifty gulden a year to provide for their protection, but we don't see a lousy pfennig of it," said Hrbeck.

"Maybe you should be raising the protection fee to sixty gulden a year."

"We tried that. The extra ten gulden went straight into the imperial coffers."

Masaryk said, "We tax them every time they pass through the gates of the city or cross the border into Moravia. We tax them for crossing the stone bridge, for buying a loaf of bread, or for selling a secondhand shirt in the *tandlmarkt* on Havelská Street. We tax them for taking a bath, getting married, and protecting the cemetery from vandals. What else is there?"

"You charge them for protecting the cemetery?" said Johnson. "Are you taxing each burial, as well?"

It struck them like a bolt from the heavens. Kopecky looked around the table. The others were equally thunderstruck.

"A tax on each death and burial," said Masaryk. "How come we never thought of that?"

"Got any more where that came from?" said Kunkel.

Johnson said, "Well, I understand that King Philip of France was making the Jews pay a yearly fee for the privilege of wearing the yellow badges."

"He *charged* them for the Jew badges?"

"Oh! Nice idea," said Švec.

"That'll teach them to undersell us," said Hrbeck.

"Provided we can get the Rožmberks to support the idea," said Kopecky.

"Count Vilém may have a soft spot for the *Zhids*, but all that flies out the window when there's money to be made."

"If the Jews are taxed so heavily, how are they managing to undersell you?" asked Johnson.

Hrbeck explained: "They're not allowed to join the Christian guilds, so the sons of bitches are able to set their own prices."

"Even their wine is cheaper," said Švec. "And I can tell you that many a Christian lad fritters away his time drinking in some dive in the *Židovské Město* with a couple of Jewish no-goodniks."

Masaryk had the servant girl bring in some *koňak* so he could propose a toast to their guest.

While everyone talked excitedly about the potential for exploiting these new sources of income, Kopecky took the Englishman aside.

"So how come you know so much about Jews?" Kopecky asked.

"Well, as you know, we don't have any Jews in England. So I've become quite curious about them."

"Fair enough. You've certainly got some fresh ideas about how to deal with them, my friend."

Johnson shrugged it off modestly.

"Now, what's your business with me?"

The Englishman's face changed, becoming quietly intense. "I'm after pearls."

Kopecky glanced at the tiny pearls sewn into the fabric of Johnson's vest.

"That's not really my specialty. You should talk to Granovsky about Oriental trade."

"Not that kind of pearl. I'm talking about *exotic* pearls."

The burgher still didn't get it.

"You know. Perls. Or Rachels. Or Hannahs. Maybe a Deborah or two."

The words dropped like water into a clear pond, and ripples of meaning spread out between the two men.

"I've heard that the Jewish women are, shall we say, somewhat warmer than the females in the northern climates."

Kopecky stroked his chin, and said, "Give me a little while to see how this plays out, then I'll see what I can do for you, my friend."

CHAPTER 11

"WHERE IS THAT GIRL?" DOLORA shouted from the kitchen.

"She's coming," said Lívia the upstairs maid as she elbowed the front door open and stepped outside. She had to empty the chamber pots into the gutter so the filth would wash downstream with the rainwater. You didn't just toss it out the second-floor window on Meisel Street, not when rich folks like the Hürwitzes might be strolling by.

The girl came in, dripping wet and staggering under the weight of a bucketful of brackish well water.

"Don't spill it," Lívia commanded.

The girl carried the heavy bucket into the kitchen, and dropped it on the tiles.

"Careful, Katya! You'd have to scrub the floors for a month to pay for a couple of those tiles, unless the master decides otherwise," Dolora warned the girl. "And you've stirred up the muck. Now we've got to wait for it to settle."

The Pinkas Shul shammes passed by the window, calling out, "Burn your *khumets*!"

"*Můj Bože!* We haven't even washed the turnips yet!" said the cook.

"That's enough shouting, Dolora. It won't make the day go any faster," said the mistress of the house, Frumet Meisel, standing in the doorway to the kitchen. "Anya, come bring the whisk broom."

"Yes, *paní Meislová*," Anya said, putting down the paring knife and wiping her hands on her apron. She followed her mistress down the corridor, tucking a few loose strands of hair under her headkerchief.

The servant girls had spent the morning scouring the Meisels' town house from basement to garret, leaving only a symbolic pile of crumbs in the corner of the front room.

The group of boys and girls from the orphanage had already finished their half-day of *kheyder* studies, and they had nothing to do but play games until the Seder started just after sundown, several hours from now. They formed two teams: boys against girls, of course. The leader closed his eyes and opened a printed copy of the five Books of Moses at random—the children called it a *khumesh*—then they started counting the number of times the Hebrew letters *samekh* and *pey* appeared, the boys rooting for each *samekh*, the girls screeching for each *pey*.

Even the children in the Jewish Town know how to read, Anya marveled. She remembered being their age, sitting in the drafty church staring at the imposing book with the mysterious squiggles on its pages, and dreading all the do's and don'ts prescribed in its impenetrable code. As the years went by, intimidation turned into admiration for the priests, who were the only ones given access to the knowledge needed to translate the secret language of God and share it with her, and her soul had filled with gratitude for this gift of divine wisdom. Imagine having God's word written in a book *and not being able to understand it*. And she thanked God for the priests.

Then about six months ago, a young man turned up at the Meisels' door, taking up their offer to sponsor his studies with the great Rabbi Loew. (Mordecai Meisel had to quit school when he was still a boy to support his mother by working in the iron trade, so he was always very generous with poor children and scholars.) The young student's name was Yankev ben Khayim, and the first thing that struck her was his sense of humor. He actually made her laugh with his plays on Yiddish and Czech words, which weren't always so chaste and pure. Most of the Jewish men were always so deadly serious around her, if they acknowledged her at all. The second thing she noticed was how thin and delicate his fingers were. Anyone in her family of butchers could have cracked his frail bones with one hand. But he had one thing they didn't have: a thousand-year tradition of public education, and when he spied Anya flipping surreptitiously through the children's books, he said to her:

"A hungry mind should be fed no matter what, for it is written, 'There shall be one Law for the citizen and the native who dwells among you.'"

"What does that mean?" she asked.

"It means that I should teach you to read the Bible in your own language."

The young man began teaching her letters and numbers so that she could begin to navigate the forbidding pages of the Christian Bible. She brought this new knowledge home to the family, and of course her parents worried at first. But soon they were demanding that the wholesale meat suppliers provide written receipts so that Anya could look them over and catch any omissions or excessive charges, which she always did, to their delight, however slowly and clumsily she might read.

Her wealthy employers also taught her the importance of separating the clean from the unclean, since any bits of food left lying around would attract invisible spirits who would bring sickness and poverty to the house. And it seemed to work. She noticed fewer babies dying of childbed fever in the Jewish Town than in the Christian homes, although the priests thoroughly condemned it as a sign of Jewish magic.

Frumet Meisel now took a candle from the mantel while Anya stood by with a dustpan and whisk broom. The children abandoned their game and gathered around *froy* Meisel, who lit a candle and made a show of searching for the last traces of *khumets* in the corner of the room. As her mistress renounced ownership of any crumbs they might have missed, Anya swept the last crumbs into the dustpan and threw them into the fire, declaring, "Any kind of leaven shall be regarded as non-existent."

Frumet Meisel patted her on the cheek and said, *"Di shikseh baym rov ken oykh paskenen a shayleh."*

"What's a *shayleh*?"

"It means the rabbi's servant girl can also answer a difficult legal question."

No, I can't, Anya thought, but she allowed her heart to be cheered by her mistress's kind words. Her shoes felt heavy and confining as she returned to the kitchen. She checked the bucket of well water. The sediment had settled to the bottom, so she began ladling some of the water into a ceramic basin.

She dropped a handful of turnips into the basin, running her fingers over their smooth white skins to loosen the dirt, and scraping off the clinging specks of earth with her fingernails. The icy water turned her fingers red with cold.

Dolora was chopping up the whitefish and carp and keeping an eye on the pots, so she told Anya to fetch the veal shank from the larder.

Veal shank, hell. More like the biggest side of beef on the block. There was enough on the bone to feed twenty people. Anya couldn't help letting out an unladylike grunt as she lifted it off the hook and carried it to the kitchen, trying not to get any blood on her apron, even though the meat had been hanging for nearly a day. She set it down on the cutting board, washed her hands in the proper Jewish fashion, and finished washing the turnips. She turned to the pile of cabbages, and began to wash each leaf by hand because the tiniest grub was enough to render the whole dish non-kosher.

She was pining for fresh green vegetables after a long winter of turnips and sauerkraut when her mistress told Katya to take over the washing and sent Anya into the dining room to prepare the main table.

Anya spread the white tablecloth and smoothed out the corners, wondering when Yankev would come back from the study house, since today was a half-holiday. The Jews had a rule against fasting on the day of the Pesach feast, but many of them skipped the midday meal in order to welcome the Seder with a heartier appetite. She was fascinated by how much leeway the Jews had when it came to interpreting their laws.

As she wiped the special set of kosher-for-Pesach dishes with a cloth and set them out, she remembered the day that she was at the cutting board tearing the leftover bits of boiled chicken from a carcass so the cook could make a Sephardic dish of yellow rice and chicken for Rabbi Mendes, when Meisel's new scholar came into the kitchen, and she asked him, "Tell me, Jew, what is kosher about this meat? How is it different?"

So he told her that it was mainly the method of slaughtering, and draining the blood. Then he told her his name was Yankev, and not "Jew," and she giggled and apologized and told him her name.

And since that moment, whenever Yankev returned from studying with the rabbi, she would feed him in the kitchen and ask what he had learned about God. A gentle lad with an inquisitive mind, he was so different from the men who hung around Cervenka's butcher shop making crude comments while she washed the ox blood off her arms. And since they both knew that they would always live in different worlds, they found it easy to speak freely about almost anything while she dried and stacked the dishes. Yankev told her that since any Jew in the congregation could say a blessing over the bread and wine, they had no priestly class that dictated the one correct way of worshiping and behaving.

She liked the idea of eliminating the rigid cadres of men standing between her and God, of having no intermediaries, no infallible rulings, and especially no *extra ecclesiam nulla salus*. Oh, the rabbis could fine you or even banish you from the community in extreme cases, but they couldn't declare that you weren't a Jew anymore. Nobody could. Even God couldn't turn His back on His children forever.

She set out the fancy soup bowls made of heavy cut glass with golden rims. All this for chicken broth and unleavened doughballs?

She peered out the front window. The rain seemed to be letting up, but she didn't see any sign of Yankev yet.

He had even taught her that the Jews didn't believe in eternal punishment— that a man named Rabbi Akiva, who lived in the second century, said that the worst sinners only spend twelve months in Hell, which they call *gehenem*, while another rabbi said that the maximum punishment lasts from Pesach to Shvues, which is only *fifty days*.

And according to still another rabbi, Moses ben Something-or-other, evil thoughts pop into our heads for no reason and should not be considered sinful, which was a nice change from the nuns who always told her that the slightest impurity of thought was as bad as the sinful deed itself. (So of course, she was *always* in a sinful state according to them.)

They even said that a Jewish woman didn't have to live out her days chained to a man who drank, beat her, or screwed around. If she could get her husband to approve the papers, the rabbis let her divorce the bastard.

She looked out the window again. Nothing. Up the block, people were hurrying by on the Breitgasse with more than the usual pre-holiday rush. Something was definitely up.

A flush of panic filled her chest. What if little Katya had been listening behind the door when Yankev told her the Jews believed that the Messiah is merely the messenger of God, not his son? What if the little servant girl had gone running to tell Father Prokop about the heretical ideas Anya was listening to? She told herself not to worry, but she still crept over to the kitchen and peeked around the door. Little Katya was still washing the cabbage, her face placid. Anya breathed easier.

She was laying the embroidered cloth on a silver tray for the three ceremonial matzohs when an iron key scraped the lock and Yankev came in, tracking in water with his boots. Rain dripped down his face, and he was breathing hard. His eyes were tense and humorless.

"Trying to beat the rain?" she asked. But she knew that wasn't it.

"No. There's trouble coming, Anya." He told her all about it, starting with how little Gerta Janek had been found with the blood drained out of her.

She called out to God and cupped her hand to her mouth. Nothing human could have done such a thing.

He told her no, it was clearly knife wounds. No doubt about the perpetrator's humanity.

She said that it didn't make sense to blame it on the Jews.

"That may be true," he said, "but I still have to leave the city tonight."

"Tonight? Why so soon?"

"You know that I'm not much of a fighter, Anya."

"But you said the Jews have three days to flush out the killer. And from what you've told me, I'm sure he got a lot of blood on his clothes."

"What difference does it make? A sharp mind is no match for a sharp sword."

"That's not what you've been telling me for the past six months, Yankele. Where will you go?"

"I hear the Turkish kingdom is pretty safe for Jews these days. Maybe I'll go all the way to Safed to study with Rabbi Vital."

"But how will you get past the gates?"

"All it takes is money, Anya, and Reb Meisel will give me whatever I need for such a purpose."

"But who will teach me—?"

"I've told you before that every Jew is a student of the Law."

But every Jew wasn't Yankev ben Khayim.

"Well, you can't leave, at least not until I show you—"

"Show me what?"

She took him by the hand and led him into the pantry. He must have really been distracted by all the troubles because he forgot to remind her that such contact was prohibited. She gave him a conspiratorial smile as she lifted the checked cloth from her basket, picked out two spongy white pastries, and held one out to him.

"Just wait till you taste my Easter buns. I just baked them this morning."

This delicacy was supposed to wait until Easter, since the recipe called for lots of eggs and sugar. Not exactly lean Good Friday fare. But she told herself it was all right because if Yankev left tonight she wouldn't be seeing him on Sunday. Or ever again. The thought made her unexpectedly sad.

"No, I can't," he said.

"It's still early, isn't it? I thought the prohibition didn't start till sundown."

"The law forbids eating *khumets* after midmorning on the day before Pesach."

"Just like the law forbids any contact between Christians and Jews of opposite sexes?" She had him there.

She still had so many questions, but someone was pounding on the front door. She heard Lívia scurrying by to see who it was, then heard two men asking to see Mordecai Meisel. There was urgency in their voices.

"Sounds like Rabbi Loew and that newcomer," Yankev said, turning away from her.

"Don't leave me like this."

It just came out. She was as surprised as he was by it.

He stared at her.

She tried to explain. "I mean—everyone comes to Prague. The problem is that they don't want to leave. Every jerk that marches through here tries to claim it as his own. And—and—well, the Jews don't. They don't want to conquer us, they just want to live here and not be bothered. So why should I hate them more than the preachers who say my Church is corrupt or the rich burghers who try to run our lives?"

One of her braids was coming undone, loose hair spilling out of her headkerchief. She had to let her hair down, re-braid it, and tie it back up again.

Yankev watched her strong, quick, movements as her hands shaped her long black hair, which was full of static charge. She caught him looking at her, but he didn't turn away. He stayed where he was, looking into her dark eyes. And he kept looking as if he had never seen a woman's eyes up close. They weren't Christian eyes or Jewish eyes, they were *her* eyes, sparkling like the stars on a dark winter night.

She felt her face grow warm as her hot young blood flowed to the surface of her skin, and she blushed. She had a feeling his hot young blood was flowing, too.

"Tell me, Yankele, how many more years do you have to study until you become a rabbi?"

"There's no set number of years. You become a rabbi when a community hires you to be a rabbi, or as soon as people start coming up to you asking, *Rabbi, is this pot still kosher?* That could happen to me at any time."

"And rabbis don't have to be celibate, like priests?"

"With all due respect, the priests have it all wrong. Celibacy goes against God's wishes."

"How can you say that?"

"Because the very first commandment in the Torah is to be fruitful and multiply. God tells Adam and Eve to enjoy each other's bodies without shame. There's none of that sex-is-inherently-evil nonsense."

"It's supposed to be about purity."

"Who told you that sex is impure? Love between a married couple is not impure, it's holy. Even the most pious scholar who studies the Torah every day of the week commits a sin if he doesn't give his wife joy on the Sabbath."

Her belly tingled as she thought of the delights of being a married woman.

"And a man does not sin if he loves his wife too much?"

He chuckled at the thought. "Only if it keeps him from fulfilling the other commandments."

She wondered what it would be like to forget everything else and touch him—no, strike that—to hug him with all her might.

The aroma of stuffed fish drifted in from the kitchen, which meant that Dolora must have already put them in the steamer. Time was running short.

"Why do all the old laws forbid close relations between Jews and the other races?"

"You know why," he said.

"No, I mean since the days of Solomon, as told in the Book of . . . uh . . ."

"It is written in the Book of Kings," he said. "Because in those days it was a sin to have such relations with idol-worshipers. But in our time, Rabbi Menakhem Ha-Meiri, *a likhtigen gan-eydn zol er hobn*, says that the old prohibition doesn't apply to modern Christians, because they worship the same God that we do."

Well, thank God for Rabbi Menakhem Ha-Meiri.

"Even if the person hasn't been baptized?"

"What difference does that make?" he said.

"Then how do you remove original sin?"

"We don't believe in original sin."

"You don't?"

"We believe that man's true sin is his inability to bring peace and justice to the world, a failure that occurs in every generation. Yes, Adam sinned, but why should the whole world be condemned to death for one man's sins? In any case, the stigma of Adam's sin was erased when we received and accepted the Torah."

"And what about Eve's sin?"

"The same."

"But the priests say—"

"The priests say that it was Eve who led Adam to sin, and that she is inferior because she was made after him, blah blah blah—"

"Wasn't she?"

"Some say they were made side-by-side."

"Oh. Well, which is it?"

"You're full of questions today."

"I don't mean to be such a *kvič*, but—"

"What's a *kvitch*?"

"A whiner."

"Oh, a *kvetch*." It was practically the same word.

"They always say that God made Adam from the soil, but didn't He make Adam from a mixture of soil and water that He molded into a man?"

"A mist, really," said Yankev.

"So God needed both elements. Why is that?"

"Actually, He needed three elements."

She stared at him a moment, drawing a blank. Why didn't he tell her? Did he expect her to know this? She looked aside, searching for an answer among the fat-bellied sacks of dried lentils and peas lining the wall beneath the shelves.

"The breath of God," he explained.

"Oh."

The smell of *gefilte* fish and matzoh ball soup was making her mouth water.

Yankev said, "The mist rose from the earth to unite with heaven, just as a woman opens herself to a man, and together they bring completion to the One above."

"Wait a minute. You're saying God needs *us* to be complete?"

"Yes."

"And that it's up to the woman to make the first move?"

"Well, this is an allegorical interpretation—"

She drew close and gave him a quick, soft kiss on the cheek. Now it was his turn to stare blankly at her.

"Well? What do you think of that?" she said.

No sound came from him.

Her arm floated around him like a nocturnal creature slinking along the forest floor searching for a companion, ready to draw back at the slightest hint of trouble. But he didn't pull away. He didn't move at all. His cloak was still damp from the rain. Her fingers dug in as if they were working the primordial soil, releasing that earthy mist and letting it rise toward heaven.

"You can't go now," she said.

It seemed like a long time before he spoke: "I shouldn't have spent so much time with you, Anya."

"What does that mean? Am I too *treyf* for you?"

"No, no, you're not *treyf*."

"Then what?"

"There's no room in the world for people like us."

"Then we'll have to make room."

"Such matches are forbidden everywhere."

"So you admit we're a match?"

For once, he had no answer.

"Isn't it right to defy a prohibition that has outlived its usefulness?" she said.

"It is not our place to decide—"

She needed to sway him with an example from the Scriptures.

"What was the name of that woman who tramped through the wilderness all the way to Bethlehem just to make a match with some man she didn't even know?"

"You must mean Ruth the Moabite and Boaz the Judean."

"And her people were the sworn enemies of Israel at the time?"

"Yes."

"And yet together they begat Obed, who begat Jesse, who begat King David, the father of our Messiah."

"She was indeed a remarkable woman," he said.

"Better than seven sons."

He smiled. "You would have made a good wife for a Torah scholar, if only the world were a completely different place."

My God, was he conceding the point? On her side of town, whenever couples disagreed, the result usually involved bruised limbs and broken crockery.

"You're not like the other men I meet."

"The novelty will wear off."

"I don't think so."

She leaned in closer, hiding nothing from him. The heat rose off their bodies, her own flowery fragrance mixing with his earthy essence like a field after the rain. Her lips met his skin. She filled her nose with his musky scent. Then she opened her lips. His skin was sweet and salty.

"You'd better stop," he said.

But it was too good to stop. She was astonished by the surge of sensations as her mouth crept up his neck, planting warm wet kisses higher and higher until she was kissing his cheek, his soft flesh, his mouth. She hadn't ever thought a kiss could feel so good, so sweet, so much larger than the inch of flesh that held it.

She pulled her head back and looked into his eyes. They both had crossed a line, but there was still time to jump back over it before they got caught. She should have walked away and forgotten that they ever met. But the attraction was too strong.

She put her lips close to his and said, "My momma always told me that if you're going to eat an apple, you might as well pick a nice juicy one." And she plunged in for another taste of that forbidden fruit.

Her master's booming voice filled the air.

"Anya, come in here! I need you." It came from the front room.

She broke away and discovered that she had hands for smoothing out damp hair and clothing, as she responded to this call from another world, heading back to a town called Prague, a place where physical relations between Christians and Jews was still punishable by death and dismemberment, depending on the mood of the judicial authorities on that particular day.

She wondered if she still smelled of the Jew.

Mordecai Meisel stood in the middle of the room, between two men in long dark cloaks. Meisel was in his mid-sixties, fattened with comforts but still robust, his silk shirt straining against the muscles he had built up hauling iron as a teenager.

She recognized one of the men as Rabbi Loew. The other was a tall Jew with a curly black beard and the same look of controlled desperation she had seen in Yankev's eyes when he first came in from the street.

"Anya, these gentlemen need to ask you a few questions."

Her heart fluttered. Did they know?

"Of course," she said, her throat tight.

The tall Jew spoke first. "Reb Meisel tells me that you know Marie and Viktor Janek. Is that true?"

Anya felt Yankev's presence as he came into the room behind her.

"Speak up, girl," said Meisel.

"Yes, master."

"Yes master, or yes, you know her?" said the tall Jew.

She was taking rapid, shallow breaths. She barely got the words out: "What do you want to know about the Janeks?"

Meisel said, "Anya, I told Rabbi Loew and his shammes that you'd cooperate, and I'd like to keep my word—"

The one he called the shammes held up his hand and politely advised Reb Meisel that anyone could see that the poor girl was nervous and that perhaps it would be better if he spoke to her alone. Meisel turned to Rabbi Loew, who signaled his approval of the newcomer's suggestion.

She relaxed enough to let herself smile at the tall stranger.

The shammes smiled back. It wasn't a bad smile, once he got the muscles working.

But when he asked if he could have a room with something he called "privacy," Yankev came forward and said, "I don't see why you need to question this girl. What could she possibly know about this matter?"

"It's all right—" she began.

Meisel silenced them both and instructed Anya to take the shammes to the storage pantry, the same pantry that she had just warmed with the heat of her passion. She wondered if he could still smell their bodies in the closed room.

The shammes avoided looking directly into her eyes by fiddling with the tops of the porcelain spice jars. His hands were huge and paw-like, as if they were made to break things. She had known many men like that.

His first question was a surprise: "Do you follow the word of God in the Bible?"

Was this some kind of trick?

"Of course I do."

"Every word of it?"

She would have said "yes" to a Christian interrogator immediately, or ended up dancing the hempen jig over their holy flames. But she had learned during her time with the Jews that they rarely expected simple answers to such questions.

She said, "I believe every word that the priests tell me. But I also know that the priests choose not to follow every word in the *khumesh*, like the commandment to celebrate Pesach after sundown on the fifteenth of Nisan."

His eyebrows shot up. She might as well have chanted the *Sh'ma* in Hebrew.

"How long have you been working for the Meisels?"

"Long enough to know the *khreyn* from the *kharoyses*."

He looked like a man who had found a priceless treasure at the bottom of a barrel of old rags, and he didn't try to hide his astonishment the way a real interrogator would. His imposing stature softened before her eyes as he leaned against a sack of grain and massaged his forehead.

She said, "You look like you could use a drink."

"I could," he said. "That's the hardest part of keeping the *mitsves* of Pesach. I can go without leavened bread for a week, but the prohibition against *khumets* includes anything made from fermented grain, with no exceptions for the restorative properties of your fine Bohemian beer."

"How do you Jews keep track of all six hundred and thirteen commandments?"

He was impressed that she knew the precise number.

"It's a matter of knowing which rules to break," he said.

A smile passed imperceptibly across her lips, and she felt a warm flush of relief. Maybe this shammes would be different from all the other men. Maybe he would be able to help her.

"And how do you know which rules to break?"

"It takes practice. Don't forget, you people have only been Christian for—what? Eight hundred years or so? And we've been Jews for more than four thousand. So we've got a big jump on you."

It took her a moment to realize that he was joking.

"What do you expect me to do for you?" she asked.

His eyes showed hope. "I need to find out what's been going on in the Janeks' house, and I can't do it myself. So I'm praying for a miracle and looking for a good Christian who's willing to help us out by talking to Marie Janek about her husband's business and also find out if any of the locks in their house have been damaged. Doors *and* windows, if possible. She won't talk to me, of course. Would you consider doing it?"

"I'm supposed to ask a grieving mother a bunch of nosy questions about her husband's business affairs?"

"No, of course not. You have to pay your respects first. Talk about other things. Ask how her husband is doing. Is the shock too strong? Will he be able to keep the shop in order? Is the business solid? That kind of thing. I can help you figure out what to say."

"You're going to tell me how to speak to a Christian woman."

"No, no, I'll have to trust your judgment, just like I'm asking you to trust mine. Look, I realize I'm just an outsider, even among the Jews of Prague. But I need you to—to—"

"To what?"

He let out a long sigh. "To do something that very few people have done for me in the last couple of weeks. To look past my crude mannerisms to the well-meaning soul within," he said, tapping himself twice over the heart in exactly the same way that a Christian would do it.

She felt herself wavering, and he must have seen it.

He looked around the narrow confines of the pantry, his eye falling on a bunch of fresh dill hanging on a hook. He cupped the lush green herbs with his hands, and inhaled their fragrance a couple of times before letting them drop.

"My grandmother—*olev ha-sholem*—used to put lots of fresh dill in the matzoh ball soup," he said. "It's pretty hard to get this time of year."

She said, "I don't even know your name."

"Sorry. I'm in such a rush I must be forgetting my manners. It's Benyamin."

"Ah. Jacob's youngest son."

"Yes," he said. "Listen, Anya, you seem like a righteous daughter of Noah.

I need you to help me save what could be hundreds—maybe thousands—of lives and keep the Jews from getting exiled again."

"You're telling me that if we catch Gerta Janek's real killers, the Jews won't have to flee the city?"

"That's what I'm hoping."

"Then my answer is yes. I will help you. We have three days, right?"

"More like two-and-a-half."

CHAPTER 12

downstairs, scratching his chest and ranting in his Spanish-Jewish dialect about needing more sleep. He stopped on the landing, and brushed the dark ringlets of hair out of his eyes.

"Oh, it's you, Rabbi," he said. "How can I be of service?"

"The earth has shaken the blind beast of hatred out of its slumber, Acosta," said Rabbi Loew. "And my shammes needs your assistance."

"What kind of assistance?"

Anya had gone. Yankev had insisted on taking her to the East Gate, where the gatekeepers had recognized her as a Christian and opened the small door for her at once, then resealed it with iron bolts. And now she was gone—my one useful connection to the Christian world outside the gates—and we were back at Rabbi Loew's house trying to figure out our next move. Yankev looked pale and tense, as if he were weighing a fateful decision.

The whisper of a breeze blew under my cloak and sent a chill right through the damp leggings clinging to my skin.

Avrom Khayim, the head shammes, came shuffling down the corridor from the kitchen, bringing a wave of tantalizing scents with him. I detected simmering chicken soup and brisket with a trace of something sweet. Apples?

"None of the locks were broken at Federn's shop, nor, I suspect, at the Janeks'," I said. "So whoever planted this false bloodcrime at our feet seems to know their way around locks."

"And?" said Yankev.

"And so I need to find a couple of experienced picklocks."

"And you expect *us* to put you in touch with such rabble?"

"No, but maybe one of you knows someone who can," I said. What on earth had gotten into the scrawny yeshiva boy?

The night watchman was the only one who dared to give me an answer: "That's easy. You want Izzy the Ratcatcher."

"Where can I find him?"

"He gets a bedroll and a roof over at the *shandhoyz*."

"Where's the shamehouse?" I said, using the night watchman's polite word for whorehouse.

None of the men would make eye contact with me.

Avrom Khayim said, "You can look into that later. We have to attend to the *minkhe* services first, then the Seder."

I turned to my new master. "Rabbi, I have to pursue this line of investigation, even if it leads me up the steps of a *shandhoyz*—"

Rabbi Loew said, "My shammes, attend to God first. He will provide the rest."

"But—"

Acosta said, "Slow down, newcomer. Do you really think the *oysgelasene froyen* won't be around later just because it's Shabbes?"

I didn't answer. What else could I do? When Isserles the Pious was quarantined because of the plague, did he bang his head against the walls and curse his fate? No, he sat down and wrote the *Seyfer ha-Khayim*, the Book of Life, and turned a disaster into a blessing.

Rabbi Loew said, "Come, Ben-Akiva, let's discuss this with the others," and drew aside the curtain leading to the study room.

"There's no time for that now. Let me go—"

"No. Wisdom must be shared in order to have any meaning."

Vey iz mir, I thought. *How long is this going to take?*

"Of course, Rabbi, but if you want me to resolve this crisis, you've got to let me follow my instincts."

"Your instincts won't do you much good unless you wait for that official contract you wanted me to draw up."

"Oh, right." How could that have slipped my mind?

"It appears that your assistant shammes needs an assistant of his own to keep track of everything," said Avrom Khayim.

"You see?" said Rabbi Loew. "It takes time to learn new things, there's no shame in that. Even the great Resh Lakish was once a circus entertainer for the Romans. Now, come."

I didn't want to face another bunch of scholars who seemed to spend their time not just splitting hairs but actually *quartering* them, but I dutifully followed the rabbi into the study room.

The rabbi's son-in-law and young Lipmann were still bending and swaying in prayer and chanting like a single creature with two heads. The boy's high-pitched voice and the man's deep, dark tones resonated from the floor to the ceiling. Rabbi Gans sat across from them, composing his chronicle in flowing Yiddish script.

Rabbi Loew didn't interrupt the mystics. He took his place at the head of the table, and invited me to sit next to him. He borrowed a quill from Rabbi Gans, slid a piece of fresh parchment across the table, and dictated the conditions of my responsibilities as the High Rabbi Loew's personal investigator. I wrote it down word for word, then Rabbi Loew took the document, signed it "Yehudah ben Betzalel" with a firm hand, and handed it back.

I handled this newly koshered document as if too much contact with my fingertips might profane it.

"Now, let's begin with the most basic question," Rabbi Loew said. "Did the accused have any enemies?"

"Sure, fifty thousand of them," I said.

"And they wonder why the Jews keep an eye on every penny," said Rabbi Gans, looking up from his work. "We need it all to buy the *goyim* off every time their pockets get a little short on silver."

Rabbi Loew said, "There is certainly no clear precedent in the Gemore for this type of situation. And without a clear methodology for us to follow, we'll have to gather a thousand bits of information, even though we'll probably end up needing only a tenth of that."

"But which tenth?" said Rabbi Gans.

I said, "We won't know that until we've gathered them all."

Rabbi Loew sat up straight in his high-backed chair and summoned all the dignity appropriate to a man passing a judgment of great weight. "Well said, Ben-Akiva. That was an excellent response."

I studied the tabletop.

"What's the matter? Does it bother you when I praise you?"

"No, I just want you to save your praise for when I *really* do something impressive."

Rabbi Loew's face was unreadable. Then somewhere beneath his gray mustache, a knowing smile appeared, and he said, "If I let you follow your instinct, what's the first thing you'd do?"

"I'd go to the Federns' place—"

"But we already went there."

"Sure, and we spoke to the wrong person. I'd like to ask Julie Federn if she knows anything about how her father's locks were opened. Children often see things that their parents don't notice."

Rabbi Loew stroked his beard, considering the wisdom of this suggestion.

I said, "She isn't exactly a child, but it's a place to start. She might know something crucial about this case without even being aware of it herself."

Rabbi Loew said, "Then go and see her right away."

I pushed the curtain aside and walked right past Avrom Khayim, who called after me:

"Where do you think you're going? You'll be late for *minkhe*—and you already missed *shakhres*."

"Don't worry, I'll be on time. I've just got to talk to a couple of women first."

"What do you mean, a *couple* of women? You better tread lightly, Mr. Benyamin from Slonim, because you're stepping on toes, you hear me? You're not a full-fledged member of the brotherhood yet. You have to earn that honor, my friend."

"Thanks, I'll spread the word."

"Be back in half an hour."

"I shall be at your service," I said, though I had no intention of returning so quickly.

What brotherhood? I wondered, stepping outside.

Rainwater flowed between the freshly laid paving stones. The street was less crowded now, but no one looked me in the eye as they pushed along the Breitgasse with that frenzy peculiar to city dwellers, or noticed when I took a quick turn down Meisel Street. The servants for the well-to-do families were too busy packing up food and clothing for the poor to notice me sloshing by, taking a little detour before going to see Julie Federn.

I passed by the Rozanskys' house in the narrow lane near the three wells that supplied the rich folks with their drinking water, but they told me that Reyzl was still at the shop. She shouldn't have been working so late on *Erev Pesach*, since she didn't belong to one of the professions permitted to work past noon today, but then, that woman never missed a chance to make a few extra dalers. It ran in the family.

I wound my way back toward Zigeuner Street, hunger slowly sapping the clarity from my brain. It was a bad day to go without eating. I needed all my strength to get through this.

The Rozanskys' print shop was just around the corner from the East Gate, but the masons had stopped work for the day, leaving stacks of paving stones in the middle of Zigeuner Street. And even though we'd been married for four years, my chest was tightening like a teenage groom's on the morning of an arranged marriage.

I held the door for two men delivering reams of broadside paper, and entered the shop. An apprentice rushed past with a tray of spare type, while the master and his assistants rolled the sticky-wet ink on the finished frames and pulled pages from the press with such rapidity it seemed as if the letters were about to take flight.

Reyzl was standing at a steeply tilted table, setting type and leading like she was born to it. I drank in the sight of her, this industrious female with her fingers covered with ink, smears going halfway up her arms, and a smudge over her right eye where she must have tried to brush away a bit of loose dark hair that the sweat had plastered to her forehead. I watched her slender hands fly from the upper case to the frame, composing the last lines on the final page of the book, backward, from left to right: "Arranged and finished by the typesetter Reyzl, daughter of Zalman, of the Rozansky family of Prague."

"Nice-looking typeface," I said.

"It should be," she said without looking up. "Jacob Bak himself designed it before he left for Venice."

I maneuvered around her, and peered at the handwritten text she was working from.

"What is it?"

"It's a book of customs for women—and for men who might as well be women," she said, finally looking up at me. Her eyes showed no fire, no flash, no blazing love or hatred. It was a look she might use on a traveling peddler selling secondhand lice combs.

I dredged up what was left of the speech I had prepared: "Look, I know I've disappointed you—"

"Don't underestimate yourself," she said. "You've disappointed my whole family."

"Your father always liked me."

"Sure, once upon a time."

My eyes fell on the backward letters in the type frame.

"So how does this story end?"

"It ended a long time ago, Benyamin."

My father-in-law's voice cut through the noise: "Reyzl! We're out of *tsadeks*. Be a good girl and—"

He saw me and stopped. Zalman Rozansky was short and stocky, his wiry beard as black as a Gypsy's.

"Oh, it's you. Is he bothering you, Reyzele?"

"No, it's all right, *tateleh*. I'm fine."

He told me, "There are sixty-eight other printers in Prague. Go bother one of them and quit wasting my daughter's time."

"I'm not wasting time—"

"Like I said, we're out of *tsadeks*, and Katz and Loeb are sitting on trays of them."

"And you want me to go over and borrow some," said Reyzl.

"Get some *reyshes* too, if you can." He turned back to me. "You know how hard it is to get materials without a royal *privilegeum* for printing in Hebrew type? And guess who's got the only one. Solomon Kohen."

Back in the 1580s, one of the Kohen brothers had shown quite an interest in young Reyzl Rozansky. The inference was clear.

"We're already pushing it past legal hours, Mr. *Slonimer*, and I don't want you slowing her down or following her through the streets, is that clear?"

"Yes, sir."

"Good."

Rozansky went back to check the latest page proofs, grumbling about his worthless son-in-law, until his words were lost in the clanking of the huge letterpress.

"So, you finally found me," she said, pulling off her apron and tossing it on a shelf.

"Finding you was the easy part."

"Then why didn't you drop everything and come right after me?"

"I couldn't just abandon all our obligations. I had to fill the orders, close the accounts, and wait until they found a replacement for me at the *kheyder*."

"And that took two months?"

"It takes a while to get things done in a small town."

"You can say that again," she said, stretching and arching her back until it cracked. I remembered how I used to massage her neck and shoulders after a long day waiting on the customers. She had always appreciated that.

I said, "You had one of the biggest dry goods stores in Slonim."

"I had to do *something* with myself or I would have gone out of my mind with boredom in that place. Believe me, the *cemeteries* in Prague are livelier than the central marketplace in Slonim."

"We could move to another part of Poland."

"And make a living doing what? Collecting taxes for the big landowners? *There's* a popular profession."

"It's a center of Jewish learning, and there's a lot of trade in the big cities."

"*What* big cities?"

"Kraków, Lvov, Poznan—"

"Every one of them full of Jew haters."

"It's worse in Germany."

"Is it? Take a look around you. Rudolf's the best king we've had in *ages*. The last expulsion was thirty-five years ago."

I followed her over to the washbasin, where she lathered up her hands with coarse, gritty soap.

"You have no idea what I gave up for you," she said. "And you never showed any willingness to do the same for me."

Ink darkened the water in the basin.

"How can you say that when I quit my position to come here and be with you?"

"Well, you can go ask for it back."

"No, I can't. I'm working for Rabbi Loew now. He's hired me to investigate a conspiracy against the Jewish community—" I said, reaching inside my cloak and showing her the new contract, but she waved it away.

"Marrying an outsider cost me all my rights to citizenship in Prague." She checked her dripping hands. The ink had faded slightly. She used more of the gritty soap. "And I want my rights back."

"There's still time for us to start over. We're still young enough."

"No, we're not."

"All right, maybe I'm not. But you are," I said. The pressure was building like a fist behind my eyeballs, and I needed to select my words with great care.

She kept scrubbing her hands.

She said, "You could have gotten a rabbinical post in Kolín or Roudnice, built up your reputation, and come to Prague as a respected member of the town council, but you settled for being a *shrayber* in that far-flung *shtetl* just because you were one of the three people within fifty miles of the place who could read and write."

"When Rabbi Lindermeyer left me without a letter of referral, I was lucky to get a post as assistant to the *Slonimer Rebbe*."

"Some luck. Exiled to a place where your spit freezes before it hits the ground."

That wasn't the only thing that froze, but I didn't particularly mind the cold in that small, northern town. At least it was predictable. And there was something peaceful about the way the snow blanketed the land for miles around.

Reyzl examined her hands. Traces of ink still remained etched deep in the lines of her palms and under her fingernails. She kept scrubbing.

They say that even your worst enemy contains a spark of the divine, but it's a lot easier to see it in a pretty young woman.

I said, "I wish that our spirits could float above all this, to the places of God's miracles, and mingle with every other soul in creation."

"That's because you've been studying with that mystical rabbi who thinks that rearranging numbers can unlock the secrets of the universe. Well, I arrange numbers every day—it's called double-entry accounting—and they haven't unlocked any secrets other than the fact that if you spend more than you take in, you starve."

"Nobody starves in our community."

"Oh, right, I forgot. We can always get a bowl of watery oatmeal in the poorhouse."

There was shouting in the street, but I didn't really notice it.

"How much time do we get here?" I said. "How many years do we have together? Can't we at least find happiness in the short time that we're here?"

"That's what I'm trying to do."

"I mean together."

Piles of gray paving stones sat outside the window, unmoved by my plight.

I said, "All this other stuff around us comes and goes with the seasons, but your love is a bridge to the next world. Union with you is like a foretaste of heaven—"

"Don't talk about that in here," she said, stepping away and examining her face in a broken piece of mirror nailed to the wall. She moistened a rag with soap and wiped at the smudge over her eye.

"Rabbi Horowitz says that there is no holiness like the union of man and wife."

"Except when the woman's womb is not strong enough to bring healthy children to term. That changes everything. Then the rabbis say that a childless man is like a dead man, which means that not having kids is practically the same as murder. So there—you can divorce me on those grounds."

My breath caught halfway down my throat. She had actually used the word for divorce—a *get*, such a short, sharp word in Yiddish—like a punch in the gut, and I had to be careful not to take the bait. I had to remain logical about this.

I said, "You've got to wait six more years before that will hold up in the *beys din*."

"All right, then have me declared a rebellious woman who refuses to have sex with her husband. You can even deduct the money from the *ksubeh*."

"I don't want to deduct money from the *ksibeh*, I want *you*."

"Then I'll tell them you're not providing for me, that you're unfaithful, and that you beat me."

"You wouldn't do that."

"I will if it's the only way I'm going to be free to remarry."

People were running by the front of the shop with panic in their eyes.

"Reyzl—" I said. This was as hard as parting the Red Sea. "Our marriage was foretold in heaven. Forty days before we were formed in our mothers' wombs, a heavenly voice decreed, 'The daughter of Zalman Rozansky will marry the son of Akiva ben Areleh.'"

"So maybe they made a mistake. Some heavenly office clerk—made a mistake. I'm sure it happens."

"But . . . I will have no son to say *Kaddish* for me when I'm gone."

She tossed the towel next to the basin.

"So get a shammes to do it. Better still, get two. They're cheap enough."

Her words cut through my conscience to the center of my soul. I felt a numbness, like a knife wound that only hurts after the blade is removed.

Then Acosta burst into the shop and called out to me: "There you are! The Christians are wrecking Federn's shop."

I was forced to drop everything and follow the night watchman outside, where I was swept along with the crowd jostling toward the East Gate in time to see a mob of lawless soldiers pulling Freyde and Julie from the looted shop.

I heard the women screaming, "Leave us alone, you *eyrev-rav!* You stupid idiots! A black year on you!"

Then one of the *Reiters* tossed a burning torch into the shop, and at that moment I knew that if I hadn't stopped in to see my wife, I would have been at the shop by now and things wouldn't have gotten so out of hand. But now it was too late. And I stood there watching my plans for the immediate future go up in smoke.

CHAPTER 13

THE VALERIAN ROOT BOILING IN the pot exuded a rank odor like no other on earth—a blend of peasant sweat, mossy wood, and rotting meat that filled the air as thick clouds of steam rose and dispersed.

The sharp-eyed observer of this alchemical experiment was a wise woman named Častava, whom the Germans called Kassandra the Bohemian, or Kassy Boehme for short. She was somewhere in her thirties, but had chosen to wander off on her own, far from the well-traveled path of wife and mother, so she still had the bright smile of a much younger woman; a smile that caught the eye of countless men who had known the thrill of seeing her light up a room just by walking into it with a glow that was nothing short of a miracle of nature. Or so it struck them. She had a high sloping forehead, eyes that changed from brown to green depending on the light, a long thin nose, all of her teeth, and according to whom you asked, either long blond hair with brown streaks in it, or long brown hair with blond streaks in it.

At the moment, she was searching for a way to distill the essence of the valerian root into concentrated drops. She didn't know what useful purpose it would ultimately serve, since an ordinary infusion made from steeping a bit of the root in hot water for a few minutes usually worked its natural magic quite nicely, easing her nervous humors and letting her get some much-needed sleep. Still, the experiment might yield some interesting results.

That venerable iconoclast Paracelsus had argued that if the active ingredients in a plant could be isolated and concentrated, the resulting tinctures would surely be purer and more effective than the natural forms of the medicinal herbs, which were full of inactive materials that diluted their potency. The first step was the easiest: extracting the water that made up most of the plant by boiling it away.

But the root of the valerian plant had very little water in it to begin with, so Kassy made a decoction from the finely ground root, and was boiling it down to its elemental form when an old woman everyone called *babička* Strelecky, or "granny," entered her tiny storefront, which served as a combination kitchen-laboratory-consulting room. The old woman had cloudy gray eyes, and deep-set wrinkles that made Kassy think of the dry gullies and stream beds high up in the Krusné Mountains, in the land of a thousand sunsets.

The old woman told Kassy that her jaw had been hurting for two days, ever since the tooth doctor had yanked out a rotten molar, telling her that she'd feel better in a day or so. Only so far she didn't feel any better, and how was she supposed to get her strength back when it hurt so much just to chew? Kassy took the old woman's hand and helped her over to the chair by the fire, easing her worried mind with kind words and the promise to send her home feeling better, absolutely no question about it. Then she had a look inside the woman's mouth. The wound was taking a long time to heal, but it showed no signs of infection. Kassy told her to gargle three times a day with warm salt water and a dash of strong drink to keep the area clean, and gave her a vial of nut-brown syrup to ease the pain.

"You'll need to take some prune juice with this as well."

"I don't like prune juice."

"This class of medicine tends to clog the bowels, and you already have enough trouble in that area, don't you?" Kassy explained. "It's the price of reducing your pain, granny."

Everything came with a price. If you wanted to take the paregorics, you had to drink the prune juice as well.

Babička Strelecky examined the brownish glop in the tiny bottle. "How much is this going to cost me?"

"Three pfennigs."

The old woman pursed her lips tightly. It was clearly too much for any medicine that wasn't a sure thing. Kassy would have charged her less, but the ingredients were expensive, and the landlord never reduced her rent just because she had trouble turning away the charity cases.

"Two if you bring me back the bottle," she said.

Babička Strelecky counted out the battered copper half-pfennigs, slipped the bottle into her apron pocket, and went on her way.

Kassy didn't think she'd ever see the bottle again, but she didn't let it bother her. God would pay her back in time.

The mixture was one of Paracelsus's rare successes, easing pain so effectively that the old alchemist had taken the Latin verb for "praise," *laudare*, and named it laudanum. His original recipe called for minute quantities of gold, lead, pearls, and other precious metals of dubious healing properties, but Kassy had modified it, dropping the heavy metals while keeping the main ingredient, concentrated juice of the opium poppy dissolved in alcohol. It worked wonders, if used properly.

She still had her doubts about using lead as a fever reducer, since classical authorities from the days of Olympiodorus of Thebes had reported that a demon living inside the metal drove long-term users mad. Not that she believed that a demon could inhabit the tiny shavings used in the Paracelsian tinctures, but she had no plans to test that hypothesis on herself or anyone else until a better explanation was forthcoming. So she kept in touch with the other wise women who used it in their medicines, curious to learn what results they had observed, and remained skeptical of the legions of naturalists who made a regular habit of overstating the effects of their drugs. She didn't want to be duped again, like the time she finally got her hands on a long-sought volume of Pliny, only to find out that he was one of the sources of the blasted myth with a hundred lives that a menstruating woman's touch will curdle butter, turn cream sour, rot fruit, and dull the blades of carving knives, and that just *one look* from her is enough to kill a swarm of angry bees in mid-flight. *I didn't realize we had such power*, she thought with a bitter chuckle, before she had thrown the dusty old book across the room and startled her orange tiger cat, Kira.

Her shelf was filled with tattered flea-market copies of books by the great masters, bearing their incontestable stamp of authority and containing complete and utter absurdities. John of Gaddesden passed down the wisdom of his age, writing about how he had cured the son of King Edward Plantagenet of

England by wrapping a bit of red cloth around the pox, which he claimed would cause it to disappear (it won't). The German Inquisitors Sprenger and Kramer were so credulous they swore that "a certain virgin" who recited the Lord's Prayer and the Apostles' Creed while making the sign of the cross had cured a friend whose foot had been "grievously bewitched" (if only it were that easy). Even Albertus Magnus repeatedly stumbled in his *Book of Secrets*, recording for all time his assertion that mistletoe and a certain species of lily could open any lock in the kingdom. Magically.

Nonsense.

But the world-famous Albertus had the epithet "the Great" permanently affixed to his name, while she barely survived on the pennies she took from the poorest patients in the city. So he must have been on to *something*.

"What's that awful smell?"

Kassy looked up from her bottles and flasks. A woman with a tangled mop of hair and dark circles under her eyes blundered into the shop, her shawl damp with rain, dragging a child dressed in rags, with snot dripping from his nose. The neighborhood of Bethlehem Chapel didn't have much in the way of palaces and nunneries, but it sure had plenty of poor people. The revolutionary leader Jan Hus had preached in this very square, and started a mass movement that became the first of its kind to successfully resist the dominance of the Roman Church and carve out a zone of religious tolerance in the very heart of the Empire. But these days it was a Protestant ghetto, besieged on all sides by the resurgent Crusaders, even if it didn't have a wall around it like the *Židovské Město*.

"What's the matter with your little boy?"

"He's got the worms."

"Intestinal worms?"

"What other kind of worms are there?"

"There are plenty of other kinds of worms. You've seen them in his stools?"

"Listen, missy, I've got five kids at home and I think I know when something's wrong with them. And what on earth is that god-awful smell?"

Kassy opened the window to let in some cold air. Then she reached for a jug of pale gray liquid and a copper funnel, and carefully decanted a cupful of the bitter medicine into a small green bottle.

"The juice of the ash tree is a reliable vermifuge—"

"A *what*?"

"Sorry. It's also called Bird's Tongue, and the boiled bark of the tree will kill the worms, but it's kind of bitter tasting. You can try mixing it with sugar or stirring it into his porridge."

"Do I look like I can afford sugar? Will you be making a fine burgher's wife of me then?"

"Here, this will help it taste better."

Kassy tossed in some dry peppermint leaves at no extra charge just to get rid of the woman, but the boy was busy petting Kira, who had been sniffing around the mouse hole, and the woman had to yank him away.

Poor boy. His eyes were glazed over and his face was pale. He probably got the worms from eating dirt. She had seen many cases in the mountain villages of hungry children trying to fill their empty stomachs with clods of earth that were full of worm eggs.

They were almost out the door when Kassy called them back.

"Now what?" said the woman.

Kassy made up something about how the juice of the ash tree bark was cool and wet, so it worked best if taken in combination with something warm and dry, like freshly baked grains, as she cut a couple of thick slices of rye bread and brought them around the counter for the boy to eat.

"What's your name?" she said, kneeling next to the boy and offering him the bread.

"Karel," he said, looking up at his mother, his eyes as big as empty soup bowls, as if he were afraid to ask if he could really have the bread. His fine golden hair was plastered to his skin in places by sweat, and his lips were dry and chapped.

"Listen to me, Karel. You must eat this here, right in front of me," said Kassy.

His mother nodded, and the boy grabbed the top slice and began stuffing it into his mouth.

"Slow down, I'm not going to take it away from you," said Kassy, patting the boy's hand. His fingers were unusually warm. Kassy felt his forehead. He was burning up with fever.

Kassy asked if she could examine him more closely. Then she unbuttoned Karel's shirt, exposing a diffuse redness all over his chest and arms—everywhere except on his face.

Kassy pulled up a stool, sat down at the child's level, and examined the rash closely. It wasn't a solid mass of red, as it first appeared to be. It was more like a collection of deep red spots that were growing together to form a confederacy. It sure wasn't worms.

"Say ah."

The boy had a hard time swallowing the bread so he could open his mouth. His mouth was red and swollen inside, particularly around the soft palate and the little lobe of flesh hanging at the back of his throat, which were covered with a viscous secretion.

"Has he been complaining of a sore throat?"

The woman shrugged, as if she were worried about opening the door to that possibility and letting in another burden.

"Any vomiting?"

"Sure, but I thought it was the worms."

"Convulsions?"

"Huh?"

"You know, any uncontrollable twitching, fits, attacks, seizures, that sort of thing."

"No, thank God."

"Does he have any pain in his legs?"

"Oh my God, *yes*," said the mother, her eyes widening. "He was just complaining about it on the way over here, but I figured he was just whining as always. What is it? What has he got?"

"What about his urine?"

"What do you mean, his urine?"

"Is he peeing normally? What color is it?"

"No, the fever must have taken it all away. The few drops that came out this morning were as red as that rash."

Oh, dear God. It was the scarlet fever, which no doctor on earth could cure. Despite all her knowledge, the best she could hope for was treating some of the symptoms, which might give the boy an even chance of surviving.

"How long has he had this fever?"

The woman hesitated. "I don't need any more trouble."

"There won't be any trouble. Now tell me how long."

"A couple of days," she finally admitted.

"All right. The first thing you need to do is give him cold baths to keep down the fever."

"Cold baths? What about spiderweb?"

"That's an old legend. It won't bring down his fever. I don't keep any around."

"You don't? What kind of a healer are you? Not even to stop bleeding?"

"Cloth works just as well," said Kassy. *And in case you haven't heard, people associate spiderwebs with witches.* "What about his brothers and sisters?"

"What about them?"

"Do they show any signs of having the same symptoms?"

"Not yet."

"Good. You need to keep him away from them, or they might catch it, too."

"What do you think he's wearing this for?" said the woman, holding up a pouch around the child's neck.

Kassy gently eased the pouch out of the woman's grip, loosened the drawstring, and opened it up. She sniffed the contents, and almost got a noseful of peony root—a deadly poison.

"Did you get this from another curist?" she said, covering her nose and waiting a couple of heartbeats to see if she felt its toxic sting.

"Of course I did. He said it would protect him from evil."

"Yes, it works like a charm, doesn't it?"

That is, if you want to kill someone. *Peony root, for Christ's sake.* But Kassy didn't feel any burning yet, which meant that she might actually live to see the sunrise on Easter morning, as she had been planning to do. So she simply said that this dosage of the herbal charm had become too dry to be effective, and replaced it with some flowering hops sprinkled with alcohol, which would at least help the boy sleep.

"That's fine for keeping down the fever, but what about getting rid of the rash?" asked the woman.

"I'm going to give you a couple of doses of an infusion made from the bark of the aspen tree, which comes all the way from the northern Americas. It's been highly recommended for bringing down fever."

"I didn't ask you about bringing down the fever, I asked you about curing the rash."

"Keep giving him water with sweet herbs that's been boiled and cooled, and with God's help, the rash might go away before long—"

"It *might* go away? There's a man down the block who says he can cure it in three days flat."

Well, he's lying, Kassy thought.

She said, "I'm sorry, but I've never seen anyone actually cure the scarlet fever."

"Don't you want to help my child? Or are you out to harm him? I don't know what your game is, missy, but we're not staying here another minute."

The woman wrapped her shawl around her son as if she were protecting him from a sorceress's evil gaze, then she picked him up and stormed out.

"Don't forget to give him the cooling baths!" Kassy called after her.

Some days are like this, Kassy thought. Sometimes the ignorance was just too strong. She did what she could, but she knew better than to press too hard against the brick wall of people's superstitions, which would stir up resentment and worse, charges that would put her own life in danger. Maybe she should have gone into the shoe trade, like her younger brother Jacob.

At least when a sick old man loosened his grip on this world and went to his reward, you could tell yourself that he'd lived a good long life, had his full measure, couldn't complain—all the usual comforting lies. But children were different. Losing a child always hit her hard, enough to make her wonder if all her mastery of the craft amounted to anything at all. Because there were things that no one should have to face alone. Things that left her wide awake in the dreary solitude of an empty bed with no hope of fulfilling her dreams. Not in this man's empire, anyway.

She boiled some water, added a pinch of St. John's Wort, and sat down to have a nice, warm cup of herbal tea, which some touted as a cure for melancholy. Kassy knew very well that there was no such thing as a cure for melancholy. Temporary alleviation, maybe, but nothing remotely like a cure. The systematic study of medicinal herbs was only just emerging from the murky realm of superstition and magic, and it didn't make her job any easier when greedy mountebanks went around making wildly exaggerated claims about the curative properties of various concoctions.

Kassy had come from the mountains northwest of Prague to make a new life for herself in the enlightened city, but she had landed in the poorest quarter and found it filled with people whose horizons of expectation were disappointingly narrow. Charlatans roamed the streets trying to sell gullible women crudely carved-up briarwood as if it were mandrake root. Her first paying job was "purging" a burgher's house of the plague by giving it a good scrubbing that any kitchen maid could have pulled off. And she found that she had to watch what she said very closely. When a passing beggar asked her how cold it would get that night, and without thinking much of it she looked at the sky and said that it might rain, she was nearly accused of "aeromancy," the maleficent practice of making predictions about the future by studying the atmospheric aether, which was closely akin to witchcraft.

And with the Roman Church reestablishing its grip on the empire, witchcraft had become a serious charge. Hus himself was arrested on the lesser crime of being a heretic, and they had burned him at the stake, then roasted his heart over the flames, pulverized his bones, and thrown the ashes into the river where they dispersed forever without a trace so that there would be nothing left of him—not even a shoelace for his followers to remember him by.

What was the matter with these blood-crazy "reformers"? Because just killing someone wasn't enough for them. No, the Inquisitors objected so strongly to a secret Jew—a Portuguese *converso* named García da Orta—publishing esoteric dialogues about exotic drugs from India that they had his body dug up and burned five years *after* his death.

She knew the real reason for this. And despite the authorities' public claims that the Jews were a low priority, everyone else on this unruly street knew it, too: by refusing to convert to Catholicism, the lowly Jews kept the fires of religious freedom burning for all to see. Their very existence defied the Papists' arrogant claim that there is no salvation outside the Church.

It was different back when a woman could escape the horrors of a forced marriage by retreating to a convent full of like-minded women, and perform meaningful and rewarding work like ministering to the poor while getting a decent education. But ever since the Council of Trent had confirmed that all of the sisters had to be cloistered, a convent was the last place she'd ever want to end up—especially when they were ruled over by men who knew in their hearts that all scientific investigation and book learning was inherently evil. End of discussion.

Maybe that's why she felt such an affinity for the Jews and their famous thirst for knowledge. "Of bookmaking there is no end," went one of their sayings. And she had seen it written in the Book of Job that wisdom can lead you to "a path which no fowl knoweth, and which the vulture's eye hath not seen." These passages aroused her starving curiosity. *Is it possible to salivate over a book?* she wondered. But since she couldn't read Hebrew, and few secondhand editions were available in Latin translation, the main sources of Jewish knowledge were closed off to her for now.

She checked on the bubbling broth in the pot to see how the experiment was progressing. More than three-fourths of the water had boiled off, leaving a brownish residue clinging to the sides of the heavy iron pot while the mixture at the bottom thickened to a dark paste. It *did* smell like something that might have been left behind by the inky black hoofprints of the Devil himself.

She rinsed out her teacup, washed a couple of pots from yesterday's experiment, and had just sat down to re-read Agrippa's comments in praise of Jewish learning when a stream of voices rushed by the window, yelling something about how a phalanx of Jesuits in long black cassocks was pushing its way into the quarter. Angry men and filthy street kids swarmed by with bits of wood and stone to hurl at the arrogant holy warriors.

She got up and lifted the lid off the big black pot, dipped her little finger in and tasted the bitter valerian extract, and had to fight the urge to test its effects that very minute. It was too early in the day to numb herself with potions. People came in at all hours with their personal emergencies, and she needed to be ready, no matter what.

As if to underscore this fact, a young woman came in who obviously needed help, though probably not for herself. Kassy saw the familiar look of desperation in her eyes, but also saw great strength and determination in them as well. And she was clearly concealing something under the folds of her apron.

"Are you Častava, the wise woman?"

"There are some who call me that."

"In the name of God and his Blessed Mother, you've got to help me."

"All right, but what's a nice Catholic girl like you doing around *Betlémská kaple?*"

The young woman opened her mouth to answer, but stopped after a couple of syllables. Kassy could tell that she wasn't especially good at lying.

"Don't worry," Kassy said. "Anything you tell me stays within these walls."

"Really?" The young woman approached, her eyes brightening.

Kassy studied her more closely. She had long black braids that had been hastily tied back with a kerchief. Her hands were chapped from washing vegetables in cold water, and her apron showed traces of animal blood. Her deferential manner indicated that she was a servant girl, but there was something else about her, a certain headstrong quality that suggested that she wasn't dependent on a serving maid's meager wages for her livelihood. She didn't have a ring on her finger or any other sign that she was another man's property, but she didn't seem to care about spoiling her beauty with heavy chores, including, apparently, butchering large animals.

"Tell me, how long has your family owned a butcher shop near the Jews?"

"You are truly as wise as they say, Miss Častava. The Cervenkas have been butchers in the *Staré Město* for five generations. My name is Anya," she said, reaching into the pocket of her apron. "And I'm coming to you because I need you to identify these herbs."

She took out a sachet filled with long oval leaves.

Kassy took the small pouch and studied the leaves, turning them over in her hands. The specimens were thin and brittle, tapering to a dull point, like bay leaves, with a thick midrib, deep green on top, and gray-green on the underside, where the veins were more prominent. She had never seen their like before, and her eyes shone as she examined this new discovery. Who knows? Maybe *this* was the plant that could cure the little boy's scarlet fever.

"Where did these come from?"

"From the New World."

"I'm not surprised to hear that. I meant, where did *you* get them from?"

"Oh. From Viktor Janek's shop, but please don't tell anyone—"

"I won't tell, I promise. But I do want to know why Janek the apothecary is trafficking in exotic herbs such as these."

"His wife says he's selling a lot—" She stopped again.

"Look, why don't you just tell me what's going on?"

Anya the butcher's daughter clenched and unclenched her fists a few times, fiddled with her apron strings, then finally revealed her big secret: "I'm working for the Jews."

"Yes, I heard they were having some trouble over in the Jewish Town. You work as a Sabbath maid?"

"Yes, but also as—something else."

"And these herbs are a key to that something else."

"Yes." Anya nodded rapidly.

"Do you know where they come from?"

"Like I said, from the New World."

"That covers a lot of territory. Any idea where in the New World?"

"Marie Janek said something about the *Viceroyalty of Kee-To*. Am I saying that right? It sounds like it's somewhere near China."

"If it's the Viceroyalty of Quito, it's in the mountains of the southern Americas."

"Oh. What is it, some kind of tobacco?"

"No, it's not tobacco." Kassy's pulse quickened at the prospect of uncovering the secret of these mysterious herbs, and their importance to the Jews. Perhaps they would lead her to some of the Jews' forbidden wisdom.

She said, "But if you leave them with me, I'll see what I can learn from them."

CHAPTER 14

FEW LANGUAGES ARE MORE ELOQUENT than German, especially when it's shouted. So we paid close attention when a preacher called Brother Volkmar climbed onto an empty beer barrel and harangued the citizenry not to hold the whole Jewish community responsible for this crime against nature. He said that they had to treat the Jews in a friendly manner, for Christ Himself was born a Jew, and such kindness would surely bring many Jews back to the faith of the patriarchs and prophets, and lead them to become real Christians.

I wasn't too sure about that last part, but since a couple of inches of crumbling wood were all that stood between us and the knife-sharpening party outside the gate, I was willing to accept this as a step in the right direction. Rambam counsels us that if we are forced to choose, conversion is preferable to death, since it allows us to live and return someday to our Jewish faith.

But when Acosta spotted another group of ragged street boys running up the Geistgasse to join the scavengers tearing up the sooty remains of Federn's shop, I swear I heard something inside that hotheaded Sephardi go *snap* from three feet away.

He started barking orders like an old soldier who still jumps at the sound of the trumpet.

"I need eight strong, fleet, trustworthy men to watch the remaining gates," he said as he went about rounding up volunteers from among the bystanders.

"Would you settle for two out of three?" said a toothless old graybeard.

"I'll settle for *one*, old man."

I saw the old man smile.

Then Acosta grabbed a *batlen* by the collar and told him to alert the butchers and have them take up their choppers and guard the flimsy wooden barrier on Schächtergasse. A *batlen* is one of those people who hangs around the shul all day in case he's needed to make up the tenth man in a *minyen*, so I was pretty amazed when he took off as if he were trying to outrace the sun itself.

Acosta drafted me to organize a human chain to transfer the stacks of cobblestones from the Zigeunergasse half a block away to the clearing in front of the East Gate, where my comrade planted himself, spittle flying from his lips as he called out the dimensions of our makeshift barricades.

Somewhere behind the dark gray clouds, the sun was getting low. Shabbes would begin in less than half an hour. But half an hour before Shabbes is not yet Shabbes, so I kept working, struggling to keep the line moving by catching the stones from the fellow on my right and passing them to the fellow on my left. The jagged rocks scraped my hands, leaving them chapped with rough white crosshatches.

The tumult must have cleared out the nearest Talmud Torah, because a group of students in long black cloaks came scurrying up the street. I was hoping for a spell of relief from them, but when I saw Rabbi Aaron leading the pack with all the signs of righteous anger clearly written in his eyes, I prepared for the worst.

"What's this?" said Rabbi Aaron, his tone confirming my expectations. Then he warned us that if we didn't stop in a few minutes, we'd be guilty of desecrating the Sabbath.

Acosta hadn't read two pages of Talmud, so I spoke up for him. "But, Rabbi, surely we have learned that it is acceptable to profane the holy Shabbes for the sake of a man like Reb Jacob Federn so that he may keep many Shabbeses," I said, losing my rhythm and nearly getting whacked in the elbow with a cobblestone.

Acosta caught the wayward stone and knelt to align it with the second row of stones.

The rabbi said that kind of talk was just what he expected from a circle of radicals like us, then he reminded me—as if I needed reminding—that as a new-comer to the community, I had no right to interfere with its internal affairs.

"And unless you honor the Sabbath by praying with us, all your earthly toil will be in vain," said Rabbi Aaron.

Acosta jumped to his feet. "With all due respect, Rabbi, here's how it's go-ing to be. You pray, and we'll defend the ghetto. It's called division of labor. It's a modern concept, so you wouldn't know about it."

"You're going to regret that comment," said Rabbi Aaron.

Half a block away, I saw Reyzl leaving the print shop and heading home for the Pesach feast.

"Yeah, we may end up regretting a lot of things," I said.

"I'd sooner commit *kidesh hashem* and die with God's Holy Name on my lips than violate Shabbes with a bunch of *fraydenkers*," said Rabbi Aaron, and several of his hangers-on nodded in unison, their close-cropped hair staying rigidly in place. Then they actually started *removing* the cobblestones from the barricade.

Rabbi Hillel says, *In a place where there are no men, try to act like a man.*

I faced Rabbi Aaron's students and said, "In all your years of study, did you people happen to skip over the passages in the Mishnah which tell us that it is permitted to violate Shabbes on a woman's account in order to deliver a baby, and to openly carry the necessary implements and heat them in a fire?"

But they acted like they didn't hear me. They just kept on removing stones as if I wasn't even there.

I wondered if they went through this at Masada, where the last of the Zealots committed mass suicide rather than surrender to their pagan enemies, or in York, England, where the Jews had taken their own lives rather than fall into the hands of their Christian attackers. All we ever get are the grand and glorious speeches about their heroic sacrifices. But I wondered if they bickered among themselves, taking sides and splitting along the fracture lines of old rivalries. Fortunately, all my years of apprenticeship in institutions of higher learning had prepared me for this type of circumstance.

Acosta looked like he was ready to split one of the disciples' heads open with a paving stone. So I said, "Haven't we learned that Rabbi Yehudah Ha-Nasi saved the Jewish nation after the Romans destroyed the Second Temple by writing down the Oral Law in spite of the prohibition against doing so? Didn't he break the rules in order to save our very souls?"

I said all this while gathering the muddy stones and feeding them back into the rotation, even as the rabbi's followers undid our work by taking the stones off the pile and tossing them back into the mud.

This bit of horseplay from a rustic *Purimshpil* went on for a few go-rounds, until Acosta recognized that he would never win a theological debate with the esteemed rabbi and his followers, and limited himself to muttering about how the toil and sweat of men like us had built the gates that allowed the rabbi and his personal band of zealots to pray in peace.

But the rabbi's band of devotees refused to listen, and it was about to turn into a tug-of-war over the muddy stones when Rabbi Aaron called them off.

"That's enough, my boys," he said. "Although removing the stones is the correct action to take, it is not worth the cost of desecrating the Sabbath."

The rabbi's students reluctantly dropped what they were doing and murmured in agreement.

Luckily, the *batlen* returned at that moment with the message that the butchers were sharpening their cleavers and gathering under the banner of the double-tailed lion.

"Good," said Acosta. "Now run and tell the other guilds to do the same."

"What other guilds?"

"The goldsmiths, tailors, and shoemakers."

The *batlen* said, "What are we going to do to our enemies? Throw *shoes* at them?"

A couple of the men in our crew laughed, but Acosta's back went rigid.

"If necessary," he said.

"I'm disappointed by your apparent lack of faith," said Rabbi Aaron. "I shall have to have a word with your rabbi."

I knew that was an empty threat, having seen how the two rabbis got along.

And with that, Rabbi Aaron whisked up his coterie of budding scholars and left us to our fate.

When they were gone, I asked, "Who are the Freethinkers in this town?"

"Anyone who doesn't agree with Rabbi Aaron."

"I figured out that part. But it would really help if I knew their names."

Acosta looked at the gray sky. I followed his gaze and saw a faint trace of the sun's rays glowing sideways across the rooftops.

"Some other time," he said, pulling me from the line and telling me to go aloft and blow the horn that announces the end of the work day.

He cut me off when I started to protest.

"We can handle it without you, *señor* Benyamin. Besides, Rabbi Loew wanted you to cover the *minkhe* services, remember?"

"All right," I said, "but promise me you won't commit mass suicide till I get back. I wouldn't want to miss out on that."

It took him a moment to realize I was just kidding, then he almost cracked a smile.

"This isn't the time for jokes."

"No, it never is," I agreed. "But it's one of the tricks we use to survive, isn't it? I bet you can still say a pretty good *Ave Maria* if you have to."

My words lingered in the air between us. The empty space was filled with the heavy clunking of stone on stone. Our barrier was already two feet high and rising, but it still wasn't big enough to be an effective defense against anything larger than a sewer rat.

I counted eleven stones before he said, "My family were *conversos*," Acosta said. "You know what that means?"

"Sure."

"No, you don't. You can't possibly know. You're the original wandering Jew."

"Aren't we all?"

He looked at me. "Do you know what it is to love the place you were born? I mean *really* love it? Do you know what it means to dance with all the pretty girls at harvest time, and drink from the same barrel of cider as their fathers and brothers, and feel your heart swell with pride when the drummers come bearing the royal colors of His Majesty King Phillip, because he's *your* king, too, and those are *your* colors as much as anyone else's?"

"No, I don't," I admitted. "I guess I don't really feel like I belong anywhere that much."

"That's right, you don't."

I had nothing to say to that.

"I had friends in the *armada* who fought in the battle at the Gulf of Lepanto. One of them died, another practically had his hand blown off. And three years later, the Turks took back almost everything we had fought for. It's still in their hands. So much for our big sacrifice."

I said, "Do you still have family back there?"

He looked down at the unmoving brick in his hands, leaving me to wonder what this man I had been thinking of as a free-spirited bachelor had left behind in the land that he loved so well.

"What the hell is this?" he said, as if he had just noticed the brick he was holding.

"Looks like we're running out of stones already."

"Then it's time to start tearing up the streets and put those new paving stones to better use."

I had a thousand questions about how we'd manage to accomplish that without more support from the townsfolk, but one look at the veins bulging in his temples silenced me on that subject.

"Take comfort, my brother," I told him, laying my hand on his shoulder. "When the Messiah comes, he will reunite the tribes of Israel, and we'll all be together again."

"You're telling me that we're so divided, it'll take a messiah to bring us together."

"That's one possible interpretation, I suppose—"

"There's always another interpretation, newcomer. Now go blow that horn before my hot Spanish blood gets the better of me."

MY BOOTS THUDDED UP THE worm-eaten steps as I climbed to the top floor of the tallest house on the Schwarzengasse carrying the horn that heralds the coming of Shabbes slung over my shoulder. Away from all the street noise, from the *toyhu vo-boyhu* of the gutter, I finally found a moment to reflect about what Reyzl had said and done, and to let it sink in that it might actually be time to say the *Rabbis' Kaddish* for our marriage, or whatever it was that we once had between us. Something that was once love, surely.

The *aggadah* says that when Adam was just formed from the earth, before he met Eve, before God breathed life and soul into him, he was a senseless clay figure called a *golem*. And that's just what I felt like.

These thoughts flowed through me like a dark river, flooding my heart with memories of how good it was when we were first together, once upon a time, how our attraction for each other was so strong, our passion so exhilarating that we felt like it could surmount any obstacle, as if no one had ever made love before us, as if the complete history of the world were leading up to that one moment of divine coupling. It reminded me how every dip and curve of her body was shaped by the same hand that completed the circuit of this great globe of ours and set the heavens spinning, how the downy fuzz on her lower back looked like precious golden threads in the morning light, and how I'd give anything to get a second chance to go back and live those days all over again, knowing what I know now, and not mess up quite so badly this time.

But this was not the moment to indulge in the luxury of frivolous thoughts—or at least what any self-respecting knight in the romance tales would consider frivolous. But what do those idiots know? Courtly love. *Ha.*

By the time I was back on the street again, merchants and beggars alike had already dropped what they were doing and were heading for the baths. All around me, Jews were hugging each other and asking forgiveness for any wrongs they may have committed during the week. Nobody hugged me or begged my forgiveness, but we wished each other a *gutn Shabbes* as I made my way back to the East Gate.

I peered through the opening. The German preacher was still perched on that barrel—the fellow had stamina, I'll give him that—only now he was praying for the Jews to see the light and free ourselves from our captivity to the Devil. All we had to do was let Jesus into our hearts, and everything would go swimmingly for us from that point on, on earth and in heaven. He made it all sound so simple. Maybe it *is* simpler for them, I thought, since most Christians don't know what it's like to live in constant fear of having their bones ground up into piecrust like a character in one of those horrible English revenge tragedies.

I thought I caught a glimpse of the imperial guards coming to protect the perimeter of the ghetto and I took heart for a moment, then felt it change to a sick tugging in my *kishkes* when I saw that it was only the municipal guards bearing an order to conduct a house-to-house search for "clues" and to inventory the contents of the ghetto.

One of the scavengers outside the gates, his hands blackened with soot, complained that the guards would get the best pickings. The sergeant turned, still clutching the order in his mailed fist, and said, "Don't worry, that Jewish gold isn't going anywhere soon. It'll still be there Sunday night."

Some of them laughed, although coming from them it sounded more like the cackling of a flock of vultures waiting for a suffering animal to breathe its last.

"What are you talking about?" I said. "The Sheriff told us we had three days to solve this bloodcrime."

"You weren't told you had three days, Jew. You were told you had till Monday morning, and I have it on high authority that the Jewish Monday begins at sundown on Easter Sunday. Now let us in."

CHAPTER 15

"SINCE WHEN HAVE THEY PAID attention to the Jewish calendar?" Yankev ben Khayim whispered hotly in my ear.

"Since it served their purposes."

"Somebody must have blabbed."

"Don't start making accusations. The *goyim* all know that our days end at sundown." In Hebrew, the hour of twilight is called the *beyn ha-sh'moshes*, the moment between the suns.

"*Shhhhh!*" Somebody shushed us.

The services were starting. I was leaning on the west pillar, facing the holy ark. I straightened up as the shul's upper shammes, Abraham Ben-Zakhariah, got up on the *bimeh* and began reciting the *Ashrey* prayer.

"*Ashrey yoyshvey veysekho—*" Praiseworthy are those who dwell in Your house.

I joined in the prayer, which normally calls upon us to lay aside all earthly concerns for the next twenty-four hours and to open our souls to God's tremendous majesty. But today we were also celebrating the first days of Pesach. Anyway, I tried. I didn't rush over the Hebrew words as if they were meaningless syllables to get through, like people sometimes do. I pronounced each word clearly, letting the cadences of the holy tongue clear my thoughts of the everyday Yiddish of the street.

But it was hard to draw a curtain between the weekday world and the spiritual realm. Unless you were one of the rich *makhers* who got the best seats near the ark, it was standing room only inside the Old-New Shul. A crush of men ten rows deep was packed in behind me along the western wall. The line went out the door and into the vestibule, and every time somebody else tried to squeeze in, a fine white dust drifted down from the scaffolding on the south wall. And there was some pretty vigorous shoving as burghers of various ranks competed for the best view, which was not at all in keeping with the welcoming spirit of the prayer. But the shul didn't have a gallery for women yet, so what did they expect? Men tend to behave better when the women are watching, even if it's from up in the balcony or behind a screen.

But the real distraction was that right before the service, as I was scraping all the old wax out of the candle holders, Yankev ben Khayim had come rushing in and started quizzing me on my knowledge of local law.

Did I know that the Jews of Prague were being held prisoner by Christian gatekeepers whose salaries we were required to pay?

No, but it didn't surprise me any.

Did I have any idea how absurd it was that the Christians believed with all their faith that the death of Jesus was God's will, and yet they still blamed the Jews for it?

As a matter of fact, I did.

Did I know that under German law, anyone who owes money on a private debt is only obligated to repay the original lender? In other words, if the lender dies, the debt dies with him.

"*What?*"

I told him if that isn't a motive for getting rid of somebody, I don't know what is—especially a merchant of fine imported goods. Plenty of people must have owed the Federns money, and a short list of their major debtors would be a great place to start.

Except that the looters were getting smarter, and the ledger was one of the first things they burned these days.

But some kinds of men are willing to blot out the figures in a lender's book with the blood of their fellows. And with Federn and his whole family under arrest, I'd have to get authorization from the emperor just to speak to them.

The prayer continued: "*Tsadek Adinoy b'khol d'rokhov—*" The Lord is righteous in all His ways.

THE FIRST GREEN VEGETABLES of the season offered us a foretaste of the Garden of Paradise, or at least a welcome change from the colorless gruel we'd been eating all winter. And yet I couldn't wait to jump to the end of the Seder so I could get back out there and knock on some more doors. I figured I wouldn't be treated like such a stranger this time, since Pesach is the night all good Jews open their doors to everyone, even the poorest outcasts, to celebrate the season of our liberation and to remind us that we were *all* strangers once in the land of Egypt.

But first we had to get through four pages of opening prayers, plus an extra prayer Rabbi Loew tacked on for the well-being of our Christian rulers.

The whole extended family was crowded around the table with barely enough room left for Elijah's cup, but it was kind of nice being squeezed in among them all. It made me feel like I belonged.

The rabbi's granddaughter Eva kept the little ones sitting still by seesawing between girlish tenderness and her family's renowned firmness. Young Lipmann watched her every gesture, looking like he'd sit through the plague of hailstones if she asked him to.

Rabbi Loew blessed the first cup of wine, and we leaned a little to the left and drank.

We washed and dried our hands, dipped the greens in salt water, then Rabbi Loew held up the middle matzoh and broke it in half with a snap that seemed to shake the walls, and for a second the supernatural took hold of our minds, as if the waters of the Red Sea had come thundering through the streets of the ghetto. Then the sound came again, reduced unmistakably to a harsh dry pounding on the front door.

It was the municipal guards coming to take inventory and search the house for contraband. They brought one of the town clerks with them, since taking inventory meant that somebody had to know how to read and write.

Rabbi Loew told one of the Jewish servant girls to show the guards around, then he resumed the ceremony.

The guards stomped through every room in the house bellowing things like, "Item: one sideboard," and relaying the words back to the clerk for him to catalog.

Undisturbed by the choppy seas around him, Rabbi Loew held up the first matzoh and said, "This is the poor man's bread that our forefathers ate in the land of Egypt. Whoever is hungry, let him come in and share it with us. This year here. Next year in the land of Israel. This year slaves. Next year free men."

We turned the page in the large Haggadah, and the first word of the next section stood out in thick black letters an inch high: עבדים

Avodim.

SLAVES we were of Pharaoh in Egypt.

In the right-hand margin, a woodcut showed a man swinging a sharp hoe. He was dressed in the tunic and leggings of a Bohemian peasant.

One of the guards said, "Item: one silver candelabra."

Another one said, "That's not silver, that's pewter."

In the beginning, our fathers were idol worshippers.

By the time we got to *But I took your father Abraham,* I could hear the guards asking each other where all the fabled Jewish wealth was hidden.

Blessed is He who has kept His promise to Israel.

The accompanying woodcut showed a shammes in a hooded cloak blowing a *shofar,* although the puffs of air coming from the mouth of the trumpet made it look like it was spitting forth fire and smoke.

Know for certain that your descendants will be strangers in a land.

A pair of women's voices in the kitchen cut through the mystical mood. Hanneh the cook was complaining what a pain it was putting the whole meal together without the *Shabbes goyim* helping her out. Yankev ben Khayim looked particularly distressed by this interruption.

Because not just one alone has arisen against us to destroy us. In every generation they have risen to destroy us.

Jacob fled to Egypt with only seventy members of his tribe, but God nurtured his people until they grew numerous and strong—the text gets fanciful here—like a *beauty with firm breasts and flowing hair.*

Here the illustrators had slipped in a picture of a young woman with a fiery halo of blond hair and a modest loincloth around her middle. The image was supposed to be allegorical, but it didn't look very allegorical to me.

And the Egyptians dealt evilly with us.

They set taskmasters over us.

And we built the cities of Pithom and Raamses. And since the artists the Kohen family used when they first printed this edition of the *Prague Haggadah* had no idea what these cities actually looked like, they carved one of them in the image of a walled European city of a couple of hundred years ago, while the other was represented by a tower just like the one at St. Andrew's Church in Kraków.

But we cried to the Lord our God.

The city guards met their match in Hanneh the cook, who threatened them with her plentiful supply of sharp implements if they poked at her delicate stuffed fish with their dirty fingers.

And the Lord heard our voice, and remembered His covenant with Abraham.

And He smote the firstborn of Egypt.

And here the illustrators went wild, depicting a group of men in modern clothing hacking and impaling babies until the blood ran out. And off to the side, someone who looked like a queen was bathing naked in a vat of their blood.

And Pharaoh commanded:

Every son that is born shall you throw into the river.

On the opposite page, men and women were throwing babies off a stone bridge with guard towers on each end just like the bridge that still stands in the center of Prague.

The next page showed an angel with a sword, even though God said:

I shall pass through the land of Egypt.

I, and not an angel.

But you can't picture God.

And I shall smite every firstborn.

With great terror.

With signs and wonders.

Although there is another interpretation of this passage regarding the plagues.

The children's eyes grew wide with wonder as we dipped our fingers in the cups and spilled out ten drops of dark red wine, one for each plague, to placate the evil spirits while reciting the names of the plagues in unison like the tolling of a bell.

But the rabbinical discussion that followed—about how we can deduce from the Scripture that the Egyptians actually suffered *three hundred* plagues— left the children squirming again, and it ended just in time for the bouncy sing-along professing our gratitude for all that God has given us when any one of his gifts *would have been enough.*

Dayenu.

Because God passed over our houses when He smote the Egyptians.

You shall tell your son on that day—

How the Holy One, blessed is He, redeemed us all.

But I have no son.

Rabbi Loew blessed the second cup of wine, and we leaned over and drank.

You're supposed to drain the cup, but I'd been fasting all day, and I was starting to lose my strength from hunger. We finally got to the *matzoh* and *maror*, the bread of freedom and the bitter herbs of slavery. A pair of opposites. So naturally, we mix them together. Take *that*, Pharaoh! See what happens when you mess with the Chosen People?

Rabbi Loew blessed the third matzoh, broke it up and passed the pieces around so that we could all take a bite.

And let me tell you, after reciting the whole ritual while the succulent smells of the sacrificial feast fill the room, that first taste of dry flat bread makes you *know* in your heart and *feel* in your soul how truly miraculous it is that God makes wheat come out of the ground for us. All we have to do is mix flour and water and—if we can actually find the time to bake it—we get bread, which is why we always say a blessing over the bread.

A man called Yeshua Ha-Notzri, better known as Jesus of Nazareth, did exactly the same thing at his last Seder, and for some reason the Christians elevated it to a divine mystery.

But even a shammes can say the blessing over the bread and wine on my side of town.

Finally a pair of servant girls brought out the first dish, hard-boiled eggs in salt water. But we weren't allowed to touch a thing until Rabbi Loew quizzed the children about why eggs are eaten during the Holiday of Spring. (They're symbolic of mourning and rebirth.) Young Lipmann clearly knew the answer, but he wasn't considered a child anymore since he turned thirteen.

"Because they represent the Jewish people," Eva said. Her answer caught me by surprise.

Who else but the Maharal's granddaughter could come up with an interpretation I'd never heard before?

"How so?" the rabbi pressed her.

"Because the longer you keep the eggs in hot water, the harder they get. So it is with the Jews."

If that's the case, then the Jews must be as hard-boiled as they come.

THE GUARDS MOVED ON TO wreck some other family's Seder.

We finished the meal, and blessed Him whose bounty we had eaten, and we drank the third cup of wine, and we said *Pour out Thy wrath*, and we sent a child to open the door for Elijah the Prophet whose cup of wine awaited on our table. And we called upon the Lord from this narrow place:

All the nations have surrounded me.

Save us, O Lord, we beg You.

For His love endures forever.

We begged Him to save us from the sword of our enemies, and asked Him to rebuild His house, and we drank the fourth cup of wine and switched into Yiddish so that even the women could join us as we raised our voices in song and asked the all-powerful God, the righteous, mighty, eternal, gentle, consoling, and loving God to build His temple speedily in our days. Soon, soon. Amen and amen, selah. *Omeyn, seloh.*

"CAN I GO NOW, RABBI?"

"No," said Avrom Khayim, butting in. "We need him to help straighten up the mess the guards made."

"I release him from those duties," said Rabbi Loew. "But keep your ears open, Ben-Akiva. Remember—when King Antiochus forbade us from reading the Torah, we read from the Prophets instead."

Meaning he wanted me to be ready to adapt to anything. I could handle that.

"And remember to trust in God even when everything seems to be going against you, because His plans are beyond our comprehension. After all, if Jonah had not spent three days in the belly of a fish, he would have drowned."

So being swallowed by a fish was actually a good thing. I bet you never looked at it that way.

"And remember to trust yourself."

He had me there.

But it was time for me to follow Acosta's advice and hunt down this rat-catcher who purportedly knew about picklocks.

So I turned to Avrom Khayim and said, "So tell me, old man, where's the whorehouse?"

CHAPTER 16

THE SHUTTERED WINDOWS TRIED TO hide the telltale glow of burning lamps, but slivers of pea-green light kept slipping out around the edges. Anyone could tell that it was a house of pleasure in the middle of Hampasgasse, right across the street from the *beys khayim*, where the earthly souls of the newly dead hid among the shadows, watching over their graves for twelve full months before joining their uppermost spirits in the World-to-Come.

Rainwater trickled down a flight of steps and collected at the bottom, where my face stared up at me out of a murky puddle. The front door was once at street level, but centuries of flooding had buried it under successive layers of silt from the river, until the street rose up to the second floor, and the first floor gradually became the basement.

The door swung easily on well-oiled hinges. The walls inside were cool and veined with dark streaks of moisture seeping down from the ceiling, but the fires were warm, and the lanterns brightened the place up pretty well for a subterranean cavern. Some of the candles must have been lit after sundown, in violation of the Sabbath, but I desperately needed to rid myself of the chill of the graveyard, so I didn't bother to inspect the fires too closely.

It might have been a roadside inn anywhere in the kingdom, except for the persistent dampness. Men with an air of prosperity gathered around the tables near the bar, hoisting cups of wine and playing at dice, dominoes, checkers, and—off in a corner, even contemplating their next chess move. Men whose grimy faces and tattered clothing told a different story huddled in the shadows under the stairs, playing cards and keeping their voices low. I found a seat near them.

The rattle of dice and slapping of dominoes triggered the old, familiar urge to lose myself in the fleeting thrills of wagering. It overwhelmed my senses as surely as if a perfumer had cracked open a vial of Turkish jasmine under my nose. It would have been so easy to shut my eyes to everything else and dive headfirst into it, but I silenced the urge by thinking about how much greater the reward would be if I saved the ghetto from destruction and won back Reyzl's love as the people carried me through the streets on their shoulders. Not an easy task, especially since one of the men at the next table would blink and swallow a few times whenever he got a good hand, telling signs that could be read from a half-mile away.

"What'll it be, honey?"

The hostess was standing over me with a tray of empty mugs and glasses balanced on her hip.

I didn't need any more wine tonight, and beer was *farbotn*. She saw my hesitation, and asked if I was here for a bit of their other line of business.

I shook my head.

The two men at the next table drained their cups and demanded a refill of wine.

"I'll get that," I said. "And bring one for me, too."

The hostess appraised me with a skeptical eye, and found me lacking. I can't say I blamed her. So I dug into the folds of my cloak, produced the rabbi's silver daler, and plunked it on the table. She didn't do anything vulgar like try to bend it with her teeth. The weight and feel of it satisfied her practiced fingertips just fine.

"Three cups of wine coming up," she said.

"Make it four cups," said the crooked little man next to me. He had leathery skin and a nub of flesh-covered bone where his right thumb should have been.

"Why the fourth cup?" I asked.

"Isn't it our duty to drink four cups of wine tonight as a symbol of freedom?" he said.

"Yes, but not all at once. And you're supposed to eat a full meal in between."

"Are you going to talk or are you going to play?" said the man with the blink-and-swallow tick. His matted hair was stiff with dirt, but under all that grit I could see that he was younger than his companion.

Their names were Israel and Beynish, and they were in the middle of breaking several commandments, but since I had skipped the Shabbes bath myself, I was in no position to pass judgment.

"So you're a scholar," said Israel, scratching the area around his missing thumb. "Then let me ask you something. Are flying insects really kosher?"

I told him that even though it is not our practice, the Torah permits us to eat certain "flying creeping things" such as crickets, grasshoppers, and locusts.

"You mean God in His infinite wisdom allows us to eat locusts, but *shellfish* are forbidden?" said Israel. "How is that possible?"

"Greater minds than ours have failed to find an answer to that question, my friend. Those laws belong to the *khukim*." The class of laws that have no rational explanation.

"In that case I got a question for you, too, mister big-shot scholar," said Beynish.

Oy vey. Here it comes. They say that a fool can ask more questions in an hour than ten wise men can answer in a year.

"Maybe you could settle something between me and another fellow. Isn't there someplace in the Gemore where they talk about women going wild and having sex with donkeys?"

I knew it.

I said, "You're probably thinking of the passage in Kesives which says that one cup of wine makes a woman radiant and attractive, but two spoil her dignity, three make her shamelessly aroused, and four make her demand sex, even of an ass in the marketplace."

"So the point of the lesson is for us to stop at three cups," said Beynish. He turned to his friend. "And you keep telling me there's no practical information in the Talmud."

"Just how big are these cups?" said Israel.

I admitted that the Babylonian units of measurement were different from our own.

"No kidding? So how big am I in Babylonian units?" said Beynish, grabbing his crotch so there would be no mistaking his meaning.

"You? About three fingerbreadths," said the hostess, slapping three cups of wine down in front of us. Drops of wine spilled onto the tabletop.

Beynish tried to look insulted while the hostess held the fourth cup in the air, unsure of where to put it.

"That one's for Elijah," said Israel.

She placed the cup in the middle of the table, and strutted away from us, her hips swinging like a ship's lantern in a heavy sea.

"But if he doesn't come for it in the next five minutes, we'll have to drink it ourselves," said Israel.

He raised his cup in his left hand.

"What do the Psalms say about not enjoying our enemy's suffering?"

"You mean *rejoice not at thine enemy's fall*," I said, citing the Proverbs.

"That's it. Rejoice not at thine enemy's fall—"

We raised our cups.

"But don't rush to pick him up, either."

They both drank deeply. I took a small sip. It didn't compare very well to the full-bodied wine served at Rabbi Loew's table.

"So how did your thumb go missing?" I said, pointing at the wiggling stump of flesh on Israel's right hand.

"He sucked on it too much when he was a kid," said Beynish.

"I lost it to a creature that was half-sewer rat and half-devil," said Israel. "But don't worry, I'll see it again someday. God's holding on to it for me until I come to claim it."

"You're Izzy the Ratcatcher?" I asked.

"Sure. Want to see my credentials?"

He reached into a leather bag and before I could stop him he pulled out a couple of dozen rat tails tied together with a bit of string and held them in front of my nose.

I leaned back, away from the smell. "What are you doing with all those? Do you have to pay the city council a thousand rat tails a year as tribute, like the Jews of Frankfurt?"

"Those days are long gone," said Izzy, shaking his head. "And by the way, it was *five* thousand rat tails a year."

"My God, how did you manage it?" I tried to sound impressed.

"This street used to be full of houses for fallen women, cast out from Christian society just like us, and every one of them had a rat problem. And also, every burgher in the city knew the way here, so there was always plenty of work to go around. Those were the days. Then they started cracking down, and now this is it. The last house of its kind in the whole *Yidnshtot.*"

He drained his cup and stared past me into the darkness. Bits of candle-light flickered like faded flames in his eyes.

I shook my head at this sad state of affairs, and refilled their glasses from Elijah's cup. I wasn't too worried about this transgression, since the Sages say that a sin done for the right reason is better than a *mitsveh* done for the wrong reason.

Izzy swallowed some more wine, and wiped his mouth with the back of his hand.

Then he asked, "So why is the new shammes in here pushing drinks in front of Izzy the Ratcatcher and his apprentice?"

Never underestimate a man's intelligence, no matter how raggedy his clothing. The masters of the Kabbalah even say that sometimes you can find a jewel in a poor man's underwear, though I can't say that I've tried to confirm that proposition.

"I'm here to learn about locks," I said.

"Then you're talking to the wrong man."

"Of course I am. But the night watchman told me you'd know who I *should* be talking to."

The chatter got kind of quiet on our side of the room, but there was move-ment beneath the stillness.

Izzy's eyes narrowed. "What are you getting out of this?"

"I don't know," I said. Redemption? Atonement? Acceptance? "I'm just trying to do what is righteous."

"Uh-huh. And what is this righteous thing you want from me?"

"I want you to take me to someone who knows about locks."

"I already told you I don't give a goat's turd about locks. Rats are my trade."

"Fine. Then let's talk about rats."

"What do you want to know about rats?"

"Oh, everything—their mating rituals, favorite foods, migration pat-terns—"

"Don't jerk me around, newcomer."

"Then give me something I can use."

Izzy looked at me as if I were something lower than a leech, but sometimes a leech is just what the patient needs.

He started reshuffling the cards, but he was just keeping his hands busy while his brain adjusted to this shift in the conversation.

"All right, Mr. Shammes," he said, his voice heavy with portent. "I might be able to help you identify any signs or omens involving rats."

"Go ahead," I told him. "I've got a charm against all rat-borne omens."

Beynish spat on the floor to ward off the Evil Eye, and locked his hands together by grabbing each thumb with the opposite fist. He probably would have tried to cross himself a couple of times if he thought he could get away with it.

Izzy licked his lips. He must have found them a little dry, because he took another sip, leaving his teeth stained purple from the cheap wine.

"You must beware of dreams in which you are being attacked by rats, for it is a sure sign that someone means to do you great harm," he said. "Finding tooth marks on sacks of meal, shoes, or any kind of clothing means bad luck, maybe even death. A sudden swarm of rats fleeing a ship or a house foretells an imminent disaster—"

"Wait a minute—" I stopped him.

"What?"

"I saw a swarm of rats early this morning."

Beynish's eyeballs nearly popped out of his head.

"Where *exactly* was this?" said Izzy.

"A few feet from Federn's shop on the Geistgasse, where the girl's body was found. And there were more inside. They came pouring out the door—"

"Wait, wait. Let's not get ahead of ourselves. Tell me about the rats in the street first."

It was the height of creepiness. The street seemed to come alive with an undulating layer of greasy pelts. Then the rats scattered and left something behind on the blood-soaked cobblestones.

"They were fighting over a hunk of raw meat lying in the middle of the road."

"A hunk of meat big enough to attract a *swarm* of rats? Did somebody happen to toss a whole joint of beef into the street?"

"I don't know, but from where I was standing it looked like there was plenty of meat left on it."

"And the rest were actually inside the shop? And they all came running out the door?"

"Well, yes. That's what I saw."

"You're sure?"

"Yes. Why?"

"Nothing. Just that it's very unusual behavior for rats. They generally creep in through holes and chinks in the walls. They're not in the habit of using the front door."

"What does it suggest to you?"

"It suggests that the rats were all in the front room, that they were unfamiliar with it, and they chose to flee through the first opening that presented itself."

"That's some pretty strange behavior, all right."

"No, I'd say it's a pretty common reaction for cornered animals."

"I mean, how did they get there in the first place? Did they follow the smell up the block and get trapped inside the store?"

"Oh, I suppose there are a lot of ways they could have gotten in there. But . . ."

He drummed his fingers on the table. I tried not to stare at the stunted digit on his right hand.

"But . . . ?"

"But—" He brought his hand up to his throat. "But it's so hard to talk with my gullet being so dry and all."

He rubbed his throat like a wanderer in the desert, desperate for water.

I ordered another round. That made him smile. In the meantime, my cup was still half-full, so I let him have the rest of it.

He took his time drinking it, then continued. "But the most likely explanation is that whoever put the body of that poor girl there brought along a sackful of live rats just in case they needed them."

"Needed them? For what purpose?"

"To distract people. It worked on you, didn't it?"

It certainly did.

"They took the trouble to gather a sackful of rats?" I said.

"It's not hard if you're willing to use good bait."

"Like—?"

"Like good cuts of meat. Did they look well fed?"

"How should I know?"

The ratcatcher shook his head as if he were supremely disappointed in me, because naturally *he* would have spotted it immediately. Then he shrugged it off as if he had gotten used to the gross incompetence of meddling amateurs.

Three more cups of wine arrived.

They drank. I sipped.

"A single piece of rotten meat in the right location will attract a few dozen rats in a couple of minutes," said Izzy.

"What kind of locations?"

He took another long, slow drink before saying, "Places where rats gather. Slaughterhouses, dungheaps, the waterfront—"

The pieces were starting to fit.

I said, "And the only kind of cart that wouldn't miss a hunk of beef that big is—"

"A butcher's cart," said Izzy. "Mystery solved." He celebrated this triumph of reasoning by draining his wine to the dregs.

"I saw such a cart," I said. "There were two men in it. The driver and somebody else."

"One to pick the lock and the other to carry in the body," said Beynish.

"They nearly ran me over, and a Christian girl, too, they were in such a hurry to get out of there."

"And you want me to help you find out which direction they went," said Izzy.

"Sure, but I think the most important question is what direction they came from."

"Why is that more important?"

"Because I might be able to answer it, if I only knew the streets better—"

"Not that way, you idiot!" A woman's voice blared, scattering my thoughts like frightened starlings.

"Ha ha ha!" A drunken man cackled, kicking his half-naked legs in the air and sending his gaily colored pantaloons flapping all around him.

"Mr. Johnson, please—!"

The hostess nearly spilled a pitcher of wine as she rushed over to help the woman drag him back into the dark corridor behind the bar.

It was just a quick flash of color, but it was enough. The man's clothes, his carefree attitude, and the unwashed turnip swinging between his legs told me it was time to abandon my drinking partners and follow the hostess into the pleasure garden behind this underground tavern.

The hostess reappeared in time to block my way to the passage.

"I've changed my mind about seeing your other line of business," I said.

"Too late. We're all full up."

Nobody had come in after me.

"Oh, I see." I feigned disappointment. "How much?"

"That depends," she said, practically batting her eyelashes at me, trying to be coy, although she couldn't have pulled off being coy with the help of a team of dray horses.

I reached inside my cloak, and her smile turned sour when I held up a piece of parchment signed by Rabbi Loew granting me license to investigate in his name.

She blinked.

"What the hell is this?" she said, looking at the Yiddish words as if they were a collection of meaningless squiggles.

"Do you recognize this signature?"

Her eyes flitted along the page like frogs hopping around Pharaoh's bed-chamber.

"Sure, but what is it supposed to mean?"

"It means don't bother yourself, I'll show myself around."

Some chairs scraped behind me as several gentlemen stood up from their games and gallantly offered to come to the lady's assistance.

"And I'll take my change now," I said, holding out my hand.

She looked like she wanted to drive a corkscrew through my palm, but decided against it. "Fine. Take your change, you cheap shammes."

She slapped a few kreuzers on the bar. At least she didn't throw them at me.

"Thanks," I said, picking them up. Then I nodded toward the middle gaming table. "And by the way, one of those pairs of dice is loaded."

I FOLLOWED THE SOUND of voices to a little room at the end of a pale green corridor, where a half-dozen women were lounging on a long couch, drinking cups of peppermint tea and joking among themselves. Some of them had their feet up on the table, exposing even more of their forbidden flesh. The only attempt to dress up the room was an embroidered tablecloth and a couple of lanterns with tinted glass emitting a reddish glow that rendered the women's soft curves all the more mysterious and alluring. I wondered what the artisans who spent their days piecing Virgin Marys together out of stained glass thought about the less-than-sacred uses of their materials. It probably kept them sane.

Many are Thy works, O Lord. There were women of every shape and size, for every style and taste, from twiggy teens to full-figured fertility goddesses, including a blond as white as bleached flour with a cross around her neck. Her name was Jana, and she wasn't just there to be someone's fantasy dress-up, she really was a Christian.

"You mean there's actually someone here who's more out-of-place than I am?" I said.

"I've never felt more at home," Jana said, linking arms with the girl next to her. "The richest men in the ghetto come to me."

"Second richest," said a good-looking slightly older woman with dark wavy hair, whose name was Trine. "The richest have their own class of whores in the Christian part of town, only they call them *mistresses*."

"What does it matter?" said a woman whose attributes were as full and round as ripe melons. "The milk of white goats and black goats is the same."

What would the rabbi say if he heard the Midrash quoted in this room, from such a mouth?

Or if he heard Jana proposition me in fluent gambler's Yiddish: "*Nu?* You wanna play the *froyen-shpil* with me for a little while?"

"He's not interested in your games," said Trine. "Can't you see that he's a scholar? You have to say, Come, let us explore the *sod ha-zivug* together."

The mystery of coupling. A term from the Kabbalah.

"So what'll it be, mister?" said one of the skinny ones, smiling at me and revealing a number of missing teeth. I guess there were men who found that sexy.

"Yeah, we don't have all night, O learned one," said Trine. "For dust thou art, and unto dust shalt thou return."

Now the Torah. If you ignored their profanities, they had to be the most literate bunch of whores in the kingdom.

I picked Trine.

She grabbed a candle and led me down a nearby corridor with doors lining both sides. Her raven hair glistened in the candlelight, and the stark shadows accentuated her cheekbones. Her skin was a bit weathered, but she must have been a *groyse yefeyfiyeh*, a real stunner, when she was younger, because she was still very attractive to my eyes. Considering how sharp-witted she was as well, I wondered what happened on the road of life that sent her down this path. Did she take a wrong turn somewhere, or did someone happen to give her especially lousy directions?

"I'm right, aren't I?" she said. "You're some kind of a scholar."

"Sure. Now, if only I could figure out what kind."

I listened closely, catching bits of Yiddish, Czech, and German conversation through the cracks and keyholes. A sallow-faced girl with layers of makeup painted on as thick as a wooden marionette's stepped around us, followed by a slow but eager-looking man with the perpetual stoop of a porter and rope burns across his hands.

"I knew you were the brainy type," said Trine. "You probably want to discuss the teachings with me before we lie down, since if we sit together and no words of Torah pass between us, then it is a seat of the scornful, but if we sit together and words of Torah do pass between us, then the Presence is with us."

My God, the Pirkey Avos chapter of the Mishnah.

"What were you before? A rabbi's daughter? Or sister? Or—"

"Or *what*?" She turned suddenly. "Keep talking like that and I'll snuff this out in your eye."

She pointed the candle at me, the flame close enough to singe my eyebrows. The creases around her eyes deepened, and I realized that with nowhere else to go, her sharp-wittedness had become dangerous.

"I'll have you know that we're doing the work of God," she said, "by keeping all the filthy men in this town from ruining the well-brought-up women from the good, pious families."

Candle wax was dripping on my cloak, and I could smell the bitter, minty herbs on her breath.

"I guess I never thought of it that way."

"Yeah, I bet there's a lot you never thought of."

She withdrew the flame from in front of my eyes.

"Do you drip hot wax on all your customers?"

"Only the ones I like."

"I'm flattered."

"Don't be."

Two shapes approached from the shadows. One was another wayward daughter of Israel, who barely glanced at me as she slipped by, pulling along a fairly well-dressed man who touched his hat as he passed and thereby managed to cover most of his face with his hand.

I let Trine enjoy tormenting me for a while, then I said, "Can we go somewhere with a little more privacy?"

"Ooh, listen to you, talking about *privacy*. That's a pretty rare commodity around here. Sometimes when all the best rooms are taken, I've got to make like a lovebird in the same room with two other people."

"Hey, you're talking to a man who sleeps in the same *bed* with two other people."

She smiled wryly. Then she led me up some narrow stairs past the kitchen to a covered walkway that bordered a square courtyard. The rain was picking up again.

We passed through an archway into a dark hallway on the far side of the building. There were only three doors, with no light coming from any of them.

This was as private as it was going to get.

I was about to make my move when the room at the end of the corridor erupted with inarticulate howlings. I started, which made Trine laugh. It sounded like someone was tearing apart a sheep, until I realized that the sounds were rhythmic, repetitive, and distinctly *happy*.

"He must have heard us coming," she said.

I was about to ask who "he" was, when she opened the door and a giant of a man in a dirty white shirt jumped all over her, flapping his arms and making those same happy *ahooo ahooo* sounds like a big baby.

"They call him Dumb Yosele," she said. "Not dumb as in stupid, but dumb meaning he doesn't speak very well. But I understand him, don't I, Yosele?"

"*Yess*." The big man spoke quickly. It turned out to be his clearest word, besides "cookie."

"And I thought I told you not to scratch your flea bites," she said, checking the scabs on his arms. "He won't stop till he's bleeding, unless we keep reminding him."

"Ow-*sigh*."

"You want to go outside?"

"Ow-*sigh*."

"All right."

"Ow-*sigh*."

"Yes."

She let him go skipping out in the rain. I'd never seen anyone over the age of five get so excited about running around with his mouth open to catch raindrops. He was getting soaked, and he loved every minute of it, laughing and letting out what for him was a joyful sound: *gaaa, gaaa, gaaaaah.*

Trine smiled just watching him.

"You should see him when he takes his weekly bath," she said. "We have to tell him *everything.* 'Wash under your arms, Yosele. Both sides. Now wash your face. Use the soap, Yosele.'"

"He bathes for Shabbes?"

"What are you, crazy?"

"Not yet, but I've been studying with a couple of real experts."

She ignored that. "Every day he fetches water from the well and food from the market, sweeps out the rooms, and carries hundredweight sacks of grain up three flights of stairs. What do you think? He doesn't get dirty like everybody else?"

So even Dumb Yosele bathed every week like a good Jew. I wondered if he could be included in a *minyen.*

I said, "You know, there are enemies of Israel who bathe only twice in their whole lives, on the day they're born and the day their bodies are washed for burial, and yet they say that *we* are the ones who have a distinctly 'Jewish' smell."

"Is that so? Well, we've got girls here who go to the *mikveh* every day and *still* don't feel like they'll ever be clean."

Her face had grown stern, and I was very much aware of the sound of falling raindrops all around us.

I listened to the raindrops for a while.

Yosele started screaming so loudly that anyone who didn't know better would think something horrible was happening to him: *ah-ha-haa, ah-ha-haa, ah-ha-haaah!*

"He's got to let it out somehow," said Trine. "But if he's happy, God's happy."

I had to agree. Watching him cavorting in the rain and loving every minute of it almost made me envy the big fool.

"We found him chained up in a stable, behaving no better than an unbroken horse," she said. "But we cleaned him up. Taught him how to wipe his own butt, make his own bed, and wait his turn for the bath. And one of these days he's going to learn how to chop wood with a sharp ax, because that's a damn heavy job for us in the winter."

Yosele finally came in out of the rain, dripping wet and leaving a trail of tiny puddles all the way back to his room, where Trine had him take off his shirt. Then she helped him dry himself with a towel. She had to keep prompting him to dry his chest, his arms, even his groin. He had no sense of shame, because instead of covering himself, Yosele found a loose piece of string and started wiggling it in front of his face and making more whooping noises.

Trine took the string away and told him to put on a clean shirt.

"He's such a big baby in a man's body. But what a body!" she said, laughing while she hung up the shirt and towel.

She lit his candle, and he promptly blew it out.

"Oh right, I forgot," she said, handing him her candle. "He has to do it by himself or it's not right somehow."

Yosele lit his candle, then blew it out, then lit it and blew it out again. He did this a couple more times before Trine said, "That's enough," and tried to pry her candle away from him. But he was in a playful mood, and wouldn't let her have it back.

"He doesn't know how strong he is," she said, struggling with his iron grip.

"Good thing."

"Oh, you don't have to worry about him. He never hurts anybody on purpose. He's totally without the *yetzer horeh*." The Evil Inclination.

She finally got the candle away from him in one piece.

"The worst is when he's sick," she said, "because he can't tell us where it hurts, so we don't know what remedy he needs, and it's so hard to watch him suffer because he doesn't understand why he feels bad."

Yosele bounced on the bed, then took a box from the shelf and dumped out some broken draughtsmen on a wooden gaming board. He lined the pieces up with great precision.

"Check-*uh*."

"You want to play checkers?" she said.

"Check-*uh*."

"We'll play checkers in an hour, all right? Now, why don't you go say the *kidesh* with the girls upstairs?"

"Uh-*tay*."

"Yes, upstairs now. Checkers later."

"Uh-*tay*."

"Yes."

"Uh-*tay*."

"*Yes*, go ahead."

"He says the *kidesh*?" I asked, after he left.

"In his own way."

And as I watched Dumb Yosele tapping his fingers on the walls along the corridor, I saw that the *sh'khineh* dwelt in him. And I felt a distinct sensation that he was in some way a specially chosen one, a holy fool sent to us as a test of whether we would take good care of him and see to it that he didn't suffer, and that God would judge us on how we treated this innocent soul.

"Most men don't have the patience to deal with him," Trine said, unlocking the door to a private room.

I followed her in.

"Now let's get down to business," she said, turning to me.

"Yes, let's." I shut the door and dropped the playfulness from my voice. "How did that Christian get in here?"

"What are you babbling about? We've always got Christians in here. How long do you think we'd stay in business if we didn't?"

"I mean tonight. How did that Englishman get in here when all the gates are sealed and guarded?"

"You know what they say. The *goy* may be *treyf* but his money is kosher."

"I don't give a damn about the money. Just tell me how he knew about this place."

"What are you, *meshuge*? All those upright Christian soldiers march in here, take one look at me, and practically have to pour the drool out of their boots."

"How do they get in?" I demanded.

"I knew there was something screwy about you. No normal man would let me spend all that time taking care of Yosele."

I took a step closer. "There's a secret passage, isn't there? Where is it?"

She cursed me.

"How do they know about it?"

She spat in my eye.

"Wow. Good aim. Now, tell me where it is before I—"

"Before you *what*? I've hurt bigger men than you."

I believed her.

Someone was pounding on the door.

"Who is it?" Trine said.

"Is everything all right in there, Trine?"

"Sure, I'm just trying to turn a big-boned ass into a man of understanding," she said. Another mangled quotation from the Sages.

What a waste of a truly gifted mind, I thought.

A passkey slid into the lock and turned with a *click*. The door opened and there stood the hostess with a couple of the girls and Izzy the Ratcatcher.

"What's going on in here?" the hostess wanted to know.

"I'm looking for the way out of the *Yidnshtot*," I said.

"Not looking like that, you aren't. You wouldn't get ten feet with that shaggy beard and that yellow bull's eye on your chest," said the hostess.

The other girls giggled at my predicament.

"Also, there's nothing happening over there at this time of night on Good Friday," said Izzy. "It's dead."

"I bet it is," I said.

"Besides," he said, "there's someone I want you to meet."

CHAPTER 17

THE MAN HUNCHED OVER the railing at the top of the stairs smiled at us, displaying a crooked line of yellowing teeth. He brushed a cloud of orange dust from his shirtsleeves, and invited us into his studio overlooking the courtyard on the Rotegasse. The room had no stove or fireplace, so it was cold enough for us to see our breath.

At first I thought that Izzy was taking me to meet a locksmith, but he told me that this man had a much more useful skill to share with me.

"So *you're* the lowly *unter*-shammes who's single-handedly trying to save us all from this false bloodcrime charge," said the man, shaking my hand.

"Not by choice. I'll take any help you can offer."

His name was Franz Langweil. He had dark eyes, pale skin, and shoulder blades that must have fused to his spine years ago because he was bent into a permanent crouch. He offered us some tea, but his mugs were so dusty that I declined. Every available surface was crowded with odd containers spilling over with minerals and powders of every conceivable color. Langweil told me he scraped out a living mixing dry pigments for the Christian artists decorating the new churches near the emperor's castle.

"A few years ago, a Jewish painter could work side-by-side with the Christians and nobody gave a damn. *Then there arose a new king over Egypt, who knew not Joseph,*" he said, pilfering a quote from the Book of *Shmoys,* "and now I'm barred from working on Christian themes. My *goyishe* friends still toss me some business now and then. Not much, but it's a living," he said. Then he coughed, and some orange particles went flying into the air. The wind carried the sounds of the city in through the broken windowpanes.

Izzy must have read my mind, because he gestured for me to be patient.

"You appreciate the finer points of the female form, I presume. Tell me, what do you think of this?" Langweil asked, lifting an oil-stained cloth, revealing a painting of a young woman. She was totally nude, facing away from us, her body floating on a sea of blue satin, her smooth, round behind in the very center of the frame. Kneeling in front of a dusky red curtain, a winged cherub whose dark hair matched the woman's held up a mirror that reflected her face, which was dimly shadowed and indistinct compared to the soft flesh that was the brightest element of this scene.

I swallowed.

Like a male animal with no control over his instincts—I swallowed.

"Notice how dark the painting is?" said Langweil.

"Sure, that's the first thing I noticed," I said, hoping it sounded natural.

"See how the blue satin turns black at the painting's edges? See how well this artist observed the relationship between light and color, simultaneously revealing and concealing the mystery of her beauty? Just look at the attention to detail," he said, handing me a glass magnifier.

I obliged him, leaning close and pretending to study the subtle shift in shading under the woman's right elbow.

"I've never seen anything like it," I said, straightening up. "She's— fantastic."

"Before your palms get all sweaty and you drop my lens, I better tell you that the man who painted this nubile young lady died a hundred-and-fifty years ago."

The warm glow in my chest drained away. This vibrant young woman appeared to be so full of life, and her warm, tender places were posed so naturally, that I wouldn't have been surprised to find the paint still wet to the touch. Now, I realized that she had probably died at least a hundred years ago. I hoped that she'd had a good long life, full of warmth and happiness, and that she hadn't died of a purulent fever a few months after she posed for this painting, which was pretty common among artists' models.

"It's called *The Venus of Colucci*. I think that was the original patron's name," said Langweil.

The iron clapper of the town bell rang three times, announcing the curfew in the Christian sections of the city, and the rhythm of the night was punctuated by the tramping of heavy boots as the municipal guards came around, barking orders and pounding on doors as they searched the ghetto for hidden treasures—which were so well hidden that not even the Jews knew where to find them.

I reluctantly bid goodbye to the ageless beauty of this unknown woman as Langweil covered her again with the oily cloth. I knew that Izzy had brought me here for a reason, but before I could ask him what it was, a window shattered in the courtyard below, and the sergeant of the guards stormed around issuing scatological curses at his henchmen.

Langweil turned to me, his dark eyes glistening as if they were made of glass. "What do you think of all this, Mr. Shammes? Some Polish stargazer can shift the center of the universe from the earth to the sun, but even in this strange new world the Jews are still hated and persecuted as heretics."

I said, "Actually, the Church's official position is that Judaism is a perfidious deviation from the eternal faith of Christianity, but not a true heresy."

"So we're in a class by ourselves?"

"I guess so."

"Lucky us," said Izzy.

Langweil asked, "Do you follow the Zoharic Kabbalah or do you prefer the Lurianic system?"

"I didn't come here to talk about this."

"Oh, but you did."

Ah, the famous mystical reasoning: Nothing is what it seems to be. Absence is presence. There are hidden meanings everywhere. He sounded like a follower of Rabbi Luria.

His manner of questioning me brought back the feeling of when I was a kid in the small-town *kheyder* where the teachers smacked your knuckles with a wooden rod if you took too long to answer a difficult question. Naturally, I thought that the World-to-Come was run like that *kheyder*, and that we would have to pass some kind of test before we got in. But in the troubled world of my daydreams, my brain would get all slow and fuzzy and I never had enough time to answer. So while other people have nightmares about drowning or being chased by demons, I have nightmares about not being able to think my way out of a simple problem.

I looked at Izzy, who directed my gaze back to Langweil, like an assistant reminding a distracted student to pay attention to the master.

I said, "I believe that as long as we live and breathe, we will never know the Creator in His true form, because in order to protect us from being engulfed by His endlessness, He had to build a barrier around us, and that same barrier also keeps us from being aware of the infinite energy that lies beyond it."

"Not all the time. There is a wise woman in the Old Town who knows how to prepare philtres that will temporarily dissolve the barrier and reveal the hidden glory of the Divine that pulsates in everything."

"Really? I must meet her, after all this blows over."

If I'm still alive by then.

"But that's quite a paradox you've identified," he said. "What would the great rationalists say in response to that?"

My right leg was getting numb. I shifted my weight and rubbed my thigh to get some feeling back into it.

"You know, I would be perfectly happy to have this discussion *on Tuesday*. But right now—"

Izzy nudged me.

I resumed my part of the dialogue. "Rambam would probably argue that the universe contains many accidents, such as time, which he describes as a side effect produced by the motion of the material objects of creation."

"We all know that the pure energy of God's emanations devolved into time-bound material reality," Langweil chided me. "The question is, how do we reverse the process and convert a material object back into God's original energy?"

"If I knew that I'd be making a living transmuting base metals into gold."

Izzy's face brightened, but Langweil remained serious, apparently waiting for my answer.

So I told him, "The *Seyfer Yetsireh* says that God created the world through some combination of the ten emanations and the twenty-two letters of the alphabet. But the Sages say that God created the entire world by unlocking the hidden energy in the single letter *hey* in the short form of His name."

"The universe is made from the energy contained in a single letter *H*? It's a good thing we're Jewish, or the Inquisition would be screaming for our heads on a platter for even thinking such a thing—"

"Before you go on, does this have anything to do with finding out who owed Federn money?"

"Yes," Langweil insisted. "Because they probably burned his ledger. Am I right?"

I didn't drop my jaw and say *My God! How did you know that?* But I came pretty close.

"Ah, the Hidden Science teaches us many things," he said. "We can neither create or destroy any part of God's creation. All we can do is alter its form. And so it just might be possible to reconstruct the contents of the ledger through a series of mystical processes that will briefly unite our souls with God's eminence."

"You're saying the words and numbers in that ledger still exist in the form of dissipated smoke?"

"Exactly."

"I see. Any chance of us being able to reconstruct the shape of evaporated footprints by examining their vapor?" I asked.

"Let's not get too far-fetched here, shall we? It's just that many times, what appears to be destruction is really an opportunity for us to begin healing God's creation."

Another mystical absence-is-presence type argument.

"You doubt me," he said.

I didn't deny it.

"For more than a hundred years, we have plowed our ashes back into the soil to bring renewal to this city," he said. "When the Jewish Town Hall was damaged by flames, Mayor Meisel rebuilt it with the alabaster ceiling that soars above our heads today. When the great fire tore through the Little Town and reached the roof of St. Vitus's Cathedral on the hill, they replaced the old roof trusses with brand-new copper ones, and laid the foundations for all the town houses you see rising up in a grander style than ever before."

"I haven't visited those neighborhoods yet."

"You don't have to. I've made a living record of it. Every disaster, every act of demolition, every laborious rebirth. Let me tell you, it's better than hanging myself with the rope from a sack of sugar so I'll have a sweet death. Come, I'll show you," he said, beckoning us to follow him around the dusty table.

He parted the ragged curtains and easily cleared the low roof beams thanks to his permanently stooped shoulders.

I had to duck under the angled beams and keep low as I entered his private wonderland.

A scale model of the city of Prague lay across three tabletops, taking up most of the artist's studio, including all the hills and valleys and the river running through the middle, with countless houses made of bits of wood and canvas. Thousands of tiny chimneys rose from roofs that Langweil had adorned with rows of orange tile, each one painted on with a brush about the width of an eyelash. Each window was distinct, whether it had four panes or six, an iron grille in front of it or ornate curlicues below the sill. Nothing had escaped his cunning eye. He had glued bits of spruce and other natural objects together to reproduce the bushes and trees in the cemetery, the rocky outcroppings on the shore, and even the ripples in the rushing water. Tiny loads of lumber were stacked by the river's edge waiting to be shipped out, and he had painstakingly outlined the details of each brick in the Old-New Shul's distinctive roof columns, as well as the faces of the Old Town Clock.

The whole thing stank of horse glue.

Yet the model was an absolute marvel. And it allowed me to appreciate how truly vulnerable we were in terms of sheer proportions. Spread out on the table in front of me, the Old Town was easily six or seven times larger than the ghetto. The Little Town and the castle were larger still, and Langweil hadn't even started on the New Town, which had the big horse and cattle markets and so many neighborhoods it needed its own town hall.

The Christians had it all: fortified walls topped with crenellated teeth in the old style, powder towers for storing ammunition, and hotels and castles that laid claim to all the surrounding high ground, while we lay in the flood plain by the river. Did the river offer a refuge? A way out?

I looked closer.

He had even labeled the streets, but I could barely make out his scribbling, which made the words look like the bending images of tree branches reflected on the surface of a pond. Then I noticed that he had put himself in his model, in the darkened window of the jail on Stockhausgasse. So he had a grim sense of humor, which was probably what kept him alive.

He'd made it sound like something he had taken up to pass the time when the steady work dried up, but anyone could see that he had spent years on it. He had spent years in this room, making a model of the city. For what purpose, exactly?

Maybe *this* one.

In his discussion of the Mishnah, Rambam says that a man may spend many years building a palace without knowing the true purpose of his labors. It may all be to satisfy God's will that a century later, a pious man shall be saved from the scorching rays of the sun by lying in the shade of one of its walls.

"Your model may end up serving a higher purpose by helping us save the ghetto from destruction," I said, drawing a circle in the air around his miniature representation of the *Yidnshtot*.

And from high above, I saw just how easy it would be to destroy it all. All those tiny bits of wood and canvas and horse glue would go up at the merest touch of a flame, the smoke curling up to be reconstituted in the World-to-Come.

Of course, we had recovered from such assaults in the past. The sands of time were littered with the remains of the proud empires that had tried to destroy us. But still, it was something to be avoided. A seedling growing from the stump of an oak is not the same as the original tree.

I studied the model, getting a feel for the layout of the city that I had been sorely lacking, particularly the area around the ghetto, noting the lines of sight down certain streets and the relationships between the angle of some rooftops and the street corners that made up the presumed itinerary of the butcher's wagon.

I focused on the street that ran south from the river along the eastern edge of the ghetto. It was the shortest route from the dockyards at Johannes Platz to the Geistgasse where Federn's shop stood (that is, until they torched it this afternoon). The shop was still intact on the model.

The wagon drivers must have had a hell of a time turning that big cart around on this narrow street, but if they had kept going straight, they would have ended up in the biggest public square in the city. So they took the trouble to turn around and tore off down Stockhausgasse, which leads to a four-way intersection at Haštal Square, where they had their choice of escape routes. But they probably wouldn't have turned back, or turned south toward Old

Town Square, so that left two possibilities, north on Kozí Street or farther east on Hastalgasse. And then what?

Something caught my eye. Langweil's model included a house with a long row of windows on the second floor overlooking a key stretch of the Geistgasse where the girl's body had been dropped.

"Do you know who occupies these rooms?" I asked.

"No one's ever asked me a question like that before," he said, leaning over to examine the spot under my finger. "It's always, *How long did it take you? What did you use to make the bushes?* But why do you want to know something like that? You don't think that a Jew had something to do with this?"

"No, no, of course not. God forbid. I was only thinking that anyone staying in those rooms might have seen something unusual, if they were up early enough."

"Well, let me see . . . hmm . . ." He made a clucking sound that for some reason I found extremely irritating at that moment. I told myself that if I would just be patient, all would be revealed.

Finally he said, "Ah, yes. The second-floor windows face the Christian street, but the entrance to this building is on the Shammesgasse. That's where Rabbi Aaron's study group meets every morning, just before sunrise."

Oy vey. Fifty rabbis in this town and it just had to be him.

Izzy said, "See? That's a whole classroom full of *yeshiva bokhers* who might have seen something if they weren't paying attention to the rabbi."

"I can't imagine Rabbi Aaron having much tolerance for inattention."

"They're probably still there," said Langweil. "They usually stay up pretty late burning the midnight oil. If you hurry, maybe you can catch them."

"This is your lucky day, my friend," said Izzy.

"Right. I figured if I stayed in one place long enough, some luck was bound to stick to me."

THE SHAMMESGASSE BARELY COUNTED as a street, even in this part of the ghetto. It was a dead end, ankle deep in murky water from today's rainstorms, and barely wide enough for two men to pass each other without scraping their elbows on the peeling plaster. The crumbling houses leaned on each other for support like a group of penniless old beggars who had turned their faces to the outer streets and gave their humble backs to this alleyway.

A wooden sign swaying in the wind marked the house we were looking for. The faded lettering was barely legible:

בחוץ לא-ילין גר דלתי לארח אפתח

A verse from the Book of Job, offering hospitality to all newcomers: *No stranger ever passed the night in the street, my door was always open to any guest.* The text was in Hebrew only, however. Rabbi Aaron may have been openly welcoming strangers, but he wasn't crazy. Any strangers who wanted a bed for the night had better know how to read Biblical Hebrew.

All that mystical talk with Langweil must have gotten inside my skull, because as I crossed the threshold, I felt a prickling under my skin as if I were leaping over a chasm, sensing for the briefest moment what the Kabbalists call the presence of God's absolute Being between the gaps in our experience of the world.

I was breathing hard, but somehow I made it up to the second floor without upsetting the balance of the universe. I listened outside the door while waiting for my heart to slow down. They must have been discussing the tractate Niddah, because they were talking about how a new bride who notices some spotting after performing her marital duty may be declared ritually clean, because the blood did not issue from "the source," a polite term for the uterus. One of the students raised a difficult question about a *married* woman who still bleeds from "that place" during intercourse.

Rabbi Aaron answered in classic Talmudic fashion, by posing another question. "Rabbi Simeon ben Gamaliel ruled that the blood of a wound that issues from the source is unclean. On the other hand, Rabbi Yehuda Ha-Nasi and our Masters declared that such blood is clean. Why the discrepancy?"

Before today I would have nodded in approval, but now the high-level debate of such a fine legal point seemed almost alien to me. We needed to act, and swiftly, or else I could practically guarantee that pretty soon we'd all be seeing plenty of blood, and that nobody would have the time to debate whether it was clean or unclean.

Rabbi Aaron wasn't pleased with the interruption, but if I learned anything in the old school it was how to kiss up to people I can't stand, so I bowed humbly and wished him a *gutn Shabbes* and did my best to avoid the charges of "working" on the Sabbath by confessing that I was here because I was lacking a crucial bit of knowledge that only he and his students could provide for me.

An intellectual problem to solve? Nothing could interest them more. They rose from their benches and formed a loose semicircle around me, asking for details. They all had the same closely cropped hair, like some splinter sect of reverse-Nazirites, as if every applicant had to chop off his hair to join their little study group.

I told them I needed to know if anyone had seen a butcher's cart pass by that morning, just before sunrise, heading south toward Federn's shop, or if they remembered seeing anything else out of the ordinary, no matter how insignificant it might seem. I reminded them that the Holy One, Blessed is He, did not create a single thing that is useless (Tractate Shabbes), and that even a snake, a scorpion, a frog, or a gnat may carry out His mission (*Breyshis Raboh*).

They nodded vigorously and told me that they had seen a number of omens that day, bombarding me with stories of how this one felt his foot or his palm itch, or that one saw a pot of milk boil over and spill on the fire, or broke a shoelace, or heard the maid singing before breakfast. All bad signs, apparently.

A young student named Bloch, with short blond hair and bright blue eyes, told me in all seriousness that he had heard thunder, and that thunder on a Friday means the Angel of Death is walking the streets of the ghetto searching for victims.

Then a skinny fellow with big ears and deep-set eyes named Schmerz claimed to have seen it all unfolding, from the swarm of bloody rats to the mob of angry Christians torching Federn's shop. He described the men in the cart that nearly ran me down as a big man with a wrestler's body and a driver whose face was half-hidden by a black mustache and beard. He said he had seen them before. But as I pressed him for details, he got that possessed look that I've seen in newly minted converts as he explained that these events were harbingers of the final split between the Chosen People and the *goyim*, and that God was punishing us because we had become too much like the Christians, but that all the horrors to be visited upon us were necessary, since they would hasten the coming of the Messiah and bring an end to the Jewish Exile forever.

And the thought came over me, creeping in from the edges of my awareness like a malodorous breeze drifting through the window, that such devotees of messianism were capable of anything, and that some wild-eyed fanatic could very well have committed this crime in the hopes of precipitating a crisis that would somehow "purify" the Jews and speed their return to the Land of Israel. So it was possible that a Jew could have done it.

I caught Rabbi Aaron looking at me with a hint of a smile, and I was so disturbed by runaway notions that I wanted to grab Schmerz by the shoulders and shake him.

I had come seeking answers that would help bring the truth to light, but I had forgotten that we also have a saying that if God wants to punish a man, He makes him wise.

I got out of there as fast as I could, my head filled with visions of the sky crashing down on us.

I ran through the streets to Rabbi Loew's house to seek his counsel, splashing through puddles and skidding on the cobblestones, and saying the nighttime *Sh'ma* the whole way:

Master of the Universe, I hereby forgive anyone who angered or antagonized me, or who sinned against me, whether against my body, my property, my honor or against anything mine; whether accidentally, willfully, carelessly, or purposely; whether through speech, deed, thought, or notion; whether in this life or another. I forgive every Jew.

I arrived wet, muddy, and exhausted, the words of the prayer still on my lips:

And may You illuminate my eyes lest I die in sleep.

CHAPTER 18

BISHOP STEMPFEL FOLLOWED A PAIR of page boys to the bedchamber reserved for eminent guests. His retinue accompanied him inside the luxurious quarters, where a roaring fire cast its glow upon the four-poster bed bearing the coat of arms of Our Lady of Terezín. The bishop dismissed the pages and asked his aides to deliver their final report of the day.

Grünpickl placed a bound sheaf of page proofs on the table beside the bed, explaining that it was a compendium of evil doings across the continent penned by an Italian brother of the Order of Saint Ambrose. The bishop nodded. Another book to review for doctrinal errors and falsehoods before final approval for publication was given. Perfectly routine.

"What else?"

Grünpickl reported that there were still no clear indications linking witchcraft to that morning's alleged bloodcrime offense, but the matter was still under investigation.

"The faithful are already calling on you to beatify the girl and set her on the path to sainthood," said Popel.

Bishop Stempfel grunted. "It would be easier if she were a boy," he said, as an attendant helped him doff his official robes and slip on a dressing gown that had been warming by the fire.

The final resting place of a martyred child-saint would bring thousands of visitors a year and much attention to the cause, but the biggest shrines belonged to the likes of Saints William of Norwich, Hugh of Lincoln, and Simon of Trent. All boys. But it was too late to change anything now.

The bishop climbed into the downy bed. The sheets were cold, like everything else this far north of Rome. He propped himself up on the pillows, but it was hard to find a comfortable position because of the inflammation in his posterior. He shivered as he pulled the covers up, then the attendant spread another coverlet on the bed and tucked it around the bishop's mid-section.

Popel was still standing there.

"Was there something else?" the bishop asked.

"My lord, it has been our practice for many years for all the Brothers of Our Lady to gather in the great hall every Friday during Lent and castigate ourselves."

"How very commendable of you."

"Perhaps you would care to join us."

"I appreciate the invitation, Brother Popel, but as you can see, I'm already suffering enough as it is."

"Oh. Is your, um, condition still bothering you?"

"What do you think?" he said, eyeing the attendant, who quickly withdrew from the chamber. The itch got so bad that sometimes when he scratched it left spots of blood on his underclothes.

Popel was about to send for the doctor, but the bishop told Grünpickl to take care of it, and to make sure he brought back *two* doctors this time.

"But that's not what you wanted to talk to me about," said the bishop.

Popel acknowledged this with a crooked smile and launched into another one of his little tirades, this one about how Christian interest in dabbling in the Jewish Kabbalah was undermining the moral virtue of the nation, etc., and that such *excrementa* (as he called it) should be condemned and destroyed.

The bishop said, "It is our understanding that the Holy Office of the Inquisition has taken great pains to ensure that the Latin translations of the Kabbalistic works have been purged of all anti-Christian elements, so that one may read them and remain a good Christian."

"True, but there is still much work to be done, my lord. This heretical book has just been brought to my attention, a book of 'poetry' by a certain Immanuel the Jew that contains passages of the vilest filth—"

"Can't this wait till morning?"

Popel flipped through a stack of pages of crabbed handwriting, the results of several weeks' labor by a team of learned professors who had been translating the offending text.

"Another banned book, Popel—?"

"My lord, I will tell you in all sincerity that if my own father had written this book, I would personally carry the torch to light the fire under him."

Popel found the page he was looking for and read a passage aloud in which a young Jew boasts of having talked a nun into breaking her vows of chastity for him, and that her passion was so aroused that "the fire of lust burned in her like a river of sulfur."

"I bet it sells very well at the Frankfurt Book Fair," the bishop murmured.

"Beg pardon, my lord?"

"I said you'll have to let me examine a copy before I make my determination."

"Very good, my lord," he said, piling the loose pages on top of the other book. "Of course, all the influential rabbis have condemned the book as usual, but that's nothing but a clever ruse. This calls for *scharfe Barmherzigkeit*." Rough mercy.

"I'll look into it."

"Excellent, my lord. Now, if you'll excuse me, the brothers are waiting for me to join them."

"By all means."

Go whip yourself bloody, he thought. Once the Lenten period of mourning was over, he'd have to talk with Popel about his misdirected zealotry. Dirty jokes about errant young men unleashing the passions of sexually frustrated nuns were as old as the seven hills, and hardly amounted to heresy, even if they did come from a randy Jewish bard.

The real problem of heresy came from turncoats like that Dominican monk Bruno, who dared to argue that there were no absolutes in space, only positions relative to other bodies. It might sound harmless, but taken to its logical conclusion, such an argument meant that there were no absolutes of any kind—no up or down, no right or wrong, and no God. The Venetian authorities would have to extradite him soon, and fortunately it wasn't too late to save the young students who had read his book. But if any young women had been allowed to listen to his lies, the bishop had no doubt that their virtue would have been thoroughly destroyed. It's a good thing women weren't allowed in school.

He steepled his fingers and pressed them against his nostrils, and considered the other extreme—men like Popel, who saw the world *entirely* in terms of absolutes, when there were many subtle complexities to take into account. To such a man, the Cossacks would seem like natural allies. After all, they hated the Jews and the Turks equally as enemies of Christendom. But dig a little deeper and you found that the Cossacks hated the Catholics almost as much as they hated the Jews. They fought the Turks, but not for the right reasons. No, they were not our friends. And they were very good at destroying things. Of course, the Cossack hordes didn't even have a country to call their own, but who's to say what might come to pass in a hundred years time with a tribe of people so determined to assert their independence?

The bishop's legs were finally warming up when the doctors came in and made him take the covers off again. His skin shriveled with cold as they poked and prodded him fore and aft. When they finally put away their instruments and let him cover himself back up again, he asked for their opinions.

The old man with the ring of white hair let the younger one speak first. His name was Lybrmon, and he had an unassuming and authoritative manner that the bishop found reassuring. Dr. Lybrmon wiped off his eyeglasses and spent a good long while stroking his trim gray beard before speaking.

"My lord, you have a fissure that will not heal on its own. We can supply you with ointments that will temporarily reduce the swelling and irritation, but a long-term cure would require stitching the wound up."

The other doctor fixed his iron-gray eyes on his rival, and sliced the air with his bony arm as he denounced such procedures as dangerously similar to the forbidden practices of Jewish doctors, who, according to the latest research at the University of Vienna, were obligated by Jewish law to kill one-tenth of the Christian patients they treated.

The bishop was skeptical. Although Pope Gregory XIII had banned Jewish doctors from attending to Christian patients for all eternity, in all lands, even those undiscovered countries which did not yet know the light of Christ, it was widely known that every noble had a Jewish doctor hidden away somewhere, and surely somebody would have noticed if all the prominent noble families were being decimated by poisonous drugs. Even Emperor Rudolf II had an influential trio of converted Jews in his court as advisers, and the bishop had heard rumors about Rudolf's personal physician, Tádeás Hájek, even though Hájek had fought on the Hungarian front as a military doctor and served as court doctor to the emperor's father, Emperor Maximilian II.

"What do you recommend?" asked the bishop.

"Virgin amber, direct from the source, my lord. It's the best thing for a toothache."

"But I don't have a toothache," the bishop protested.

"You may not feel it, but the ache which manifests itself at one end often begins in the mouth."

The bishop looked to Dr. Lybrmon, who quickly concurred with the elder doctor's opinion.

"In that case, fetch forth the virgin amber."

"As you wish, my lord. Although we might not be able to procure it until sometime tomorrow."

"Fine, fine. Now go."

The bishop dismissed the physicians, and settled back into bed. He shoved aside the papers Popel had left for him, and untied the ribbon around the bundle of page proofs he needed to examine. He skimmed the introduction, then flipped through the pages to get a general overview. By all appearances, it was a detailed, case-by-case catalog of the spread of witchcraft to every village, town, and region of every country in Europe, illustrated with a few dozen woodcuts depicting strangely compelling scenes of Satanic adoration. Men lined up to tread upon the cross and kiss the devil in that most hideous and shameful place. The Devil placed his mark upon their bodies, usually on the men's eyelids, armpits, lips, and shoulders, and on the women's breasts and privates, confirming what Gödelmann had noted in his new book, *Tractatus de magis*.

The book also furnished clear proof that devils can fornicate with women by preying upon their gullible nature and uncontrollable carnal lusts. It was clearly a work of immense importance.

He turned the pages over till he came to the chapter on soporific spells. A woodcut depicted a woman in bed, with her breasts showing and a passive smile on her face, as three well-dressed and deceptively comely young witches offered her a goblet containing a potion that had clearly drugged the woman into such a stupor that she was blissfully unaware—or possibly unconcerned— that her breasts were on display for all to see. He *had* to learn more about the uses and content of this potion, because, naturally, it might help make the accused more compliant during interrogations.

His eyes nearly glazed over as he stared at the picture, and he felt a stirring under the bedclothes, and he was considering what to do about it when Popel burst into the room, half out-of-breath, and said, "We've brought in a pair of witches, my lord."

The bishop flipped the pages shut, his unsightly bulge fading to invisibility as he made a show of flapping open the sheets and climbing out of bed.

"What do you mean, a pair?" he demanded.

"A mother and daughter, my lord. The mother has already undergone a couple of hours of rough questioning."

Those idiots!

"I gave them strict orders not to start without me," he said, as Popel helped him put on his robes of office.

"I'm sorry, my lord, but we had no control over this. They were arrested by the local authorities."

"On what charges?"

Popel checked the *Blutschreiber's* report. "It says they cursed a crowd of good Christians, made the sign of the Devil, spun around three times, and uttered more of those blasphemous Hebrew curses."

"What are their names?"

Popel ran his finger down the page. "Freyde and Julie Federn."

A pair of Jewish witches, eh? As Popel grabbed a lantern to light their way down the steps to the dungeon, the bishop wondered if the daughter was young enough to be a virgin.

שבת

Samstag

Sobota

Saturday

Behold, the Guardian of Israel does
neither slumber nor sleep.

—PSALMS 121:4

CHAPTER 19

I BLINKED AWAKE, AND BREATHED easier as I came to full awareness that the dream was over and the creeping things had vanished. It felt good for a second, but then I remembered where I was, and it took a good long moment for the spirit of God to come flooding back into me. I closed my eyes and thanked the Lord in His mercy for having returned my soul to me.

A shadow loomed above me, and I heard Acosta's voice: "Well, blessed art Thou, O Lord, Who revivest the dead. Now get the heck out of that bed and let me have my spot. I've been up all night."

I told him as quickly as I could that I was worried that we might have a deranged messianist in our midst who believed that stirring up Christian hatred would prevent assimilation and thereby preserve our separate Jewish identity. But he dismissed my fears.

"Do you really think anyone has to encourage the *goyim* to hate us? Now I'm asking you nicely to get the hell out of my spot."

I got up, washed my hands, and said the *reyshis khokhmah* prayer: *The beginning of wisdom is the fear of God*. Then I sat on the edge of the bed and pulled on my old, worn boots, one of the few things I could count on these days to keep out the rain. One of the few things I could count on, period.

The Holy Writings tell us that God speaks to us in dreams, and that if we do not pay attention to this subtle form of communication, we will suffer for it. So I went looking for Rabbi Loew, and found him in his study-room, getting ready for the morning prayers with his daughter Feygele and his son-in-law Rabbi Ha-Kohen. Yankev the mystic and young Lipmann were also there, putting on their *tallises*. Rabbi Loew's daughter barely glanced at me as she stepped out of the room in her best Shabbes clothes.

As her steps faded away, I said, "Have any of you recently studied the passage in Brukhes which says that a dream is one-sixtieth of a prophecy?"

The others stood there shaking their heads, but Rabbi Loew said, "Why? Did you have a prophetic dream of some kind?"

"It certainly felt like it."

"Then you must tell us about it."

After the quiet isolation of Slonim, I had forgotten what it was like to have all but the most intimate acts open to public observers.

"What are you waiting for?" said Rabbi Ha-Kohen. "No wisdom will come of this if you keep it to yourself."

"Aye, for an uninterpreted dream is like an unread letter," said Yankev.

So I told them about my unsettling dream, and Rabbi Loew's face grew serious.

"What were you running from?" asked Rabbi Loew.

"I don't know. I just knew that I had to get away."

A feeling that I'd always known.

"That would explain the final part of your dream," said Rabbi Loew. "The part where you saw the *Shmir*."

"The what?"

The fringes of Isaac Ha-Kohen's *tallis* stopped swinging. Even the books on the shelves seemed to straighten up and listen closely.

"Ach, my *talmid*, you need to study the *aggadic* literature in greater depth."

"The time will come for that."

He looked me in the eyes and accepted this as a promise to study with him further.

"A story," he began in classic rabbinic style. "In the early days of creation, a mighty reptile was formed. A *tanim hagodl*, a great worm named Shmir, as it is called, that has the power to flood the world with just a swish of its tail. And while we would be virtually powerless to subdue it ourselves, the demon king

Ashmedai was able to imprison the creature in a deep pit beneath the waves and seal it with the seal of Ashmedai."

He gripped my forearm and turned it over as if he were looking for traces of the strange seal still written on my body.

"And you will continue to wear the invisible bonds of slavery until you summon the will to confront the forces within you that are driving your actions."

It was too early in the morning to absorb all of this. How was I supposed to go around knocking on doors and calling people to shul while trying to fathom how close I came to waking the sleeping dragon that is guarded by the king of the demons?

"A bad dream can sting worse than thirty lashes," said Rabbi Loew, trying to reassure me. "But you must believe that God would not build the moral foundation of the world on such shaky and unstable ground as human reason alone. It is precisely *because* the world appears to have no order or justice that the Holy One, blessed is He, created us with His commandments imprinted on our souls. But we will have to talk about this later, my *talmid*. It's time for you to call the faithful to shul."

THE STREETS OUTSIDE THE GHETTO were empty of Jews, who had either gone into hiding or melted into the countryside. So the rabbis added a couple of streets to my rounds, which turned out to be a maze of alleys north of Hampasgasse that dead-ended near the riverfront. And I had to pound on all those doors with my fist, since we're not supposed to use the *kleperl* on Shabbes.

I could smell the dankness in the rotting wood.

I heard noises coming from inside, foul and unpleasant noises, and a black mood gripped me by the shoulders.

> *The hand swoops down and knocks me to the floor. The clenched teeth open wide and snap at me. I press against the floor with my eyes squeezed shut, until the angry whirlwind rushes over me and leaves me shivering in its wake.*

I did my best to shake it off.

Rabbi Akiva says that God foresees all, but still gives us permission to act freely, which suggests that the Almighty is willing to permit a fair amount of random cruelty in the world.

I must have been lost in those kinds of thoughts for a while, because I suddenly found myself up against the iron fence, looking across the cemetery at the stragglers scurrying into the Klaus Shul for the *shakhres* services. And I had to squeeze through a break in the fence and cut across the cemetery or else I'd be late—again.

The *beys khayim* was filled with tombstones. Well, what did I expect to find crossing through the cemetery? But these marble stones were positively *crammed* together, some of them leaning on each other for support, others, the old ones, nearly falling over. And the Bohemian Jews had decorated their brand-new tombstones in the latest fashion, which meant that instead of austere monuments bearing silent witness with the eternal Hebrew letters, I was surrounded by living symbols of who the inhabitants were in life. Everywhere I looked, the carvings depicted animals that represented the family names of the deceased—a fox for the Fuchs family, a deer for the Hirsches, a rooster for the Hahns, a crouching lion for anybody named Judah or Ariyeh—or symbols of their professions, like a pair of shears for the tailor, its blades tilting menacingly toward me, or a water-jug for the Levite, which looked like it was about to spill over into the apothecary's mortar and pestle.

I had to get out of there before the spirits of the dead closed in on me, but my path was blocked by the sudden appearance of a gravestone carved with the hand of God breaking a blossoming branch from a tree that spread over a female figure, which must have meant that it was the grave of a young, unmarried woman. And the text confirmed this: "She had trouble all her days and did not have years."

I felt a deep sadness for her, whoever she was.

But the dead would have to wait. I barely had time for the living, and the sun was already running its course.

Rabbi Gans told me that Mordecai Meisel built the Klaus Shul about twenty years ago, several steps below street level, for two reasons. One sacred: because the Psalm says, "Out of the depths I have called unto thee, O Lord," and one profane: in order not to provoke the Christians by building a shul as splendid as one of their churches. (Although he had apparently grown bolder in recent years, employing his favorite Italian architects Fodera and Tannuzzo to build the Meisel Shul, which was on its way to becoming the biggest and most lavish building in the ghetto.)

The benches in the Klaus Shul were only half-full, since the shul was located on a bad street and presided over by a strict reformist whose views were unpopular with the rich families. But in the rear of the shul, behind a rope separating them from the rest of the worshipers, a group of women of the night huddled together on a low bench, following along as the *zogerke* translated the Siddur into Yiddish for them.

I washed my hands again and joined the service just as the first *balkoyre* was called up to read from the Torah. On the first day of Pesach we always read the part where Moses tells the Israelites to smear the blood of a lamb on their doors to keep the Angel of Death away. You might think that such divine protection allowed them to sleep easily. And yet they remained awake and vigilant all through the night, listening to the howling wind as the Destroyer walked the streets.

I probably wouldn't be able to sleep through that, either.

The second reading was the passage from *Bamidbor* that commands us to do no manner of servile work on the fifteenth day of Nisan, just in case I had forgotten what a bad job I was doing of keeping His commandments.

We also read the passage from the prophets where Joshua circumcises all the tribesmen of Israel with razor-sharp bits of flint stone (some of the men cringed involuntarily at those words), then a captain of the Lord's army appears with a sword in his hand and tells Joshua how to defeat the people of Jericho, who had shut their gates against the children of Israel so that no one could go in or out.

And when the walls fell, the Israelites destroyed everything in the city— men and women, young and old, oxen, sheep, and asses—everything except for a harlot named Rakhav and her family, who had been kind enough to harbor our messengers.

It made me wonder if it was really such a great idea building walls around people, whatever the reason. Sure, it offered you short-term protection. But on the other hand, your enemies knew right where to find you, all crammed together like sheep in a pen.

Rabbi Loew finally lifted the silver pointer from the sacred scroll and laid it aside, then he gave his sermon in plain Yiddish.

Oddly enough, he didn't say much about the current standoff with the Christians, beyond reminding us that no nation has the right to rule over another and that every nation has the right to be free. Instead, he suggested that certain members of the community bore some of the blame for our dismal situation, having sought a false sense of stability by siding with the wealthy burghers who were nothing but a pack of wolves who always wanted more and more of everything.

No wonder the shul was half-empty.

Then he drove the nail in deeper by railing against the leaders of the community for not attending to the needs of the poor.

"Rava said that the righteous could create a world, if they wanted to," he declared, his words resounding off the cold stone walls. "But what do we find here in the *Yidnshtot*, where a handful of rich Jews own two-thirds of the property, while the rest of the community owns a little sliver of nothing? I have told you many times over the years that the only legitimate use of property is to provide us with our basic needs, and that any surplus wealth must be used to benefit the whole community. Doesn't the Lord promise us that *there shall be no poor men among you*?"

Dvorim.

He finished with the usual prayers for the health and well-being of Emperor Rudolf II and the rest of our Christian rulers. We had just started a Psalm—the one that goes *Vatabeyt eyni beshuroy, bakomim olay mereyim tishmanoh oznoy* (My eye has seen the downfall of my adversaries, and my ears have heard the torture of the evil ones who rise against me)—when a shopkeeper's assistant came rushing in and announced that a royal carriage had just pulled up at the South Gate with orders to take Rabbi Loew up the hill to meet with Emperor Rudolf.

Rabbi Loew interrupted the Psalm amid hushed gasps and told me to get Rabbi Gans so that he could include this momentous event in his chronicles, then he directed the congregation back to the verses.

Rabbi Gans lived somewhere near the Pinkas Gate, but I couldn't bring myself to cut through the cemetery again, so I had to run all the way around to the east, then south, *then* west on Pinkasgasse. Some straight-and-narrow types gave me a black look as I sped by, even though they should have known not to pass judgment without knowing the circumstances, since a man is permitted to run on Shabbes in order to perform a *mitsveh*.

If it is true that *an empty table holds no blessing* (Zohar), then surely Rabbi Gans was blessed many times over, because I found him finishing a large breakfast that easily fulfilled the obligation to celebrate Shabbes with three full meals in order to renew ourselves and all creation as well.

Rabbi Gans invited me to look around his study while he got ready. He had an impressive library of at least a hundred volumes, so of course I leafed through some of them while waiting for him to return. He had a copy of Rabbi Loew's *D'rush No'eh b'Shabbes Hagodl*, A Fine Sermon for the Great Sabbath, published by Kohen of Prague three years ago, which had sealed the Maharal's reputation as a troublemaker in these parts. In it, he was openly critical of the newly created office of Mayor of the *Yidnshtot*, and many other practices of the community government, denouncing corruption and ignorance wherever he saw it, which was pretty much everywhere. But I was surprised to find it shelved near a well-worn copy of dei Rossi's *Meor Enayim*, a book that Rabbi Loew detested because the Mantuan author had claimed that the Jewish calendar, and therefore our whole system of telling time from the creation of the world, did not square with known mathematical principles.

Rabbi Gans may have hidden it well beneath his apparently placid exterior, but it was clear from even a glance at the titles on his shelves that he was bravely following our teacher Rabbi Isserles's command to read what the great Christian scholars and other "idolaters" had to say on matters of science. His writing desk was littered with papers, and he appeared to be working on several manuscripts at once, on such topics as math, astronomy (this one was full of charts showing the phases of the moon and such), and what looked like a lengthy history of the Jews in Bohemia. This text opened with a citation of Moses' command to "Remember the days of old" (*Dvorim*, again), and a courtly bow to "our lord *keyser* Rudolf, may his glory be exalted."

Next to it lay a treatise on optical devices, and the first draft of his latest project—the chronicle of this week's events. I was tempted to skim through it to see if my name appeared anywhere in the manuscript, but I didn't want to disturb the collection of glass lenses arrayed on top of the pages, either as part of an optical experiment or merely as paperweights, I wasn't sure which.

There were also several letters, including one from a kinsman named Joachim Gans, who apparently worked as a mining engineer in England without disclosing his Jewish identity, describing the results of an innovative method of manufacturing saltpeter, the main ingredient in blasting powder.

Rabbi Gans returned while I was trying to improve my knowledge of the mystifying ways of women by thumbing through his copy of the *Sheyn Froyenbikhl*, an instructional guide for women on manners, religion, and marital duties that was printed in Kraków when we were both students back in the old days.

"Are you ready?" I said.

"Is one ever ready to meet with one's emperor?"

"I wouldn't know. What's he like in person, anyway? And please don't give me any of that may-his-name-be-elevated stuff that you had to write in that book."

Rabbi Gans smiled at me. "People will still be asking that question a hundred years from now. *Keyser* Rudolf is a hard man to know. He has much of the regal stiffness of his Spanish uncles, but he has always been a dedicated patron of the sciences. He has a long history of being subject to dark periods of melancholia, but after Prince William of Orange was killed by a Catholic zealot's bullet fired at point-blank range, he became even more reclusive, and began searching for magical elixirs of eternal youth and such. Perhaps he hopes that one of his Jewish alchemists or mineralogists will be able to find a cure for his melancholia, although that didn't stop him from renewing the Jew badge edict. And he once approved the expulsion of a handful of Jews from a town in Moravia, but aside from a few such incidents that we will have the good taste not to bring up, he's been as reliable a friend and protector as any of the Christian monarchs."

"That's not much of a standard to measure by, is it?"

"What else have we got to measure by?"

We stepped outside. The sky was shrouded by gray, as if the earth itself were in mourning, but thank God it had finally stopped raining.

Rabbi Gans studied the sky for a moment and said, "Did you know that the natural day is one degree longer than the normal rotation of the eighth sphere of the heavens?"

"Really? How much of a difference does that make?" I thought maybe he knew of a scientific way of negotiating for more time.

"About one-fifteenth of an hour."

"You mean—four minutes?"

"It adds up significantly over the course of a year."

And there I was thinking we had a chance.

If only we could literally *buy* the time we needed, I'd have laid down 100 *gildn* for an extra ten hours. Hell, I'd have taken *five* hours at that rate.

We met up with Rabbi Loew at the sign of the Lion of Judah, and took the Narrow Lane toward the South Gate.

On the way, Rabbi Gans told me all about his latest book, *Tsemakh Dovid*

(The Offspring of David, which sounded like a messianic title to me). It was already at the printing house, and, *keynehore*, it would be coming out any day now.

As we approached the gate, a group of traditionalists stood at our backs and carped at us for working on the Sabbath. I responded with the words of Rabbi Yokhanan ben Nuri, who says that anyone who goes forth on a mission such as ours is allowed 2,000 cubits in every direction, while Rabbi Loew simply stated that the Torah permits the wise men of each generation to create new laws. But the traditionalists had us outnumbered. Then, on the other side of the big gate, two rows of municipal guards stood before us in two straight lines, with a narrow, well-defended path between them leading from the small door in the gate to the open door of the royal carriage.

"You are Rabbi Loew?" said the footman, his nose crinkling as if his polished boots were unsuited to our muddy streets.

"I am," the great Maharal replied.

"Then get in, Jews. The Kaiser has granted you an audience and you mustn't keep him waiting."

"I'm afraid that we'll have to."

You would have thought that—*kholile*—Rabbi Loew had cursed the name of God from the way the footman's face jerked back in shock. God forbid.

The footman managed to cough up something that might have been a *What?*

"It's Shabbes," the rabbi explained calmly. "We can't ride in a carriage, or any other mode of transportation. We'll have to walk."

Two thousand cubits uphill.

And walking at the old man's pace would take up a lot of time.

CHAPTER 20

IT HAD BEEN A LONG night, and he could tell that they weren't going to get anything else out of the old woman for now.

The one called Freyde was hanging by her wrists, her blood coagulating in the gears of the great machine. The correctors should have taken greater care not to foul up the engine's intricate workings, but even with black hoods obscuring their features, it was clear that they were getting tired. They just weren't putting their backs into it anymore.

"Christ, it's worse than pulling out poison ivy," one of them muttered.

The *Uffzieher* was beautifully efficient for such a light form of questioning—all you had to do was secure weights to the criminal's legs and yank the wretches up in the air, then drop them again. Repeat as necessary. Simple. But as long as God permitted the Devil to give his minions the strength to endure it, some of them even laughed as the instruments of persuasion were applied, knowing that the Evil One would protect them from any form of pain.

All except iron.

Oh, the legions of the faithful had made fantastic technological advances in the battle against evil. Led by the Germans, of course, they had conceived and executed glorious feats of engineering that could loosen the grip of the strongest demons on the souls of the possessed and wrestle the truth from the most recalcitrant sinners. The very word *engine* exhibited its divine origins in the Latin *ingenium*, meaning wisdom, skill, natural capacity, derived from *genium* and related to the Greek *genea*, birth, race, family, and akin to the Latin *gignere*, to beget. In other words, creation itself.

But no one had ever improved on good old-fashioned iron and fire. Who could resist the beauty of the smelter's fire, its orange glow reflected on the brawny chest of a good Christian as he forged the weapons of God's truth? It was a wondrous sight. But the punctilious lawmakers, safe in their velvet-cushioned armchairs, had stipulated that the hot irons were only to be used as a last resort, when it would have saved everyone a lot of time if the examiners were allowed to *start* with them.

So they had to go through the motions while the court scribe dutifully wrote it all down.

"All right, cut her down," the bishop ordered. "It's time to try the girl."

The girl let out a muffled cry as the correctors seized her.

"Now, that's more like it," one of the correctors said through his mask.

The bishop conferred with the official observers—the two archpriests and the scribe—who were reading over the transcript of the previous session.

"Did you notice how she didn't even shed any tears?" asked Zeman.

"None but a Jew could show such unnatural stubbornness," said Popel.

But it was worse than that—it was a clear indicator of the presence of witchcraft.

"We will have to continue questioning her later," said the bishop. "Right now, the correctors need a break in order to recover their strength. Send for a pair of able-bodied replacements."

"My lord, there are no replacements at the ready," said Zeman.

"Why not?"

"Because it's the day before Easter, we didn't think we'd need a second shift—"

The girl let out a high-pitched wail as she was dragged before the engines of persuasion.

The bishop turned. "Quiet down over there. Can't you see we're trying to talk?"

"Sorry, sir."

They stuffed a rag in the girl's mouth.

He turned back. "Witches are to be questioned on the feast days, and on the fast days, and even at the hour of the solemn Mass. The Devil takes no holidays, and neither should those who fight against him. I need men around me who would hold witch trials on Easter Sunday itself to protect our citizens from this scourge."

Both priests agreed wholeheartedly, and Zeman volunteered to go and fetch some replacements.

The bishop reached inside his robes until he felt the reassuring crunch of the salt crystals that the archbishop had blessed on Palm Sunday, effectively doubling their protective powers. Then he crossed himself and approached the girl with a confident manly stride.

Her eyes were brimming with tears. Or at least they appeared to be genuine tears. Then she reached out to him with her bound hands.

He stepped back, for an Inquisitor must never let an accused witch lay a finger on him.

"Bind her arms, for God's sake."

"Right away, sir."

It was just a precaution, but he needed to determine what class of witch he was dealing with before any contact was made. Such was their command of the black arts that certain witches had the power to render the whole cross-examination legally useless through some confounded manipulation of the senses. And all it took was a simple touch.

They tied her arms to the Up-Yanker's blood-sodden rope.

"Your mama really bled a lot for such a small woman," one of the correctors said, close to her ear.

The girl jerked away, and a sound came through the cloth that was little more than a muffled animal howl.

"And take the gag out of her mouth."

"Done, sir."

He faced the girl directly. She was deathly pale, and visibly shaken from having spent the night watching them question her mother. He hoped this would make his task easier, but he harbored no illusions about the compliancy of witches. It was sometimes easier to exorcise a devil than it was to convince a witch to speak the truth.

He decided to probe delicately before he cut to the heart of the matter.

"You are charged with using magical charms to threaten innocent Christians."

But her throat was so parched that she could barely speak.

"Give her some water."

The correctors were surprised by this request.

"I said give her some water."

They did as they were told. She had trouble swallowing.

"Now, speak."

"Yes, yes, I'll speak," she said, gulping down the water. "Just promise me—that you'll let—my mother go. Please."

Her words poured out in quick, shallow breaths, as if she were truly about to faint. And she was already perspiring. Bishop Stempfel leaned in a bit closer, his nostrils twitching as he took a deep, practiced sniff. Good. It was the sweat of fear.

"Do you still maintain that you did not use magical charms?"

"What charms are those, my lord?"

"You know very well what charms."

"No, I don't. I swear."

"*Stuck!* Read back the charges."

"Yes, my lord."

The scribe flipped through the court record, and read out the exact words of several eyewitnesses, all of whom testified that the accused did most brazenly and egregiously shout strange curses at a group of God-fearing Christians.

"We never did any such thing, my lord."

The bishop was pleased, for there was no surer sign of guilt than this obstinate and insistent profession of innocence.

"Show her the record."

"Yes, my lord."

The scribe stepped into the circle of glowing firelight, and showed the girl the place in the transcript where a terrified witness had been coaxed into sounding out the dreadful syllables of the Jew's curse.

She was a little slow to react, so one of the correctors grabbed a fistful of her hair, jerked her head up, and directed her gaze at the writing.

She tried to pretend that it was nonsensical.

"*Aer . . . reff . . . rääff . . . ?*"

"Yes. What does this mean?"

"I don't . . . Oh, *eyrev rav*—!"

"Stop her tongue!"

The corrector clamped his hand over her mouth.

Good Lord, that was a close one. Where on earth was Zeman with those replacements? The men were getting careless.

The girl tried to speak, so he warned her that if she spoke improperly to him again, he would have her hung upside down and cut in half, groin-first, with a two-handed saw.

It was the worst punishment they had, even worse than burning at the stake. It was usually reserved for sodomites, but he could always make an exception. Witchcraft was such a heinous crime, the prosecutors routinely suspended the usual rules of evidence and coerced confessions in such cases.

The girl writhed and tried to shake her head, but it was tightly secured between the corrector's fists.

He gestured for the corrector to release her mouth.

"Mind what you say, love," said the corrector, loosening his grip.

"Tell me," said the bishop. "Are you not a virgin?"

"What does that—?"

"Answer yes or no," the corrector advised her.

She spoke very cautiously, another clear sign of guilt: "I don't understand. Are you asking if I *am* one or if I'm *not* one?"

"Don't get smart—"

The bishop waved the corrector off, and stepped closer.

"Are you a virgin?"

"Yes, my lord."

He looked her over, slowly and carefully.

"And so no man has known you?"

"Yes, yes, it's true, so help me God."

She certainly portrayed the virgin convincingly enough.

"Then tell me the truth about the curse words."

"They aren't curse words. It just means common riff-raff. It's in the Bible."

"There are no such curses in the Bible," Popel said, spitting the words out.

"Perhaps she means the Bible in Hebrew," the bishop suggested.

"Yes, yes, the Bible in Hebrew."

"Where in the Bible?"

She didn't know exactly. She just knew that the words were used to describe the masses of poor Egyptians who joined the Israelites on the road from Raamses to Succoth. It was somewhere in Exodus, or so she claimed.

"So, if I follow what you're saying, it isn't a curse, which we all know is a form of witchcraft, but rather, it's some kind of code word used to secretly invite non-Jews to join you in a flight from the authority of the Church, which is heresy. So which is it?"

Popel stood in rapt admiration of the Inquisitor's mastery of the art of interrogation.

"Are you encouraging non-Jews to join you in a flight from authority?"

"No, we're not! I swear it!"

"Then it *is* a curse."

"No—!"

The bishop turned to the scribe. "Be sure to note how she constantly alters her statements and contradicts what she said before, which is why we must start all over again."

Now *that* upset her.

"They're just words! Harmless words—"

"Harmless words? Do you deny that God brought the world into being through the *power of words*?"

"But that's the word *of God*—"

"Of course the words are harmless *by themselves*. But in the mouth of a witch, they become commands to all the devils in hell to come forth and do their evil bidding. What words do you use to conjure these devils? What are their names?"

"Their *names*?"

"Answer the question, Jew," Popel interjected.

"We do not call on any devils, we call on God alone."

"Aha, now we're getting somewhere. So you admit that you invoke the name of God to perform this sacrilegious magic?"

"It's not sacrilegious."

"But it *is* magic," he said, pressing her.

"We believe in *miracles*, which come from God—"

"Then why can't you tell us what the names are? Why are you keeping them a secret?"

"Because it's forbidden to say the name of God out loud."

"That only refers to the Ineffable Name. What about all the other secret names that you employ for your magical ends?"

He looked into her moist and bloodshot eyes.

"I promise that you will leave this room unharmed if you just give me those names," he said.

"But I don't know them."

"You expect us to believe that?" said Popel.

"Why are you answering badly? Why can't you tell us the names?"

"Because knowledge of them is the domain of men alone."

The bishop was struck by this admission. It certainly fit the evidence.

"Why do you insist on telling lies?" said Popel, who hadn't made the connection.

One of the correctors leaned on the machine, clearly bored by the slow progress. "Of course she hasn't told you the truth, we haven't even put the frigging weights on her yet."

But the bishop called Popel aside and explained that the girl's mere knowledge of forbidden practices was not enough to proceed with prosecution in this matter. They had to have *proof* of actual witchcraft.

So they agreed to follow the standard procedure.

The bishop returned and made a show of entreating the correctors to release the girl.

The correctors shrugged and loosened the ropes just enough to allow her to lower her arms. The bishop had them offer her some more water, then he softened his voice and told her that she could save her mother and herself from beheading or (if the judges were being lenient) strangulation, and then being burnt at the stake, if she would simply confess the truth and tell him the names of the unbelievers who dared to use the name of God to conjure devils and perpetrate other acts of evil.

He saw the last bit of hope drain out of her, and the only thing that she confessed was that she couldn't possibly comply with his request.

The bishop looked down at the girl's tender little feet, and started slowly shaking his head, as if it deeply disturbed him to have to do this.

"Then you leave me no choice but to insist that you be examined in the usual way."

The correctors perked up like a pair of Rottweilers picking up the scent of raw meat. They retightened the ropes, yanked the girl's arms over her head, and proceeded to strip off her clothes.

She screamed, as they almost always did, then the bishop cringed from a sudden pain in his gut. So he let Popel take over the search.

They commenced shaving all the hair off her body, including the secret parts that must not be named, in search of the truth. Now, in the bishop's native Germany, it was not considered delicate to shave the *pubes*, so he turned and looked the other way.

But it wasn't long before Popel triumphantly ejaculated, "Here it is. The mark of the Devil."

"That's not the mark of the Devil," the girl insisted. "That's a birthmark I've had since I was a child."

"That's just the sort of perverse lie the Devil would make you say."

The bishop examined the spot closely.

"Keep looking," he said.

"Yes, my lord."

The girl stiffened but gave little resistance as they continued to shave her down below, because the masked men approached the task with some measure of propriety. But their patience was wearing thin, and they were much rougher with the thick, dark hair on her head. And halfway through the process, their efforts were rewarded.

"My lord, come and look at this."

The bishop bent close to look. The girl had a curved scar nearly two inches long behind her left ear that was much lighter than the surrounding skin, just like so many other scars he had seen that had been made as a result of carnal copulation with the Devil.

"Stick it with pins," he commanded.

And when the girl felt no pain in that place, he knew that the mark could only have been made by the Devil's claw. And that changed everything.

The girl insisted that she had gotten the scar years ago when a drunken Christian hit her in the head with a bottle and left a deep gash, and that ever since that day she had no feeling in the area, but he knew that they would soon get at the truth. And so he gave the order:

"Begin the *Inquisitionsprozess*."

THEY PUT YOU THROUGH THE same paces every single time, thought Bishop Stempfel. First they denied all the charges, then you induced them to tell the truth, and you went back and forth with the same questions over and over until the easy ones broke and the stubborn ones dug in their heels, while the scribe mechanically copied it all down. Every question, every answer, pausing only to change quills or stifle a yawn.

Perhaps the court scribbler had seen it so many times before that he no longer appreciated how challenging it could be to bring a case like this to trial. There had to be sufficient grounds before they could proceed, and the ability to unearth such evidence (and justify the time and expense of a trial) varied widely depending on the skills of each Inquisitor. It wasn't always easy to define a particular example of witchcraft. You just had to be able to recognize it in whatever form it appeared.

The new team of correctors had arrived, bringing youthful energy and a fresh perspective to the proceedings. The bishop sat on the edge of the orange circle of light, keeping warm by the embers where the irons lay heating for use.

He watched the two priests closely. Zeman had a more nuanced approach, extracting critical information from the young witch about the Sabbat feast, where the food was apparently so bitter and foul that it made the participants vomit profusely (what foul lengths these witches go to satiate their perverse desires!) but he couldn't get her to confess that the meal consisted of the flesh and blood of young children, to say nothing of the corpses scavenged from the graveyard or harvested from the gibbet.

Popel was clearly more effective, focusing on the crucial issue—namely, that we *know* that witches fornicate with devils. The question is, *How* do they do it?

"What is the Devil's member like?"

"I don't know."

Here the interrogator administered some pain.

"What is it like? Is it hard or soft?"

"It's hard. Hard as steel."

"No, it isn't." *Pain.*

"My brother," said Zeman, "some say that it is hard. Some even say that it is forked."

"Is it forked?"

"I don't know." *Pain.* "Yes—!"

"*Yes?*"

"No—?"

"Which is it?"

"Yes! No! It's both. It's hard for some, soft for others."

"You mean it *is* forked?"

"Yes. Please. My arms—"

"Is sex with the Devil pleasurable?"

"Yes." *Pain.*

"Yes?"

"No! No, it isn't."

The Inquisitor was impressed with Popel's technique. After a short apprenticeship, he was already learning how to jump between topics just to keep the vile race of sorcerers off balance.

"We are well aware of the fact that the pact with the Devil must be written in blood. But we would like to know what *kind* of blood it is."

No answer. *Pain.*

"I don't know."

"What kind of blood? Jewish blood? Babies' blood? Menstrual blood?"

But she stubbornly insisted that since she had never signed such a pact, she didn't know how to answer, and the pain had to be applied again and again.

Bishop Stempfel watched as the correctors tilted the witch's head back, jammed a funnel into her mouth, and told her they were going to pour molten lead down her throat. They used iron tongs to lift the steaming pot from the brazier, then they carried it over, and she shrieked before realizing that she was being drenched with ice water.

The correctors laughed. "What's the matter? Did you think we were *really* going to pour molten lead down your throat?"

"What kind of men do you take us for?"

What an excellent deception! The bishop smiled, knowing that he would be able to honestly report that the Inquisition was in good hands here in the heart of Protestant Bohemia.

Then he felt a tap on his shoulder, and received word that the doctor was waiting for him in the next room.

He reminded Popel to focus on getting the names of the other witches involved in this crime, be they Gentile or Jew, then he gathered up his robes and removed himself from the darkened chamber.

The light in the other room was so bright it hurt his eyes at first. The interrogation must have entered its tenth hour or so, since the sun had climbed midway up the meridian. He had lost all track of time.

The doctor was pleased to announce that he had secured a worthy maiden in order to administer the virgin amber treatment, which was the only proper cure for the bishop's condition.

But the bishop was shocked by the brazenness of this alleged virgin, who showed no modesty whatsoever as she lifted up her skirt, squatted over a golden chamber pot, and began to relieve herself like an animal with no knowledge of morals or shame. What he saw reminded him of a horse.

He demanded an immediate halt to the activity.

"What is the matter, my lord?" asked the doctor.

"If I am to submit to this revulsionary procedure, I must confirm that she is indeed a virgin."

The doctor's assurances were useless, and the girl was made to lie down on a hard wooden table.

He could hear Popel in the next room, switching tactics again and demanding to know the name of the city where the secret society of rabbis had met this year in order to decide which community would kidnap and kill a Christian victim. Why did the *Kindermörderische Juden* pick Prague this year? To further divide the Christians? Speak!

The young virgin spread out before him was a truly devoted Catholic girl, willing and ready to make this sacrifice for a higher cause, and yet he couldn't help being disgusted by the idea of any female who would actually submit to such a degrading procedure. Ugh! She hadn't even washed herself first. Fortunately, he had been so preoccupied that he hadn't washed his own hands since yesterday morning, so he had a nice layer of dirt to protect himself from the filthy juices defiling the area. He felt his own nethermost twinge as he pried her open and confirmed the presence of an intact piece of shiny film.

He straightened up and bestowed his approval, and a lackey fetched the golden chamber pot.

AT LEAST SOME PROGRESS was being made. When he was in Saxony three years earlier, they had burnt 133 witches in a single day. But it was nowhere near enough, since they were turning up *everywhere*—in Trier, in Arras, Trèves—the list went on and on.

The bishop spat on the floor to clear the taste from his mouth.

He had even heard of cases of men who took a woman home to bed only to discover that by some witchcraft, the woman had been transformed by the

Devil into a man—that is, the Devil had used his cunning to make it *appear* so, since only God can actually effect such a transformation.

The others withdrew as he approached.

His lips drew back into a tight smile, making his shiny bald pate look like a giant Easter egg with a crack forming around its middle.

"Leave her to me, now," he said.

CHAPTER 21

THE COPPER PFENNIG CAME SKIPPING over the cobblestones with a distinctive metallic *ping* and lodged in the mud that lay in our path. I looked up, tracing the path of the coin back to its point of origin, where a band of foot soldiers stood smirking at us.

It was one of those gray days when all the colors are dull and flat and people's faces look as if they have no blood in them at all.

"Pick it up, Jews," they said.

I resolved to keep marching straight ahead, keeping my eyes fixed on the King's Way twenty yards onward, but when a little girl plucked the *fertl-pfennig* from the mud, wiped the dirt off it and offered it to us, Rabbi Loew acted as if the coin had dropped from the sky:

"Heaven is indeed generous, my friends," he declared. "For who could imagine that this lowly farthing would provide the daily bread for at least a dozen little children? Praise be to God."

At least the coin didn't land in one of the steaming piles of offal that clogged the gutters near the Little Square. From the broad spatter marks on the paving stones, it looked like half of the *goyim* dumped their chamber pots right out the window.

We followed the royal carriage onto the King's Way, which stretched for a hundred miles behind us to the east. The common folk cleared out of the road and stared open-mouthed, craning their necks to get a glimpse of the celebrated personage they assumed was inside the gilded carriage.

So most of the people paid us no mind as we quietly invaded their territory. The streets were unfamiliar to me, and I couldn't help marveling at all the elaborate house signs, from the golden pikes near the South Gate to the white swans and silver harps near the stone bridge.

The entrance to the bridge was defended by a square tower with a pointed arch wide enough for two lanes of traffic. Above the archway ran a couple of rows of crested shields adorned with the usual eagles and lions, presided over by a trio of statues—a pair of kings with some saint perched between them, all cupping cross-topped orbs in their left hands and gilded scepters in their right.

Sentries stood under the arch collecting tolls and other taxes and fees. When they saw our Jew-badges, they decided that we had to be well-connected merchants, and tried to charge us a daler each to cross the bridge. They laughed when we tried to explain that we were three humble Jews on our way to see the *keyser*, until the royal footman intervened, peering down from his privileged perch and explaining to the sentries that the levy had to be waived in this instance.

The sentries had little choice but to agree, but they got back at us by holding up traffic in both directions and making us stand with our arms and legs apart so they could pat us down with unnecessary roughness and intimacy. Then, while the frustrated travelers cursed and *kvetched* in Czech and German, the guards pawed through the cloth bundle Rabbi Loew was carrying. Then they made us remove our hats and shoes so they could "search" them for any weapons or substances that might harm the emperor's person.

The bridge itself was nearly five hundred yards long. Covered wagons and nobles on horseback jostled for position alongside peasants carrying baskets of dirty vegetables to market. Pilgrims crossed themselves as they passed a tall wooden crucifix set in its own special niche about one-third of the way across the span.

"Boy, that Jesus fellow sure gets around," I muttered to the east wind.

Rabbi Gans shushed me, and nodded toward the severed heads that were fixed on pikes at various intervals along the bridge. He pointed out which were the common criminals and which were the rebellious subjects, whose grisly remains were left on display for years as an example to all.

A few hundred yards upstream, a long wall with crenellated teeth angled down the hill toward the river's edge like the jawbone of some fallen giant. Rabbi Gans told me this was the Hunger Wall, which Emperor Charles IV built to help his subjects through a couple of lean years by paying them in food to build a wall that no one particularly needed. He also told me about how Charles's son, Prince Václav, used to disguise himself as a poor journeyman to see if the workers were being cheated (they were), and how, after he put in a grueling day in the vineyards, he instituted a number of changes, shortening the workday for the agricultural laborers and giving them a longer meal break as well.

"If only more of the privileged would walk in another's shoes, just for an hour," he said, "or put on a badge and see what it's like to be a Jew for a day, the world would be a better place."

The gunpowder tower on the far side of the bridge was swaddled in billowing sheets of canvas. Dust flew as workers chiseled away at the squat structure, remaking it in the new style. A breeze off the river raised a white cloud of grit as we approached it. So I closed my eyes. When I opened them, a witchlike gargoyle with a hooked nose and sagging breasts was grimacing at me from a rainspout over the archway.

The castle hadn't seemed quite so imposing from across the river, but as we got nearer, it appeared to grow tremendously, taking up an ever larger slice of the sky. I knew from Langweil's model that it wasn't simply a castle, it was a whole complex, including a four-hundred-year-old basilica, a cathedral, a convent, the queen's summer house (although there was no queen at the moment), the old palace, as well as a new palace, which was still under construction. It seemed like half the city was still under construction.

The main language on this side of the river switched over to German, and all around me Catholic symbols proliferated on the churches.

IF ONE COULD DRAW an imaginary line in the air, straight from the South Gate to the main entrance hall of the castle, it probably *would* measure two thousand cubits. But we nearly doubled that figure by trudging up the winding streets of Little Town behind the carriage, sidestepping horse manure whenever we needed to, which was more often than I would have preferred, and by the time we reached the top of the Royal Road, my nose was dripping from the cold and my underclothes were soaked with sweat.

The wind picked up, cutting through my protective layers and conspiring with my own perspiration to chill me to the bone and compound my misery. It may have been late March on the Christian calendar, but up here it still felt like early February.

How could it be that the emperor's castle was colder than my crowded little attic room? Maybe it was the stone walls, the castle's location on a windy crag overlooking the city, and the sheer size of the rooms. The main hall of the old palace was big enough to hold a jousting contest with mounted knights in full armed regalia. Rabbi Gans told me that they did in fact hold jousts here until the 1570s, and that the huge entranceway on the far side of the hall had been purposely built with wide, flat steps so the knights could ride into the hall on horseback.

Next to the Riders' Steps was the entrance to the Supreme Council chamber, whose four-columned portal, with twin columns on either side connected by a round arch over the doorway, looked exactly like the title pages of the Talmud and other rabbinic writings, which were themselves modeled on traditional descriptions of the main entrance of Solomon's Temple. This resemblance to our ancient symbols of wisdom and justice gave me some hope.

A lackey dressed in the Italian style, with bright red velvet with gold accents, nodded curtly and told us, "The *Obersthofmeister* will be with you shortly."

What the heck is an Obersthofmeister? I wondered. Somebody big, I guessed.

We shuffled around, stamping our feet and trying to keep warm, while the lackey reminded us for the third time not to be put off by Kaiser Rudolf's manner, which many of his subjects perceived as cold and distant. And all I could think of was that it must be pretty bad when *a German* thinks you're cold.

Eventually *Obersthofmeister* Wilhelm von Stein Tafelfrung Gruber appeared wearing a tight-fitting black doublet with matching hose and a silver badge of office pinned over his left breast, and graciously led us from the old hall through a string of galleries whose regal placidity was being turned upside-down by new construction projects. He swept us past an open balcony that provided a splendid vista of the royal city, spreading toward the horizon in every direction, and filled with the roughly 60,000 Christian subjects who outnumbered the inhabitants of the ghetto by at least twenty to one. We passed through the *Wunderkammern*, whose cabinets contained such oddities as a unicorn's horn, a set of rusty nails from Noah's Ark (though the Torah makes no mention of iron nails), and, from the collection of Emperor Charles IV, a couple of drops of the Virgin Mary's breast milk (clearly another miraculous occurrence), and some spines from the original crown of thorns. I was disappointed that they didn't have the original wine-stained tablecloth from the Last Supper, although the King of Hungary is said to have possessed a piece of it.

The curator of Emperor Rudolf's collection was an Italian Jew named Strada, who was too busy admiring himself in a full-length mirror to acknowledge us as we passed through the art gallery. Rabbi Gans told me that the emperor had sired at least three children by Strada's daughter Katharina, though he had yet to legitimize them.

The largest paintings in the *Kunstkammer* were pastoral landscapes crowded with fleshy gods and goddesses bearing trumpets, shields, and plumed helmets, when they were wearing anything at all, but I thought the most interesting works were the small-scale portrait of the emperor as a bowl of fruit and some pen-and-ink drawings of costumes for some kind of celebratory parade, illustrating the diverse ways of dressing up a man as a demon or disguising a horse as a three-headed dragon.

That gave me an idea about how we could transform an ordinary-looking creature into a frightful one, but we had to keep moving, for the clock was already striking. This particular clock featured a Turkish soldier with an oversized head who shifted his eyes from side to side and raised his curved scimitar every time the little bells chimed.

Then an odd chattering came spilling out of an adjoining gallery. It sounded like a group of men were fighting in there, but the *Obersthofmeister* informed me that it was only a troupe of English comedians rehearsing a play.

"Does the *keyser* speak English, too?" I asked.

The *Obersthofmeister* replied, "His Majesty has mastered five languages, in addition to Czech, with some knowledge of English as well."

Since English is a cousin to German, which is itself a sister to Yiddish, I was able to recognize some of the words, and I wasn't terribly reassured by what I heard. One of the main actors appeared to be representing a Jew, complete with a false nose and beard, who was bragging about how he liked to go about poisoning wells, double-crossing friends, and filling the jails with Christians bankrupted by his usury, all of which has blessed him with "as much coyne as wull buye the towne." I couldn't say exactly what the last sentence meant, but it sure didn't sound like a love letter to Christians. I wondered if the author had ever seen a Jew, since the English King Edward had exiled us from his lands more than three hundred years ago. Not that it would have made much of a difference, I suppose.

Still, I found myself hoping that Emperor Rudolf's English wasn't so very good after all.

I had expected the ostentatious displays of wealth that we had seen so far, but I was utterly amazed when we passed through a library containing *thousands* of books. It didn't seem possible for one man to own so many books. And it brought me no comfort when I spotted several titles in English.

Rabbi Gans tried to comfort me by observing that such an intellectually curious sovereign simply *had* to be a friend of Israel because of our longstanding reputation as a nation of wisdom and reason, but I wasn't convinced.

Finally, the *Obersthofmeister* led us into an antechamber, where a page boy drew back a curtain, and announced us, pronouncing the Maharal's name in the Czech manner: "Rabbi Yehuda Liwa and his entourage."

The inner chamber wasn't as large as the banquet hall, but it was every bit as cold. A green porcelain stove in the corner did very little to heat the room. Its lacquered surface was doubtless hot to the touch, but the heat completely vanished into the air just a few feet away.

The emperor himself was sitting with his back to us, gazing into the metal tube of some strange optical device. Beside him lay an open book with large illustrations that matched some of the plants and minerals cluttering up the table. I caught a glimpse of a frown as he turned, but it changed into a smile the moment he saw us.

The emperor stood up and greeted us warmly. We bowed our heads, but he insisted on shaking our hands as if we were his equals, and he stopped us from taking off our hats.

"Keep your head coverings on, for I know it is your way."

We thanked His Majesty for this privilege.

He instinctively struck a pose with all the straight-backed dignity befitting a monarch.

He was about forty years old, with sad, intelligent eyes and a strong chin ennobled by a curly black beard. He dressed in the latest Spanish fashion— simple, austere clothing with clean lines, and draped with the sort of long black cloak one might expect a magician or a sorcerer to wear. This was the man who was next in line for the Spanish throne if Prince Don Carlos turned out to be too mentally unstable to rule, though I wondered how one went about determining mental instability in a country that once banned all scientific study, expelled most of its non-Christian scholars, and then, with no one left to persecute, turned on each other, finding witches and heretics in every closet and under every bed, before seeking out fresh victims in the New World.

"Please, take your seats," he said.

We took our seats.

"It is my great privilege to welcome such learned men as yourselves to my *laboratorium*. There are so many questions that I wish to ask of you."

"And we of you," said Rabbi Loew.

"My councilors inform me that you, alone among the rabbis of the Jewish Town, have instructed your fellow Jews to study mathematics and natural sciences in order to understand the world, and ultimately the Creator."

"Your councilors have spoken correctly," said Rabbi Loew.

"Excellent. But I understand that you also believe that human science will always be inferior to Kabbalistic and Scriptural studies. So perhaps you could teach me about how one might use the Kabbalah to decode the secrets of creation."

Is that why he granted us an audience? To talk *Kabbalah*?

Rabbi Loew was better schooled than I in the ways of the powerful, and he responded with great enthusiasm to the emperor's request.

"It would give me no greater pleasure than to discuss these matters with you, Your Grace, since the Law encompasses all forms of knowledge, and leaves out nothing."

The emperor actually rubbed his hands together like a little boy. "Then please begin by telling me what you know about the manipulation of numbers and letters, for I have been told that you are a master of that art."

"Very well, Your Majesty," said Rabbi Loew. "It is a fitting place to begin, since there are many points where Jewish and Christian numerology intersect. In both systems, the number one typically represents unity and truth, while the number four often symbolizes the four corners of the physical world—"

"I'm not interested in the similarities, I'm interested in the differences."

"Of course you are. I see that Your Highness is hungry for new knowledge. Blessed is the Lord, who has bestowed such wisdom upon you. I must tell you that Jewish numerology is distinct from its Christian counterpart in a variety of ways. For example, among Christians, the number thirteen is unlucky. But for the Jews, it is no such thing. For the Ten Commandments are actually thirteen in number, since the second commandment is actually made up of four distinct utterances."

"Fascinating," said the emperor. "Pray continue."

"Yes, Your Majesty. Moreover, there are thirteen measures of divine mercy described in the Book of Exodus, and thirteen principles of faith that we praise in song at the end of the *mayrev* services on Shabbes and holidays."

"So you're saying that the number thirteen may not be unlucky, after all," said the emperor, thoughtfully stroking his beard, and presenting the very image of that rare species of monarch who is actually willing to listen to advice from someone outside his closed circle of councilors. "Then how would you answer those Christians who say the world will end six years hence, in the year 1598?"

"There is no valid numerological reason to believe that will happen."

"Especially when everyone knows the world will end in 1666," I said.

"And who is this?" said the emperor, looking directly at me.

"This is my student, Benyamin Ben-Akiva."

"Ah, the sexton. I've heard about you."

"You have?" I said, genuinely surprised. "I see that Your Majesty is very well informed about the goings-on in the ghetto."

His Majesty was pleased to hear this report. He smiled a little, but he said nothing. He must have had informers in every corner of the city. A wise precaution these days, since the latest firearms were small enough to conceal beneath a man's cloak.

I explained that in the farthest reaches of eastern Poland, one could still find scattered groups of Old Believers and messianic Jews who believed that the world would end in the year 1666 of the Christian calendar.

"And you don't support this view," said the emperor.

"No, I do not."

"Why not?" He appeared to be genuinely concerned that the end was nigh. I did my best to explain my position without using the words *because only an idiot would believe such a thing.*

"It's always a risky proposition to try to predict the exact year of an apocalyptic event. Rabbi Abravanel was convinced that the Expulsion from Spain was a sign that the Messiah would come within his lifetime—and he died in 1508. Even the great Ari of Safed got it wrong when he declared that 1575 would be the year of our redemption. Only the most unreasonable fanatics insist that they know for certain what the future brings."

"Then I must be an unreasonable fanatic," said the emperor, his chin sagging as he yielded to the heavy pull of his melancholy humor. "Because I *do* wish to understand the cosmos in its totality."

I tried to rescue the emperor from the depths of his despondency. "Then may I recommend that you read the works of Rabbi Moses Cordovero? His *Pardes Rimmonim* has just been published in Kraków."

The emperor's eyes brightened. He grabbed a pen and a sheet of paper from the workbench and handed them over to me. "You must write down the author and title for me."

I made no move to take the writing implements from him.

"What's the matter?" he said, unable to hide his irritation, for clearly the emperor was not used to having his wishes ignored.

I explained that writing is forbidden on Shabbes.

"Ah, yes. The People of the Book are not allowed to write anything at all, isn't that right?"

"To be precise, the law refers to two letters at once—"

"Even in Latin?"

"In any alphabet. Although the penalty is less if it isn't permanent."

"So it would be permissible to write the words in wax or in chalk, or something equally impermanent?"

"Only if an emergency genuinely requires it," I said, looking to Rabbi Loew for approval. The rabbi raised an eyebrow and gave me half a nod. So I guess this counted as an emergency.

The emperor produced a slate and a piece of chalk. I scratched in the words, ספר פרדס רמונים, or The Book of the Garden of Pomegranates, and told him that the title page looked very much like the entrance to the Supreme Council chamber. We readily agreed to procure a copy for him, and he said that he would put his translators to work on it right away.

"Now, tell me what this Rabbi Cordovero says."

Great. Another digression, I thought.

Were we ever going to get Jacob Federn and his wife and daughter out of captivity? What was with these confounded Christian monarchs, who wielded tremendous power but were constantly tormented by the feeling that something was missing from their lives? It was no mystery to me, since their power was maintained by plundering whole continents, planting their flag on every patch of ground they could conquer, and enslaving the people they found there.

Such men could search forever without finding the answers they were looking for, spending their whole lives searching for such chimeras as the Fountain of Youth or the Elixir of Life.

"Before we discuss Rabbi Cordovero's views on the wonders of creation," I said, "Rabbi Loew has a message for you from Mordecai Meisel, mayor of the *Yidnshtot*."

A thin veil of frost swept over the emperor, and I finally caught a glimpse of the famous coldness that everyone had been warning me about.

Rabbi Loew thrust the document before the emperor.

"It is a petition, Your Majesty. For privileges."

"What sort of privileges?"

"We are asking if you could transfer the accused named in this document, Jacob Federn, from the municipal prison to the imperial prison, and to free his wife and daughter, who were arrested yesterday afternoon."

"I'm afraid that the women are the property of the Inquisition, and so it is out of my hands," said the emperor. "But I shall make some inquiries."

"Your Majesty is most kind and gracious," said Rabbi Loew.

"As to the accused, the transfer has already been made."

"It has? Where is he?"

"Here in the castle. In the Daliborka Tower."

"May we speak with him?"

"I will grant you that privilege," said the emperor, taking the document from the rabbi's outstretched hand.

Rabbi Loew and Rabbi Gans bowed and expressed their gratitude for the emperor's kindness and wisdom.

The frost slowly melted as the emperor read certain parts of the text aloud, perhaps for our benefit, perhaps not.

"Everlasting and Most Benevolent Sovereign . . . seeking your protection . . . sanctuary laws . . . right to display the flag of David . . . tax exemption for the new synagogue . . ."

Meisel had some nerve slipping that last part in.

Nevertheless, the emperor summoned his scribe. The curtains parted, and in came a crooked little fellow with a nose as sharp as a hatchet blade and a pair of black dots where his eyes should have been.

"Take up your pen," said the emperor.

"Yes, sire."

The scribe hunched over the writing table, poised to scribble down the emperor's words.

Emperor Rudolf II assumed a regal posture and began to dictate. "Whereas Mordecai Meisel the Jew has unhesitatingly given us loyal service and support whenever it was needed, and whereas he has lent us thousands of dalers for some little trinkets besides, and whereas he has sent representatives of his people to me on this day seeking imperial protection from false blood libel accusations, be it resolved that Mordecai Meisel, by virtue of his position representing the whole of the Jewish community, shall be granted immunity from paying taxes on the newly constructed synagogue."

The pen stopped moving, then haltingly started scribbling the emperor's words again.

"Moreover, this privilege shall pass on to his heirs in perpetuity. This synagogue shall be a haven from abuse and oppression. No officers of the law shall enter it, nor may any person enter Meisel's home in order to disturb him or interfere with his private affairs without the express permission of the emperor."

He broke from his pose to sign the document. Then he affixed his seal, and the scribe withdrew to dispatch the order.

"Now, let us discuss Rabbi Cordovero's views on the Kabbalah."

Rabbi Loew said that for the initiate, it was better to start with the *aggadah*.

"My time is short," said the emperor, and he commanded Rabbi Loew to instruct him in the ways of the Kabbalah.

"Very well, Your Majesty," said Rabbi Loew. "But where can such wisdom be found? You will not find it on any printed map of the world, marked with an *X* like a pirate's treasure, for it lies on the other side of reason and judgment and that branch of alchemy which surveys the earth with measuring rods and assigns the highest value to gold. It lies on the side of inquisitiveness and kindness and mercy, which is symbolized by the metal that we value more highly, namely silver."

The rabbi paused to allow the emperor to absorb this bit of information, which ran counter to the most commonly held beliefs about our people.

"Even the very dust under your feet may contain hidden mysteries," said Rabbi Loew. "So it is with the Jews, who may be scattered like the dust of the earth, but as hard as men may try to trample us with their boots, we will persist, like the dust, and will not go away. In this same way, the source of truth may not be a glittering jewel like the much-coveted Philosopher's Stone. It may initially appear to be of little value."

"Then I may have just the tool you need for such a quest," said the emperor. "You must observe this, for it is a most amusing curiosity. Step this way."

He led us over to his workbench and swept his hand toward the cylindrical device that he had been peering into when we first entered the chamber.

"A Franciscan friar who men call Dr. Mirabilis and some of the Italian oculists have known for some time that a convex lens that can form an image of a faraway object will, if combined with an eye-lens with the correct—uh, *focal point*, I believe is the term—will magnify the image. So come forward, and if any of you have something that you'd like to see magnified, pray put it here. This apparatus only works with opaque objects. That is, it can't bring the invisible to light, but virtually anything viewed here might reveal something hitherto unseen of its own peculiar texture. Why, even the dirt under your fingernails may provide clues as to what you had for breakfast."

"We don't have any dirt under our fingernails," said Rabbi Gans. "We cleaned them for Shabbes."

"Oh. Yes, of course."

There was an awkward silence, then suddenly my hand flew to my chest as if it had a will of its own, searching for the shape beneath the folds of my cloak, in my inner pocket, finally clutching the pouch that I deposited there with such ceremony the day before.

"This, Your Majesty," I said, removing the pouch. "I want to examine this."

"What is it?"

"It is a sample of material that I collected from the floor of Federn's shop. It may contain traces of the killers' essential humors."

It was a good thing the emperor was so fascinated by our "Jewish knowledge," because when I dumped the contents out on a sheet of paper, he did not flinch or curl his lip in contempt, but eagerly took a pinch of the sweepings and placed it on a metal plate beneath the brass cylinder. He repositioned the device, aiming it more toward the light, and fiddled with one of the knobs until the image came into focus.

"There," he said. "Yes, some of it certainly looks like ordinary dirt, but there are quite a few sparkles of light reflecting off what appear to be tiny bits of quartz. I'd have to summon the court geologist to be certain, but I'd say that this dirt has probably been combined with sand."

"Sand? From where?" asked Rabbi Loew.

"It must come from the riverbank," said Rabbi Gans.

The emperor went on: "And this looks like a hair from somebody's head, or perhaps an eyelash, since it's so short and raspy-looking, and what must be a tuft of coarse fabric of some kind, and—I say, this is rather odd."

"What?"

"It appears to be a strand of fine silver thread."

"The shop had been swept clean for Pesach the night before," I said. "And the Federns weren't wearing any clothes with fine silver thread that morning."

"Have a look for yourself."

It certainly appeared to be as the emperor had described. There was no mistaking the look of real silver, even though the true object was barely visible to the naked eye.

There was general amazement.

"This comes directly from God, who is lighting the way for us to find the guilty ones," said Rabbi Loew.

But enough amazement. The hour was getting late. So I said, "This is all very well and fruitful, Your Majesty, but we actually came here to ask *you* a question."

"Really? By all means, you may ask me anything you want."

I saw the rabbis' brows darken with trepidation.

"Will you grant us permission to examine the body of the victim?"

The rabbis' eyes screamed *Are you crazy? How could you even think of asking such a thing?*

"The young Christian girl?" said the emperor. "I don't know. Imagine the reaction from the people—and the Church—at a time like this, when we need to keep a united front against the Turkish menace—"

Rabbi Loew appealed in the name of justice.

Rabbi Gans promised that we wouldn't touch the young girl's body with our hands or with any magical implements or with any implements that might even be *perceived* as being magical.

But none of that worked, until I submitted it to His Royal Highness that he graciously allow us examine the body "in the interests of science."

He finally granted his *heavily conditional* approval. We asked him to put it in writing, just in case.

He did. Then he summoned one of his attendants and asked the young lad to accompany us to the royal dungeon.

CHAPTER 22

THE DUNGEON WAS NOT IN the new part of the castle. The imposing round tower lay at the farthest end of the old battlements along the rim of the "stag moat." Maybe they called it a *moat* to mislead would-be attackers, because it was in fact a natural gorge a couple of hundred feet deep. I didn't know much about old-style warfare, but the north side of the castle seemed to be *very* well defended.

The emperor's attendant led us on without looking at us once. We followed along, not ready to speak our thoughts aloud in the presence of a Christian servant, even one as young as this lad.

The Daliborka was a thick-walled tower built to withstand a siege. No soaring arches, tall windows, or decorative details got in the way of its primary purpose of breaking the spirit of all who entered.

Rabbi Gans told me that the tower's most famous resident was none other than Sir Dalibor of Kozojedy, a knight who actually fought for the rights of the peasants. He ended up being imprisoned in this tower for so long, they named it after him.

There must be an easier way of getting a building named after you.

The tower clung to the edge of the precipice. Its barred gate beckoned to us, and we had to turn our backs on the light of day and tramp down a flight of stone steps to reach the top level of the prison. Two guards were about to bar the way by crossing their spears (they love doing that), but the emperor's attendant said some special words in the Silesian dialect, and the heavy iron door creaked on its hinges and we were in.

The first cell occupied the entire top floor. Any room this spacious was clearly meant for an aristocrat. It was also *very* cold, since no prisoner was being kept here at the moment. Except for the red brick floor, everything was stone, with a big, empty fireplace and man-sized windows that looked out over the whole city. It was actually a pretty nice view, but the price of the room was too high for me.

A passing bard had penned some lyrics and hung them on the wall:

When I was young, once upon a time,
Outside my hut, the birds did sing.
Now I live in a palace
But no birds sing outside my window.

We descended a narrow, tunnel-like staircase, and had to duck our heads under the low archway. This cell was much darker than the one above, with small windows in deeply recessed alcoves and a few wispy gray ashes in the pitifully inadequate fireplace where a lone candle had burnt down to a hard puddle of wax. An iron ring hung in the middle of the low ceiling, above a barred hole in the floor that must have led to the lowest level of the prison—a dark, windowless room with no doors, steps, or fireplace at all, but plenty of rats, judging from the scratching sounds of hundreds of tiny claws stirred by our arrival. The jailers probably lowered the hopeless prisoner through the hole by means of a rope or chain and closed the lid tight and forgot about him. Or her.

A slice of bread lay untouched on a tin plate. Jacob Federn had chosen to go hungry rather than eat leavened bread during Pesach.

Federn's lips were chapped and slightly blue with cold, but so far the emperor's intervention had spared him from being tortured.

His eyes lit up when he saw us, and he raised his arms to greet us, although he was too weak to lift the heavy iron shackles more than a few inches.

"My friends, have you come to get me out of here?"

"I'm afraid that we are still working to solve that particular problem," said Rabbi Loew.

Federn's arms fell with a heavy clanking of iron chains.

"But they did allow us to bring you this," said the rabbi, handing over the small bundle tied up with a rag.

Federn's fingers were so stiff with cold that Rabbi Gans had to help him untie the rag and spread out the contents—a cold piece of stuffed fish with a pinch of *maror*, a half-dozen round matzohs, a sealed bottle of wine, and a pair of thin, white Shabbes candles.

Federn nodded toward a tin cup of water, and I retrieved it for him. He cupped his hands, and I poured out a bit of the water so that he could wash his hands and dry them with the rag.

"They wouldn't even let me make a Seder," he said, as if he needed to apologize to us for this transgression.

Rabbi Loew made this wretched place a little bit holier by chanting a verse from the Psalms: *"Ki mikol tsoroh hitsiloni uve'oyvay ro'asoh eyni."* For from all trouble He has rescued me, and upon my enemies my eye has fallen.

I wondered why he chose that passage until he said, "There is your Seder. And your matzoh as well."

Then I realized that the rabbi had chosen a verse with three successive words beginning with the letters *mem*, *tsadek*, and *hey*, which form the word מצה, or *matzoh*, and thus contain the essence of the Seder in a few short words.

We couldn't light the candles, so we just said the Shabbes blessing.

Federn's lips trembled as he said the *brukhes* over the bread and wine. He took a bite of matzoh, a sip of wine, and when this little ceremony was finished, he hungrily gobbled up the fish. Between bites he asked me to pour some wine into the tin cup.

"There's still some water in here," I said.

"It's left over from the prisoner before me," he said, his mouth full of fish.

That explained why he hadn't touched it. It was extremely dangerous to drink from another man's cup, especially in a filthy place like this. If the other man had contracted a fever or some other illness, the harmful spirit of that illness could have slipped out of his mouth and into the water.

I dumped out the remaining water and filled the cup with wine.

What wonders a crust of bread and a cup of wine can do to cheer a man's heart! I waited till Federn was sipping his second cup of wine and nibbling on his second matzoh before opening up the subject of our visit.

"*Reb Federn* is so formal," I said. "Is it all right if I call you Jacob?"

"Why shouldn't it be all right?"

"Listen to me, Jacob," I went on. "If you want to get out of here, you've got to be cleared of all charges. And in order to do that, we need to hear what happened in your own words."

"You were there. You saw everything. What else is there to say?"

"No, I didn't see everything," I said. "For example, I didn't see what happened there three days ago."

"What do you mean, three days ago?"

"I mean that what happened in your shop started at least three days ago, if not long before that."

I pressed on before Federn could respond: "By the way, we found a piece of silver thread on the floor of your shop. Do you have any idea how it could have gotten there?"

"How should I know?"

"Did any of your recent customers wear silver thread?"

"How do you expect me to remember that?"

"So it could have been anyone."

"*Vey iz mir*, I'm freezing to death up here and he's talking in riddles."

"Are you acquainted with Viktor Janek, the father of the victim?"

"Uh . . . only slightly."

"But well enough to get into an argument with him?"

"What are you talking about? I don't remember any argument."

"You don't remember talking with him?"

"Do you remember every conversation you've ever had?"

"You were seen arguing with Viktor Janek in front of your shop. That was three days ago. Surely you can remember that far back?"

"Why are you speaking as if I were the guilty one?"

"I don't know. Why are you *reacting* as if you were the guilty one?"

"Everyone's guilty of something," he said defensively.

"Don't I know it," I said. But something in the room had shifted, and I had to shift with it.

"It must be hard to run a Jewish shop outside the gates, with all those *goyim* staring at you as if you've got horns growing under your hat, your wife carping at you for not putting aside more money, your daughter getting ready for the matchmaker—do you have any idea what a decent wedding costs these days?" I asked my companions. They clucked their tongues and condemned the latest trend among rich merchants for increasingly lavish wedding parties.

I went on: "And the municipal guards always chiseling away at you in return for their 'protection.' Oh, you don't have to tell me, I saw enough of that Kromy fellow to get the idea. And, well, a man gets desperate, doesn't he? Anybody can understand that."

Federn stared at me. In the dusty light, he looked like a man who had a lot of secret compartments tucked away deep inside himself, under lock and key. And he was trying to decide which compartment to open.

After a while, Rabbi Loew said, "You realize that you are telling us something even when you *don't* answer."

I said, "I can't help you unless you tell me the truth."

Federn finally turned the key on one of those tiny compartments. "We were arguing about money."

"We already know that," I said, as if it were common knowledge in every corner of the city.

Rabbi Loew squinted at me skeptically, but he held back and let me press on. "Between *kesef* and *mammon*, money takes all kinds of forms. What was the *specific* problem about money?"

"We were arguing because he owed me money."

"Wait a minute." I leaned closer so he couldn't look away as easily. "You're saying he owed *you* money?

"Well, to hear him tell it, I owed *him* money. And that's what we were arguing about."

"How much money?"

"It doesn't matter."

"I see. So it must have been a trivial amount. Then why would you bother arguing about it?"

"You think a Christian merchant needs an excuse to argue?"

"Why did he owe you money? For what?"

"You want to know what he owed me money for?"

"That's the question I asked."

He was just killing time.

Somewhere outside his cell, high above the clouds, the sun was hurtling past the midpoint of the heavens toward another distant twilight. It took every drop of patience in me to sit there as if I had all the time in the world to wait for him to decide what he was going to say.

Eventually I said, *"Let thy yea be yea and thy nay be nay,"* I warned, quoting the Bava Metzia tractate. The Council of Elders says that going back on your word is one of the seven deadly sins that provokes God's fiercest wrath, and I was pretty sure that Federn knew it.

Rabbi Loew spoke so softly that it almost felt as if his voice were coming from inside my own head: "Sometimes when we pray for certain things, the gates of prayer may be open or they may be closed. But when we truly repent our misdeeds and pray for forgiveness, the gates are always open."

A scouting party of red-eyed rodents came creeping up through the hole in the middle of the floor. They must have smelled the fresh food.

I said, "You know, it's really hard to keep those little creatures from biting you, especially when you can't maneuver to defend yourself. And it only takes a couple of days for the sores to fester. That alone can kill you."

"God works in strange ways," said Rabbi Gans.

"You shouldn't have put yourselves out for me," Federn confessed. "I'm not worthy."

"One man is equal to the whole of creation," Rabbi Loew said, but the words also came from the mouth of Rabbi Nathan, gone these many centuries, for we are taught that whenever we quote a teaching in the name of the one who composed it, the lips of the teacher still whisper from the grave.

A low moan floated up through the hole in the floor, but I didn't have time to think about who it was.

"Look, we all bend the rules every now and then," I said. "It's the only way to survive in a repressive society like this, am I right?"

"That's right," Rabbi Gans agreed.

"And we all make mistakes. With all the laws the Christians impose on us, it's impossible to remember them all. We're always violating some edict or other, and nobody in the community would hold it against you if you did. The only thing they care about is whether you're going to admit your mistakes and do something about making restitution for them. And for it to mean anything, you have to do it *now*, while we still have a chance to fix the situation."

Federn laughed bitterly. "You think you can fix the situation? I thought you rationalists didn't believe in miracles."

I did some more pretending that I had all day for this.

"The longer you make us wait, the worse we have to assume your actions were," said Rabbi Gans, playing up his part nicely.

"Listen Jacob, I know what you're going through," I said. "I've been in some pretty tight spots myself. I'm sure you didn't want it to turn out this way. You only wanted to provide for your family the best way you knew how. You just didn't get a chance to put things right before all this happened."

"Yes, that's it exactly," said Federn.

"So tell me about it."

Federn's eyes flitted from me to the rabbis.

"Don't look at them, look at me," I said.

But Rabbi Loew said, "When the Israelites came to the wilderness of Sin between Elim and Sinai, the Holy One, Blessed is He, sent us the manna from heaven. And on the sixth day, He sent us a double portion for Shabbes. Do you know what this means, Jacob? It means that even when a man has no money for *challah* and wine, he must prepare for Shabbes as best he can, and have faith that God will provide for him."

Federn said nothing.

I gave him one more *noodge*. "Look, it's going to come out anyway. But if you talk to us now, maybe we can keep everyone from hearing the news from the wrong people. Isn't that what you want?"

Maybe it was the redemptive qualities of the bread of affliction—the dry, unleavened bread that he could barely swallow—or the fact that Pesach is also called the Festival of Freedom, that fragile ideal that he was particularly receptive to at the moment, but Jacob Federn finally started talking.

"We started out by clipping dalers," he said.

I tried not to show any reaction.

"Janek knew a couple of metalworkers who would melt down the shavings and mold them into coins," he said.

How could he? After the blood libel and other sorcery-related crimes, the charge that the Jews debased the currency by counterfeiting coins was the worst kind of trumped-up nonsense the Christians could throw at us, which they did periodically and with great enthusiasm. When Archduke Ferdinand tried to expel the Jews from Bohemia in the 1540s, he cited counterfeiting as one of the principal reasons. But no Jew ever believed that we actually did such things.

I wanted to spit in his face for justifying the lowest accusations against us.

"But that didn't last," I said.

"No, it was too risky."

I'll say. They'll put you in the iron maiden for counterfeiting. Even with the spikes, it can take three days to die in one of those things if they do it right.

"So you turned to something else."

"Yes. Janek said he had connections to a certain merchant on the coast of the German Sea who had figured out a way of shipping rare and expensive spices up the Elbe River so that we wouldn't have to pay import duties or taxes, and so increase our profits."

"Thanks for the economics lesson. You know, short-changing the emperor is possibly the only mercantile activity that's even *more* dangerous than counterfeiting."

"That was our mistake. We should have 'rendered unto Caesar,' as the saying goes."

"Yes, but how would you have made any money that way?"

"Oh, I—" He stopped.

And we hit another wall. Just when we were starting to get somewhere.

"You *what*? Something worse than what you've already told me? It must be pretty bad if you can't even bring yourself to say it."

A few more precious moments of my life slipped away, never to return.

"We're wasting our time here," said Rabbi Gans, making a show of leaving. "Let's go."

"Not yet," I said, as if I had the authority to tell a learned rabbi what to do. "I still haven't heard anything worth killing somebody for."

"True, for even thieves must have some kind of honor between them, or the confederacy would fall apart," said Rabbi Loew, borrowing a line from Halevi's *Kuzari*.

Federn pulled up sharply at the word *thieves*.

"That's just it," said Federn. His chains rattled emphatically. "We agreed to split the cost of a chest of very expensive herbs, but when it came time to divide up the goods, Janek cheated me and gave me a short weight. So I got mad, and I held a grudge, but what could I do? It was only a verbal agreement, so I had no way to claim what was rightfully mine. Is that not something that a man would want revenge for?"

"It's not enough to kill someone over," I said.

"What do you know about these things? I—" He took another long, sweet pause. "I cannot speak of it."

"You must tell us," said Rabbi Loew, summoning his severest Day-of-Atonement voice.

I said, "You know, I came here to help uncover evidence of your innocence, and instead I keep uncovering evidence of your *guilt*."

"We got in an argument," said Federn. "Janek cursed me in the most hateful way, and I got crazy with anger and I told him that—"

"Yes, go on."

"I told him he would live to regret what he had done to me."

"How could you say such a foolish thing?" said Rabbi Loew. "Such curses can easily bring charges of witchcraft against the whole community."

"I was enraged. I wanted to beat his skull against the pavement and instead I let my tongue take over and commit the violence for me."

I knew exactly what that felt like.

"*Oy vey iz mir*, you really fouled things up," said Rabbi Gans.

"But we can't allow you to lose your life through a slip of the tongue," I said. "The Talmud clearly states that *no man should be held responsible for the words he utters in anger*."

Rabbi Loew eyed me closely. He could tell that I was up to something, since I had changed a crucial part of the phrase.

It worked. Federn looked at me hopefully, as if I had invoked a little-known legal precedent that would get him out of this barrel of pickles.

"But you still haven't told me how you managed to turn a profit even when you were short-changed by your partners."

He got that cagey look of the petty shopkeeper double-checking to make sure that all his little money boxes are securely locked and fastened.

And that's when I lost my sense of decorum.

"You give me that stuttering it's-too-shameful-to-mention act one more time and I swear I'll drown you in your own swill bucket," I threatened. "You were clever enough to commit the sin, and you can at least be man enough to tell us what it was."

It was Rabbi Loew's turn to play the voice of reason. "More important, your wife and daughter have been seized by the Inquisition, and if you have any concern for them, you had better tell us everything."

That broke through the wall of lies and prevarications. Federn gazed at his leg irons, unable to meet our eyes as he confessed in a low, quiet voice that he had "made ends meet" by selling medicinal herbs to Christians and Jews at highly inflated prices, which was forbidden by the *Shulkhan Orekh* on the grounds that it violated God's holiness, and by the Talmud, which specifies that *for a Jew to cheat a Gentile is worse than to cheat a Jew, for in addition to breaking the moral law, it brings contempt on the Jews.*

The good news was that this went a long way toward clearing him of a motive for murder, but he was still a pretty big disappointment to us all.

After Federn's words had settled like dust in the crypt, Rabbi Loew broke the stillness and said that this illustrated the truth of Rabbi Assi's teachings— that the evil inclination begins as a spider's thread, but ends up as thick as a cart rope. For whoever is envious of his neighbor's goods will soon find himself giving false testimony against his neighbor, and so on up the ladder until eventually he is driven to steal from him and finally, to shed his blood.

Federn sat there looking stunned, while I tried to figure out where this new trail might lead. At least one or two of the municipal guards must have known about this illegal arrangement, and that fellow Kromy struck me as a real *gabenfresser*, a gift-gobbler, our word for a corrupt official with a sideline in petty bribery, and just the kind of man who had the necessary skills and motivation to carry out a high-stakes murder-and-extortion scheme. And I knew just the woman to talk to him, if only I could get a message to her.

But—*Good Lord*—how was I supposed to get her a message when I wasn't allowed to write? Oh, the hell with it. The Torah teaches us to put life before the commandments. (With three exceptions, and I wasn't planning on committing idolatry, adultery, or murder anytime soon.)

"One more question," I said. "How many people owe you money?"

"Ha! Half the neighborhood."

"But who owes you the most? Or is the most difficult to collect from?"

"I'd have to check my ledger."

Good luck. How are you at reading smoke signals?

"Nobody in particular comes to mind?" I asked.

"Not really. The amounts were so trivial."

Of course they were. A man like Federn couldn't afford to let anybody run up a huge debt that he couldn't collect on. Only a handful of merchants in the Jewish Town could manage that. But as far as I knew, only one of them had petitioned the emperor with a special request for protection.

"It's time to go," I said. "If erasing an old debt was the motive, we've been talking to the wrong man."

"SO WHAT ARE YOUR PLANS NOW?" asked Rabbi Gans.

"We still have to free Reb Federn in spite of what he's done," I said.

Rabbi Loew quizzed me: "What does the Mishnah say on the subject of man's freedom?"

"*The only free man is the one who studies Torah.*"

"Correct."

"And the meaning in this context—?"

Rabbi Loew held up his hand to silence me as the emperor's attendant presented us with a copy of the royal decree, signed and sealed, permitting us to examine the young victim's body *without touching it*. Then the attendant escorted us to the nearest gate, in the shadow of a massive square tower with a pointed roof and one tiny window peering out of its blank stone face. It was called the Black Tower, a name that fully conveyed the spirit of the place, for it stood atop a dark passageway connecting two gated arches. A strong breeze was blowing up the hillside, raising the hems of our cloaks and scattering dirt in our faces. We blustered through this windy tunnel and stepped out into the light, where it was still breezy, but quite a bit warmer.

A patch of green was splashed with shiny gobs of butter-yellow flowers blooming by the wayside. I slowed down for a moment, taken with the astounding natural beauty of the flowers, amazed at the simple miracle of nature going about its course without regard for the plight of humanity, and at how such rejuvenation could flourish in the middle of all this chaos.

It's a well-worn saying, but it's true: You don't appreciate life until you look death in the face.

When you look around on a spring day like this and see flower buds sprouting, you realize that every moment of life is a precious miracle. Just the fact that we're here to see and smell the first flowers of spring is a blessed miracle.

"Come along now," said Rabbi Loew, tugging at my sleeve. "The day is short, the labor is much, the workers are sluggish, the reward is great, and the Master is impatient."

The Pirkey Avos again, as relevant as ever.

"Yes, Rabbi."

But from where I stood on this high place above the rain-gorged river, the taste of nectar in the wind and the marvelous sight of the mother of cities nourishing her children briefly filled me with a sublime poetic urge to embrace the bustling world around me.

"At least we're breathing the air of freedom, unlike our brother Jacob," I said.

"Do you honestly believe that?" said Rabbi Loew, his voice rising. It sounded like Our Master and Teacher was challenging my assumptions again.

So I said, "What I mean is that before all this happened, he was already living in a prison of his own making, and perhaps now that he is being forced to confront his errors, he will be able to free his mind from the Evil Inclination, and his body and soul will follow."

"Let me explain something to you," he said. "As long as we are subjects of the imperial crown, and of the mercantile system that reduces all that is human to a commodity to be bought and sold in the open market, none of us is any freer than a forgotten prisoner living out his days in the darkest cell."

"Metaphorically speaking, you mean—"

"Not in the least. We all saw quite clearly today that the emperor is in no way inherently superior to other men. And if any man is capable of being emperor, that means that the imperial state is not a divine creation at all, but a human creation, full of human flaws. And therefore our only hope is that some day, when humanity has left its ignominious childhood behind, the monarchical state will wither away, since one of its primary goals is to place unnatural restrictions on the freedom of men like us."

Serious words indeed, not to be spoken publicly in a Christian language.

"So again I ask, where to now?" said Rabbi Gans, anxious to change the subject.

"First we must execute the emperor's decree," said Rabbi Loew.

"That'll be a barrel of laughs," I said.

"Then what?"

"One of the clues we uncovered today is a thread," said Rabbi Loew. "And a thread is always found on the tailor."

Metaphorically speaking.

CHAPTER 23

KASSY WAS TIRED, BUT ELATED. She had been up all night, boiling the strange new leaf into a tisane and testing it on a mouse she had pried away from Kira. Satisfied that the pale green mixture wasn't poisonous, at least, she had tested it on herself, and found that a tea made from this new leaf was a mild stimulant, and that the more concentrated tincture was a stronger stimulant that greatly eased the darker moods of melancholia.

An herb that relieved the symptoms of melancholia. Imagine the possibilities if she had found a way of counteracting its debilitating effects! Her pulse was surging and her mind was abuzz, as if she were strolling barefoot through a lightning storm, and she felt that anyone who had never experienced the sublime pleasure of finding an elusive answer to a long-standing problem has never known true joy.

But the best answers always led to more questions, and now she wondered how the Jews were involved in this, what they knew about this herb, and what other secrets they possessed that could shed light upon the dark places beyond the limits of her knowledge. She was more determined than ever to defy the restrictions and penetrate the man-made barriers around the ghetto in order to study with the Jewish alchemists. And she couldn't wait to tell Anya, the Jew's maid, about her thrilling discovery.

Her worktable was still covered with iron filings from a series of trials with Magnesian stone, reminding her that she had to give the whole place a good sweeping before any stray bits of metal contaminated any of her current experiments. But all that—the mundane reality of dirt, sweat, and obligations—could wait until after she recorded her observations, so she quickly brushed the filings onto a sheet of scrap paper with the side of her hand and set them aside, clearing a space for her notebook and a relatively intact specimen of the Peruvian leaf.

She dusted off her hands, and flipped open her notebook, creating a slight turbulence that nearly sent all the metal sweepings spilling onto the floor. She was focused on setting down her observations as she slid the scrap paper out of the way, when the most extraordinary thing happened. The iron filings on the paper arranged themselves in series of expanding arcs emanating from two point sources. She stared at the undulating pattern for a moment, not sure if this was really happening or if sleep had somehow crept up on her and this was all an exceptionally vivid dream. When she held the paper up to examine it, the pattern collapsed, and she realized that she had caused this phenomenon by laying the filings across the thin bar of iron that she had magnetized as part of yesterday's experiment. She held the paper over the flat slab of metal again and gently shook it to distribute the filings evenly, and to her supreme astonishment the bits of iron realigned themselves in the same pattern of loops radiating from the two ends of the magnet. Like an apostle witnessing the Ascension, she slowly turned the paper and shook it some more, and the pattern reconstituted itself once again. Somehow the tiny iron filings were giving substance to a constant invisible force.

She was so absorbed in the process of mapping out a couple of weeks' worth of experiments that she didn't pay much attention to the clanking of steel boots on the paving stones outside. Another confrontation between the Society of Jesus and the Hussite sectarians, she thought, when something rammed the door to her lab so hard the wood split.

All of her plans, solid or barely formed, even those lying just past the visible horizon like undiscovered islands—all were broken from their orbits by the sound of splintering pine and scattered like so much sawdust as the next shuddering impact broke the door in two.

Kira skittered away and hid under the dish rack.

Spike-toed boots kicked the last dangling pieces of planking out of the doorframe as if they were stray bits of driftwood. Glass rattled in the rack as a contingent of squires stormed in like a pack of hounds, and as in a dream gone wrong, she couldn't move a muscle to stop them. And in an instant, Kassy was surrounded by eight bodies protected by several layers of chain mail and steel, as if her humble healer's shop were a strategic location on a foreign battlefield.

Four sets of mailed fists seized her under her arms and knees and lifted her off the ground as if she were made of straw, while two men in black-and-gold jerkins slid a heavy basket under her. The steel-faced men struggled to keep her in the air the whole time as they set her in the basket. Then they drew the straps tight, and raised her higher so that the four of them could carry her out the door all trussed up like a bundle of laundry.

And during all this, someone with a commanding voice had been giving orders not to allow her to touch anything or secrete anything upon her person, and to turn her rooms upside down looking for any instruments or ointments or other objects of witchcraft.

A bolt of fear shot through her and remained quivering like an arrow shaft buried deep in her chest. Images of the rack, the *Uffzieher*, and the water board flashed before her eyes, all of them light forms of torture whose use was so routine that the courts had ruled that confessions obtained with them were "freely given." But what really made her skin crawl was the Witch's Chair. The spikes on its arms and back were made of wood, but it had an iron seat you could fry an egg on once they heated it up. The Austrian judges were especially fond of this one.

"You are charged with dispensing a potion containing a suspicious ingredient known as bird's tongue."

Kassy's fingers closed around the cross hanging from her neck as the commanding voice read aloud the legal document that would seal her fate:

"And so by order of the Imperial Code, we hereby sentence the herbalist and accused aeromancer, Kassandra Boehme of the Bethlehem Chapel district, to public exposure in the pillory while wearing the *Schandmask* for a period of ten hours, and thenceforth do banish her from Prague and its environs for the remainder of her days. Furthermore, her worldly possessions shall be confiscated and divided among the loyal Christians to whom that office falls."

The guards shoved the leather Mask of Shame over her mouth, making sure that the iron choke bit pressed down on her tongue to keep her from speaking any more. Then they shackled her legs together and carried her off to the pillory.

THE HASP WAS COMING LOOSE, so the correctors used a heavy mallet to drive a pair of spikes through the metal and into the post. With a dull clang, they chained her alongside the other troublesome women on the platform in Old Town Square.

Kassy scanned the horizon to see if anyone noticed her, or took pity, or if she had any enemies in the crowd, because she could withstand this punishment as long as no one tried to torment her with rotten vegetables embedded with nails, or sharp stones. At least they hadn't hung a sign around her neck calling attention to her crime. But it was hard to see through the eyeholes in the mask.

Only now did she have time to reflect on Kira's fate.

Who'll feed her? she thought. Her furry little companion would survive on natural wit and instinct, but would she find a nice, warm home and be cared for? All she could do was hope.

Her second biggest concern was her undelivered message for the butcher's daughter, Anya, although she had no way of knowing if it would still matter by the time she was released.

Then she saw them. A few paces behind the jeering mob, trying not to draw too much attention to themselves. Evelina the midwife's helper and a couple of Father Jiři's young partisans, standing together with grim, determined faces. As she fixed her gaze on them, they discreetly held up a few torn-up books that they had "looted" from her shop in order to save at least *something* from the wreckage of her life for the long journey ahead. It was such a relief to see some sympathetic faces in the square, and to know that she wasn't completely alone in this world.

Because she knew that there was plenty of good work for a wise woman to do in the hills of northern Bohemia.

And she knew how lucky she was to have gotten off so easily.

CHAPTER 24

A LINE OF RIGID, UNIFORM bodies suddenly emerged from the swirling masses of humanity on the far side of the stone bridge like a fleet of ships gliding through the misty waters of some inland sea. And the people melted away like clouds of gray-green fog before the fixed figureheads of municipal authority.

The sheriff stood square-shouldered, his heels planted firmly in the earth, and when we approached him, he informed us that he and his men were here to escort us back to the ghetto. That was his plan, anyway, until we presented him with a copy of the emperor's decree.

"What's this?" he said.

Rabbi Gans started reading it out loud: *"Our Sovereign Emperor Rudolf, a just and pious ruler—"*

"I can read, you know," said Zizka, taking the decree from Rabbi Gans and looking it over.

We awaited his reaction.

He said, "So the emperor takes your gold and returns the favor with his protection, and I have no say in the matter. You Jews certainly know the ins and outs of every legal document in the land, don't you?"

I admitted that textual perspicacity was one of our strengths.

"Do you really have to go through with this?" he asked, slapping the decree with the flat of his hand.

"I'm afraid so."

"Because a lot of people are not going to like it."

"No, they're not."

"It says we are obligated to accompany you at all times for your own protection," he said.

Each of his men was carrying a double-edged broadsword, all shiny and freshly sharpened.

I said, "Just don't protect us *too* closely, all right?"

The sheriff shook his head with bitter amusement. And we stood there silently, while the currents of people washed around us, until finally he said, "All right, let's get this over with," and waved us on.

We started down the King's Road toward the main square, with the armed patrol falling in behind us.

Zizka said, "But no matter what this decree says, I can't guarantee your safety if you arouse the people's anger by mishandling the child's body in any way."

"We all share your concern," said Rabbi Loew. "And you may rest assured that we do not intend to force the dead girl's spirit to reveal her killer's name or anything else that might trouble her. We just want to see what she has to say for herself."

A couple of guards stopped short with a clanking of metal. Zizka ordered them to get a move on, while we kept walking.

"What are you saying?" said Zizka, catching up with us.

Rabbi Loew explained, "What you Christians think of as the human soul is actually made up of several different elements. Although the young girl's eternal soul, which we call the *neshamah*, has already returned to the Creator, her *ruakh*, or spirit, will cling forever to the mortal remains that housed her in life, and the active spirit of her *nefesh* will float between the two, mourning the body for seven days while drifting back and forth between the girl's home and her final resting place. Some say this lasts a whole year. In any case, it is with the *nefesh* that we might be able to communicate during this period, although I need to warn you that it takes a tremendous effort for the dead to speak to us."

"I would imagine so," said Zizka. "But what if her spirit won't speak to a Jew?"

"Then she may choose to speak to us through other means."

We were coming up on The Blue Pike, a public house packed with laborers and artisans who had finished work for the day. They bubbled out into the street, and I greedily eyed their sweaty steins of Bohemian lager.

Zizka asked what we hoped to learn from seeing the girl's body.

Rabbi Loew said, "It is not a matter of merely seeing the girl. Anybody can *see* her. Even wild animals are observant of their surroundings. But only men like us, Sheriff Zizka, are capable of combining our observations with the wisdom and understanding needed to determine if the child met with some accident, or slipped and fell on a knife, or if some other blameless tragedy occurred. And so we may learn many things from what the body tells us, and also from what it doesn't tell us."

"I don't need any more riddles today, Rabbi. How can you learn anything from what it *doesn't* tell you?"

"You know the tale of Jonah and the whale, don't you?" said Rabbi Loew.

"Every little schoolboy knows that one," Zizka growled.

"But have you studied it closely? Ah, I didn't think so. For in the Book of Jonah, the prophet says that when the people of Nineveh repented of their sins, they covered themselves in sackcloth and ashes. But what, you may ask, were the terrible sins that aroused the wrath of God? The Bible doesn't tell us. However, since the text does *not* say that the Ninevites went around smashing their idols—idolatry being one of the very worst sins in the eyes of God—we may deduce from this that they were *not* idol-worshippers, which is why the Holy One, blessed is He, gave them a chance to repent."

Zizka slowly dropped his street-fighting attitude. It took him a while to shift from the flinty lawman who spent much of his time breaking up drunken brawls to the rational being capable of analyzing a complex problem like this one, but I believe I saw a slight softening of the sheriff's hardness.

He said, "You mean, if they had smashed idols, the Bible would have mentioned it?"

"That's it precisely," said Rabbi Loew.

Rabbi Gans said, "They say that Rabbi Simeon could tell whether a man was a Jew, a Christian, or a Moslem from the way he played at chess."

"Well, this isn't a bloody chess game, Rabbi," said Zizka, as we reached the main entrance to the Old Town Hall.

We were shown into a large room built in the style of the last century, with a high ceiling, exposed beams, and four tall windows casting the dull shadows of four identical Christian crosses across the floor. The gilded arch over the doorway culminated in an elaborate seal of the city—three towers in a row behind a stone wall topped by a pair of lions holding a helmet and a crown, all done in polished hammered metal.

A long table occupied the middle of the room, draped with a crisp white sheet that outlined the shape of a young child.

Two sentinels stood guard over the body.

The sheriff gave a nod, and one of the guardsmen yanked the sheet off with alarming swiftness, exposing the tiny, broken body to our prying gazes. The girl's eyes had not been fully sealed by the sleep of death, and a sliver of dull white showed between her eyelids like a hard piece of eggshell. Her lips were blue and bloodless, and her nightdress was still encrusted with reddish-brown stains that testified to the full horror of her fate.

"Doesn't look like she 'fell on a knife,'" said the sheriff.

Some of the mystics will tell you that there is no such thing as death, that all matter and form are illusory, and that this world is merely the antechamber to the World-to-Come. But even so, it is better not to have children than to bury them, because if the order of this world means anything at all, it's that your children are supposed to outlive you. By a day, even by an hour, your children are supposed to outlive you.

These thoughts were interrupted by the sound of insistent pounding.

Rabbi Loew began by asking the spirit of the girl to forgive us in the presence of these many witnesses for any wrong that we might commit in the course of our examination. But he was also keenly aware that there's nothing worse than losing a child, no matter how chosen your people are or which day of the week you call the Sabbath, because he suddenly began to recite the prayer for the dead.

"May His great Name be exalted and sanctified."

Rabbi Gans and I joined him in saying, "Amen."

Angry voices echoed through the hallway behind us.

"May He who makes peace in the heavens bring peace to us all."

We all said, "Amen," and took three steps forward.

"You better stay away from her!"

An unruly mob was filling the doorway.

"Good Lord, who let them in here?" asked Zizka.

Some minor official squirmed to the front of the crowd and proclaimed, "The people's desire to observe these proceedings shall not be denied."

Right. He probably remembered the *last* time the people brought their outrage to the Town Hall.

Rabbi Loew tried to assure the present company that it is forbidden to disrespect a corpse, and that any Jew who even comes in contact with one must be purified with the ashes of a red heifer on the third and seventh day, a very expensive and mystifying procedure even to this day, but nobody was listening.

"And I said you better not touch her!" someone yelled.

Zizka emptied his lungs calling for silence.

When he had everyone's attention, he said, "The emperor has given them his permission to examine the body. But they are not permitted to touch her. They may not even touch her clothes."

That wasn't in the decree.

"How are we supposed to do this without even touching her clothes?" I asked.

Then a woman's voice cut through the din.

"Why don't you let *me* touch her?"

All heads turned toward a tall woman with long dark braids pushing to the front of the crowd. It was Meisel's Shabbes maid, Anya. The death threats shrunk to low hisses and murmurs, and the room became eerily quiet as she stepped forward.

It made sense that a butcher's daughter wouldn't be terribly squeamish about handling bloody flesh, but I didn't know where she got the courage to stand in the middle of the room like that with all eyes upon her.

How did she find us? Presumably, word had spread rather quickly about the city guards escorting three foolhardy Jews through the center of the Old Town. But whatever the reason, she was a godsend, because a Christian like her is not susceptible to the ritual uncleanliness imparted by a corpse, nor could she transfer it to us through any form of contact.

"What do you say to this?" asked Zizka. "Will you allow this woman to assist you in your examination?"

"Why shouldn't we accept her offer?" said Rabbi Loew. "Women can be quite practical at times."

He was probably just trying to put the crowd at ease by expressing some kind of common sentiment that made us appear more human in their eyes.

"All right, all right, just get on with it," said Zizka.

"First of all, you're going to need more light," said Anya, reaching for a standing candelabra over by the wall. A guard seized it from her and planted it near the head of the table so roughly that one of the candles tumbled to the floor. Anya stepped on the flame and put it out. Then she picked up the candle, touched its smoking wick to another candle's flame, and fit it back into its socket.

Who else among those present would have known that the Jews cannot handle fire on Shabbes? Surely this young woman's place in Heaven was assured.

"Now, let's see what this speechless little girl can tell us," said Rabbi Loew. Then, barely above a whisper, he asked me, "What was her name again?"

"Gerta," I said. As if I could ever forget the name that roused me shivering from my bed on *Erev Shabbes*.

"Don't worry, Gerta," he said tenderly to the pale corpse. "We won't harm you. Do you hear me, Gerta? We won't even touch you. Your hair won't even tremble from our breath."

The cluster of curious faces in the doorway bobbled around as the forces behind them jostled for a better view. Rabbi Loew waved his fingers, beckoning Anya to come closer.

Like it or not, we had an audience closely scrutinizing every move we made, every gesture, every utterance. But Rabbi Loew knew how to hold an audience as well as any preacher in the kingdom.

He took a moment to address them. "My friends, you all know me to be a righteous man who spends his days delving beneath the outer garments of the Torah to uncover the truths that lie there. So you understand that we should have no trouble applying this process to the far flimsier garments with which ordinary men clothe their lies."

There was movement among the gaping mouths in the doorway, and some heads began to nod.

In hushed tones, Rabbi Loew instructed Anya to undo the top button of the girl's shift. Anya did as he requested, then she spread the fabric apart, revealing the long, jagged gash running across the victim's neck.

A shiver of revulsion rippled through the crowd so palpably that a bit of it went rolling through me as well.

I leaned in to get a closer look at this gory trench cutting through the girl's soft flesh like the deep red line dividing the land of the living from the land of the dead.

"Very strong and savage," said Rabbi Loew. "And yet, oddly hesitant. They appear to have made several tries."

"Not the easiest way to get it done," said Anya.

We waited for her to expand on this, but she seemed a bit uncomfortable with her public role as the expert on butchery.

"Please explain what you think that means, no matter how unpleasant it may be," I said, stepping closer to her side.

"It means that whoever did this may have been as savage as the rabbi said, but he wasn't very good with a short-bladed knife."

"And what can be deduced from this?" Rabbi Loew asked us.

We conferred in low but audible voices, because we actually wanted the people to hear what we were saying. We even incorporated Anya's observations in our responses, and concluded that the men we wanted were most likely a couple of experienced mercenaries, old hands in the murder-for-hire trade, but that the specific manner of death was new to them.

Why? Because they had never needed to extract a couple of pints of blood from their victim.

And where was the victim's missing blood? We had every reason to fear that it had been collected in order to be used against us, probably with the intention of planting it at Federn's shop or somewhere else inside the ghetto.

Zizka followed our dialogue closely without interrupting us once.

We asked Anya to undo the rest of the buttons, which she did. Then she gently pulled back the nightshirt as far as it would go, exposing the bruises on the girl's chest, mostly purple and reddish welts that she must have gotten at the hands of her murderers. But there were some other odd shadows on her skin as well.

"Could you bring that candle a little closer?" I said.

Anya twisted a candle from its socket in the standing candelabra and held it over the girl's chest.

"Hold it down here," I said, indicating the right side of the girl's chest.

She brought the candle closer, bathing the area in light and bringing out the details of several faded brown welts and a couple of faint greenish-yellow ones.

"No wonder they didn't want us to look at her," I said.

"What?"

"This girl bears marks from at least three separate beatings over the last couple of weeks."

"How can you be so sure?" said Zizka.

"Believe me, Sheriff, I know the difference between fresh and old bruises."

"Then we need to examine her much more thoroughly," said Rabbi Loew.

"Absolutely not," said Zizka.

"Just above the waist," I offered. "As part of the investigation."

Zizka stared at the marks indelibly recorded on the girl's skin as clearly as if they had been inscribed in the court register and sealed with wax.

Just as a fool is not aware of being oppressed, the flesh of a corpse does not feel the knife, said Rabbi Loew, citing a particularly appropriate—and cynical—bit of Talmudic wisdom.

Zizka finally conceded, but the girl's nightdress wouldn't open any wider at the top. The sheriff deliberated for a moment, then unsheathed his dagger and brought it close. His blade hovered over the girl's dress as if he could already hear the merchants hawking pieces of this holy relic for a price, before he cut through the thin fabric, including the places that were stiffened with dried blood, as delicately as if he were bisecting a butterfly's wing, and laid the cloth out on the tabletop. When he repeated this process on the girl's left side, the fabric fell away, revealing a blackened half-inch hole between her sixth and seventh ribs.

Street-hardened men sucked their breath in through their teeth.

"What infernal wound is this?" said Zizka, pulling away and giving us the evil eye.

"Perhaps we could better answer your question after we examine it," said Rabbi Loew.

"No! You stay away from her!"

"Use your head, Sheriff," I said. "Why would we practically *beg* you to expose the area if we were responsible for that wound?"

"To divert suspicion from yourselves, of course."

"I have to admit, that *would* be pretty clever of us. But I could think of much better ways of doing it."

"I bet you could."

Zizka wasn't about to yield ground in front of his people. I suppose I wouldn't either, if I were in his shoes. But did he really believe everything he was saying, or was it just for show? He seemed like too much of a realist not to be swayed by evidence that he could plainly see with his own eyes, even if it went against the received wisdom of his countrymen.

But that still left us in a tough spot, unless I could find a few sympathetic faces in the crowd and convince them to help us get past the gang of credulous cretins blocking the door, which was the only way out of the room that didn't involve hurling a chair through a couple of square feet of stained glass.

So once again, I put all my hopes in the magic of words.

"If I remember correctly, Pliny the Elder tells us in his *Historia Naturalis* that death occurs only when the tide is ebbing. What time was the high tide yesterday?"

A crusty old boatman who knew the ways of the riverfront answered that the high tide was at about two hours after midnight by the Christian clock, or what we would call the eighth hour after sunset by our reckoning.

"That puts the time of death sometime between the second hour after midnight and her discovery about four hours later. But we would need to examine the body to confirm this."

There were a few stirrings from the groundlings, then some voices in the crowd called for the sheriff to allow it, as their morbid fascination with our grisly endeavor temporarily overcame their desire to see us punished.

Zizka finally grabbed the candle from Anya and bent down to examine the mysterious wound himself. But he didn't stop me from pressing in close beside him so I could get a good look at it, too.

It was unlike any sword or pike wound I'd ever seen—deep, round, and hollow in the center, as if a giant bloodworm had bored straight through her chest. Traces of dark particulate matter formed a ring around its edges. Under different circumstances, my first move would have been to probe the wound carefully to get a sense of its depth, but obviously that was impossible.

I certainly never expected Zizka to tell me truthfully what was on his mind, but that's just what he did. "If I didn't know any better, I'd say that was a bullet hole."

"A bullet hole? From what kind of gun?"

"Looks like we'll have to search the ghetto and find out."

"Come on, Sheriff, your men would have found it during yesterday's search—"

"I wouldn't be too sure about that."

"What Jew could possibly get away with carrying a weapon of this kind?"

I said. "You people haven't even let us carry *swords* for a couple of hundred years."

"And it's a good thing, too," said one of the guards.

"Because that law's easy to enforce," said Zizka. "You can't hide a sword. But you could easily conceal a short-barreled German wheel-lock pistol."

"You're saying this wound was caused by a German-made weapon?"

"I'm saying it's *possible.*"

"Well, then I guess you're right. There's only one way to find out."

"What's that?"

"Find a German wheel-lock pistol and fire it into the body of a suitable substitute—say, a thief cut down from the gibbet—then compare the two wounds."

"It'll be Judgment Day in Hell before I let you mutilate a Christian corpse in so barbaric a fashion."

"I agree that it's barbaric, but saving a life supersedes the prohibitions in the Bible."

"But it *doesn't* supersede the prohibitions in the Carolinian Law Code, which you have *repeatedly* reminded me—"

Suddenly Anya spoke up: "Why don't you test it out on the pig's head we've got in our shop? It's still fresh—"

"What on earth are you talking about?" said the sheriff.

"My daddy always said that a pig wounds just like a man."

"But we can't even *touch* the carcass of a pig," I protested. I moved closer to her and confided, "I'd be unclean until I took a ritual bath, and I don't know when I'm supposed to fit that in because the rest of my day is looking pretty full right now."

"Well, then, I'll just have to touch it for you," said Anya.

Someone send a call up to God and ask Him if one of His angels is missing.

"This is madness," said Zizka.

"No, the bloodcrime accusations are madness," I said. "This is our best chance so far this week to dispel the baseless rumors with a physically verifiable fact."

Zizka paced up and down like a caged tiger who still remembers the taste of freedom, ignoring the kibitzing from the spectators, until he finally decided to send one of his men to fetch a variety of pistols from the municipal armory and bring them to Cervenka's butcher shop.

Rabbi Loew asked for a basin of water for us to wash our hands in.

"What—*now*?" asked Zizka.

"Yes, now."

"Why do you Jews need to wash your hands so often?" said Zizka.

"It is customary after viewing a body or a burial," said Rabbi Loew.

But several of those present clearly saw it as further proof that the Jews practice sorcery.

OUR STRANGE PROCESSION ADVANCED ACROSS the Old Town Square, attracting a dozen or more curious souls as if it were growing a long human tail. Some of the newcomers were probably just tagging along, hoping to catch a glimpse of some genuine Jewish magic before the scourge was eradicated once and for all by the righteous emissaries of the Church of the living God, or simply to have a story to tell their grandkids.

But remarkably, I did not see hate in all of their eyes this time.

We followed the sheriff as he led us through the square, until we passed directly in front of the public pillory. Whether he did this as part of his rounds or simply to intimidate us once more with the spectacle of all those rebellious women chained to the pillory posts, I can't say. Either way, it was an effective demonstration, because some of them were writhing and gesturing madly at us while fending off wet chunks of horse manure, much to the delight and merriment of the spectators. But the other women stood by and stoically accepted their punishment, with every feature but their sorry eyes obscured by the grotesque masks.

Anya averted her eyes from the disturbing sight. Then after waiting long enough for it to seem accidental, she fell into step beside me and asked me how I came to know so much about the ways of Christians.

"By living among them, the same as you."

"And you were able to get along?"

"Most of the time."

A couple of guards glared at her, but she deflected their steel-eyed glances by assuming the role of a disinterested interpreter inquiring about Yiddish vocabulary.

"Tell me, Jew, how do you say *brother* in your language?"

"We say *bruder*."

"So it's just like German. And what about *sister*?"

"*Shvester*. But I wouldn't go around saying that it's 'just like' German."

"And how do you say *war*?"

"*Milkhome*."

"Now *that's* different. Is it Hebrew?"

"Yes, but you could also say *krig* if you really wanted to."

"Which *is* just like German. What about *peace*?"

"*Sholem*. What's your word for it?"

"*Mir*."

"Oh. Same as in Russian."

"Yes. And how do you say that something's cheap, or not of much value?"

"You mean, in the sense of poor quality?"

"No, I mean in the sense of someone making promises they don't intend to keep, and leaving you empty-handed."

"I'd say, they promised me the moon and the stars, but I ended up with *bubkes*."

An unlikely tinkle of laughter spilled from her mouth and brightened the gray air around me.

"What's so funny?" I asked, but she waved me off. "Come on, tell me. I could use a good laugh."

She drew a breath and held it long enough to smother the ticklish urge, then she let it out and told me, "*Bobkes* is our word for a goat's turd."

"Then I guess the two words must be related."

The guards lost interest. Anya and I managed to find a few other words that our mother tongues had in common, words like *nudnik*, *tshaynik*, and *pupik*, then she lowered her voice, and as casually as if she were commenting about the weather, she asked me, "Do you believe that you can be mysteriously drawn to somebody you've only just met?"

"Sure. They say it happens when you meet someone whose essence was formed next to yours inside the massive cloud of primordial energy that preceded the creation of man."

"Who says that?"

"One of the Kabbalists. I don't remember which one—"

"So you mean, that person is like your heavenly soul mate?"

"I suppose you could put it that way—"

"And what happens if you get separated from your soul mate?"

"Then I'd say you have your work cut out for you. It's like digging for buried treasure. The Talmud says you have to go out and find it, since the treasure isn't going to come looking for you."

"So this famous Talmud offers the same old *seek and ye shall find* that I get from the Sunday sermons?"

She looked a little disappointed.

"Well, it's a little more active than that. It's also a lot easier when you have the right tools. And you have the right tools in abundance."

"How do you mean?"

"Do you really need me to explain it?"

"I guess I do."

"Fine, fine. We have a saying, *Eyn hor fun a meydls kop shlept shtarker fun tsen oksn.*" One hair from a girl's head pulls stronger than ten oxen.

"Meaning—?"

"Meaning love can move mountains."

"Who said anything about love?"

She was pretending that she wasn't involved in something, but she couldn't control the flush of pink rising to her face.

She asked, "And do the rabbis have a saying about women like me?"

The rabbis had plenty to say about women like her, but I just chose the good ones: "They say that even the daughter of your enemy can be righteous, and that the righteous of all nations have a share in the World-to-Come. Didn't the priests teach you that Pharaoh's own daughter defied his wishes and saved Moses from the river even though she *knew* that he was one of the Hebrews' children?"

"Yes, but I haven't thought about that sermon in a *long* time. But where is it written that these acts of kindness and charity outweigh the rest of the commandments?"

She sounded just like a yeshiva student preparing for an oral argument before the *beys din*, and her earnest level of commitment brought me back to the days when the world was still a wide road spanning infinite horizons, and anything was possible.

"It's in the Jerusalem Talmud," I said, with the sweet sting of pain for a world long past reverberating like a dying echo in my head. "At the beginning of tractate Peah."

"And what the Talmud says is law, right?"

"Well, yes and no."

I could tell she wasn't satisfied with *that* answer.

"It depends."

"It *depends*?"

"The Talmud encourages us to look at every side of an issue, every detail, no matter how trivial, because the work of finding a satisfactory answer is never done."

"But how do you enforce a rabbinic opinion if it's not enshrined in law?"

"We don't."

"Then what do you do?"

"We learn to live with conflicting opinions."

Something you folks should learn to do.

But the moment finally seemed right, and I probably wasn't going to get another chance like this. So I lowered my voice to a whisper and asked her to talk to the wives of some municipal guards to see if they had heard anything about Janek's shady dealings with Jacob Federn. When she told me that Kromy was her neighbor, I had to keep from shouting, *Which house?*

"It's time to put that little theory of yours to the test," said Zizka, as our rag-tag procession arrived at the butcher shop.

Had he been listening? If so, he had more than enough evidence to hand Anya over to the Inquisition for harboring un-Catholic thoughts. But I was getting the feeling that he wasn't the type to turn in a fellow dissenter from the Roman Church.

Anya broke away and ran inside to explain the situation to her father. But old Cervenka still looked bewildered as she grabbed an apron, gave him a peck on the cheek, and disappeared through the back door of the shop. She returned in a moment carrying the pig's head in an enameled metal tray, and set it down on the counter.

Zizka's men finally arrived, carrying armfuls of weapons of various sizes. The sheriff cleared a space on the counter and spread the weapons out, looking each one over and eliminating the most unlikely prospects, explaining his rationale as he went down the line.

"A rifled arquebus like this one takes a lot of skill, but in the right hands, it will discharge a ball that can penetrate the thickest armor. And the long barrel makes it more accurate over long ranges, but I can't see a kidnapper concealing this thing under his cloak."

It was about three feet long. He picked up another, larger weapon.

"Spanish matchlock. Heavy weapon, fires bullets weighing ten to a pound that would unhorse a knight on a charging steed at forty paces. But too unwieldy for anything besides battlefield use. Hardly practical for our purposes."

He was certainly in his element. He picked up another weapon and set it aside immediately.

"Double wheel-lock. Too expensive and unreliable."

He separated three short-barreled pistols from the remaining weapons. He selected one and recognized its style in an instant.

"Italian-made," he said, laying that one aside.

He took a bit longer examining the next one, paying particular attention to the fluted wheel and cocking mechanism.

"There are some technical peculiarities which suggest that this one was made by French gunsmiths," he said, putting it down. He was left with one pistol about two feet long with a heavy butt.

"Here we go," he said. "German-made. Plain barrel without ornamentation, such as an ordinary soldier might use. Some wear on the grooves, but it should do nicely."

He and his men began the intricate process of loading the pistol with ball and wadding and powder and whatnot, tamping it down, then winding up the spring-lock mechanism. I didn't know much about this kind of gun, but the spring-lock must have been very strong, because even Zizka, with his huge hands, was straining to get the tension right. When he was done, he let the cock down into the priming pan.

"What does your Torah have to say about the correct way to fire a pistol at a pig's head?"

"The Torah is silent on the matter," said Rabbi Loew. His quiet dignity did not invite a retort.

Zizka shrugged, and told Anya and her father to clear out of the way. Then he raised the heavy pistol and aimed it at the pig's head. He was standing about ten feet away from the target, and his hand was remarkably steady as he slowly put pressure on the trigger.

A crowd of the faithful had gathered to witness this singular event. They stared wide-eyed, huddling close to their neighbors, many covering their ears in anticipation of the earth-shattering explosion.

I could see the muscles tensing in Zizka's hand.

When the moment came, the gun jumped as if even it was surprised by the concussive shock and the cloud of acrid smoke that engulfed the sheriff's arm. The noise hit me like a solid blow to the chest, the same kind of jolt that caused my rude awakening on Friday morning, and the sulfurous smell of death wafted out into the street and assailed our noses and stung our eyes. Frightened babies started screaming in the nearby houses, and their mothers cursed us in the name of St. Vitus as the dogs began to howl.

Zizka's men moved in, waving their arms to disperse the smoke, and suddenly I was pressed on from all sides as everyone regardless of rank tumbled into the shop to get a look at the splattered pig's head. Someone stomped on my foot, but I concentrated on holding on to my purse strings as the sheriff's men forced the crowd back into the street. Finally, Zizka had them make an opening so that the three of us could come forward and examine the pig's head.

Rabbi Gans was the most experienced anatomist among us, so we let him go first and study the filthy creature close up. His eyes blazed with that old spark, and it felt just like when the two of us were Freethinkers back in Kraków and the spirit of the age flowed through us all: We were going to shatter superstitions and sweep away the darkness with the blazing light of observation and reason. It was a shame that he hadn't brought along one of his glass magnifiers.

There were no other marks on the swine's flesh besides the plain round hole in the pink, hairless hide, with a faint ring of dark particles around it, just like the girl's wound.

Rabbi Gans cocked his eyebrow and said, "Fascinating."

"It certainly looks like the same kind of wound," declared Rabbi Loew.

"That doesn't prove a thing," said Zizka. "It just tells us that the girl *might* have been shot with a gun that was similar to this one."

Suddenly he was a skeptic?

"Fair enough, Sheriff," I said. "But you know as well as I do that every weapon leaves a unique kind of wound. A knife leaves a slit, an épée leaves a triangular puncture, and that girl had a round gunshot wound in her left side just like this one. There aren't many people who have access to a gun like that, and it's something a Jew would not possess. Besides, as you have so ably demonstrated, you couldn't fire a gun like that within a furlong's distance of the ghetto without waking up a thousand people."

"And what does this suggest to you?" said Rabbi Loew.

"If I were to accept your premises," said Zizka, "it would suggest that the girl was shot at some distance from where she was eventually found."

"And then they rushed her to Federn's shop so they could dump her there," I said. "She hadn't even lost all her color yet."

"But what about the knife wound?"

"Obviously, the purpose of the knife wound was to drain some of her blood in order to create a plausible excuse for blaming it on the Jews," said Rabbi Loew.

"But why the two different weapons?" said Zizka.

I had my own thoughts about that: "It would fit with our assumption that even these hardened hired killers couldn't bring themselves to slit a little girl's throat. So they shot her first, right through the heart, then they finished the job after she was dead. But they were in a hurry, and they made a mess of it."

Not that there's a clean way of cutting someone's throat.

"What makes you think that they were hired?" asked Zizka. "What proof do you have?"

"None yet. Just the simple equation of an expensive gun and a piece of fine silver thread, which adds up to a wealthy person being involved in some way. And I don't know of anyplace on earth where the wealthy need to do their own killing."

A couple of the guards actually seemed to nod in agreement with me.

"Silver thread? What silver thread?" said Zizka.

"The emperor himself witnessed the discovery," said Rabbi Gans, and he began describing our visit to Emperor Rudolf's cabinet of wonders.

"Why are you so intent on pursuing this?" said Zizka.

"You mean, besides averting a communal disaster?" I said.

Rabbi Loew looked at the wounded pig's head, then back at the sheriff. He said, "Because someone has already cheated that poor girl once, and we would be cheating her a second time if we didn't seek out the cause of her death."

The townspeople trembled at the thought, and for a moment Hussite and Catholic were united in their mutual fear of vengeful spirits.

Rabbi Loew explained that anyone who cheats the living can still ask for forgiveness and make it up to the injured party, but anyone who cheats the dead can never be forgiven.

But Zizka wasn't listening. His eyes had taken on that faraway look of a man who has gone to a place deep inside himself, a place where convictions crumble under pressure and are reforged into enduring proofs that must be weighed on a just and true balance. And the scales were tipping.

"I must admit that it could have happened in the way that you describe it," said Zizka. "But we must—what was that word you used? *Investigate*. We must *investigate* more."

Eyes widened. I could almost hear the men and women thinking, *Did he just take their side?*

Then tongues began to wag. But it was a smaller percentage than I expected, so maybe we were actually making some converts among the folk.

Maybe we had a chance after all.

I told Zizka that if he really wanted to be a hero to his people, he should start looking for two men who came tearing through the streets early Friday morning from the direction of the waterfront in a butcher's cart filled with enough goods to conceal a sackful of rats and a dead body.

"To conceal *what*?"

"You heard me right the first time."

"I was afraid of that."

"Because if our reasoning is correct, there are a couple of cold-blooded murderers at large on the Christian side of town."

"More like a couple of hundred," Zizka muttered. "Why are you telling me all this?"

"We have a saying, Sheriff: *If there's a fire at your neighbor's house, you, too, are in danger.* It just depends on which way the wind is blowing."

The sheriff nodded as if he genuinely believed what I was saying. He told us that bargeloads of meat were transported every morning from the big slaughterhouses on the other side of the river. Then he gave the order to bring us back to the ghetto and make sure that we stayed there this time. For our own protection, he said.

The guards eagerly complied, corralling us and shoving us forward through the crowd.

In all the confusion, Anya suddenly appeared by my side and slipped something into my hand. The guards looked to Zizka, but he turned a blind eye to it, so they just shoved her out of the way with a few choice curses about blood and honor. As we were led down the street and the crowd began to disperse, I opened my fist and saw what she had given me. It was a folded slip of paper, and scrawled on the outside in Yiddish script were the words, *To be opened in the event of my death.*

CHAPTER 25

ANYA'S HEART WAS RACING, and her fingers tingled with a strange numbness, forcing her to concentrate as she fed the chunks of raw pork into the grinder.

Her mother collected the ground meat in a metal dish and added it to the contents of a large wooden mixing bowl.

Anya flipped the last slice of pork onto the cutting board with a wet slap, and carved it into strips. She felt a drop of cold sweat run trickling down the hollow of her back.

When all the meat was ground up, Anya switched over to grinding up the fennel seeds and other spices while her mother washed the vegetables.

Jirzhina said that the smell of the spices always reminded her of the time Anya was a little girl and she ate a whole jar of spiced peppers when her daddy was supposed to be watching her.

"I know, Mama. You've told me," said Anya. She let the familiar feel of slicing vegetables slip over her tired muscles like a well-worn blanket, a comfortable routine that meant that somehow, life was going on and all things were still possible.

"We used to keep you in a vegetable crate under the counter when you were only a few months old," said Jirzhina with a sigh, the same sigh she always made whenever she talked about bygone days. "And as soon as you learned how to walk, you figured out how to open the cash drawer and you threw all the money into the street."

"I guess the beggars were very happy that day," said Anya.

"On other days, too. You acted like the coins didn't belong in the store."

They mixed all the ingredients in the bowl until their hands were coated with globules of congealing pork fat, then they stuffed the skins with the prodigious portions of meat that made Cervenka's sausages known throughout the quarter as a sign of God's plenty, and the perfect way to celebrate His resurrection on Easter Day.

Anya and her mother carried the trays of fresh sausages into the shop, where Benesh was chatting with a couple of men in mud-spattered breeches. One of the men smiled at her. He had a broken tooth, and he stared at the sausages the way all the penniless wayfarers did, with a certain emptiness in his eyes.

"That was quite a show you put on before with that pig," he said, and suddenly he got the bright idea of reminding everyone about the time some butchers drove a herd of pigs from the docks all the way through Jew Town and what a terrific joke it had been. The two men laughed heartily, and they clearly expected Anya to laugh along with them. She smiled faintly.

"Don't worry about her," Jirzhina explained. "She's lovesick."

Oohs and *aahs* followed as predictably as night follows day and regret follows indulgence.

"I've got to go now, Mama," said Anya, heading back inside to wash the pork fat off her hands. She slipped more than a dozen sausages into a burlap sack to take with her as gifts—or more accurately, bribes. Then she packed a few other things she might need as well.

"Are you going to meet Janoshik and see the pageants in Old Town Square?" Jirzhina asked.

"Um . . . yes."

Anya didn't like having to lie to her mother. But she *was* heading to Old Town Square, eventually, and if the pageants happened to be passing through at the moment she was there, she would surely see them, so it was only half of a lie, really. But she had several other stops to make first.

"It sounded like he had something special planned for you," Jirzhina hinted.

But Anya was already on her way out the door.

The two men watched her go, as Benesh told them, "You can say what you want about the Jews, but no Jew ever stole anything from me."

The man with the broken tooth turned it into a joke about how Cervenka's famous pork sausages could be sold as magical charms to keep the Jews away.

Everything is a joke to such men, thought Anya. They could afford to joke. They didn't know what it was like to scurry around like a mouse in a house full of cats, expecting to be pounced on at any moment, which is exactly how she had felt ever since she handed that note to the Jewish *shammes* in front of a crowd of witnesses.

She wondered what all those Hebrew scribblings meant. She knew it was something important by the way Marie Janek had slipped the note to her without her husband's knowledge, saying that Janek kept it around "just in case." Anya only hoped the Jews could tell her what it all meant.

The first stop on her list was right next door.

The Kromys were arguing, as usual.

Ivana Kromy was a big woman who usually gave as good as she got from her thick-headed husband. But only what the Germans called a real *Hausdrache*, a house-dragon, could have held her own against him all the time.

Kromy was contending that it is God's will that the husband be the head of the wife, and that her first duty is obedience.

She answered by swinging a soup ladle at him, but he deflected it and smacked her so hard it made her eyes water. Her pale face looked like a ball of wet dough, with veiny red splotches providing the only color in the crevices around her nose and cheeks. Their six-year-old boy Hanuš jumped in and pummeled his father with his tiny fists. But Kromy swatted the boy away and took a stout switch down from the wall. The boy shrank back, knocking over a sack of turnips, which only made his father angrier. Kromy called the boy a worthless piece of garbage who would never amount to anything, just like his brother.

He emptied the dregs of a bucket of beer into a tankard and drained it. Then he wiped his mouth on his sleeve, and finally noticed Anya standing in the doorway.

"Well, what do you want?" he said.

Anya had come expecting to find Ivana alone, since Kromy was supposed to be on duty at this hour. She had planned to act as if she were dropping by to catch up on the latest gossip in order to find out what the guard's wife knew about Janek's involvement with Federn, but Kromy's presence changed all that.

"I brought you some *klobása* for Easter Day," she said, reaching into her sack and holding out her peace offering of half a dozen fat sausages.

"Give them here," said Kromy, snatching the string of sausages from her. He inspected them closely, smiled with approval, then ordered Ivana to fry them up for dinner. "I'm going to be hungry when I get back. There's some trouble at the South Gate to the *Židovské Město*."

"What kind of trouble?" asked Anya.

"Didn't you hear?" said Kromy, grinning as if he were enjoying her distress. "They arrested some more Jews for killing that girl."

"But I thought they already had that shopkeeper in custody—"

"You know as well as I do that there's no such thing as *one* guilty Jew," Kromy said, looking her over the same way he did the sausages.

"So we're supposed to keep the peace," he said, heading for the door. "Which always turns out to mean protecting the damn Jews. But orders are orders."

He drew himself up and sauntered out, but he didn't slam the door this time.

Anya watched him go, trying to think good Christian thoughts about him because she knew that's what she was supposed to do. Only God was in a position to judge another man's soul, and even a repellent human being with no visible redeeming qualities had just as much right to life as she did. But in her heart she also knew that no one would ever be safe from such insensitive brutes until their kind were banished from sight or buried six feet under ground.

When Anya turned back, little Hanuš was trying to set the straw seat of a chair on fire with a piece of kindling.

She tried to stop him: "No! Hanuš, don't—"

But before Anya could intervene, Ivana whirled around and slapped the stick of wood from the boy's hands, then she drew back and smacked him across the face as hard as she could.

And so it went with the Ivana and Josef Kromys of the world. Anya accepted that. What bothered her was that they were passing it on to the next generation.

She converted that thought into a useful strategy, and asked Ivana about her other children. Ivana wiped her eyes with a kerchief and said that she hadn't seen her eldest son Tomáš in a while because all he did was work on the docks all day and drink all night, and he didn't come around much anymore.

Anya said that it must be hard to accept, but Tomáš probably saw his share of filth and corruption working in a place like that, and Ivana cut her off to regale her with the latest dirt on how a secret society of Jewish merchants had figured out a way around the laws against selling new clothes to Christians by making a tiny rip in a brand-new set of apparel, then selling it as "used" clothing, then sewing up the rip in less than two minutes while the customer waited, and how she'd have given anything to see their faces when they were caught with the goods.

Once they got on to the topic, Anya learned more than she ever wanted to know about a variety of Jewish plots to annihilate the Christians once and for all. Did she know that a sinister cabal of Jewish alchemists had been stockpiling supplies for a scheme to poison the air with some kind of toxic smoke? Ivana couldn't explain precisely how this deadly cloud of smoke would be restricted to Christian houses, but she had no doubt that the Jews were clever enough to carry it off. Anya tried to steer the conversation toward Janek's association with Jacob Federn, but that only led to another tirade.

"How can you work for those Jews?" Ivana asked. "They're not like us."

"Oh, they are so very much like us," Anya replied.

"Except that they perform sorcery with Christian blood."

"No, they don't."

"Then what do they use—animal blood?"

A loud screech pierced the air. The little boy was pulling the cat's tail. Then he twisted it while the tormented animal tried to seek refuge under the table, and Ivana didn't lift a finger to stop the incessant caterwauling.

Anya left the Kromys' place in a rush, drawing more than her usual share of glances from shop windows and doorways. She felt their eyes on her back all the way down the block, their vigilance reminding her that some of the law books still punished the crime of sex between Christians and Jews with death by fire.

She visited the homes of several other wives of city guards, and from their widely disparate accounts of Janek's illicit ties to Jacob Federn, put it all together into a story that went something like this: Aside from the usual claims that each one owed the other money, Janek once tried to seduce the Jew's daughter Julie when she was only eleven or twelve years old, but she pushed him away and told her father, who threatened to expose Janek unless he was duly compensated. The price of Federn's silence was said to be a percentage of Janek's lucrative trade in imported herbs and spices, which was illegal since Federn wasn't a Christian burgher.

And with her sack emptied of sausages, she headed for the Old Town Square.

Some soldiers languishing on the fringes of Haštal Square tried to have some fun at her expense, but she told them to get out of her way or they'd learn how good she was with a butcher knife, and pushed right past them. They chuckled and complimented her spirit, and a pair of them showed their appreciation by removing their plumed hats and bowing as if a gracious lady were passing by.

She kept walking, putting some distance between herself and the watchful eyes of the well-meaning neighbors, until halfway down the block, when a hand came out of a doorway and grabbed her by the shoulder.

Anya's heart jumped and she pictured how far she could run before they caught her and dragged her back by the hair as she waited for the rigid voice of male authority to say, *You must come with me now, Fraulein.*

Instead it was a tiny female voice that said, *"Bitte sehr!* I've got to have a *Liebestrank* from the Jews. Can you get me one?"

Anya turned. "A what?"

Janoš Kopecky's kitchen maid Erika was cowering in the doorway as if she were afraid to be seen talking to her. "A love potion. Everyone knows the Jews have all kinds of recipes for love potions."

"What am I, the expert on all things Jewish?" said Anya.

"Well, aren't you—?"

"I don't really have time for this right now," said Anya, turning away.

The girl was devastated.

So Anya said, "Look, it's very simple. All you have to do is write your beloved's name on a piece of paper and hold it up to a candle flame until the paper starts to burn, and the person whose name you have written will burn with unquenchable desire for you."

The girl gave a tiny shiver of delight, but an instant later her worried look returned.

"But who will I get to write his name?"

Anya looked up and down the street, then stepped into the vestibule and took out a stubby pencil and a slip of paper. She tore off a tiny piece of paper and stood with the marvelous implement hovering in mid-air, poised to write.

"What's his name?"

"Janoš."

Anya stopped just short of making the first stroke of the *J*. It was a common enough name, but all the same she was about to ask the girl if she was sure she wanted to go ahead with this. The young maid sorely needed to have a heart-to-heart with someone.

But Anya had too many other things on her mind, so she wrote the name out carefully, letter by letter, folded the paper twice and handed it over.

The girl scurried away as if she were the fair damsel in a romance saga running off to join her gallant lover for a secret tryst.

Anya finally slipped unobserved into the crowd at Old Town Square, hiding beneath the streams of bright fabric hanging from the branches that were giving form to the wind and painting the air with flickering tongues of yellow and orange. The Church of Our Lady of Týn stood by impassively, her severe black spires sticking up like knife blades in the featureless sky. Merchants decorated their booths with parti-colored Easter eggs while the festive pageant wagons rolled through the middle of the crowd like ships borne aloft on a sea of upturned faces.

But Anya was not distracted by all the color and commotion, looking neither to the left nor to the right as she steered a course through the waves of people to that place where earlier in the day, one of the women in the pillory had called out something that sounded vaguely like her name. It had been too muffled for her to be certain, but she couldn't live with that doubt and she had to find out for sure.

She knew it as soon as their eyes met. Despite the mask, she recognized the brownish-green eyes, reddened with fatigue though they were. It was Kassy the wise woman who had called to her, and now she was a prisoner of the municipal authorities. The masked woman came forward as far as her restraints allowed, and kneeled as Anya approached the platform. Anya could barely make out what Kassy was saying because they had clamped a bit over her tongue, but she was able to slip her the pencil and paper to scribble down the essentials before the city guards stepped between them and shoved Kassy back with the butt-end of a pike.

Anya hurried away before they could question her and plunged back into the crowd, clutching the scrap of paper to her chest. When she had scrambled far enough away, she read the note and realized that Kassy had discovered the secret of the strange herbs, and that she had to deliver this message to the Jews right away. But she had one more thing to take care of first.

The nearest confessional was in the Church of the Holy Spirit.

She was hurrying up the steps to the church when a decrepit beggar rattled his cup at her.

She was about to rush past him without a second glance when the beggar said, "Going to confess now, aren't you?"

She stopped and looked him over with a critical eye, since so many of these beggars were charlatans skilled in the arts of painted scars and feigned injuries. But one of his legs was clearly stunted and shrunken from an old wound, and his outstretched hand looked like it had weathered nearly eighty winters or more.

"How did you—?"

"Late afternoon, last Mass before Easter, and a pretty young lady in a hurry," he said. "It always means a confession."

"And what if it does?"

"Maybe nothing. But if I were you, I'd watch what I said to the bastards."

Anya was shocked by the beggar's words. But then she saw the indelible mark, half-hidden under the worn sleeve on his right arm, of a single word spelled out in faded red letters: **Fryheit.**

The German word for *freedom*.

Which meant that he must have been a veteran of the great revolt, when thousands of armed peasants stood up to the nobles and paid for it with their blood.

Anya couldn't think of a reply. All she could do was reach into her apron and drop a coin into his cup with a helpless *plink*.

The church was cool and dark inside, and steeped in the age-old scent of sanctity, which embraced her like a lover and filled the whole of her being. The comforting smell enveloped her as the yellow chunks of incense gave themselves to the smoldering fires, and in doing so released the smoke that rose heavenward from the swinging censers and began the slow transformation to ashes.

The priest was droning on and on in a low voice, but she could barely follow what he was saying. Her eyes were fixed on the dark, narrow entrance to the confessional while the priest's Latin phrases paraded by like disembodied dancers in a strange carnival of emotions, their sounds elongated and stretched beyond meaning.

She had always been among the faithful who got swept up in the pageantry of the Church, and celebrated the act of prayer as the gift of joyous meditation that it was supposed to be, not as a dose of medicine to be gulped down with a shudder, a bitter pill to be endured.

But the beggar's words haunted her.

She sat there going over it all from the beginning as one Christian soul stepped out of the confessional booth and another took his place.

She heard the invocations, but except for the occasional *ora pro nobis*, which meant *pray for us*, the priest's words held as much meaning as the sound of pebbles dropping into a fast-moving river, and she wished that she could simply open the Good Book and read the passages aloud for herself and for others. But even if they let her come forward and sully its illuminated pages with her dish maid's hands, she would find that it was written in that same archaic and inaccessible cipher as always.

Anya watched the fragrant wisps of smoke curling lazily around the pedestal supporting the closed book, and she thought back to the gentle way that Yankev had instructed her in the ways of the Bible.

But the dove found no rest, he had said, his voice warm and penetrating as he indulged her desires and patiently showed her how to sound out the phrases in the Noah story of the Book of Genesis. Then he explained that this passage also meant that Israel will dwell among the nations, but her people will find no rest among them.

And she relived the moment he first read to her from the Prophets: *But the Lord said to Samuel, Pay no attention to his appearance or his stature*, he said, the holy words resonating around their makeshift study table next to Mrs. Meisel's pantry, and he prompted her to read the rest. And as she slowly put the sounds together into words, it felt like she was absorbing the greatest magical power ever invented right through her skin. She could feel it suffusing throughout her body and coursing freely through her veins, and she still remembered every word of that passage: *For things are not as man sees them; a person sees only what is visible, but the Lord sees into the heart.*

And when Yankev saw her eyes glistening with emotion, he told her one of his Midrash stories about a princess who married a kind but simple man from a remote village. But the princess was always sad, even though the man always gave her the best bowl of porridge in the village. *Nu? What did he expect? She was a princess!* She had tasted delicacies from all over the world, and she would *never* be satisfied with the "best" porridge his tiny village could offer. In this same way, Yankev explained, man's eternal soul will never be satisfied with material wealth, because the best this world has to offer can't compare with the sublime and everlasting beauty of the World-to-Come. And so all those deluded souls who seek to satisfy their earthly appetites with riches and comforts are like that foolish man who could never figure out why the best bowl of porridge he could provide would never satisfy his princess.

The curtain parted and the confessional awaited, dark and beckoning, like the mouth of a subterranean passage to another realm, a portal to another world.

She needed to reach out to that world, and she couldn't do it by just sitting there feeling sorry for herself.

So Anya got up and left the church. She ran down the steps, sweeping past the beggar as she raced homeward.

She couldn't do what she needed to do without first letting her parents know where she was going.

But as she turned down the lane where her parents lived, she saw Janoshik standing with the sullen priest he had threatened to denounce her to the day before. Janoshik pointed her out, and when the two men started toward her, a small cry escaped from her lips, and she turned right around and ran straight to the ghetto without looking back.

Smoke was rising in the distance, but it seemed as if the fires had already been extinguished.

She was panting for breath when she reached the East Gate and announced to the stunned guards that she wanted to be allowed inside.

"Huh?"

"You're sure about this?" they said.

"I am."

"Because this is a one-way gate, sweetheart."

"Just let me in."

They opened the small door a crack, and let her squeeze through the narrow gap and slip inside the ghetto.

She ran through the streets as if guided by some instinctual force until she found Benyamin the shammes. His face was scratched and his muddy clothing smelled of smoke.

"What happened?" she said. "Where's Yankev? Have you seen him?"

"I'm sorry to have to tell you this," he said evenly. "He's been arrested."

CHAPTER 26

I SMOOTHED OUT THE NOTE as flat as I could on the rabbi's table, hoping that a couple of missing letters might be revealed in the paper's creases and bring some sense to the matter. But it didn't help any. Aside from Federn's signature at the bottom, the message appeared to be a random string of words:

Be strong . . . stifle . . . something . . . *light together with darkness . . .* something something something.

"It must be a code of some kind," said Rabbi Gans.

As soon as the sheriff had escorted us back to the East Gate, I unfolded the note the butcher's daughter had given me. She must have gotten it from the Janeks, and Rabbi Loew decided on the spot that our first priority was deciphering this strange message, so once again I had to put off talking to Mordecai Meisel about who his biggest debtors were.

"Maybe it's an acrostic," said Rabbi Gans.

"I can't think of any words that start with *amakh*," I said, stringing together the first three initial letters, א-מ-ך or a-m-kh.

"Then maybe it's an *at-bash* acrostic. In that case, the initial letters would be *tes-khof-mem*—" His voice trailed off. There weren't any words beginning with that combination, either.

"Or a simple substitution where each letter stands for the one next to it?" I proposed. *Beys-nun-lamed*? Another linguistic dead end.

"First of all, are we sure that's Federn's signature?" I asked.

"It certainly looks like it. Besides, who else could have written it?"

Rabbi Loew had been sitting quietly at the table, stroking his beard and studying the document. Our speculations trailed off and we found ourselves paying attention to his silence.

"Take a moment to look at the words," said Rabbi Loew. "Look at them. Each word has a unique meaning."

"Forgive me, Rabbi, but how is *oymets* unique?" I said, indicating to the first group of letters. "It appears in many places."

"As a verb," said Rabbi Loew. "As a noun it only occurs in one place."

"But how do we know which it is without context?"

"Here is your context. Look at the next word."

Oymets means to show might or courage, as in, *One people shall be mightier than the other*, in *Breyshis*, or, *Only be strong and very courageous*, in Joshua. As a noun, it would mean something like *fortitude*.

The next word was *makhanok*. If I treated it as another verb turned into a noun, then its meaning would shift from *strangle* to *strangulation*. Was this the pattern he wanted me to see? The next word was *kelekh*. I had seen it somewhere before, but I couldn't remember where. The term was so rare that I had forgotten its meaning. I looked over the rest of the document and confirmed the pattern. Even the phrase *or im khoyshekh* was unusual.

I said, "Each one of these words is extremely rare."

"Better than that," said Rabbi Loew. "Each one of these words or phrases occurs only once in the whole of Scripture. Moreover, they all occur in a single book."

I studied the word formations again, trying to conjure up the relevant phrases. My eye ran over the second word about eight times until I remembered where I had seen it: *My soul craved strangulation, preferred death to life. I loathe it. I shall not live forever; leave me alone, for my days are emptiness.* Only one man in the whole of the Tanakh spoke like that. All the way from the Land of Utz, the man we know as Iyov, whom the Christians call Job.

"All of these words are from the *Seyfer Iyov*." The Book of Job, which as I recalled, uses *kelekh* to mean both ripe old age and faded strength.

"And the secret to cracking this code is that all these words are unique," said Rabbi Gans.

"As unique as Job himself," said Rabbi Loew. "A man so complex he is given more distinctive attributes than our own father Abraham."

"Complex and bitter," I said. "But how is that relevant to our situation?"

"Where do you think his bitterness comes from?"

"Where else should it come from? He's been abandoned by everyone, including his wife."

"Not so. His three friends remain," said Rabbi Gans.

Friends who only know how to talk, not to listen.

"More than that," said Rabbi Loew, "Job admits that he has never felt secure, or at peace, that he has lived his life in constant fear of disaster in a world that is ruled by blind fate rather than a just God. He still doesn't realize that God may have chosen to increase his suffering in order to teach him something, the same way that a little discipline is good for a child's education."

"You don't learn anything by getting smacked," I said. "It doesn't teach you anything except how much it hurts to get smacked."

Rabbi Loew sat there tapping his middle finger and avoiding eye contact. "You have a great deal of the serpent's bile in your innards, Ben-Akiva. And you mustn't let it eat away at you. Look at these other words—*or im khoyshekh, metil, kidoydey, soysokh*. They refer to eternity and to God's most powerful earthly creatures, the gentle beast known as Behemoth and the terrible serpent whose name is Livyoson."

Or, the Leviathan.

"But nobody is even sure what *metil* means," I protested. "Rashi calls it a *burden* and Ramban calls it a *sledgehammer*. *Kidoydey* probably means sparks, *soysokh* some kind of slingstones or catapult. What does that have to do with—"

The dragon-like creature from my dream.

Rabbi Loew nodded as if he had read my mind. "Perhaps now we can begin to interpret your dream, my *talmid*. Ramban says that we will curse the day that man's destructive nature wakes the fearsome Livyoson from his slumber. But God makes a promise that whoever takes on the challenge of fighting the Livyoson shall be rewarded."

"Fight the Livyoson?" I said.

Canst thou draw out Livyoson with a hook, or press his tongue down with a cord? Canst thou put a hook into his nose? Who can pry open the doors of his face? His fangs are terrible all around. Flames spew from his mouth, kidoydey *leap out. Strength lives in his neck. He treats iron like straw, brass like rotted wood. He will not flee before an arrow. He looks upon the* soysokh *as so much straw, he laughs at the shaking of a spear.*

"How can anyone fight such a creature?"

"That's what most men would say. And yet these same men, who can't find the courage to challenge one of God's own creatures, presume to challenge the ways of God Himself. But you are different from them, Ben-Akiva. You have the strength to face such an adversary."

"But God will listen to a rational argument. A sea monster doesn't respond to such—"

"There is something that you are not seeing, Ben-Akiva. It has been suggested that the Livyoson represents man's aggressive nature. It could therefore be said to represent the Evil Impulse itself. Why, then, did God make him?"

The *Tehillim* say, *livyoson zeh yotsarto l'sakhek boy.* There is the Leviathan You formed to play with.

"The Psalms of David say that God made Livyoson to be His companion. So the most fearsome creature on earth is a mere plaything for Him. But if we pursue your line of reasoning, it also could mean that God created the Evil Impulse for his own amusement."

"And what could possibly account for that?"

"My guess would be that things were getting pretty boring up in Heaven."

"Angels don't get bored," said Rabbi Gans.

"How would you know?"

Rabbi Loew kept up the inquiry. "What does Rabbi Samuel ben Nakhman say about the Evil Impulse?"

I quoted Rabbi Samuel: *"If it weren't for the Evil Impulse, no man would build a house, marry a wife, beget children, or engage in trade."*

"Exactly. You can't slay this beast because it lives inside your own breast. Livyoson is the anger raging within you, with no mind or soul directing it, not some sea monster to be frightened of. But unless you learn to conquer it, this inner serpent will eventually rise up and destroy you. So what you need to do is absorb the best part of it while leaving its irrational and destructive part behind. You must harness its strength, its determination, its perseverance, and use them to your benefit, because the difference between raw power and controlled power is like the difference between a wildfire that destroys a whole neighborhood and the metallurgist's smelting fire that purifies the finest gold. Once you have learned to channel this power, you shall find great strength within yourself and be like Rabbi Hanina ben Dosa, about whom they say, *Woe unto the man who meets up with a venomous lizard, and woe unto the venomous lizard who meets up with Rabbi Hanina ben Dosa*."

I found it hard to believe that Federn intended to send me such a profound and detailed message. His wife said he was no great scholar, but then, who am I to say? When the Angel of Death comes and takes away your only cow, who can say that he didn't originally come for *you*?

"There is one other phrase in the *Seyfer Iyov* that does not recur in Scripture," said Rabbi Loew, returning to the document on the table before him. "*At this my heart trembles, leaping from its place*. The absence of this expression from our list is most curious, and forces us to ask why it was not included with the others to form a complete list of the unique words in the *seyfer*. Clearly it deserves special attention."

There it was again, that unmistakable mystical logic, which Rabbi Loew used to pull all the disparate elements of the message together into this spiritually uplifting summary of its contents: *He who gathers the strength to strangle the opposition and defeat the enemy within will live to a ripe old age, even to eternity. The heart leaps at the thought, but first, you must harness the iron pillars of Behemoth and the fiery sparks of Livyoson, and then, like them, you will fear nothing, not even the most dreadful machines of war.*

Rabbi Loew's explanation of the deeper meaning of this message was interrupted by the frantic, Sabbath-breaking clanging of the bell in the Jewish Town Hall only a block away—the only such "Jewish" bell in all of Europe.

We dropped everything and ran out into the street. Markas Kral, the shammes from the Pinkas Shul, came running up the Narrow Lane and told us that a fracas had broken out at the South Gate. The city guards had shown up with arrest warrants bearing the names of several prominent rabbis and were demanding to be allowed entry. A mob of *Judenschläger* had gathered under a homemade battle flag, and were threatening to storm the ghetto if the guards weren't allowed in.

By the South Gate. Near Reyzl's house.

I reached inside the doorway and grabbed the big wooden *kleperl*, then I set off in the direction of the Narrow Lane. Others followed.

"Whose names were on the warrants?" asked Rabbi Gans.

"You're on the list yourself," Kral answered. "Right after Rabbi Horowitz, Rabbi Loew, and Rabbi Sheftels."

I slowed down. "Rabbi *Abraham* Sheftels is here in Prague?" I said. He, too, had studied with Isserles.

"You know who else is here?" said Gans. "Rabbi Jaffe."

"He's on the list, too," said Kral.

Rabbi Mordecai Jaffe, former President of the Council of the Four Lands, had also studied with the great ReMo.

"They're arresting all the Freethinkers," said Rabbi Gans, like a prophet announcing a dark epiphany.

"And anyone else who has been a thorn in the side of the town leadership," said Rabbi Loew, since he was not a Freethinker, but was on the list as well.

"All except the newcomer."

"Right," I said. "Who knew that being ignored could be such a blessing?"

"There appears to be a pattern to all this," said Rabbi Loew. "And we must ask ourselves who would benefit from denouncing all their major political opponents to the Christian authorities?"

"You're not suggesting that our fellow Jews would do such a thing?" said Rabbi Gans.

"It's an awfully one-sided list."

I took my leave and hurried along toward Reyzl's neighborhood.

Halfway down the block, Jews were abandoning their homes and fleeing to the Meisel Shul, which the emperor had just designated as a sanctuary.

I broke into a run.

Acosta the watchman came charging all the way from the East Gate leading a small group of men carrying hooked poles and oxhides. He intercepted me and told me to turn around and head to the Schächtergasse to alert the butchers.

"Send someone else," I said, stepping around him.

But I stopped short when Rabbi Loew called my name quite sharply and told me to go and escort the orphans to safety. He had gotten word from a nun called Sister Marushka that she had convinced the Christian authorities to grant the orphans temporary asylum in the Agnes Convent, and it was my job to deliver them to her outside the South Gate. I admit that I had been hoping to rush in and heroically rescue my wife from an ugly situation and somehow win back her favor. But that childish fantasy had to yield to the call to save upwards of thirty innocent children from witnessing another human sacrifice on a mass scale.

I rushed up Belelesgasse to the orphanage, thinking about the endless litany of *Kaddish* prayers for absent parents that must emanate from that roomful of children. But when I walked in, they were having their matzoh and broth and listening to a lesson on what to do if they are ever confronted by a demon (one solution: always carry a coin or two to buy it off).

Even the mindless mob of idiots should allow a group of orphans to pass through unmolested, I thought. But the children knew that something was up. A strange man had interrupted their lesson, and their eyes grew wide with wonder. I wished I could do more for them. I would have given anything to take just *one* boy or girl away from here and give them a warm, loving home. But then I'd have to leave the rest behind, and I couldn't do *that* either.

So I told the children I was taking them someplace special where they would be safer until things returned to normal. Then I herded them together like a flock of lambs and set off down the Narrow Lane toward the South Gate, holding the *kleperl* aloft like a shepherd's crook and fending off the flood of refugees streaming in the opposite direction. I always seemed to be swimming against the tide in this place.

The runoff from yesterday's rains had inundated the area, and the lower end of the street was a sea of mud. The small door to the gate was partway open, and a handful of defenders gathered around Rabbi Loew like the last remaining pieces in a chess game protecting their king as he stood with his foot on the threshold calling Sister Marushka's name and demanding to know the charges against himself and his fellow rabbis.

The sergeant of the guard replied that all of the men on his list were wanted for illegal possession of the proscribed and heretical books of Rabbi Moses ben Maimon, also known as Maimonides.

"Books you can't even read," Acosta said, and he spat in the mud.

Rabbi Loew lamented the shortsightedness of his accusers. Hadn't they learned that wherever they burn the books of Rabbi Moses ben Maimon, eventually they will burn the Talmud and even the Bible itself? Even the freedom-loving Parisians had been goaded into burning twenty-four cartloads of Talmudic writings in a single day.

Acosta saw me approaching with a swarm of children in tow.

"I ask for butchers and you bring me orphans," he said, with his palms turned up like a merchant appraising a shipment of bruised cabbages.

"But at least you brought something," he added, nodding toward the *kleperl*. "I brought these—"

He opened his cloak and showed me a pair of well-worn cutlasses tucked into his belt.

"I thought we weren't allowed to carry swords," I said, pointing to one of his weapons.

"That's not a sword, it's an exceptionally large dagger."

A bystander with the closely cropped hair and beard of one of Rabbi Aaron's disciples saw this display and reprimanded Acosta: "On Shabbes, a man should not go out with a sword, a bow, a shield, a lance, or a spear."

"Only if they're being used as tools or implements," I said. "It's acceptable if they're ornaments."

"So they're ornaments, all right?" Acosta told the bystander, who frowned and turned away in disgust.

"Do me a favor," Acosta said.

"Anything."

"When I die, don't bury me anywhere *near* that schmuck."

"Sure, if that's what you really want."

"Swear it."

"All right, I swear."

"Good. You know, I've been working in Rabbi Loew's house for a couple of years now, and I've never had a moment to study with him. Maybe I'll get to study with him in the World-to-Come."

"Don't get ahead of yourself. The *Zohar* says that if we are to be destroyed, it will never be on Shabbes."

But time was passing, and our shadows were growing longer by the minute. Shabbes would be ending within the hour.

Rabbi Loew appealed to the populace to show some compassion and let the orphans through, but the *Judenschläger* weren't having any of it, buzzing and jeering at his concern for the sad-faced children of exile.

Acosta's lips tightened and his face grew white, as he kept his fury just below the surface like an old world thunder god, waiting for the moment to strike. All he said was, "I once saw a crowd of Castilians torture a full-grown ox just for fun. They do things like that. That's their idea of entertainment."

He took several deep breaths while the sergeant of the guard tried to persuade the crowd to allow the orphans to leave the ghetto unharmed. Where on earth was Sister Marushka?

"Enough of this," Acosta said to me. "There is a time to lay down the glove and take up the sword."

"Only trouble is they have a lot more swords than we do."

"Better a noble death than a wretched life."

"That's a mighty fine sentiment, but are you sure you're ready for this?"

"One hundred percent ready. How about you?"

"One can never be one hundred percent ready for anything like this. It's not possible."

"All right, I'm ninety-eight percent ready. You?"

"I'm the other two percent. Let's go."

Acosta gave a tight smile. "I promise to put in a good word for you with God the next time I see Him."

The two of us led the children forth into the crowd, which grudgingly parted, standing like a wall on either side of us. And as we marched into their midst, I finally spotted Sister Marushka waiting for us at the other end of the gauntlet.

Our enemies watched the children closely, as if they were counting heads of cattle. Suddenly a shout went up.

"Hey!"

"Hold on there—!"

One of the *Judenschläger* elbowed past the guards and laid his hand on a lump of fabric crawling along amid the cluster of children. He grabbed on with both hands and effortlessly hauled a grown man to his feet. Yankev ben Khayim popped into view looking pale and petrified, his knees barely holding him up.

"What the hell is this?"

"Please don't—"

"See how they repay our kindness us with deception and trickery!" said a town official, who must have gotten it straight from one of those anti-Jewish pamphlets, because I couldn't believe that anybody really talks like that.

The *Judenschläger* descended on Yankev ben Khayim, others made for

Rabbi Loew. We had no time to think. Acosta plunged into the crowd, trying to save Yankev. To their everlasting credit, the city guards closed in to protect the children and deliver them into the arms of Sister Marushka, while I waded into the sea of bodies, beating a path to Rabbi Loew.

A couple of Christian *bulvans* were setting a pair of dogs on him. I charged into the men, knocking them to the mud, then drew back and smacked one of the dogs as hard as I could with the club and sent him off with a swift kick in the rear. The other dog growled and leapt at me. I held out my left forearm for it to latch onto but all it got was a mouthful of gaberdine, and as the damned thing tried to sink its teeth into my flesh, I grabbed its front paw with my free hand and yanked up sharply until I heard a pop. The dog yelped and dropped to the ground. I shook my club at him, and he showed more sense than some people I know and limped away.

The two men came back at me. I lunged at them with the *kleperl*, jabbing one in the stomach with the sharp end of the stick and kneeing him in the face when he doubled over. As the other man closed in on me, I faked a jab at his face, and when he held up his arms to block me, I spun the shaft around and hooked him by the ankle and yanked him off his feet.

I threw my arm around Rabbi Loew and half-carried him through the small door to safety. Then something clubbed me from behind and I went down in the mud, pain shooting through my shoulder.

The mob tried to push through the small door, but Acosta's crew fought them off.

I groped around in the mud until a hand reached down to help me. Waves of pain spiraled through my shoulder. I slowly raised my hand, my quivering fingers drawing upward at the promise of a friendly encounter, when that other hand inexplicably closed in mid-air, without my fingers in it, and my arm sank back into the mire. The face of the bystander with the close-cropped hair loomed over me.

"I'd be happy to help you *tomorrow*," he said. "But never on Shabbes. On Shabbes, we need not seek protection, for Shabbes itself protects us."

The face drifted away and silence filled its place.

I knew it wasn't right, but I couldn't help feeling that if by some miracle I managed to survive this day, I was going to remember precisely which members of the community had turned their backs on me when I needed them the most, or promised to help me but never did.

I twisted around and looked up the block for any sign of reinforcements, but the street was deserted, except for a couple of terrified observers peeking around the corner at Joachimstrasse. They looked like servants from the Rozanskys' house, but I couldn't really tell from where I was lying.

I sat up, rubbing my shoulder, and slowly got to my feet.

Outside the gate, the municipal authorities were leading Yankev away under heavy guard, which undoubtedly saved his life, or at least prolonged it by a day or two. And it looked like Sister Marushka was being allowed to guide the children to safety.

But Acosta was surrounded. He was keeping a ring of twenty men at bay by jabbing and slicing at the air between them, spinning around to threaten the ones creeping up behind him, and cursing them all in the harshest Judeo-Spanish idiom. You didn't have to know a word of Ladino to get the gist of it. They had vastly superior numbers and a plentiful supply of weapons, but rather than get in close, they decided to pelt him with stones. And before I could get enough feeling back in my shoulder to hold a weapon effectively, sharp stones clipped him in the ear and over the eyebrow. The wound over his eyebrow started to bleed profusely, then time slowed down as he took one in the neck— his neck bone jerked aside, and all of a sudden he turned into a limp sack of human skin, stumbling forward, already beginning the awful transition from a vibrant human being to a wet hunk of meat, fat, and bone.

He went down, and the mob fell on him, poking, kicking, and stabbing, while others stood off to the side and did nothing. And never before had I understood so strongly how there are times when doing nothing can be a deadly sin.

The rest of the mob turned on us. A few more Jews had turned out to help, but only five of us were armed—with inferior weapons—and my right arm was still tingling, so we couldn't hold them off for long, and they soon overran us and the looters poured into the ghetto. Some of them began prying the mezuzahs from the doorposts, either for the silver and brass or for the magical properties that some Christians ascribe to them. Others smashed shop windows and grabbed what they could. They shattered mugs, glasses, and other vessels as they plundered the shops searching for the gold that they *knew* the Jews were hoarding.

There just *had* to be more gold in the ghetto.

The Jews were sitting on a mountain of gold.

Oh, they're clever, all right, the cheap bastards. They've got it hidden somewhere.

A shopkeeper stood by watching the invaders destroy his livelihood. He did not try to interfere as they shredded his ledger and tossed it into the gutter.

He calmly addressed one of the looters: "So, Václav, I guess you don't owe me four-and-a-half dalers anymore."

The man could only stare back for a moment before continuing the rampage.

They also ransacked a print shop. Unable to find gold, they turned their wrath on the books, tearing the covers off and sending loose pages flying out the window into the mud. The galleys for Rivka bas Meyer's *Meynekes Rivka* were scattered like a deck of playing cards, her guide for housewives on baby and child care fluttering down together with a set of pages depicting two angels supporting a shield embossed with a pair of hands giving the priestly blessing. The largest word on the page was just beneath the angels, and even upside down from twenty feet away I could tell that it said בראשית. *In the beginning*.

Proof of the *Zohar*'s observation that if there is quarreling among men, even God's anger does not frighten them.

Then one of the raiders came across a large book full of magical symbols and markings in thick black letters an inch high that looked like this: עבדים. *Slaves*. He tore out a fistful of pages, till he got to a page showing a group of men in European clothing chopping up infants and filling a tub with their blood so that a queen could bathe in it.

It was an ordinary set of woodcuts illustrating the place in the Haggadah where the Egyptians butcher and drown the male children of Israel in the Nile. But to the Christian illiterates, it must have looked like a bunch of men in modern dress slaughtering babies and collecting their blood, and they saw this fanciful image as indisputable proof that the Jews practice ritual murder.

They screamed like madmen and held up the offending book to the crowd, whose demands quickly became a chant: *Burn the book! Burn it!*

Their outrage knew no bounds. They broke apart the store's shelving and tore up the floorboards in order to start a bonfire in the middle of the street with books and anything else that would burn.

The Christians ignored us in their frenzy. No one bothered us as we stood around, helplessly watching the flames grow hotter, since it was suicide to step in against fifty men, at odds of eight-to-one against.

At least the cool, wet mud would keep the fire from spreading to the nearby houses, for the moment.

But they had already taken the life of a man whose like is not to be found the whole world over, and unless they allowed us to retrieve his body, there would be no one to wail over his coffin.

One of the Christians spotted a trickle of silver flowing from the bonfire, a sure sign that someone had missed a bauble and thrown it into the fire with the rest of the trash.

And the Lord heard our voice, and remembered His covenant with Abraham.

I felt them before I heard them, as a vibration under the soles of my feet like the pulse of a beating heart.

All eighteen members of the butcher's guild and their apprentices came streaming down the street with a force six men wide and four rows deep brandishing meat cleavers, bone saws, and flaming torches. Every butcher in the *Yidnshtot* was marching shoulder-to-shoulder behind the emblem of their guild, a massive heavy metal key topped by the figure of a lion wielding a sharp ax, and there was no space between them.

They saw the fire, and charged the mob with butcher knives and torches held high, raising a fierce battle cry.

The no-goodniks looked upon their foes and froze.

The moment had arrived.

While our enemies readied themselves for the frontal assault, my four comrades and I belted out a war cry and attacked from the side.

Torches blazed and smoked, blades swished and slashed, hooks caught slivers of bleeding flesh, and the invaders soon decided that they didn't want to die for a handful of melted silver.

The *Judenschläger* taunted us as they retreated, saying that they had taught us a lesson so we wouldn't hold up our heads so high the next time we saw them coming.

We used the hooks to pull down the bonfire, then we kicked the logs around in the mud and smothered the flames with the oxhides.

The *Judenschläger* withdrew through the shattered door, but said they'd be back tomorrow with a hundred men for every man who was here with them today. Right after Easter Mass at Our Lady of Terezín, which ends at midday.

I said that the municipal authorities had given us until sundown on Easter Day.

And they said that *they* were giving us until midday.

I asked the sergeant if we could at least recover the body of our friend.

"No. He had illegal weapons on him. He was a lawbreaker, so we will leave him for the birds."

And that's exactly what they did.

Rabbi Loew stepped out of the narrow confines of the stairwell that had served as his refuge during the mayhem and surveyed the damage. The mob had completely gutted a couple of shops and torn up a couple more, going through them for whatever they could scavenge, not exactly working with a fine-toothed comb.

"What should we do, Rabbi?" I asked.

"We do as Rabbi Hillel said. We close the gates, and we do not rely on a miracle."

CHAPTER 27

ERIKA'S HEART WAS TWITTERING like a hummingbird's as she hurried down the Langergasse with the name of her beloved clutched in her fist. She could feel the force of the magic writing surging through her palm, as if the ink itself were pulsating with power.

Why wasn't that butcher girl working for a rich and influential burgher? she wondered. With all her knowledge of word writing and such, why was Anya Cervenka still working for Meisel, that Jew? How could she stand being that *close* to them? Of course, the master's wife always looked very kindly upon the Jews, but she was an ignorant cow who obviously didn't know any better. Anya was *smart*.

Master Kopecky's private chambers were growing cold, so he was receiving visitors while propped up in his large ceremonial bed in the sitting room, wrapped in a velvet gown and several layers of soft woolen blankets. The two *Reiters* paced around in their muddy boots, describing some street fight they had witnessed with great passion and glee, laughing and swearing and punching the air with their fists to punctuate their story.

"But in all fairness, those Jews put up a pretty good fight."

"They did all right."

"I think they defended themselves bravely."

"Ha! We'll see how brave they are tomorrow."

Erika rolled her eyes at the thought of the Jews distinguishing themselves at anything besides devilry and theft.

She stole into the larder at her first opportunity, set a candle on the table, and finally let her fingers open like the petals of a newborn daisy. Her palms were a little moist, so the paper stuck to her skin and she had to peel it away. She hoped that it would still burn the way it was supposed to. She smoothed the paper, caressing it with her fingertips as if it were her lover's skin, then held it up before the flame so the light would pass through and bathe the name of her beloved with a golden glow. She could feel her pulse pounding between her thumb and forefinger, but the bit of paper barely trembled as she moved it closer and finally let it dip into the white-hot center of the flame. The paper went up in a flash, and stuck to her fingers as she tried to shake it loose.

The door swung open as the last stubborn bit of the paper flew from her fingers and fluttered to the floor in a swirl of smoke and ash.

The other maids laughed at her, and told her to get busy churning the cream for the master's supper.

She followed the maids back to the kitchen and poured the cream into a big porcelain bowl. She found a whisk and started stirring the cream with it. But when the cook sent her back to the larder for some more sugar, she took the long way around so she could peek into the master's sitting room. And on the way back, the long-awaited miracle occurred.

"Who's puttering around out there?" said Master Kopecky.

She stepped into the doorway, turning slightly to show off her profile. "It is I, my lord. How may I be of service?"

The master needed a moment to think about that. "What have you got in your hand?"

"Sugar, my lord. For the whipped cream."

"Is that what you're supposed to be doing now?"

"Yes, my lord."

He told her to go to the kitchen, get the bowl of cream, and bring it back with her. He said his wife wouldn't be back from church for at least another hour and he wanted someone to keep him company while he read.

Some wife, she thought. Erika could hear everything through the walls, and she knew that the master and his lady's conjugalities were so infrequent that their marriage was barely valid under German common law as far as she was concerned. Now, if *she* were in her lady's place, well, things would be a lot different.

She sat down by his bedside and stirred the cream until it started to thicken. She stuck her finger in the bowl and licked the cream off it. It still needed more sugar. She poured some in and kept stirring.

The master read to her from an old book of pious stories, choosing a cautionary tale in verse about a group of villainous Jews who lived off foul usury and villainy.

"Our first foe, the serpent Satanas, That hath in Jews' hearts his wasp's nest," he began, as she beat the cream harder.

These Jews conspired to stamp out the world's innocence, one child at a time.

"This cursed Jew seized a child and held him fast, And cut his throat and in a pit him cast."

She stuck her finger in the bowl and licked the cream off again. It still needed more whipping.

"I say that in a privy they him threw—"

She drew in a breath and felt herself blush.

"What's the matter?" he asked. "The word *privy*?"

"Ooh, my virgin ears," she said, playing at being bashful.

He smiled at her little game.

"Interesting," he said, leaning in for a closer look. "Tell me, what other virgin orifices do you have?"

She stopped stirring the cream, stuck in her finger and slowly licked off the sweet, heavy cream. It was ready to eat.

A few moments later, the master opened a small drawer in the bedside table and took out a shiny silver band. He offered it to her and promised that there would be more.

Then his voice became a bit earthier, as if his tongue had thickened, and he said, "And now, as they say in the Good Book, the wolf shall lie down with the lamb."

CHAPTER 28

"I'M GOING TO HELL, aren't I?" said Anya.

"There are worse places," I said.

"Like where Yankev is right now?"

"Don't worry. I'm sure that we'll be able to bail out your boyfriend one way or another."

She sucked in her breath with an audible *huh!*

"How did you know?" she whispered.

"Some things can't be hidden."

She lowered her eyes. The paving stones had been torn up to build the barricades, leaving the street full of mud puddles.

"I can't go back home now," she said. "You know that, right?"

I nodded. I was well aware of what she had given up for us, and I saw the despair in her face reflected in the puddles. I needed to ask what she had learned about the Janeks, but that could wait another minute. My heart was telling me to put my hand on her shoulder, but I had to draw it back again.

I said, "I want you to know that God will reward you for this, and that He will love you more than the rest of the nation of Israel."

"You're just saying that to make me feel better."

"No, it's in the Midrash. It says the Jews had to witness the parting of the

Red Sea and the thunder and lightning at Mount Sinai in order to accept the Torah. But the convert who saw none of these things, yet chooses to accept the Torah, is dearer to God than His own Chosen People."

"Do you really think there's room in this world for two people like Yankev and me?"

"Of course there is. Maybe deep in the Ukraine somewhere, but there's got to be a place for you out there. You didn't . . . uh . . . ?"

"No, we didn't."

"Good. That makes it easier."

"He said I was forbidden fruit."

"Right. And we all remember what happened the last time."

She rewarded me with a smile, then she gathered a handful of material from my mud-spattered cloak and rolled it between her thumb and forefinger. "Why don't you come with me to Meisel's house and we'll get all this mud washed off your clothes?"

"And what am I supposed to wear while waiting for them to dry? I don't have anything else—"

Someone was knocking on the East Gate.

"Who goes there?" barked the watchman. But he took one look through the peephole and rushed to unbar the small door, which creaked open to let in two broken women. Freyde and Julie Federn barely had the strength to step over the sill and limp through the door, clutching each other for support. They looked like the emaciated figures in a Christian painting of the Last Judgment.

Something else was odd about their appearance, and it took me a moment to realize that Julie's eyebrows were missing, and that the outline of her head beneath her kerchief was far too smooth, which meant that it must have been shaved completely bald.

We rushed over to help. Anya took Julie's arm and swung it over her shoulder like a girl who was used to carrying heavy cuts of meat, and Freyde practically collapsed in my arms.

Since their home had been looted and burned, we brought Freyde and Julie to Rabbi Loew's house, where the remaining servants took them in. I followed close behind, but Rabbi Loew pulled me aside and told me to go out and call the people to shul for the *minkhe* services.

"But I need to hear what the women have to say."

"It is better for them to be with other women right now. Besides, your duties as shammes are more important."

He said that because the afternoon service on Shabbes is the holiest moment of the week, when the *Riboyne shel Oylem* pays the closest attention to our prayers. So I made my rounds as fast as I could, going from door to door and knocking only twice instead of three times to let people know that there had been a death—Acosta's death. And behind all those closed doors, I heard tears and comforting voices, prayers for salvation, and parents making hasty marriage arrangements for their young children in case they didn't live to see the day themselves.

The mood was black.

And I wondered if next time, perhaps I could get an easier job—say, working for Rabbi Gans's cousin, the one who specializes in making gunpowder.

THE KLAUS SHUL WAS PACKED with worshippers, huddled close for warmth, and Rabbi Loew's face was glowing from the flames of twenty candles as he led the congregation in prayer. But the people hung their heads and mumbled their responses.

Then the rabbi's voice shook the rafters like a trumpeter's blast: "We must not cower in constant fear," he said, "nor give in to despair and hopelessness. We must never lose our courage in the face of oppression, for as the Sages say, *as long as a man breathes, he should not lose hope.*

"It would do us all good to remember how many times the Jews were saved on the third day of a crisis: Joseph freed his brothers from captivity on the third day, Jonah was delivered from the fish's belly on the third day, and *Moyshe Rabbeynu* received the Torah on the third day at Mount Sinai. The Midrash also comforts us with the promise that *God does not allow His righteous to remain in dire straits for more than three days.*

"But if the worst should come to pass, we need not fear dying for the Sanctification of His Name. There is only *one thing* that we need to fear, and that is the deceitful parasites who live among us and who line their purses by collaborating with the authorities at the expense of the rest of the community. Such hypocrites are *worse* than any other kind of sinner."

He stopped. "Why?" he asked.

The word echoed around the vaulted chamber.

"I'll tell you. Because the man who commits a sin might actually believe that what he is doing is right, but the hypocrite *knows* that what he is doing is evil, yet he publicly pretends that it is for the good of all."

A few people were sidling conspicuously toward the exit, but Rabbi Loew wasn't finished with them yet.

He lashed out at his detractors, saying, "And by far the lowest form of hypocrite is the *moyser*." The informer. "Even the great rationalist Rambam—may his light shine on—says in his *Mishneh Torah* that it is permissible to kill a *moyser*, and that it is even permissible to execute this sentence *before* he has informed."

Incredulous murmurs rustled through the rows of benches.

But Rabbi Loew didn't give them a chance to object. "And on this night, one begins the counting of the Omer," he said, returning to the order of the service.

The Omer. Forty-nine days that often coincide with disaster for the Jews. The Crusades and countless other massacres, and all the plagues that have befallen us, always seem to come out of winter hibernation right about now, all rested and ready to inflict maximum damage on the populace. So it's really a time to hold our breath and count the days, hoping that if we make it all forty-nine days to Shvues we might actually stand a chance of surviving another year.

When the service ended, I straightened up the chairs and benches and swept the aisles as quickly as I could, and begged the rabbi to let me go and speak to Freyde and Julie Federn.

"That can wait."

"Then at least let me talk to Reb Meisel."

But he said, "Shabbes isn't over yet, and I expect you to attend the second Seder."

I could see that it was futile to insist.

The sky outside was blanketing the cemetery in a magical shade of purple. It was the *time of favors*, a mixture of holy and regular time when it is neither day nor night, when God is at His most merciful, a time that lasts until three stars appear in the sky.

So Rabbi Loew and I put aside all other thoughts and recited solemn and mystical prayers as we plodded through the streets to his house, while the twilight came and went in the blink of an eye, without stopping to let us grasp at its magic.

HANNEH THE COOK BROUGHT IN a silver tray of yesterday's *gefilte* fish, which she had garnished with tarragon in the Bohemian style, and set it on the Lord's table, which is made holy by the family gathering around it.

Sixteen people crowded around the table, and there was still an empty seat for our fallen comrade. And Lord knows what deprivations Yankev was suffering at that moment.

Poor Anya wasn't even supposed to be here. But since she was trapped inside the ghetto with us, she had fallen into her regular role as Christian servant girl, watching the Seder with fascination.

The rabbi's granddaughter Eva came around and filled our glasses with wine. We washed our hands, bowed our heads, and said the blessings, then Rabbi Loew broke the matzoh and passed it around the circle.

Rabbi Loew also said a special prayer for Emperor Rudolf, whose intervention had secured the release of Freyde and Julie Federn.

The two women looked waxen and haggard, but they managed weak smiles when Anya brought them both steaming mugs of tea. They both had sworn that they didn't tell the Christian authorities anything that could be used against the community. And now they sat at our table wearing borrowed clothes, with their whole bodies shaved like the captive Joseph preparing for an audience with Pharaoh.

Rabbi Loew conducted the meal as if it were a continuation of the *minkhe* service and we were his congregation.

"The Sages tell us that our fathers were freed from slavery because they kept themselves apart and did not try to adopt Egyptian customs," he said. "But the danger is even greater these days, when the fashion is to act like the *goyim*."

Rabbi Isaac Ha-Kohen and Avrom Khayim nodded in agreement.

Rabbi Loew went on: "Although we are dispersed throughout the world, we must remain a people dwelling alone, and limit our contact with the nations of the world, and not try to imitate their ways, or we will lose our identity as a people."

Anya was leaning against the doorframe with one foot in the kitchen and the other in the dining room, and I could only wonder if the rabbi knew something about his young pupil's budding relationship with the *Shabbes goye*.

Then Rabbi Loew looked around the table and warned us that such dalliances would delay the coming of the Messiah.

"But Rabbi, the *Seyfer Hasidim*—" I started over, repeating the title for Anya's benefit: "The Book of the Pious says that any Jew who marries a non-Jewish woman who is kind-hearted and charitable will find her to be a better wife than a woman who is Jewish by birth but who lacks these virtues."

My eyes met Anya's.

"But you are talking about when a member of a foreign tribe becomes a Jew," said Rabbi Loew. "That is a completely different matter. See what happens when you don't take the time to stop and replenish yourself? Your mind is losing its sharpness, Ben-Akiva."

"Have some more *gefilte* fish," said Perl, serving out another portion, as if more food were the solution to my problem.

I obliged the rabbi's wife and accepted the second helping of fish. But soon it was time to end the Seder.

"Next year in Jerusalem," said Rabbi Loew. "*Borukh atoh Adinoy*, Lord our God, Ruler of the Universe, Who creates the fruit of the vine. Amen."

Then we switched to Yiddish and everyone took a turn with a verse, beginning with Young Lippman:

"Mighty is He. He will build His temple soon—"

"Speedily in our days," said Eva, finishing the phrase.

"Soon, soon," said Peshke the street cleaner.

"Soon, soon," said Samec the *mikveh* attendant.

"God build His temple," said Avrom Khayim.

"Speedily in our days," said Freyde and Julie, with surprising strength. Some of the color had come back to their faces, and I wondered what miracle had brought about this swift recovery. "Soon, soon."

"*Omeyn!*"

The tea that Anya brought them appeared to do a world of good.

The clattering of dishes aroused me from my ruminations, and my glance fell on the mugs of tea that Anya was removing from the dining table. She caught my eye and signaled to me, so I got up and followed her into the kitchen and over to the washbasin, where she handed me one of the mugs. When I didn't do anything with it, she held it right under my nose. The dregs of the tea smelled bitter, and the pale green leaves stuck to the sides of the mug. I pulled one away and examined it. It seemed to be a wet leaf like any other.

Anya told me in a low voice that she had learned that Jacob Federn had been secretly supplying these herbs to a number of women in the ghetto who were using them to treat the symptoms of melancholia.

"I didn't realize there was an epidemic of melancholia in the ghetto," I said.

"Ghetto life can be very frustrating for a lot of women."

"But why all the secrecy? What's so special about these herbs?"

"Janek was sneaking them into the country so he wouldn't have to pay any taxes on them."

So these were the famous goods that Janek and Federn were distributing in their illicit partnership.

"So what do we do now, Mr. Investigator?"

"That depends. What news did you bring me about the locks on Janek's doors?"

"I did better than that. I brought you one of his keys."

WE STARTED WITH THE HOUSE at the sign of the Fat Milk Cow at the lower end of Embankment Street. Poor drainage had turned the alley into a marshland, and we had to slog through several inches of brackish water to reach the doorstep. I knocked on the soggy wooden planks, and my knuckles came away covered with greenish flecks of mold. I was brushing the mold off my fingers when the door opened, and I found myself staring into the fearful, pleading eyes of the woman who had come to Rabbi Epstein on Friday morning seeking protection from her husband's cruelty.

Who knows what pain we could have prevented if we had only responded sooner?

A young girl who must have been her daughter was sitting on a wobbly stool sewing a patch on a rather tatty pair of leggings. Maybe it was the dim light, but she appeared to turn a little green when she saw me, and she hopped off the stool and ran into the other room.

"Yes, I must be quite a sight in these muddy clothes," I said, ducking my head under the doorframe and stepping inside.

The woman's name was Havvah, and she said that her husband the locksmith would be home any minute. The Fettmilchs' front room was cold, and saturated with the kind of moist, chilly air that penetrates the bones. It was barely illuminated by a damp wood fire that produced little heat but plenty of smoke, and soot coated the furniture like the drifting remnants on the day after the plague of darkness.

This weak flower of womanhood didn't stand a chance under these conditions, and it's a good thing Anya was there, because Havvah wouldn't even *look* at me.

So the two women huddled together by the fire and whispered things not fit for a man's ears while I sat on the wobbly stool and soaked up the heavy sense of depravation permeating the room. I wondered how many houses felt this dreary, whether in the ghetto or among our Christian neighbors, then I closed my eyes and tried not to think about the minutes ticking away. I even started rocking back and forth and reciting the tractate Sanhedrin just to keep myself occupied.

I had made it all the way up to the words, *If one comes to kill you, be first and kill him*, when Anya tapped me on the shoulder and said, "I can tell that something truly awful has happened to her, but she can't bring herself to tell me what it is."

"Then she should go to the rabbi," I said. "We could even take her with us. I'm sure he wouldn't mind—"

And at that moment, which required the utmost delicacy, Lazarus Fettmilch burst into the house. His dirty blond hair stuck out at all angles as if he had just stepped out of a whirlwind, and his face flushed with rage when he saw me.

"What are you doing here?" he demanded, clomping toward me and leaving dark puddles wherever he walked.

When I explained that we were here to ask him about the key to a certain lock, he told us what we could do with our locks and keys, then he threw us out. The door slammed, then we heard a heavy crash as he screamed at his wife and daughter for letting us in.

Anya gave me a pained look, then she told me that Havvah had anticipated her husband's foul mood, and had given her the names of several other locksmiths in the ghetto.

"That's just what we need. You've done a terrific job, Anya," I told her.

"Then why don't I feel terrific about it?"

"Because you've just seen the face of a lost innocence that can never be completely recovered."

She stopped and faced me.

"What?" I asked.

She regarded me as if taking my full measure, and said, "So there *are* other Jews like Yankev. And I thought he was so unique."

"He is unique, he's just . . ."

"Just what?"

She stood with one hand on her hip, shifting her weight from one foot to the other.

I searched for the words, but even when I found them I couldn't meet her eyes. *He just tried to escape from the ghetto without you.* So I looked away and said, "Just like the rest of us. He's toiling forever toward perfection without ever achieving it."

"Yes, that's him, all right." She clasped her hands and hugged them to her chest like any young woman dreaming of her lover.

"Thank you for everything," she said, reaching out to me. I backed away abruptly.

"We still have a mission to complete," I said.

And a grim mission it was. We passed through households weighed down by the iron claws of melancholy, from grimy hovels tucked away in dark passages to three-story town houses on Golden Lane, before we found a locksmith who could tell us that it would be a simple matter for any competent cracksman to pick the lock that went with the heavy key that Anya held in her hand.

I still didn't see how two big men could have crept into the Janeks' bedroom and taken their little Gerta away without waking them up. And the only possible explanation that occurred to me was that Janek must have let them in himself. But why?

Then Anya filled me in with the facts about Janek's attraction to young Julie Federn and the trouble it had caused him. And I wondered if Janek had conspired with the men to use his own daughter somehow as a way of getting back at Federn.

But surely he never expected them to *kill* her.

So where did they shoot her? And how come nobody heard it? They must have taken her *somewhere*, like the other side of the river, then put her in a butcher's cart when they got to the waterfront. Everything was coming together like the threads in a tapestry, but I was too neck-deep in it to see the patterns, and I needed to step back to get some perspective. And with a yarn this tangled, I'd have to step awfully far back to make sense of it.

MORDECAI MEISEL'S DINING ROOM was lined with display shelves crammed with shiny silver pitchers and trays and decanters, all so intricately carved and decorated it was hard to believe anybody ever used them. Rabbi Gans sat at the table composing the rich man's will while Rabbi Loew stood by and acted as a witness.

Meisel had come to Rabbi Loew begging for help, worried that since he was childless, if he died in the next day or so without a proper will, the state would take possession of his entire fortune, which was worth more than 400,000 *gildn* at the time. After giving it some thought, Rabbi Loew finally declared the situation an emergency, and announced a suspension of certain rules due to the extraordinary circumstances.

Gans read back the laudatory phrases that he had set down so far: "I, Mordecai Meisel, a prince among men and a pillar of the community, who feeds the poor and hungry with the choicest meats and flour, who built a hospice that serves both Christians and Jews, who helped to fund the Church of the Savior, who lent the Jews of Poznan 10,000 gulden after the great fire of 1590, who has chosen every year to give two poor girls dowries so that they might get married—"

"I don't need to hear the whole *shpil* again," said Rabbi Loew, taking Rabbi Gans's pen and making a stiff and uncomfortable *X* at the bottom of the page. Despite the circumstances, it was that difficult for him to write a single letter on this holy day.

"Can you add one more item to the list?" I said, still shaking off the chill from our nighttime trek through the ghetto.

"What's that?" asked Meisel.

"Raising the money to bail our friend Yankev ben Khayim out of jail."

Anya looked up at me with the kind of admiration usually reserved for saints and other do-gooders.

Meisel caught the exchange and his eyebrows knotted up, but he found it in his heart to say, "Why certainly, my boy, certainly. Will five hundred dalers be enough?"

"We might be able to bribe our way into the stockhouse with that, but I don't know how far it'll go toward getting us back *out* again. Everything is so much more expensive in this town, including the price of a man's freedom."

"You're right. We'd better make it a thousand."

We all thanked Meisel for his generosity, especially Rabbi Gans, who had the gift of eloquence in such things.

"There is one other matter, Reb Meisel," I said.

"Yes?" said the mayor, facing me with an open smile, as if he expected me to add a few choice pearls of my own to the long string of compliments.

"I need the names of your biggest debtors."

If he was disappointed, he didn't show it. No wonder he was such a successful merchant.

"Jews or Christians?" he said.

Damn. I had been trying not to think about the possibility of broader Jewish involvement in this affair. Time was running short, and I couldn't afford to waste another minute of my most precious resource chasing down dead ends. I had to concentrate on the most likely scenarios, which certainly sounded like a good plan—*but which were the most likely scenarios?*

"Both, I guess."

Meisel started to recite the names off the top of his head, and there were so many that I had to ask him to start over so Rabbi Gans could write them all down for me.

"Is all this writing really necessary?" said Rabbi Gans.

"I'm afraid so," I said. "And be sure to make separate lists for the Jews and Christians."

"What are you going to do with the list of Christian names?" said Meisel.

"I'm going to give them to the sheriff."

"And you think that will do any good?"

"It might or it might not."

That left a hole in the conversation big enough to drive a team of oxen through, until Rabbi Gans said, "Then we'll just have to believe that it might."

"Yes, exactly," I said, trying to sound convincing.

Meisel started with the Jews first, and Rabbi Gans copied down all the names in a single column:

B. Shtastny
I. Rabinowitz
M. Vinchevsky
L. Finkelstein
M. Pacovsky
J. Stein
F. Weiler
E. Bavli
K. Halpern

Rabbi Loew closed his eyes as if the mere sight of the list was too much for him, then he reopened them and said that a few of the names belonged to the people who had left the shul in protest during his sermon.

My ears filled with silence for a few seconds, and I thought of the Arab saying, *Better a thousand enemies outside the gates than one enemy inside the gates.*

"Now let's get on with the list of Christian debtors," I said.

"Should we include *keyser* Rudolf in the list?" asked Rabbi Gans, as we gathered around him. "I didn't think so," he said, answering his own question.

The list of Christians ran slightly longer:

L. Mutz
K. Obuvník
E. Feuermann
M. Dietrichstein
J. Kopecky
P. Grubner
A. Straka
J. Fenstermacher
L. Belickis
S. Jacobus
A. Hesse
P. Bleisch

L. Kompert
T. Wolff

None of the names meant anything to me, but Anya peered over my shoulder, put her finger on the fifth name and said, "Janoš Kopecky the butcher? How much does he owe you?"

"Around five thousand dalers," said Meisel.

"Why would a butcher need that kind of money?" I asked.

Meisel said, "Kopecky may have started out as a butcher, but he always had plans to expand into other areas. So he borrowed the money to build a new slaughterhouse outside the city."

"A slaughterhouse that makes deliveries every morning," said Anya. "By boat and horse cart."

A bright spot must have lit up in the middle of my brain, and I saw it all at once.

Anya read the look on my face and knew exactly what I was thinking. "The meat shipments come from the other side of the river," she said.

I turned to Meisel. "Then I'm going to need a couple more dalers."

THERE IS A PASSAGE IN *Melokhim Beys*, the Second Book of Kings, in which four lepers sit outside the gates of Samaria, a city abandoned to war and famine, and discuss their fate. Simply put, if they go to the enemy camp and beg for food, they will probably die, but if they stay where they are, they will *surely* die. So they decide they have nothing to lose and head for the camp of the Aramaeans.

And for the first time, I understood their situation completely. Maybe it was the spirit of my recently fallen comrade speaking through me, but I couldn't stand around any longer and just wait for the Christians to come and get us. We had to go out there and learn what we could about the routes of the daily shipments of meat from Kopecky's slaughterhouse.

I said, "We have to divide up the names on this list and question every one of these Jews *tonight*. And then, one of us has to sneak out of the ghetto sometime before daybreak and go to the waterfront disguised as a Christian."

"I nominate you," said Rabbi Gans.

"Do I look like a Christian to you?"

"Why not use the real thing?" said Meisel, indicating Anya.

"I don't think she'll be able to show her face out there for quite a while," I said.

"Oh. Right."

"You're the only one who can do it," Rabbi Loew said to me.

"What about Shlomo Zinger?" I said. "He's a good actor, he knows his way around the streets, and he has a trunkful of Christian clothing—"

"He also drinks like a fish, in case you haven't noticed," said Rabbi Gans.

"Besides, his face is too well known," said Rabbi Loew. "But yours isn't."

"How can you say that? Half the people in the city saw me being led around Old Town Square by an armed escort. They'd recognize me in an instant—"

"Not after I get finished with you," said Anya.

"You know the Christian ways better than any of us," said Rabbi Loew.

"Not that well."

"I heard you know the Psalms in Latin," said Rabbi Gans.

"Is that true?" said Meisel.

"Only about twenty or thirty of them." It even sounded lame to me.

"You know how they think. You know how to act like one of them. You're the only one of us who can pass for a Christian."

"I—" This would have been hard enough to say under any circumstances, never mind in front of four witnesses.

"You what?"

I told Rabbi Gans to put away his pen. He hesitated a moment, then laid the quill aside.

"What is it, my *talmid*?" said Rabbi Loew.

"Rabbi . . ."

"Yes?"

"It was Jews."

"What do you mean, it was Jews? What are you talking about?"

"I mean that I was raised by Jews."

"But you said you lived among Christians."

"Yes, that's what I told you. But I only lived among Christians for a few months, and the rest of the time with Jews. I guess I didn't want people to know that I'd gotten this—this way that I am—from living with people who were supposed to be such pious and respectable Jews."

I couldn't help biting off the words and spitting them out, and I felt my heart beating faster.

Rabbi Loew said, "It doesn't matter what lies you had to tell to survive. There are many minor sins on the road to a great *mitsveh*. What matters is that you're here now, and that you're the only one capable of performing such a *mitsveh*."

"Am I?"

Rabbi Loew drew closer to me. "Why didn't you do something to change your living situation, if it was so unpleasant?"

"What did I know? I thought it was normal to live like that."

"So the man you knew as your father called you a brute and you believed it. And those children in the *kheyder* said you were slow and stupid, and you believed it. But it's not true. And you have to stop believing it."

"I don't believe any of it. I'm not a child in *kheyder* anymore."

"Part of you still is," said Rabbi Loew, and I was stunned by the undeniable truth of his words, which burnt through the fog of years in an instant. "Surely you carry scars from all that hateful treatment, but the worst scars are not visible on your skin. They are buried deep inside you, so deep that you may not even be aware of them yourself. In spite of all your accomplishments, inside you lurks a frightened child who harbors a natural desire to get back at his tormentors, even if that leads you to do things that ultimately make you fail in order to confirm your hidden belief that you don't deserve to succeed."

There was a long silence as everyone took a moment to examine their own inner souls. Did they recognize a bit of themselves in me?

"You still think Zinger's the right man for the job?" said Rabbi Gans.

I let out a long sigh and said, "Maybe after this is over, we could all go to the New World and live among the Indians. I hear that the tribes along the Mohawk River have a non-aristocratic form of government."

"But they're heathens," Rabbi Gans protested. "They've never heard the word of God."

"I bet they've never heard of Jew badges, either."

I WALKED TOWARD THE SOUTH Gate alone. All around me, Jews were preparing for the final confrontation, prying up floor planks to shore up the barricades and breaking apart furniture to stoke the fires in which our metals would be melted down and reshaped into weapons. Everything but books. Never books. For the Sages say, *When precious metals are lost, there are replacements for them. But when a Torah scholar dies, who can replace him?*

Because we would never beat them with arms alone. We needed a diversion of some kind, something so terrifying that the Christians would forget about their all-consuming quest for Jewish gold.

I spun around and headed straight back to Rabbi Loew's house, where I asked him to send someone to find Zinger and have him meet me at the whorehouse on Hampasgasse in about an hour. Rabbi Loew raised an eyebrow, but he must have sensed the unleashed power of the beast raging within me because he agreed without argument.

Then I asked him to round up a few trustworthy men and meet me at the South Gate in ten minutes.

"How many do you need?" he asked.

"*Fifty useful men are better than two hundred who are not,*" I said, quoting the *Talmud Yerushalmi*.

"How about three?"

"That'll have to do."

Then I hurried back to the South Gate, pounded on the door, and asked to speak with Sheriff Zizka.

"Don't you ever sleep, Jew?" said the guard.

"Just get the sheriff for me, will you?"

Zizka wasn't in a great mood when he finally arrived, and his mood didn't get any better when I handed him the list of Meisel's Christian debtors and asked him to go talk to them for me.

"It's too late now," he said. "We'll have to go around in the morning."

"But—"

"I said it's too late now. Got it?"

"Right, got it."

"What did I tell you?" said Rabbi Gans. "You can't trust these *noytsriyes*."

"Why are these other men with you?" said Zizka.

"They're here to help gather the remains of our friend."

"Your friend?" said Zizka, looking over his shoulder at the inanimate heap of bloody rags lying untouched in the middle of the street. "Why?"

"He was a bit rough around the edges," I said, giving a hasty, poor man's eulogy. "But he had as much right to breathe as you or I. And now he's gone. That's why."

I somehow managed to convince Zizka to let us through the gate to collect the pieces of the man who had been our night watchman and friend.

Rings of torches had been planted in the earth outside the gate, with clusters of *Judenschläger* sleeping in loose circles around them like an army gathering strength for the morrow's battle. We gathered Acosta's remains by the glow of their flickering torches.

"Here now, what are you going to do with all that?" asked the guard as we treaded past him with our grisly burden.

We're going to cleanse his corpse as best we can, wrap him in a shroud, and give him a decent burial.

I said, "We're going to re-attach his limbs and give him new powers so that he'll be bigger and stronger than he ever was before."

"What? You can't do that—"

"Can't we? Just watch." And we shut and sealed the gate.

But no matter how smoothly things went, I had a feeling that it was going to be a long night.

CHAPTER 29

I KNOW I DID A variation of this stunt yesterday morning, but that was to a different audience, and besides, it's not playing the same trick twice when you do it fifty times bigger than before.

"This idea of yours had better be good," said Rabbi Ha-Kohen, since he wasn't even supposed to be in the *same room* with a corpse, much less handle the bloody remains.

We laid our comrade's shattered limbs on the floor of the shed and washed them as clean as we could with some old rags and a bucket of warm water that quickly turned pinkish-red and ice cold.

We wouldn't allow Rabbi Loew to sully his hands with this task—he had to remain separate from us if this plan was going to work.

I spread out the tools and began cleaning the dirt from Acosta's finger-nails with a tarnished silver scraper.

"We need to tap into their deepest fears," I explained, "and convince them that we can bring this soulless clay to life and make an unstoppable creature that does our bidding."

Rabbi Ha-Kohen dropped his arms to his side and glared at me. "You made me go through all this for some worthless *bove mayses*?"

"You're not seriously thinking about trying to create a golem, are you?" said Rabbi Gans.

"Not creating one. Making them *think* we're creating one."

Rabbi Ha-Kohen stared at his bloodstained hands. "You talked me into breaking a commandment for *this*?"

"Yes, but are you truly aware what *this* is, Rabbi?"

Something like doubt clouded his eyes, for once. It must have been an unfamiliar feeling for him, and at any other time I might have taken a moment to enjoy his discomfort.

I put it another way: "What did the Egyptians say when the Angel of Death struck down all the first-born in Egypt, and Pharaoh told Moses and Aaron to take their flocks and leave?"

"They said, *We are all dead*."

"Right. They panic. They think they're all going to die, and they panic. And you know what happens when people panic? They believe every rumor, no matter how outlandish, and they scatter, trampling each other as they try to escape the danger."

"If they don't try to kill us all first for being sorcerers."

"There's always that risk. But it's time for us to make the leap."

"You almost sound like *him*," said Rabbi Ha-Kohen, referring to our dearly departed comrade-in-arms. "Besides, how gullible do you think they are? Even the *goyim* know that we can't bring a lump of clay to life."

Fortunately, the Sanhedrin *Bavli* was still fresh in my mind. So I answered, "And Rava says that if the righteous desired it, they could create a world."

Rabbi Ha-Kohen had a counter-argument on the tip of his tongue, but Rabbi Loew stopped the debate before it could run its course: "I agree," he said.

Rabbi Ha-Kohen waited for more.

"Although my *talmid*'s plan of action has its dangers, I see very few practical alternatives," said Rabbi Loew. "And since it may well provide us with a way of holding our enemies off for a day or so, we must accept it as the *di beste fun di eser makes*." The best of the ten plagues.

That seemed to settle the matter.

I laid the scraper aside and picked up a polished silver comb.

"This may hurt a little," I said softly, as I combed my friend's hair out of his half-closed eyes, making sure not to tug on the roots too hard. Rabbi Loew set out a pair of decorative scissors and commenced the solemn task of cutting the fringes off a *tallis*. Then we lifted up our Sephardic brother, wrapped him in this sacred shroud, and laid him out on a plain wooden board. I had never seen him put on a regular prayer shawl during the time that we had shared a thin strip of bedding in the rabbi's attic, but we have a saying, *All brides are beautiful, and all the dead are holy.*

Rabbi Gans held a sputtering torch in one hand and led our simple procession through the maze of crooked headstones. The rats scattered as we squeezed past the monuments, Rabbi Ha-Koen and I shouldering the bier together, with Rabbi Loew following after, taking great care to keep his hands clean for the ceremony. All the while, I was keeping four cold torches hidden under my cloak, belted to my body.

Rabbi Gans led us along an invisible path to the highest point in the cemetery, so the Christians would be able to see us from the top of the embankment on the other side of the wall.

A distant church bell tolled the hour, but I lost count of the number of rings.

Rabbi Loew pulled his prayer shawl tighter against the dampness and quietly began the truly spiritual part of our little ceremony.

"The mystics say that on the day of his death, a man feels as if he has lived but a single day, because this world is but a temporary shelter, and the World-to-Come is our true home. And so we are never fully at home in the world," he said. "Our *khaver* Mikha'el Acosta wasn't a scholarly man, but just as one ear of corn is not exactly like another, we will not see his like again, and we are all diminished by his passing."

"*Omeyn,*" we said.

"You knew him as well as any of us, Ben-Akiva. Would you like to say a few words?" he asked.

I thought of so many things—quotes from the Psalms, the Prophets, the mystics, the Rabbis—but in the end I just swallowed and said, "He knew how to react to a situation without having to stop and think about it. He was one of those men who always seem to know the right thing to do and the right time to do it, which comes as close to the definition of a hero as anything I can think of."

"*Omeyn.*"

We couldn't recite the Mourner's Kaddish without a *minyen*, but I couldn't help hearing the words in my head: *Yisgadal v'yiskadash shmey rabo* . . .

Rabbi Loew continued the invocations while I undid my belt and let the bundle of torches slip to the ground.

"May his memory be for a blessing, may his merit protect us, and may his soul be granted eternal life, for his resting place is Eden."

We lowered Acosta's body into the narrow grave, so far from the soil of his native land, and took turns scattering a bit of earth from the Holy Land over his limbs, mixed in with spadefuls of sandy earth deposited by the river. And so the departed was laid to rest.

Then we started to play the drama game the way our mother Judith taught us during the reign of King Nebuchadnezzar. Rabbi Gans planted the torch in the freshly dug earth and receded into the shadows while I took center stage.

"Master of the Universe!" I cried. "When will you redeem us?"

The answer seemed to come from the bare branches swaying in the breeze: "*When you have gone down to the very bottom of the pit. In that hour I shall redeem you.*"

"It is time to revive his soul," I announced.

By the reddish light of the flaming torch, I made a show of swinging the *kleperl* high above our heads, and bringing it down hard, banging on the ground three times to wake the spirit of our comrade.

Then I inclined my head so I could present the powerful wooden staff to Rabbi Loew.

Rabbi Loew cleared his throat and spoke loud enough for his words to drift over the wall.

"First we set out a cup of wine, for the dead are always thirsty."

Rabbi Gans played his part well, scrambling to fulfill the rabbi's instructions.

Rabbi Loew commanded him to draw three concentric circles around the grave, and Rabbi Gans dutifully took the *kleperl* and inscribed the circles in the earth with the magical staff.

Then Rabbi Loew initiated the ritual in earnest, raising his arms up to heaven and declaring, "O, Ancient One, O Patient King, O Fourfold God, O Guardian of Israel who neither slumbers nor sleeps, look down on your helpers—I, Yehudah ben Betzalel, who was born under the sign of the wind, Isaac ben Shimshon, who was born under the sign of water, Benyamin Ben-Akiva, who was born under the sign of fire, and Dovid ben Solomon, who was born under the sign of the earth. Combine the power of these elements into the soil which we now form into a man, and breathe the breath of life into his nostrils."

On the other side of the wall, a motley group of Christians was gathering on the horizon, the light from their torches glowing like wolves' eyes in the night.

Rabbi Loew went on: "Hear our prayer, O Lord, Whose eyes saw our unformed limbs while they were still in the womb and wrote them in His book," he said, paraphrasing the only occurrence of the word *golem* in the Bible—the Psalms, which he now recited in Hebrew: *"Golmi rohu eynekho, ve'al sifrekho kulom yikoseyvu."*

We kneeled in the earth and fashioned a man of clay while Rabbi Loew said the magical words, *Ato Bra Goylem Devuk Hakhomer V'tigzar Zeydim Khevel Torfe Yisroel.* Make a Golem of clay who will destroy all the enemies of Israel.

Then the three rabbis walked around the lifeless mound of clay and proclaimed that the damp earth had dried, while I kept my head down and carefully unwrapped the torches, cradling them in my arms to protect them from the moisture. Thank God the tips of the torches were still dry. Then they made a second round and declared that the creature's limbs had joined. On the third round they cried out in wonder, beholding that God was imparting vitality to the earth, which began to glow from the heat. On the fourth and fifth rounds they swore that his organs had formed and his orifices had opened, on the sixth round the life force entered through his nostrils and the fires of creation burned as brightly as a blacksmith's forge.

I was on my knees, preparing to ignite the bundle of torches as the rabbis paraded around me, throwing distorted shadows in every direction.

"I didn't realize this would be such hard work for you," said Rabbi Gans.

"Hey, if making a golem were easy, anyone could do it," I said.

Rabbi Loew shushed us as they began the seventh and final circuit, calling on the prophet Elijah.

"O, *Elyohu hanovi*, we know that you are a man of God, and that the word of God in your mouth is truth, and that God sends us the gift of life through you when we inscribe the word *truth* on the forehead of this man of clay, so that by the time the sun rises, our golem will walk the earth!"

Rabbi Loew bent his aging bones as if he were writing the word *emes* in the mound of dirt, and the flames shot up into the air, nearly scorching the branches overhead. Then I threw a wet blanket over the torches and snuffed them out with a sizzle. But I turned away too late, and the smoke went up my nose and into my eyes, and the others had to drag me away from the pyre. I lay in the wet grass, coughing and hacking, and blinded by the sudden plunge into darkness.

As soon as I was able to see the plumes of smoke rising, Rabbi Gans kneeled beside me and suggested that we might be able to combine our make-believe golem with another frightening effect. Using his lenses and other materials to construct what the Christians call a magic lantern, he could project a grotesque image such as a likeness of the devil on the walls and gates, or even low-lying clouds, and terrorize the enemy—if only one of us could paint such an image, in all its terrifying aspects, on a flat pane of glass.

"I know just the fellow," I said, as the rabbis helped me to my feet.

I could see the flickering outlines of people on the embankment as they scurried away to spread the word about our Jewish magic.

I brushed myself off and described the way to Langweil's studio. Then we washed our hands, and left the cemetery. Rabbi Gans hustled off to search for Langweil, and I told Rabbi Loew that if all went well, I'd be back under his roof within an hour.

"Where are you going?"

"I'm going to bring our friend back to life."

ZINGER SAT IN THE MIDDLE of the circle of gaily painted women, doing what he did best, getting cheap laughs and bringing a little levity to their earthbound souls.

"There are certain words that just shouldn't exist," he said. "Like *bishopric*. I mean, what are you supposed to think when they say a word like that? I don't know about you, but I'm pretty sure I don't want to think about what a *bishopric* is." His shoulders quivered in a stageworthy shudder.

The girls all laughed.

"Look, we don't have much time," I said. "Could we get on with this?"

The hostess looked me over with the green eyes of a jealous goddess. "And what have you been doing, rolling around in a mud puddle?"

"Mud would be a step up from what I've been rolling in," I said. "Where's Trine?"

A few titters escaped from their shiny red lips.

"Keep your pants on, Mr. Shammes. She's coming."

The girls tittered again. I didn't like it any better the second time. I reached into the circle, grabbed Zinger by the hand, and pulled him away from his adoring audience.

The hostess made a number of comments about my questionable parentage as I directed Zinger to the archway and marched him all the way back to Trine's room.

I knocked on the door, but she didn't answer. The space under the bottom panel yielded no clues, so I crouched down and looked through the keyhole— *yes, I admit it*—but it was too dark to see anything. But the one next door was letting some light slip through.

I found her in Yosele's room, taking the knots out of the big fellow's hair with a wooden comb.

I made some quick introductions, but Zinger just stood there staring at this overgrown child, seemingly at a loss for words, which was fine with me because I wasn't in the mood for idle chatter.

"He's like a trained bear," Trine said, dragging the comb through Yosele's thick, matted hair. "We've trained him to sit at the table, and use a knife and fork, but he's still a bear. And sometimes he goes back to being one—" she said, pulling at a particularly tough knot.

"Well, what do you think?" I asked.

Zinger looked him over. "Well . . . with some raised shoes, maybe even a pair of special stilts concealed under extra-long pantaloons, only a couple feet long, nothing too obvious, then if we cover his clothes with a layer of mud and smear his face and hands with earth, it just might work—"

"Wait a minute," said Trine. "What might work?"

"We need to make him look like a golem," I said.

"Oh, no, you don't. Not with my Yosele. Who do you think you are, Rabbi Elijah of Chelm? You wouldn't even know how to keep him out of the pantry. Why, if I let him have all the sweets he wanted, he'd blow up like a fatted calf."

"That's exactly why we need your help."

"And what do I get out of this marvelous deal?"

"A chance at redemption."

"Who are *you* to offer me redemption? Besides, I thought I was beyond redemption."

"No one is cast off forever."

Meanwhile, Yosele kept busy by lining up a set of wooden blocks with faded Hebrew letters that must have been painted on quite some time ago. But when I tilted my head, the pattern became clear: ק‧א‧ץ ה‧ו‧נ‧ט ע‧פ‧ל. He wasn't just lining them up arbitrarily, he was spelling out the words *katz, hunt, epl.* Cat, dog, apple.

"How did he learn to do that?" I asked.

"By imitating me. He can learn to imitate anything you teach him."

I wondered what else he was learning to imitate from such a teacher.

"Good," said Zinger. "Because we need him to scare the *goyim* into crapping themselves."

"I don't like the sound of that," said Trine, stroking Yosele's head with her thin white fingers. "It sounds dangerous. And he's really very gentle, you know. He's not like other men his size—"

Suddenly Zinger clapped his hand to his forehead. "And you could be the White Lady!"

"You want me to play dress-up, it'll cost you."

"You're joking, right?" said Zinger. "Nobody wants to screw the White Lady."

"You'd be surprised."

"Who's the White Lady?" I said.

Zinger told me that once upon a time, the White Lady was one of the Rožmberks, but after she died under circumstances that have been lost in the misty corridors of time, she took to haunting the family estate, and that ever since then, whenever she is seen wandering along the battlements or the banks of the river, wrapped in a flowing white veil, it is a sure sign that death will follow in her footsteps.

"And men pay for this . . . experience?"

Trine nodded.

"Well, I guess that's one way to deny the fear of death," said Zinger.

Lord, what a world.

I reached inside my cloak and tossed a few gold pieces on the bed.

"Will that cover it?"

Trine glanced at the shiny gold ducats. A knowing smile blossomed on her lips. "I heard you were working for Meisel."

"I'm working for all of us," I said. "And I need to use the secret passage to get out of the ghetto. Tonight. And I'm going to need a diversion that only he can provide."

I waited.

I couldn't force her to do this. And she'd made it clear that we wouldn't get Yosele's compliance without her help. So I lowered my eyes, and begged her to show some mercy.

"Please . . ." I said, clasping my hands before I could think about what I was doing.

Yosele was bouncing on the bed, flapping his hands, and letting out happy howls of contentment. Trine put her finger to her lips and shushed him. He imitated her, putting his finger to his lips and saying *Shh*, and he quieted down.

He really *did* do whatever she asked him to do.

She said, "You want to use the passage now?"

I started breathing again. *It's just nerves*, I told myself. *Just nerves.*

"No, I'll be back in a couple of hours. I need to take care of a few things first."

Rabbi Loew says that deep inside our brains, we remember everything, all the way back to *Moyshe Rabbeynu* and before, all the way back to Adam and before, all the way back to the first moment of creation, because every atom of our being comes from God, and complete knowledge of God's creation flows through us, if only we would pay attention to it.

I tried to concentrate on this profound cosmical reality, but as I walked past the cemetery, a dog howled in the distance, a clear sign that the Angel of Death was approaching the gates of the city, and that the hour of redemption was close at hand.

Would God forgive my actions? Or would He disapprove of all the compromises that I had to make?

Please God, I prayed, *just grant me the wisdom and the time and space I need to finish what they started. Just give me a few more hours, Lord, before I start down the path of no return.*

Even the sounds of hammering and sawing had faded as the spirits came out to play with Lilith and all her demons, who are at their most powerful on Saturday night. And I had to remind myself not to try to win them over with a joke, because *demons don't have a sense of humor*. Only men who can feel and bleed know what real laughter is. It's one of the things that make us human.

As I went sloshing through the puddles, my mind was flooded with visions of the days to come when study-houses will be turned into whorehouses, youths will insult their elders, and God will cause it to rain on one city and not upon another, bringing famine to the land, and then pain, and then the Torah will be forgotten, and man will destroy his brothers in endless wars, until the Messiah comes. And I recited the Psalm that begins, *He who dwells in the shelter of the Supreme One,* because it contains the verse, *loy siro mipakhad loyloh, meykheyts yo'uf yomom—You shall not fear the terror by night, nor the arrow that flies by day.* And I tried to take comfort in the knowledge that my body was just a mortal shell for my eternal soul. But it really didn't help much.

I POUNDED ON THE DOOR beneath the stone Lion of Judah until a sleepy-eyed servant girl let me in. I was creeping down the long hallway to meet Anya when Avrom Khayim reached out from behind the curtain and grabbed me by the sleeve. I tried to shake him loose, but he took hold with both hands and pulled me into the other room.

"All right, but this better be—"

I stopped. The inner room had been transformed into a sacred space, all decked out with red cloth like a church when they're ordaining a new priest. Three men stood side by side in long hooded robes, each one holding a tall candle. There was a small square carpet on the floor in front of them. Avrom Khayim raised his candle, and took his place among the other men, whom I now recognized as the other three shammeses—Markas Kral, Abraham Ben-Zakhariah, and the last one, who must have been Saul Ungar.

Avrom Khayim spoke for them all: "Reb Benyamin Ben-Akiva of Slonim, assistant shammes at the Klaus Shul under the High Rabbi Loew, in recognition of your recent activities on behalf of the community, and the ongoing sacrifices and dedication to the profession that we have witnessed, we have gathered on this solemn occasion to induct you into the Ancient and Fraternal Order of *Shammashim.*"

That's wonderful, but can't this wait? I thought, my patience and energy rapidly dwindling.

Thankfully, the ceremony only lasted a few minutes, and when it was finished, Avrom Khayim said, "You are no longer a lowly assistant. Rise up and join us, Brother Benyamin, for you are now a full-fledged member of the Brotherhood of Shammeses."

They hugged me and shook my hand, slapped my back and kissed me on both cheeks, and at that moment, I couldn't have cared less about the honor they were bestowing upon me.

When I finally got away from them, I made my way to the pantry where Anya had set up a barber's chair, just for me. She was sharpening a pair of scissors when I came in, and she looked up and offered me a smile. Then she held the scissors up and gave me the universal sign that we were ready to begin:

Snip snip.

CHAPTER 30

"Relax," said Anya. "Becoming a Christian is easier than you think."

"For some."

She was trying to give me one of those farmer-style bowl-cuts, but that only works with straight hair, and she was quickly learning that you can't cut tight Jewish curls in half.

"Christ, it's like shearing a sheep," she said, rubbing her palms. Then she ran her fingers through my hair, gathering up the sheaves of half-curls so she could cut them short.

"If only your hair was straighter," she said.

"You mean, like Yankev's?"

She gripped the roots of my hair, and I thought I'd better say something to ease her mind before she cut my ears off.

"Stop worrying," I said. "He's a scholar in good standing, with Meisel's backing. Rabbi Loew will address the Community Council first thing in the morning, and they'll make sure that your Yankev will return safely."

Good Lord, listen to me. "Your Yankev." Their relationship was supposed to shock the world, but it had already become part of my routine. Either that, or it just didn't matter anymore, like trying to fix a squeaky door during an earthquake. You don't bother oiling the hinges when the walls are caving in.

Meanwhile the curly locks were falling off my shoulder and drifting to the floor.

I told Anya that any Jew who is forced to convert is forgiven. "Rambam advises us to confess and not choose death."

"And how many of the ghetto's leaders are followers of Rambam?"

She was right, of course.

Rationality no longer walked these streets. Rationality had gone into hiding to avoid being persecuted during the long reign of terror that would darken our windowpanes for the next hundred years, until some future Prince Charming as yet unborn breaks the spell with a kiss.

"Wait—the hair's getting in my eyes."

I tried to brush all the loose hairs away, but there were too many of them and they kept sticking to my palm.

"At least I can see them now. I thought they were light brown, but they're really kind of hazel," she said. "I've noticed that you talk about eyes, a lot. Why is that, do you think?"

"Just keep cutting," I said, blinking.

"I wonder," she said, her gaze boring into me like a carpenter's bit. "Maybe it's because so much depends on how we see each other. Is that it?"

Like the Rabbi said: *It's not what is, it's what people believe.*

"Yes," I agreed. "I couldn't have put it better."

When did this butcher's daughter learn to be so curious? From whom did she inherit such a lively intellect? God's ways were often unfathomable, but they were not always *completely* hidden from our eyes. We must remember that Rambam's mother was also a butcher's daughter, so who was I to say that one day this woman might not be blessed with a son who turned out to be a second Rambam?

I caught a glimpse of another world, like a painting covered with the sheerest gauze. It was a world just like this one, a world where Anya was dressed in fine clothes, a fleeting vision in shimmering brocade. She had matured handsomely, and was smiling as she held her arms out to the bright young scholar who was her son.

But in what world would that happen? Perhaps in a dream world, but not in ours.

Our world was a shimmering bubble falling inexorably to earth. Would it bounce, as bubbles sometimes do, or would it burst apart in a spray of rainbow-colored droplets?

Ibn Ezra says that a short life with wisdom is better than a long life without it, and if he were here with us on this sleepless night, I could just picture him shutting himself up in his room to write poetry undisturbed while awaiting his final hour upon this earth.

But for us, the seconds were ticking by, and we still had to figure out how to bluff our way past noon tomorrow.

The last of my curls spiraled to the ground. Anya brushed the tufts of hair from my shoulders with a kerchief as if I were a shedding animal, then she wiped her hand along the back of my neck to remove the itchy hairs that had been tormenting me by getting under my collar.

Her hands were warm despite the cold.

She wet a comb and dragged it across my head, yanking my close-cropped hair in directions that God had never intended it to go, trying to create the illusion that my hair was naturally straight. After taming my shaggy mane with enough water to mop the kitchen floor, she held up a hand mirror so I could see what I looked like with short straight hair plastered to the top of my head.

I looked half-Christian. The crown of my head felt strangely cold, while the bottom half bristled with a rabbinic beard that was strangely out of place.

"Time for the beard, isn't it?" she said. "Are you sure you're ready for this? Or does it violate some kind of precept?"

"The great ReMo of Kraków—*olev ha-sholem*—always taught us to deviate from the law under exceptional conditions, or when considerable personal loss is at stake."

"Like right now."

"Yes."

"And what other deviations are you prepared to commit?"

"Whatever the need of the hour requires."

"Rabbi Isserles said that?"

"He did."

She studied my beard from various angles, then started clipping away at it.

"This Rabbi Isserles sounds like a very practical and wise man. A real . . . uh . . . what's the word? A *hasid*?"

"You probably mean a *tsadek*."

"What's the difference?"

"A *hasid* is a pious man who always keeps to the letter of the law, and a *tsadek* is a righteous man who finds meaning in the gaps *between* the letters of the law."

She pursed her lips and pondered that for a moment. "Well, I guess that means I'd rather be righteous than pious."

"Then it sounds to me like you belong in the same room with the *tsadeks*."

"Tell me—" she said.

I waited.

"Why is it that our senses can fool us into believing that we want something very much, but once we hold it in our hand, it doesn't turn out to be what we expected?"

Before I could answer, she changed course like a ship turning hard to lee. "I mean, for example, why do so many things smell better than they taste?"

If we had actually been aboard a ship, I would have hit the deck to avoid the swinging boom.

So I said, "You know, I've never thought about that before. But it is an excellent question. It opens the door to many possibilities, which is the sign of an active and vigorous intellect."

She was trimming the hair at my jawline, and she paused. I thought perhaps it was because she was so pleased by my compliment, but she had only stopped so that I could answer her question.

I considered the problem, and said, "The most logical explanation would be that our sense of smell is more refined than our sense of taste."

Her eyes flashed. "Of course. That makes perfect sense. It's remarkable."

"It's not so remarkable."

"Yankev didn't know the answer."

"Well, he's still young—"

"Don't—"

She stopped my mouth with her hand.

"You're very kind to say so, but . . . I'd say that you're the only *tsadek* around here," she said.

"I'm no *tsadek*," I said, as she resumed the delicate procedure of clipping the wiry hair around my lips and chin. "If I were, I wouldn't be in this mess."

"We're all in this mess together," she said.

"I don't mean *that* mess."

"Then what particular mess are you talking about?" she asked, straightening up. She had finished with the scissors and comb, so she laid them aside and wiped her hands on her apron. Then she picked up the bowl of shaving soap and started stirring it with a shorthaired brush.

She dabbed my face with lather, leaning close enough for me to catch her scent.

I told her about Reyzl, how at first it was an adventure with her, roughing it on the road east and setting up our own little place together. I was very attentive to her, and the easy revelation of conjugal joys was a blessing as well. But then she started missing her family, and the big fairs and market days, and the traveling players coming through with the latest gory English dramas— just the kind of entertainment that a great city like Prague offers. And it didn't help any that her stepsisters married up while she was stuck in near-poverty.

Anya barely acknowledged what I was saying as she sharpened the razor on a leather strop like a priestess preparing to sacrifice a ram.

I told her that I gave up my position as a scholar in Slonim because I didn't want to lose Reyzl. But I didn't want to lose my status as a scholar, either.

"Well, you can't have it both ways," she said, as she brought the razor near my cheek.

She hesitated, the razor poised to strike. "So your skin has never been touched by a razor?" she asked.

"That's right."

"Amazing."

I kept silent as she delicately cleared the underbrush from my cheeks like a young wife gathering herbs from her garden.

"Have you tried talking to her?" she asked.

"Of course I have."

"And?"

"It didn't go too well."

"Then you'll just have to try again."

"What's the use?"

"Now what kind of an attitude is that? When you're studying a difficult question, mister scholar, does the answer always come to you right away?"

"Of course not."

"Well, sometimes it's the same with a woman."

A surge of warmth spread through the middle of my chest as she wiped my face clean with a towel and held up the mirror.

"Well, what do you think of your new look?" she asked.

A bare face with bright pink cheeks stared back at me. I'd started growing the beard when I was a young teenager, and the line of my lips held a manly shape and definition that I had never seen before.

"It's like looking at the face of a long-lost relative," I said. "A distant cousin or something. Someone who's not me, but I can definitely see the family resemblance."

She ran her fingers along the smooth part of my cheek to test the quality of her work.

"Not bad," she said.

Then: "Better a Jew without a beard than a beard without a Jew," she said, tweaking me. "Now we just have to get you out of those muddy clothes."

"Right. And where am I supposed to find a change of clothes?"

Her lips spread wide, forming a lovely smile as she rummaged around in her bag and pulled out a rough tunic with a rope around the middle.

"Good Lord, woman. What else have you got in that bag?"

She practically winked at me as she handed me the set of Christian clothes that she had brought with her.

Her hands were *so* warm.

I wondered whose clothes they were, but I didn't ask.

"There's just one other thing," she said.

Something about her voice made me stop and look right at her.

"You should definitely go and see your wife again. Go and tell her—" She swallowed, and I thought I saw wetness forming in her eyes. "Go and tell her your real feelings, before going out there and facing God-knows-what dangers."

"Why not? If I'm going to hang, it might as well be from the highest tree."

"I hope that wasn't an attempt to sound heroic."

I gave her a quick pat on the shoulder, but my hand lingered there, like a bridge connecting two people on opposite shores. I believe she felt it, too.

I told her what Rabbi Nathan says: "You know what a *real* hero is? Someone who turns an enemy into a friend."

"WOULD YOU LIKE A *VAYNSHL?*"

"No thank you, Mrs. Rozansky," I replied, shuffling my feet like an awkward sixteen-year-old.

"*Nemt epes in moyl arayn,*" she said, offering me a bowl of sour cherries.

Ah. So *that's* what a *vaynshl* was. We call them *vishnya* in Slonim.

"You don't need to offer me anything, Mrs. Rozansky. I know it's late. I just need to speak to Reyzl."

"Reyzl's not home," said her father, his clay pipe clamped between his teeth. He was smoking that fancy New World tobacco which burns up a day's wages with a few quick puffs.

They couldn't stop staring at my newly shaven cheeks.

Finally, Mrs. Rozansky said, "She's staying at a friend's house at the bottom of Three Wells Lane."

Reyzl had moved *closer* to the breach in the gate?

"Why?" I asked.

Zalman Rozansky blew some of that expensive smoke at me. "You'll have to ask her."

ONE MORE FLIGHT OF STAIRS, I thought. One more crooked flight of stairs leading to another narrow hallway.

My knocking had roused the landlady, which was a grievous error. She had looked me over, declared that she ran a respectable establishment, and insisted on coming with me, climbing the steps at the speed of honey flowing uphill. We finally got to the third landing and she knocked on the door.

"Reyzl! There's someone here to see you."

"Just a minute, Mrs. Leibstein."

The floor creaked as feminine footsteps approached.

Reyzl's eyes were laughing when she opened the door. They froze when she saw the strange man on her threshold, then her face went flat.

"Oh, it's you. What do *you* want?"

"Want me to toss him out?" said the landlady.

"No, it's all right, Mrs. Leibstein. Thank you."

Mrs. Leibstein gave me a look that a less rational being would have taken as a curse, then she hobbled slowly toward the stairs so she wouldn't miss a word.

"What have you done to yourself?" Reyzl asked.

It was cold in the hallway, but Reyzl just stood there in her thick woolen nightgown, glaring at my hairless face.

"Do you have any idea what time it is?" she said, crossing her arms.

"Uh . . . No."

"It figures." She dropped her arms, turned her back to me, and stepped into her room.

I followed.

The bed sheets were rumpled, but I hadn't roused her from bed. She had been going through her things. There was a pile of clothes and other items next to a small trunk on a table by the window.

"Make it quick," she said, selecting a long black skirt from the pile.

"What are you doing?"

"What does it *look* like I'm doing?" she said, shaking out the skirt. "I'm going to stay with some friends in the Christian quarter until it's safe to come back."

She carefully folded the skirt and packed it in the trunk.

"If you're going to run away, why not come back to Slonim with me?" I asked.

"I am *not* running away! It's just for a few days till—oh, forget it. I don't have time for this now," she said, stuffing cosmetics into her blue purse with the gold tassels.

"You don't have time for *me*?"

"What are you going to do, start breaking furniture?"

"I've learned not to do such things since you left," I said. "I try not to react like that so much anymore."

"Not *so much* anymore? How about not reacting that way at all?"

"Believe me, I'm working on it."

"A couple of years too late, Benyamin."

She shoved a pair of silk slippers into the trunk.

"I'm trying to do better—"

"And where on earth are the Imperial protectors? Weren't you supposed to talk them into providing us with some protection? Any sign of *keyser* Rudolf's troops out there?" she said, waving her hand toward the window.

Her gesture made the candle flicker wildly.

"How are you going to get past the *Judenschläger*?" I said. "Where are you going to hide? Unless I can punch a hole in their defenses, you won't get twenty paces past the gates."

"Won't I?" she said, yet I sensed a wavering in her manner.

But she was still winning the war of words. How was I supposed to summon the strength to fight off hordes of Jew-bashers when I couldn't even convince a headstrong woman to listen to me for five minutes? And suddenly I felt extremely tired. I sat on the edge of the bed before my whole world collapsed like a house of cards.

The Guardian of Israel does not sleep. But I was no Guardian of Israel.

The candle kept flickering by the window, burning through its fleeting life and sending up a thin plume of smoke that would soon be the only sign that it had ever existed.

"Don't send me away like this," I said. "The ReMo says not to turn away a poor man without giving him *something*, even a dried fig."

Reyzl stood there, trying to decide between a white blouse and a red blouse, holding them up and examining them in the light as if trying to weigh their beauty against their usefulness over the next few days. Finally, she gave up and laid them both on the trunk.

Then she came over and sat next to me on the bed.

"Rough day, huh?" she said, patting me on the back with some of her old familiarity.

"Rough week," I answered. *Rough year. Rough life.*

"I can tell. You didn't used to give up so easily."

I let that one ping off me.

"You're just overtired," she said, rubbing my shoulders.

"I could do this if I just had some help. I can't do it all alone."

"The problem is that you're too tired and cranky to approach this logically."

"I'm not—"

"You're a good man, Benyamin. And when I first met you, you were the smartest boy on the block—"

"But it was an awfully small block."

"Listen to me. You're not thinking clearly. You need to rest so you can restore your energy and think clearly."

"I don't have *time* for that—"

"What do you mean? Didn't you always tell me that whenever a man eats and sleeps to keep up his strength so that he can carry out God's commands, those activities become holy and sacred as well?"

I closed my eyes and thought of God. After all, they say it's better to talk to a woman and think of God then to talk to God and think of a woman.

"At least you're trying to change things for the better. I can see that," she said. "And I believe that if anyone can save us, you can. But you can't do it if you're too tired to think straight. You need to relax and rest so you can get an early start tomorrow."

"Relax? How can I relax at a time like this? I shouldn't even have come here—"

"No, you did the right thing by coming here," she said, reaching behind her head.

She unpinned her long, dark hair, and shook it loose.

O, taste and see that the Lord is good.

It had been such a long time that her body was just like new to me. Her breasts were as sweet as two ripe apples, young and erect, like the very first time.

I breathed in as if I wanted to take in the moment and hold it inside me forever.

Then it hit me. I had to tell her.

"Wait. I'm not clean."

"Neither am I," she said, indicating that her period had ended but she hadn't taken her ritual bath yet. But by that point, I wouldn't have stopped for all the money in the world.

Two opposites converged, forming a divine circle, the very essence of life, and yet something beyond life, a union of souls for a brief instant. But even one hour in Paradise is good.

Her hands caressed my newly shorn head, and she couldn't help giggling.

"Good Lord, it feels like I'm making love to a Christian."

And her lips unfolded like a rose opening toward the sun.

זונטיק

Sonntag

Neděle

Sunday

Pay attention that you not ruin or destroy
My world, for if you ruin it, there will be
no one after you to repair it.

—GOD

Koheles Raboh

CHAPTER 31

A BLAST OF COLD AIR woke me, and my head felt strangely exposed. I put my hand to my cheek, felt its sandy nakedness, and wondered what world I was in. Then I remembered I had changed myself into a Christian.

Reyzl stood by the window, fully dressed, wrapping a hand mirror in a woolen shawl, and stuffing it into her trunk.

The icy draft had brought a strange man in with it, a hunched fellow clutching a bag full of papers and other scribal implements. His crabby hand stayed on the doorknob, as if he feared that he might have strayed into the wrong room.

"Come in, Reb Avreml," said Reyzl. "You're letting in the cold."

"Where's the second witness?" said Reb Avreml, pointing his long nose at me, which in the pale shadow of a tallow candle looked as shriveled as a pickle that had been steeped too long in brine.

"Isn't Reb Leibstein with you?"

"Coming, Miss Reyzl," said a boxy man with an unkempt beard, who at least had the decency to look uncomfortable with his assigned role in this affair. But the landlady trotted in with all the bubbly anticipation of a food vendor at a bullfight. *God damn it*, she was actually enjoying this.

I pulled the blankets around me and reached for my clothes, but the foreign garments piled on the chair weren't mine.

Oh, right. They were now.

How long had I been asleep?

It was still dark out, but a faint glimmer of the dawn's first light outlined the chimney tops outside the window.

Suddenly I was wide awake. How much time had I lost? And what did they need witnesses for? Some strange Bohemian fertility rite to mark our reconciliation? Were they going to shower us with seeds and tell us to be fruitful and multiply? Somehow, I didn't think so.

The scribe laid his tools on the night table and unfolded a document that consisted of long passages of unadorned Aramaic laid out in uncompromising rows of plain black letters, and instead of taking up the iron pen of the court scribe, he took up the kosher quill that a rabbinical scribe uses to create a Torah, a mezuzah, an amulet fulfilling the commandment to *bind them as a sign upon your hand*, or a bill of divorce.

"Husband's name?" he asked.

"Benyamin Ben-Akiva from Slonim," Reyzl answered, shutting the lid of the trunk.

The quill traveled from inkpot to parchment and scratched in my name.

"What do you think you're doing?" I said. "You can't write a *get* at the wife's bidding."

"Wife's name?"

"Reyzl bas Zalman Rozansky of Prague," she said, closing the latch with a distinctive *click*.

Reb Avreml inscribed Reyzl's name on the parchment.

"And you're writing it on a *yontef*?" I said.

"The rabbis have given us special permission due to the current emergency."

"I don't think this is what the rabbis had in mind."

"Shows what you know. Cause?" The pen hung in the air, waiting.

"The groom does not provide enough to support his bride," said Reyzl.

"He readily admits that this is the case?" said the scribe, sniffing at me with his pickle-nose.

The *get* wouldn't be valid without my approval. Otherwise, it was a thoroughly illegal and invalid document that would never stand up in court. I had it in my power to cling to her until she relented.

In theory, that is.

Then Reb Avreml advised me that the city fathers had already decided to place me under house arrest and keep me from leaving the ghetto in my—ahem—ridiculous costume, unless I approved the *get*.

God knows what strings Reyzl had pulled to get the rabbis to allow this.

I could have fought them on it. I could have battered through whatever flimsy cordon they used to hold me back, but then what? I couldn't fight the whole community by myself. (Right, it takes at least *three* people to do that.) And the community was clearly supporting their native daughter's cause.

Reb Meisel and Rabbi Loew would have backed me up, but Reyzl knew that I didn't have the time to summon them and make my case.

I nodded, but it wasn't enough. They needed to hear the words. For the record.

Finally, I said, "Yes, I admit it."

Scribble, scribble, scribble.

And so I approved the *get*, irrevocably divorcing my lawful wife, Reyzl, and giving her permission to marry another man, as witnessed on this, the 16th day of Nisan, 5352 years from the Creation of the World, by Reb Avreml ben Shloyme the scribe and Reb Rossl ben Shimon the rent collector. Then Reb Avreml folded the document and sewed it up with a special needle and thread, and placed it in Reyzl's hands.

And that was that.

"MAYBE I'LL SEE YOU SOMETIME at the great fair in Lublin," said Reyzl, trotting down the stairs as if she couldn't wait to get out into the open air.

I followed in silence, carrying her trunk on my shoulder.

"There's no one else, in case you were wondering," she said.

No one else *yet*. She didn't have to say it, but I bet she had a lot of possibilities.

"But I'm glad that you're finally giving me a second chance to produce an heir for my father, even if it's with another man," she said. "It shows a great heart and a charitable spirit on your part, and I'm thankful for it. Really I am."

I had nothing to add to that, although I certainly wondered who would be benefiting from my great heart and charitable spirit.

We descended into darkness, to an eerie nether region inhabited by the musty smell of damp stones—the bare bones of the original ground floor, long buried under layers of silt. I had to feel my way along the mold-covered walls with my free hand, but I still stumbled a couple of times, while Reyzl's step never faltered.

I finally saw the small window embedded high in a buttressed wall, a square shape only vaguely lighter than the surrounding blackness.

"I didn't realize there were so many ways out of the ghetto," I said.

Her eyes twinkled at me in the darkness.

"What about your parents?" I asked.

"It's safer if we split up. My father has his own way of taking care of things."

"I'll bet he does. Then why do you have to leave?"

"You saw what they did to the Kaminskys' print shop," she said. "I'd rather be alive and penniless than die defending my wealth. But if God wills it, we'll start over and build up the business again. Now, don't just stand there gawking at me. The least you can do is help me out the window."

I set down the trunk and shoved it closer to the wall.

"What about last night?"

"You needed a few hours' rest," she explained matter-of-factly. "Now I need you to go back out there and make the world safe for me and my people."

So she thought of last night as nothing more than a noble sacrifice for the good of the community?

But after a while, there was nothing left to do but cup my hands for her dainty feet and raise her to the level of the window. She undid the rusty catch herself and pushed open the tiny windowpane.

"I need another boost."

I raised her some more, till she could pull herself up and wriggle headfirst through the tiny opening to the dark alleyway above. Her legs danced in the air for a moment while she shifted her weight, then her long skirt vanished before my eyes.

Darkness. Then she thrust her head back in.

"My trunk, please."

I picked up the trunk and handed it to her.

"I will never forget you, Reyzl."

Her face was expressionless.

"Goodbye, Ben."

I STOOD THERE THINKING ABOUT the time we saw the Bremen Town musicians, and danced the night away without feeling the time go by, fitting together so tightly in each other's arms. Those were the days. But that was a long time ago, and getting further away by the minute.

SOMEONE WAS POUNDING ON the door.

I heard footsteps and heated voices. And as I felt my way back toward the stairs, one voice cut through the noise.

"What do you mean, he's not here? He *has* to be here. We need his help."

Anya's voice.

I bounded up the stairs, taking them two at a time, and came upon a scene straight out of a Roman tragedy. The landlady was blocking the doorway as Anya and her beloved Yankev stood on the threshold pleading their case. Like a pair of mirror opposites, Anya's face was flushed and passionate, while Yankev's was pale and trembling.

One look at Yankev's face and I knew. We all knew.

He had shown weakness, and they had broken him. They had tortured and tormented him until he talked, and Yankev was now a *moyser*, the lowest form of human life in the world. In fact, in the eyes of the community, he was now *subhuman*.

Anya said, "We need to hire a boat to take us across the river before—"

Before they whip him, break his bones, stuff him in a barrel, and dump him in the river.

"Before it gets too light," I said.

"Yes. And I'm afraid we'll need some money," she said, somewhat embarrassed to be asking for such things, and perhaps more than a little disappointed in the man she had chosen.

"Why are you taking up with this *paskudne moyser*?" said the landlady. "A man who is weaker than a couple of helpless women?"

"What can I say? I fell in love," she said.

"You fell in *something*, all right," said the landlady.

"What did you tell them?" I asked Yankev.

"We have to warn the rabbi," he said, keeping his eyes on the ground. "The Inquisitors said they'd be coming for the whole community with something called a *sub poena*, whatever that means."

"It means *under the penalty* of punishment, you putz," said the landlady.

"There's no need to get like that," Anya said.

"*What did you tell them?*" I asked. I wanted to grab him by the neck and shake him till his head fell off.

"He'll have to explain later—" said Anya.

"The Catholic authorities hold court sessions on Easter Sunday?" I said. "Even the Jews aren't working today."

"Why not?"

"It's the second day of Pesach," said Yankev, his voice shaking like a reed.

"I thought—" I stopped myself. I was going to say, *I thought you people respected your own Sabbath.*

"What are we going to do now?" Yankev whined.

"Well, for starters, you better learn how to say *Good morning* in Slovakian," said the landlady.

It was a harsh way of putting it, but Anya agreed.

"It is the Moravian custom to offer refuge to all exiles," Anya said. "In keeping with the commandment, *Thou shalt not deliver unto his master the slave who escapes from his master unto thee. He shall dwell with thee, even among you, in that place which he shall choose.*"

I told Yankev, "You'd better thank God for this woman, because she's your only salvation."

Then I took them to Rabbi Loew, but the Lion of Judah refused to bless their union.

"He's not worthy," said the rabbi.

"No, but she is."

"And even if he were, weddings are not permitted during the forty-nine days of mourning."

The sky was getting lighter with every passing minute, and I had no choice but to take the anxious couple down to Mordecai Meisel's house to beg a few gold pieces from their former benefactor. Anya directed us to the back entrance, where we found the cook hanging a leftover piece of Pesach matzoh over the door to protect the house from the Evil Eye during the coming year. At our insistence, the cook went and roused the master and brought him back to the kitchen.

"Why don't you take refuge in my shul?" said Meisel, adjusting the belt on the red velvet dressing gown he had thrown over his nightshirt. "The *keyser* has decreed that it shall be a sanctuary to all in need of his royal protection."

"Forgive me, Reb Meisel," I said, "but right now the best thing you can do for this poor bride is to present her with a dowry that will allow her to flee the city."

Anya averted her eyes, but I'll say one thing for the old fellow: Mordecai Meisel was one rich man who had not forgotten what it was like to be poor.

In the end he gave the unfortunate bride a generous dowry.

"Oh, and one other thing," I said.

"Yes?" said Meisel, tapping his foot as if we were pushing the limits of his hospitality.

"We could also use a glass with a few drops of wine in it."

His expression took a whirlwind tour through the regions of confusion and surprise before coming to rest in the land of understanding and acceptance.

"Very well." He instructed the cook to bring us a glass of wine from the sideboard. She grudgingly left to fulfill his request. "So tell me, what kind of wedding is this supposed to be?"

There was an awkward exchange of glances, before I stepped in to fill the silence.

"She probably knows more about what it takes to be a Jew than he knows about what it takes to be a Christian," I suggested.

We all looked at Anya, but she had already made up her mind.

"Yes," she said. "I think it would be easier for me to become a Jew than it would be for Yankev to become a Christian."

Something changed in the room. We took a moment to meditate on this, in silent reverence for this Christian maiden's willingness to sacrifice her freedom and safety for her husband's sake.

Then I did my duty and posed the question: "Why do you want to become a Jew? Don't you know that the Israelites are hated, oppressed, and despised wherever they go?"

"Yes, I know."

"Yet you still want to become one of us?"

"Only if you will accept me. I mean *truly* accept me."

Her broad brow and Slavic cheekbones were untouched by paint, or rouge, or the dyer's brush, as the rabbis say, yet she was radiating a noble beauty from every angle of her face.

"We shall," I said. "For if God can send an angel of the Lord to Sarah's lowly handmaid, Hagar, when she was exiled in the wilderness, then surely we can find it within ourselves to welcome the newcomer with all our hearts. Indeed, God commands us to love the convert like a newborn child."

Tears were forming in Anya's eyes, reflecting her deepest gratitude. Or maybe she was weeping for the world she was leaving behind.

The cook returned with the glass of wine and handed it to me with a disapproving look. Then she set about foraging through her utensils with a great clattering of metal. I just hoped she wasn't looking for the carving knife.

"Are you ready to go through with this?" I asked.

"I am," said Anya.

"Not in *my* kitchen, you don't," said the cook, seizing a soup ladle. When I looked to her for explanation, she said, "The pope has forbidden such secret marriages."

"Since when have we given a damn what the pope thinks?"

"Since he started burning Jewish books," said Yankev, who suddenly looked like he was sorry he'd spoken.

"It is no matter, since I would rather obey Christ than the Church," said Anya. "And doesn't it say somewhere in the Talmud that deeds of kindness are equal in weight to all the commandments?"

"Yes, it does," I said, admiring her *chutzpah*. "Your native wit just needs the right whetstone, Anya. And any teacher in the land would be happy to have a student with a mind as sharp as yours."

I couldn't resist touching her shoulder as a sign of our mutual feelings for each other.

"And I said not in my kitchen," the cook repeated, swatting my hand off Anya's shoulder with the back of her ladle.

"It's all right," said Anya. "I'm just—"

She didn't finish, but I think the word she was looking for was "overwhelmed."

I cocked my head in Meisel's direction.

Reb Meisel was fiddling with the waist cord of his velvet dressing gown. And if I didn't know better, I'd say he was actually growing uncomfortable with the idea of displaying his full generosity before his own servant and the increasingly narrow-minded community of elders that she spoke for.

He pinched the velvet cord till his thumbnail grew white, and he said, "Yes, perhaps it would be better if you did this outside my house."

Yankev couldn't bring himself to meet my gaze as we stepped into the alley.

The sky was growing dangerously bright. It was going to be a beautiful day for somebody, but at the moment the light was our enemy, as if we were demons of the night. And all I could think was that a short time from now, the Holy One, *borukh hu*, would be opening three books, and the names of the righteous would be written in the Book of Life, and the names of the wicked would be written in the Book of Death, and the people who fall between the two would be kept in suspense for ten full days, awaiting God's final Judgment. Would God find us deserving of life or death? For if God can find fault with His own angels, as Rashi says, what more can we expect of a mere mortal?

I positioned the young couple for the ceremony, with nothing but sooty bricks for a bridal canopy.

"Wait a minute," said Anya. "Don't you have to be a rabbi to do this?"

"He's as close as we're going to get," said Yankev, raising his eyes from the ground. His face was an elongated mask of contrition.

Anya's face was more complex. There was joy in it, for any marriage is a joyful affair, but there was also anguish, like the face of a *kheyder* child who's afraid to ask a question out of fear of getting slapped with the wooden ruler. Or maybe I was just seeing the sweet sadness of a young woman who knew that it was our fate to take divergent paths, and that we newfound friends would likely never see each other again.

Love can be painful at times, but sometimes it's all we've got. So I took a step closer and raised her chin with my fingertips, and spoke to her softly like a father to a beloved daughter.

"Rabbi Loew says that the people of Israel are prone to great extremes— they are either outstandingly righteous or terrible sinners," I said, doing my best to fit Yankev's behavior somewhere onto the grand surveyor's map delineating the borders of human experience.

"He also says that someday, when the Messiah *ben Dovid* comes to establish his kingdom and usher in an era of two thousand years of peace, the world will know that he is descended from a non-Jewish mother on one side, just as

King David was descended from a Moabite and King Solomon from an Ammonite. May your union be so blessed."

Rabbi Loew also says that the Messiah's predecessor, the Messiah *ben Yoseph*, will be slain during the final battle between the nations of the world to destroy Israel. But I didn't mention that.

I stepped back and beheld them both.

I held up the glass of wine. It was made of fine crystal, more fitting for a rich man's dining room than this dull gray alley, but its facets caught the light and transformed it, endlessly folding in on itself and illuminating some wondrous inner world like a chandelier in a hall of mirrors, before being trapped in the sharp-angled corridors from which no light can ever escape.

I went on: "Our masters say that whenever a man and a woman come together in the spirit of all that is pure and holy, the Divine presence is with them."

Then I said the blessing over the wine. "*Borukh atoh Adinoy, eloheynu meylekh ha-oylem, boyrey pri hagofn.*"

"*Omeyn.*"

"Now repeat after me: *I will have thee as my wife.*"

"I will have thee as my wife," said Yankev, his voice tight with emotion.

"And you echo his words." I had to prompt her: "*I will have thee as my husband.*"

"I will have thee as my husband," said Anya, like a woman who had just awakened from a pleasant dream, only to find the real world drab and cold by comparison.

"Now, I don't know how they do it in this *meshigene* town, but where I come from the bride protects the groom from jealous demons by walking around him three times, although some do it seven times."

"Then we better make it seven times," said Anya.

Her feet traced seven circles around her bridegroom as the sky grew lighter and lighter.

"Is that all there is to it?" she asked when she was done.

"Almost." I said the seven benedictions, then held the glass to the groom's lips. He swallowed what little he could, then I held the glass to Anya's lips. She took a sip, then I handed the glass back to Yankev. He took it from me, turned to the north and hurled the glass at the blackened bricks. It shattered into a hundred pieces, scattering the hordes of spiteful spirits and sending shards of wine-soaked glass flying toward their greenish eyes.

"*Mazl tov!*" I said.

They kissed. It was a hurried glancing peck with dry lips, but they would have plenty of time for deep and soulful kisses later.

"When you get where you're going, you'll have to go through the proper legal formalities and immerse in a *mikveh*," I told Anya. Only then would she be a full-fledged Jew, and ritually cleansed.

She looked worried.

"He'll show you what to do," I said, which brought a smile of relief to her lips.

I guided the newlyweds to the secret passageway beneath the whorehouse, which snaked dimly through the sunken ghosts of ancient houses for half a block or more before connecting to a house on the other side of the high wall.

I started up the steps, but Yankev grabbed my sleeve.

"Don't go," he said. "I mean, it could be dangerous. You better let me go first."

I let him go first. Anya watched him climb the steps, admiring his bravery.

Then she reached into her sack, brought forth a shiny golden ring with a clasp in the shape of a fishhook, and clipped it to my ear.

"*Ow!*"

"You're going to the waterfront," she said. "And every true sailor knows that a gold earring will keep a man safe from going down with the ship."

"Good thinking," I said, trying not to show any pain.

We started up the steps. Yankev lifted the latch and stuck his head out the door, then motioned for us to follow. We emerged through an unmarked door to the street, where the glowing skies in the east threatened to expose our activities.

It was time for us to separate. But Anya suddenly seemed to remember something, and said that she had one more thing to give me. She slid her fingers under her collar, undid the clasp, and removed the medallion and thin gold chain that she had been wearing around her neck.

"Come closer," she said, and she slipped the chain over my head. "To complete your disguise."

The chain was still warm from the touch of her body.

I looked at the medallion.

"It's St. Jude," she said. "The patron saint of lost causes."

She threw her arms around me and gave me a parting hug, pressing so close that I caught a whiff of her sweet smell, which reminded me of an early spring flower, while Reyzl had always reminded me of a late summer rose.

She gave me a quick kiss on the cheek before she broke away.

Yankev bowed his head, but he didn't offer me his hand, saving me the trouble of having to refuse it.

I didn't know what to say.

But when the words came, they came straight from the heart. "I wish you both happiness. You truly deserve it."

And I watched them go, hugging the shadows as they headed east along the riverbank like a pair of beggars fleeing the city.

Part of me actually envied the young couple. For in spite of all their troubles, their life together was just starting. They had the skills and knowledge to make their way, hope for the future, and most of all, they had each other.

It's not good to be alone.

And I couldn't help succumbing to the sadness of something that would never be. A third child with my wife. One who lived.

It didn't matter if it was a boy or a girl.

Because a man lives on through his children.

Your body dies either way, but without children, without a son to say Kaddish for you, you do not live on in memory. Death is truly the end.

At least Anya and Yankev had each other, I thought.

And then I heard the sound of trumpets.

CHAPTER 32

THE SAUSAGES SIZZLED IN the pan, shrinking and browning around the edges, oily bubbles of fat hissing and popping as the eel merchant poked them with a sharp stick.

The fish market was nearly empty at this hour, and the cross atop the Agnes Convent hung over the wide, empty space before us. I'd almost forgotten what open space felt like.

And my head still felt cold.

Knots of Christian revelers gathered at the river's edge, piling merrily into boats that ferried them to the other shore, where pockets of early risers dotted the fields, waiting to see the sun dance on Easter day.

And for a moment I envied the Christians' freedom to misbehave without thinking about the consequences, because no matter what they did, no matter what rules they broke, they would wake up tomorrow in a sane and stable world. We had no such assurances.

The blare of trumpets had heralded the thunderous arrival of a company of imperial guards to escort the Inquisitor's envoys with their writ of *Sub Poena*. And before the dust had settled, the foot patrols had stormed into the ghetto and began rounding up Jews, while the horse guards spread out and took up positions outside the gates to "protect the emperor's property," as they put it.

There were only three guards at the Northwest Gate, mounted on imposing armored steeds, but their protection was more symbolic than substantive against the growing number of angry faces accusing them of being pawns of the Jews.

And I had to stand by watching it from a safe distance. The hardest part was pretending to enjoy it.

The eel merchant laughed as he prodded the sausages.

"Tell me please what you are laughing at," I said.

"Those idiots won't be happy till every friggin' Jew is killed, converted, or chased out of the kingdom," he said. "Too bad the Jews know how to fight back."

"Yes, they say that six kingdoms have tried to destroy these Jews, and they're still here," I said, trying to speak Czech with a Polish accent. "But surely they are no match for a kingdom as powerful as this one."

"Where'd you say you were from?"

"From the good town of Czestóchowa."

"Where's that?"

"It is in the distance of two hundred miles of Prague."

"Uh-huh. Ain't that Poland?"

"Yes, in its western part."

The sky was brightening, and musicians in matching red-and-yellow outfits hustled toward the main square, while the imperial guards kept things in order by trotting alongside a steady stream of dark-clothed Jews flowing southward from the gates. It looked like the whole population of the *Yidnshtot* was being rounded up and herded to some church on the south side of the ghetto.

A couple of filthy street boys chased after the Jews, pelting them with rotten scraps of fish. But they soon ran out of ammunition.

"So you wanna buy some eels?" he said.

"No, thanks."

He stabbed a sausage too deeply, and it released some juices that spattered in the grease. The eel merchant jerked his hand away and cursed, then he licked the spot and prodded the sausages more gently, turning them just a little. They were slowly browning all the way around.

"Then you must be after something else," he said.

"Well, actually, uh—"

"You've made it plain enough," he said, spearing a sausage and transferring it to a battered metal dish. "Go ahead. Take one."

"Oh, no. I couldn't."

"Shut up and take it already," he said, spearing another sausage and blowing on it. "My mom sent them. Best damn sausages in town."

Now what? Should I pretend to bite into the sausage and spit it on the ground or into my sleeve when he wasn't looking? No, the two of us were too close together and there were too few distractions for anything like that to work.

"You've been staring at them long enough," he said, stuffing his mouth with meat. "I know you want one."

I decided that my first priority was to keep my Christian identity intact and not jeopardize the plan.

"May God repay you," I said, taking one of the sausages. I started to say a silent *brukhe*, and had to stop myself. *What's the blessing for pork?* There wasn't one, of course. So I bit through the crisp skin and chewed, the warm juices spilling across my tongue and down my gullet. It tasted just like any other sausage meat, really.

So I stood there munching on pork sausage and watching the flow of people shrink to a trickle as the ghetto was emptied of Jews. The two street boys grew bored with their game and drifted back across the square.

My companion took a swig from an earthenware jug, wiped his mouth on his sleeve, and offered me a swallow. "Here, this'll take the wax out of your ears," he said.

"*Ne, děkuji*, it's a little too early in the morning—"

"Don't they celebrate Easter in Poland?"

I had to keep up appearances, so I took a swig of the raw alcohol, which cut through the pork fat and burned all the way down. I shivered a bit, which made the eelmonger laugh.

"What'sa matter? You never had *slivovice* before?"

"Ours is smoother," I said, coughing.

He laughed and slapped me on the back, hard. Right on my bruised shoulder. It hurt so much tears came to my eyes, and I figured it was time to jump feet first into the void before he noticed anything.

"You know, forty days of Lent is an awfully long time to go without certain pleasures," I said. "And I'm looking to buy some top-quality meat."

"With what money?" he said. "You look like you don't have a half-a-pfennig to sew up the holes in your breeches."

I dug into my pocket, took out one of Meisel's silver dalers, and dropped it into the metal tray.

One of his eyebrows arched, then he plucked the coin from the tray and put it in his mouth to suck the grease off it. He took it out of his mouth and examined both sides of the coin, and his lips curled up into a lopsided smile.

"Well, that changes things now, don't it?" he said. "How much meat were you looking for?"

"A whole cartload."

His eyes became two slits.

"What do you need that much meat for?" he asked.

"Actually, I'm more interested in the two men who were driving the cart."

His eyes looked east, west, and south.

"Something wrong?" I asked.

"Nothing," he said. "It's just that the sheriff's men came around yesterday, poking into everything and asking a lot of questions about a cartful of meat."

"The municipal guards are no friends of mine."

"I bet they're not. But you can't be too careful."

"No, you can't."

His gaze became distant.

I waited for his answer while my stomach grumbled, punishing me for eating that *treyfene* sausage.

Finally, he called out to one of the street boys: "Marko!"

He tossed the kid a copper farthing.

"Watch the stand till I get back."

THE PUBLIC BATHS THAT MORDECAI Meisel had built for the community lay empty and abandoned, and the rowboat heaved against the dock as we climbed aboard. I grabbed the bowsprit and got a palmful of splinters for my trouble. Carved into the main beam above my hand was a creature with three faces, sharp ears, and a pointed tongue. It was wielding a sword and a drinking horn, like a pagan idol.

"I see you've met Svantovit," he said. "Our protector since the olden days. He's got three faces because he watches over the past, the present, and the future."

And from where I was standing, the future didn't look too good.

I pulled some of the splinters out of my palm and squatted on the bench seat for a closer look at the three-faced idol. It was skillfully crafted, though not by a master.

"I carved that myself," he said.

"It's pretty good. You should have been apprenticed to a woodcarver."

"My old man made damn sure to crush that idea pretty early on," he said, handing me a piece of kindling from the cooking fire. Its tip was glowing reddish orange.

"That's too bad."

"What's the difference?" he said, slipping the painter and shoving off. "Make sure you keep that ember protected from the wind."

"That would have made me angry as hell."

"What'd you say your name was?"

"Vasil."

"Well, listen to me, Vasil. I could teach you things about anger that would curl your hair," he said, putting his back into it and steering us in the direction of the old mill on the other side of the river.

The castle rock loomed over us, casting its wide shadow across the water.

Off to the east, between the water and the sky, a disturbance shimmered like heat rising from an oven, and suddenly the bright orange lip of the sun appeared with a flash and bled across the horizon like molten fire. Distant cheers filled the fields, as the rounded rim of the sun slowly rose from its nighttime wanderings beneath the mantle of the earth.

"Yeah, I hated my old man, too. So how far are we going?" I said, eyeing the unfamiliar terrain. Langweil's model of Prague didn't include the area north of the Vltava.

"Don't worry, I'll get you there in plenty of time. What's the big rush?"

"No rush," I said, trying to push the conversation along. But the rolling of the swells did not sit well with me, and I burped up the taste of that forbidden sausage.

"I just need a couple of men who can keep quiet about what's in the meat wagon. Know what I mean?"

The sun rose higher. Easter morning was going to be beautiful. The air was sharp and clear, the colors brighter, the texture of the stones visible from a greater distance. I could even make out the severed heads on the stone bridge, though they were too far away to tell the common criminals from the rebels.

"That kind of quiet costs more than a few dalers," he said.

"I can get it."

"From where?"

"That depends."

"On what?"

"On finding the two men who drove a shipment of meat from Kopecky's slaughterhouse down the Kreuzgasse early yesterday morning."

"Oh, *them*. Sure, I saw them. Whadaya wanna know about them?"

The waves buffeted the small craft, and I wondered just how deep and swift the current was in this part of the river. The combination of pork sausage, rolling swells, and that slug of firewater was definitely getting to me.

"Where are we headed?" I asked.

"You see that?"

He pointed to a dark, gaping hole in the side of the earth.

"Six feet high and half a mile long," he said. "Eleven years of digging and it's almost finished. It's gonna supply the water for the pond in the emperor's garden."

"So it leads straight to the Royal Game Park?"

"Pretty much. So what's so special about those two drivers?" he asked.

"I've heard they can keep their mouths shut."

The taste of that *treyf* came bubbling up from my gut again.

"You know, I always figured that the easiest place to dump a body would be the river," I said, gripping the gunwales and trying to keep my breakfast down.

"Nah. It might float back to the surface."

"And you wouldn't want that to happen."

"Course not. Is that what you need such quiet men for?" he asked.

I didn't answer.

"I mean, who's paying for this?"

"You don't need to know that."

My jaw clamped tight as another wave of nausea came over me.

When it passed, I said, "Can you just tell me what they looked like?"

"Is that what you're after?" he said, pulling us close in to shore.

"Unless you happen to know their names and addresses."

"Better than that. I can take you right to their hideout."

He jumped over the side and steadied the boat. I followed his lead and dropped to the ground, where my boots sank into the muck, and together we dragged the boat up onto the shore.

I still felt fairly woozy.

The mouth of the tunnel was easily six feet high and more than ten feet wide, with wooden supports shoring it up every few yards. I couldn't imagine the labor involved in cutting a tunnel this size half a mile deep into the side of a mountain, just to supply the emperor with fresh water for his man-made pond.

The water was only about a foot deep at first, but after a couple of steps, it got much deeper and came pouring into my boots, the water so icy cold that it hurt. A few more steps and it had climbed up to my knees.

"There's a dry spot over here where they keep the torches," he said, stepping into a recess cut into the rock. He took the smoldering twig from my hand and ignited a pitch-soaked quarterstaff with it.

The cave lit up, and I drew back from the sight of bleached bones and shrunken skin laid across a rock. But it was only the dried carcass of a fox or a raccoon.

The eel merchant led the way, and I followed the smell of burning pitch for a good fifty yards or so before he said, "So what's your trade then?"

"Oh, this and that."

"Come on, I know how to keep my mouth shut. Ask anyone."

I made him think he was dragging it out of me.

"I feed the melancholiacs' habits," I said.

"What's that mean?"

"It means there are many rare and imported herbs that can lift the spirit, and there's plenty of money to be made supplying them to the melancholiacs."

"You must mean the *rich* melancholiacs."

"My goods don't come cheap."

"You apothecary types sure have it made." He shook his head and chuckled at me. "Selling pipe dreams to the rich, following strange men down dark tunnels—"

I sensed it coming before he swung the torch at me. I backed up through the knee-deep water as he kept swinging the torch in furious arcs that made his face glow orange on one side then the other. Then I backed into the bare rock face, and the only thing left to do was lunge toward him as he tried to set fire to my clothes. My tunic was too damp to catch right away, but then a sharp burning bit into my shoulder and I pulled away, off-balance. He barreled into me, and I fell backward. We both hit the icy water, which slapped me in the face like the flat edge of a sword. Thankfully the flame sizzled and went out.

I went under. He dropped the torch and tried to hold me down, the water chilling my veins and numbing my senses. But I've learned a few things about severe cold in my time and even though my limbs should have been deadened by the cold, I still found his fingers and pried them away from my throat.

We broke the surface and fought and kicked and grabbed and punched, churning up the water like a boiling pot, until he let out a snarl that echoed through the tunnel and tried to bite me in the neck, his teeth glistening in the darkness. My hand groped around in the water and finally found the extinguished torch. I brought it up and tried to stuff it into his mouth. He clawed the air trying to grab the torch, but I spun it around and whacked him in the groin, and when he dropped to his knees, I got behind him, pressed my knee between his shoulder blades and held the rod against his windpipe.

"You better say your prayers," I hissed into his ear.

I wanted to beat his skull against the rocks until there was nothing left of him but wet skin and a few clumps of hair.

Instead I waited until his head sagged loosely and he crumpled over, then I took the rope from around my waist and tied his hands behind his back. When that was done, I splashed his face with water, hauled him to his feet, and marched him back the way we came.

"Lucky for you I'm a God-fearing man," I said. "What's your name, anyway?"

"Tomáš," he said, his voice all hoarse.

"Your full name."

"Kromy. Tomáš Kromy."

"Well, Tomáš, you've just done the worst thing you could possibly have done to me."

"Yeah? What's that?"

"You wasted my time."

"So file a friggin' lawsuit against me."

Great. Now I had to rush back to the ghetto without having learned anything useful about the men who drove the butcher's cart.

But when we emerged into the light, I saw that the gates of the *Yidnshtot* had been breached, and the smoke and sparks were flying upward.

And Tomáš just loved that. It even made him smile.

CHAPTER 33

THE WHOLE STINKING CITY was a mess, thought the bishop. Even on Easter day, the holiest day of the calendar, a day that was supposed to unite all Christians, the Bohemians were dancing their little jigs on the east side of the square and the Germans were doing the same on the west side, but they might as well have been half a world apart. And some idiot on the city council had foolishly given free rein to a bunch of Venetian architects whose undisciplined demolition crews had turned this quiet neighborhood of old stone churches, elegant gardens, and stately town houses to rubble and mud.

The unruly mobs of people shoving to the front of the church reminded him of a bunch of farm animals jostling for a spot at the feeding trough. They were practically climbing over each other just to get a glimpse of the glittering gold monstrances, instead of solemnly contemplating the mystery of their salvation and preparing to receive the Body of Christ. But what they lacked in politeness they made up for in passion. They smote their chests three times while repeating the confessional *por mi culpas*, and they filled the coffers with their pennies, buying scraps of the martyred girl's dress, locks of her golden hair, and other holy relics to take home and worship, which clearly demonstrated the sincerity of their devotion.

One of the Fuggers was there to ensure that every penny was properly recorded.

And to top it off, some *Dummkopf* had decided that today would be the perfect day to cram the whole population of the *Judenstadt* into a single church and force them to listen to a conversionist sermon. So the town sheriff had to drag his men out of bed and pull them off other duties just to handle the crowds.

And now thousands of Jews were standing out in the cold, waiting to have their ears inspected for wax or cotton plugs before they were allowed to enter the church. They were patted down one by one and directed to stand against the north wall while guards patrolled the marble tiles armed with pikes and paddles in case an impiety was whispered or a drowsy head nodded off.

As the Mass dragged on, the bishop's eyes wandered to the face of Jesus in a high relief of the Last Supper. It was odd how the sculptors had elected to carve such deep worry lines into the Savior's brow, when the current preference was to depict the passive tranquillity of a being who was not of this earth. This Christ who stood before him was a man of flesh and blood whose halo receded into nothingness. You could barely see it. Bishop Stempfel would have to have a talk with the master craftsman and remind him that such literalism was dangerously close to the Protestant heresy.

The same was true of *Die Silberlinge*, another high relief sculpture of the silver-tongued Judas betraying his master for a bag of coins. The sinister group of conspirators hid their crooked features behind their cloaks as they whispered to each other, in stark contrast to the open and honest faces of the other witnesses to the Passion. And all of them except Judas wore the pointed "Jewish hats" that were still common until quite recently, when they were replaced by the yellow badges. And so the moment of Christ's capture, the judgment of Pilate, and the Stations of the Cross all depicted Jews as living memories in a way that made it look like the Jews were *still* betraying Christ. No wonder the common people hated them so much.

Once the guards established order, Brother Popel began his sermon, which relied on stitching together tried-and-true phrases, and included whole passages repeated word-for-word from the mundane lectures at the Jesuit college.

The bishop looked upon the Jews, and saw their cheeks sunken with hunger and their thrice-turned clothes falling to shreds before his eyes. Where were all the gold teeth and diamond brooches that the Jews had allegedly acquired by squeezing the Christians for so many years? It could have been a clever subterfuge, but it wasn't easy to fake sunken cheeks.

So Brother Popel wasn't going to save any souls by telling these world-weary Jews that they needed to learn the *true* meaning of the Old Testament by abandoning their false interpretations of it and focusing on "the plain sense of the text," which he tried to quote in Hebrew.

When the bishop saw that the Jews were desperately trying to keep from laughing at the priest's awful pronunciation, he interrupted the sermon by ringing a little bell he kept on a nearby table for just such a purpose.

The priest's words echoed and died, and all eyes turned toward the bishop, who summoned Brother Zeman and instructed him to read aloud from the Book of Exodus.

Zeman approached the rostrum with his chest puffed up like a gamecock's. He licked his fingers and turned the pages of the massive gold-trimmed Bible until he found the place that the bishop had indicated. Then he took a couple of practice breaths, and launched into a long passage in Latin.

When he finished, he looked up from the book, exulting in this moment of glory, and the sound of his heavy breathing could be heard from a great distance off.

Zeman looked lost for a moment, then his years of training took over.

"*Verbum Domini*," he chanted.

"Amen," the congregation responded.

But before the Mass was ended, upon the bishop's signal, Popel announced that a great debate was about to occur in which the Jews would be called upon to defend their false interpretations of the Bible. There was much stirring among the Jewish folk while Popel coolly laid out his materials, including books and other documents.

After a brief but intense discussion, an elderly rabbi stepped forward and asked for permission to speak. The bishop graciously granted him this privilege with a nod of his head.

"State your name for the *Statschreiber*," said Popel, indicating the city secretary who was scribbling away at his portable writing table.

"Rabbi Yehudah Liwa ben Betzalel," said the old rabbi, his surprisingly robust voice reverberating through the nave and transept.

So this was the famous Rabbi Loew, thought the bishop. That ought to make this whole dreadful affair a bit more interesting.

But the name *Betzalel* drew gasps from some of the less-educated Christians, and the bishop heard words like *Beelzebub* and *Azaziel* being whispered up and down the aisles.

The bishop carefully adjusted his seat cushion. The area down below was still tender, but his condition had improved slightly since Dr. Lybrmon had begun treating him with salves and sutures. He had also said something ridiculous about laying off the spices. That doctor certainly had an odd manner about him, and the bishop wouldn't have been the least bit surprised to discover that he was one of those closeted crypto-Jews. They were everywhere, trying to blend in, but he could smell one from twenty feet away.

The renowned rabbi bowed slightly and addressed Popel by name: "Father Hermann, you say that we possess the Law, but we misinterpret it, and we need you to tell us its correct meaning. Are you therefore saying that God made a mistake and delivered the Torah to the wrong people?"

There was an atmosphere of hushed expectation under the vaulted roof.

But Popel didn't have to think about that one for very long.

"The Bible clearly states that the Torah was delivered to Moses at Mount Sinai," he replied. "But the Jewish people were not chosen because of any special merit on their part. They were merely chosen to serve as caretakers of the Law until the light of Christ could come and illuminate its true meaning."

He nodded once for emphasis, like a field-tennis player scoring a difficult point, but Rabbi Loew lobbed it right back.

"If that is truly the case, then it must follow that we remain His chosen people whether we deserve the honor or not, and so the Christian position that God has abandoned us to exile due to our lack of merit must likewise be dismissed."

Popel blinked.

"What are you implying?" he said.

"I am merely suggesting that there is evidence which supports the proposition that God predetermines some events, but not others," said Rabbi Loew.

"Are you suggesting that the world is governed not by design but by *accident*?"

"That would certainly explain a lot."

There was some laughter from the Bohemian side of the nave.

"Enough of this clever Jewish talk," said Popel. "For I have it on the highest authority that one of your own, a certain rabbi's apprentice named Yankev ben Khayim, has this very day confessed to using the blood of a Christian girl to perform all manner of vile alchemical and Kabbalistic magic."

It was a hard shot up the middle, and a good portion of the crowd reacted with horror, as Popel surely knew they would. Rabbi Loew tried to even the score before it tipped any further against him: "And I cite the authority of your own Pope Innocent IV and King Charles of Bohemia, who prohibited their subjects from bringing ritual murder charges against the Jews."

It was a good point, but the moment didn't last.

Popel said, "My Lord, we also have a written record which shows that this Jew named Yankev also confessed to harboring desires for the flesh of a Christian woman."

The Bohemians shrugged it off, but the Germans were scandalized. The bishop actually felt sorry for Rabbi Loew, who could have held his own in a rational debate with a dozen of the bishop's best-trained priests, but once the Germans' emotions were aroused, the rabbi's logic was useless.

Finally, Rabbi Loew said, "A man will confess to anything under torture."

"All we did was put him on the water board for a couple of hours," Popel said dismissively. "And yet he was ready to confess to the sin of *bestialitas*."

There was confusion on both sides of the nave, and Popel had to explain that having intercourse with a Jew is the same as copulating with a dog, which is why it's called bestiality.

Although a good lawyer could probably get the charges reduced to sodomy, but it didn't really matter since the punishment was the same: burning at the stake. The bishop remembered the old days, when sexual transgressors were torn apart by wild beasts, but since so many of them were women these days, the judges had gotten lenient in their sentencing.

"If one man sins, will you be angry with the entire community?" asked the rabbi. "For even your Lord Jesus had a thief and a traitor within his most trusted circle of apostles."

"A traitor who was a Jew."

"They were *all* Jews! Christ himself was born a Jew."

"In outward appearance only."

Ah. That was the ace. Rabbi Loew had finally run afoul of the boundary marker of faith, which held that the divinity of Christ filled the heavens before the first day of Creation, and therefore predated the existence of Judaism. The bishop shifted in his seat, waiting to see how the rabbi would get himself out of this trouble spot.

The rabbi weighed and tested his words, then said, "In your Gospel it is written that Jesus cried out, *Father forgive them, for they know not what they do.* If Jesus is indeed your Lord and Master, then why don't you obey his command and forgive us?"

Some of the congregation sat there scratching their chins and considering this point, while others leapt to their feet and cursed Rabbi Loew for using the Lord's name in such a way. Popel responded with a brilliant rhetorical strategy that turned the tables on his adversary. "First tell me how *you* would explain that, Rabbi."

The hall grew hushed, expectant.

"I think we can all agree that there are natural differences between the nations of the world," the rabbi said.

Many of the people nodded.

"And so it is natural for people to react differently to the same events."

The rabbi paused to see if they were still following him.

"Therefore, when someone speaks out against my faith, I do not try to stop him from speaking. I listen in order to understand his position so that we may clarify the matter."

The rabbi went on: "Some believe that one's faith is strengthened when people are forbidden from speaking against it, but that is not so. What strength does a man show when he forbids his opponent from defending himself?"

By God, even some of the Germans were agreeing with him on that. Think of the converts we could make with a man like this rabbi on our side, thought the bishop.

Popel rushed in. "You make it sound as if we are talking about the difference between hard-boiled eggs and soft-boiled eggs. What about when the other man speaks *blasphemy*, as in this heretical book which was published in Italy barely ten years ago?"

He held up a copy of dei Rossi's *Meor Enayim.*

The rabbi let slip an oath in his Judeo-German dialect that sounded like "*Weh ist mir.*"

Popel challenged him directly. "This arrogant and impious author dares to question the traditional chronology of the Bible! What do you have to say to *that*, Rabbi?"

"I would advise every pious Jew in the land not to read such a book, or even to hold it in his hands. Such heretical words deserve to be burned in the fire."

"Then you agree that the Inquisitional authorities have the right to prohibit certain books?"

"I didn't say that. I said it *deserves* to be burned. But the rabbis have discussed the matter and have reached a compromise, and have ruled that the book is forbidden to any person under the age of twenty-five. That is our way."

"Most cunningly does Satan mask his magic under the appearance of religion," said Popel, quoting directly from the unpublished *Compendium Maleficarum*. "For know you all that this selfsame Jew, this Yankev ben Khayim, did confess under torture that the book that you revere above all others, the perversely heretical Talmud, which is written in the infernal alphabet of the Chaldeans that can only be read by magicians and sorcerers—"

He brandished the volume like an assault weapon, and the crowd drew back in terror of the strange writing.

"—which you Jews are flooding the country with like so much excrement from your filthy printing presses, does state quite clearly that *Jesus practiced magic*, and it compares Christianity to a form of heresy."

The predictable uproar followed, and the city guards had to come between the hordes of outraged Christians and the fearful tribe of Jews huddled together for warmth, their knees trembling beneath their tattered cloaks. The Christians accused the Jews of conspiring with the Turks to take over Germany, like the time they helped the Moors occupy the city of Toulouse (even though the Moors never occupied that city), of splitting the Church in order to strengthen their own position (even though Martin Luther hated the Jews almost as much as he hated the Catholics), of using magic to cause a recent series of bad harvests (even though such magic is prohibited in the Torah), of betraying Jesus to the Romans (even though Jesus had given Himself up freely and voluntarily), and of plotting to exterminate the entire Christian population by poisoning the wells, just like they did in Toulouse (again).

Enough with the Jews, already, thought the bishop, drumming his fingers. I've got *real* heretics to pursue. The place is practically crawling with them. Why, in the district of Obermarchtal alone, with a population of fewer than five hundred souls, they had executed *fifty* witches in the past two years.

The bishop called for order, which was soon restored with the help of Vilém Rožmberk, who was always preaching moderation in matters of religious differences. The bishop gave Rabbi Loew one final opportunity to defend his position.

"I am greatly obliged to you, Your Grace," the rabbi said. "It is indeed unfortunate that the Rabbis who wrote the Talmud did not always have a complete understanding of the many ways in which Christians view the life of Jesus. But there is still much that can be learned from the ancients, who saw fit to abolish capital punishment, while in many countries today one can still be hanged for stealing a loaf of bread. They also established the principle that any statements made under duress cannot be used to incriminate a person in a court of law. Surely these rulings should be carefully considered, even in expurgated form, rather than be consigned forever to the flames, Your Grace."

When the bishop made no reply, Rabbi Loew continued: "And as to the charges that we use blood to perform magical spells, Your Grace knows very well that the Laws of God strictly forbid the use of blood for any such purposes. Moreover, I defy any of you to come forward and swear on the Bible that you have witnessed a single Jew committing one of the crimes for which we stand accused. For it is written, *He who suspects the innocent suffers in his body*."

The bishop nearly jumped out of his seat.

"Where is that written?" he demanded.

"It is in the Tractate Yoma, Your Grace."

The bishop sat back and carefully rearranged his robes, and in the spirit of the moment, he proposed a compromise. The Talmud would not be seized and burned, but instead all copies would be submitted to the Inquisitional authorities for redaction and censorship of the most distasteful parts, continuing the policy established by the late Archbishop Brus of Prague. The people seemed generally satisfied with this solution.

However, in order to limit the instances of contact between the faithful and the Jews, Christians were henceforth prohibited from entering synagogues on festive occasions, from eating and dancing with the Jews in mixed company, and from working in Jewish homes as servants. Nor would any Christian parents be permitted to send their sons and daughters to study the liberal arts or any other type of arts under a Jewish instructor.

The terms seemed reasonable to all, including Rabbi Loew, and everyone was about to begin the closing prayers when a wild-eyed man who somebody called Federn burst into the church as if the hounds of hell were at his heels and declared:

"All right! I did it! Take me! I stabbed her with a knife and burned her flesh with red-hot pincers! I strangled the girl and danced on her grave!"

Rabbi Loew clapped his hand to his forehead, as if to obscure his own eyes from this dreadful apparition, and uttered the word *Gewalt!*

The man called Federn said, "All I ask is that you take me and spare the other Jews from your wrath."

And the chaos seemed to follow him like a whirlwind, as all those present beheld that out in the street, the Ship of Fools had run aground and all hell was breaking loose.

CHAPTER 34

TOMÁŠ SAW THE FLAMES CHEWING up the timbers, and the son of a bitch just laughed in my face, knowing that I couldn't turn him over to the Christian authorities in the middle of a siege. And I could just see myself trying to convince the Rabbinical Council to take charge of a Christian prisoner until Monday morning when things *might* be quieter. So I had no choice but to saw through his ropes with his own scaling knife and let him go, even though he had tried to kill me for a handful of dalers.

He rubbed his wrists and showed me a mouth full of crooked teeth, laughing as he ran away, until he plunged into a cloud of smoke and disappeared.

And I stood for a moment and watched the flames threatening to consume the ghetto, and I recalled how Rabbi Isaac, the Ari of Safed, reasoned that in order to make room for creation, God had to withdraw into Himself and leave a place that was empty of His presence. I had never fully understood how that was possible, but for the first time in my life I knew that I was standing in a place where God was *not* present.

The Destroyer had been set loose, the slaughterer who makes no distinction between the righteous and the wicked.

Some of the Jews were returning safely from the forced march, only to face the ordeal of getting "baptized" in the icy waters by Bohemians who called it the Vltava River and Germans who called it the Moldau. Such linguistic trivialities made no difference to the Jews.

"Let's do the whole fokken lot of them," said one of the water-soaked ruffians, fingering the blade of his weapon.

Nobody stopped me as I ran through the nearest gate and crossed over into a scene from a Flemish painting of an army of madmen plundering their way to the mouth of Hell.

The ghetto was largely empty of Jews and undefended, and any Jews discovered among the ruins were being forced back into the flaming doorways they had just escaped. And that German preacher they call Brother Volkmar was standing on the wreckage of a vegetable cart and stirring up his followers: "Take all you want! It's not theft to take back what the Jews have stolen from us through their obscene and onerous usury."

Usury? Not that old warhorse again. I had seen the list of debtors with my own eyes, and I knew that only the richest burghers had significant debts with Jewish moneylenders. It always amazes me how easy it is for a silver-tongued orator to take something that affects only the rich and get the masses of people to believe that it affects them as well.

He went on, aggressive German consonants exploding from his lips like hot lead pellets from an arquebus: "It is our bad luck to harbor this group of outsiders within our borders like some sort of a malignant disease."

We'd been in this part of Germany for *seven hundred years*, but we were still considered outsiders.

"And it is our duty to cast out these aliens who *still* refuse to convert to the one true faith, or face the judgment of God Himself for allowing their blasphemy to go unpunished."

Brother Volkmar then proposed his radical solution to the problem, which came straight from a fifty-year-old pamphlet called *On the Jews and Their Lies*, which is a really crappy title if you ask me (it gives away the ending). First, he said, the faithful should burn the Jews' synagogues, then level the ruins and cover the ground with dirt so that not a stone remained; then the Jews' valuables should be confiscated and their homes burnt, their travel privileges taken away, and they should all be made to live in a great big stable, like gypsies; their prayer-books and Talmuds should likewise be burned and their rabbis forbidden from teaching on pain of death; and finally, they should be given the flail and be sent into enforced labor to earn their bread by the sweat of their brows instead of living off the blood of innocent Christians.

I reached down and picked up a heavy wooden support post ripped from somebody's staircase, while Brother Volkmar told anyone within listening range that the Jews had been torturing and persecuting the Christians for centuries, poisoning wells, stealing children and slitting them open in order to cool their own savage humors with Christian blood. And I stood there hefting the baluster and imagining the damage I could do to Brother Volkmar with it.

But Brother Volkmar was only one man, and the reality in the streets of the *Yidnshtot* was that there were more slaughterers than chickens, as we say in Yiddish.

My only chance was to try to reach the house on Hampasgasse and hope that our man-made golem was ready. I shoved my way through the crowd and raced off down the Schilesgasse.

Come on, God, I prayed. I'm down to my last pfennig here, and I need at least a daler to buy a break. You're my last chance. If You're ever planning on helping me, now's the time. Send help. Send Elijah. Do *something*. At least send me strength if nothing else.

Rabbi Joshua says, *One who walks in a place of danger prays a short prayer*, but I chose a whole Psalm, the one that begins, *Yosheyv b'seyser elyon, b'tseyl Shaddai yislonon*, He who dwells in the shelter of the Supreme One, under the protection of Shaddai he will abide, because that Psalm is supposed to protect against weapons (especially daggers). But soon I had to switch to Latin, *Qui habitat in adjutorio Altissimi, in protectione Dei coeli commorabitur*, which wasn't the same at all, and the looters *still* looked at me askance as I ran past them mouthing the strange words.

I rounded the corner, and came upon a spectacle that must have spilled from the feverish brain of a madman. Three Christian boys were gleefully gathered around a sack dangling from a hook. They were taking turns beating it with sticks. Something was inside the sack that might have been alive. It might have been shaped like a baby.

I struck the boys about the face and neck and quickly drove them off. Then I lifted the sack off the hook, took a breath to steady myself, and peered inside. It was an orange cat, bloodied beyond recognition.

The sick taste of that abominable sausage climbed up the back of my throat. I swallowed hard, and stifled the urge to retch. I was miserable enough as it was.

A narrow shaft of light marked the path of the rising sun along the street. We are told that the sun has only stood still for three people—Moses, Joshua, and a folk hero named Nakdimon ben Gorion—each of whom needed more time to complete their divinely inspired tasks.

And it struck me that for the past three days, I'd been begging for more time, and now I couldn't wait for the day to end. *Bring on the blackness, O Lord, let the earth swallow me whole.*

For it is written that *He orders the sun—and it does not shine.*

How I longed for such a thing to come to pass.

But they also say that a man must not lose hope, even when the sword is laid upon his neck.

THE FOOT PATROLS HAD CLEARED out every dwelling on the street but one. Somehow they had bypassed the bawdy house on Hampasgasse.

Maybe *that* was the miracle I'd been asking for.

I found my co-conspirators in the back room. They had blocked the passage with empty crates, making the short hallway look like a storage area.

"Where the hell have you been?" said Trine. "You said you'd be back in a couple of hours."

"And what happened to all your hair?" said Zinger.

"Sorry," I said. "If I could control the world—"

"There'd be fewer Hamans and more Purims," said Trine. "Now, let's get you out of those damp clothes. Come on, don't be shy. You think you've got something I've never seen before? That's better. Here you go."

She handed me a set of clothes that a Christian water-carrier might wear.

"Don't you have any Jewish clothes?" I asked.

"Jews don't get drunk, pass out, and leave pieces of their clothing behind," said Trine.

I had to agree with that.

"So where *are* your clothes, big boy?" asked Trine.

"I left them at Rabbi Loew's house."

She eyed me curiously, but I was cold and wet, and didn't offer much in the way of interest.

When I was ready, they took me next door to Yosele's room. There was a mound of fresh earth on the bed that turned out to be a living, breathing human being. Trine patted his face and said it was time to get up. Yosele's face and arms were smeared with mud, and his matted hair was stiff with dirt. He truly looked like a creature made from the clay of the graveyard, and when he put on the elevated boots that Zinger had fashioned for him, he stood more than seven feet tall. And the floor shook so much when he took his first lumbering steps that dust fell from the rafters.

"You remember Reb Benyamin, don't you?" Trine asked.

"*Yes*," said Yosele, in that stiff way of his.

"You're going to go with him and do what he says, all right?"

"*Yes*."

Yosele grabbed my left hand and nearly crushed it with an awkward handshake.

"Be nice, Yosele," said Trine.

"*Yo-se-le*," he responded, repeating what she said.

He had the strength of ten men, but he was still as clumsy as a three-year-old child.

All the same, I tried to explain what we were about to do.

"Listen, Yosele. It is written that when a man performs a *mitsveh*, God sends an angel to protect him, and that when he performs two *mitsves*, God sends two angels. So if we're trying to save a few thousand souls, that means God should be sending a whole legion of angels to protect us."

"You're not thinking of taking him out there by yourself, are you?" said Trine. "I'd better go with you."

"No, it's too dangerous for you out there."

"If it's too dangerous for me, it's too dangerous for him."

"I'll watch over him, I promise."

"No, I'll go with you," said Zinger.

"You're not scared?" said Trine.

"After the sheer terror of stage fright, my dear lady, nothing else even comes close." Then he told me, "I am ready to die by your side defending the *Yidnshtot*."

"Don't be in such a rush," I said. "There'll be plenty of time for dying later."

"You have a dry wit, shammes," said Zinger.

Yosele grunted something that none of us could understand.

"What was that?" Trine asked.

"Ba-oo."

"Bathroom?"

"Ba-oo."

"Bedroom?"

"Ba-*oo*."

Trine shook her head.

"Even I don't understand everything he says," she told me. "Just be careful with him. He's such an innocent, you mustn't let anything happen to him."

Yosele grunted.

"He's just saying what we're all thinking," said Zinger.

A little laughter brought us some relief, and we parted company with fading smiles on our lips. And for all I knew, they would be the last smiles I would ever see.

The hardest part of being a warrior is waiting for the moment to strike. I peered over the basement steps to see what was happening on the street. The north end of Hampasgasse was blocked by the fires, and a mob had gathered at the south end by the entrance to the Klaus Shul. A couple of looters trotted by carrying a heavy log and enlisted the help of some of the other would-be thieves to batter down the shul's heavy wooden door.

As the door gave way, the gang of looters started clawing at each other to get at the bucketfuls of treasure that they were convinced were buried beneath the stone floor, just waiting to be unearthed. That's when I grabbed Yosele's arm and we ran across the street to the cemetery, appealing for strength in the Name of God: *May Micha'el be at my right, Gabri'el at my left, Uri'el before me, and Rapha'el behind me*—

"A-puh."

"Not now, Yosele."

We ducked into the cemetery.

"A-*puh*," said Yosele, pointing to a headstone that was carved with an image of the Tree of Knowledge of Good and Evil. A trio of plump, ripe fruits weighed its branches down.

"Apple?" I said.

"*Yes.*"

"I don't have any apples with me. You'll have to wait till later."

"A-*puh*."

"Later. I promise."

We cut through the cemetery to get to Rabbi Gans's house, because we didn't have a moment to lose. A thick column of smoke was already rising from the roof of the Pinkas Shul, and a gang of *Judenschläger* were kicking over the grave markers of several generations of mothers, wives, and daughters.

What kind of a person thinks it's fun to knock over *gravestones*?

The same kind of person who burns books in a language he can't even read because books are mysterious and frightening objects to him.

I told Yosele to get down low just as I was doing.

"A-*puh*."

"No apples. Later apples."

"G'ape."

"No grapes either."

He kneeled next to me, his mud-caked forehead reminding me that there was something I had forgotten to do.

"I'm not going to hurt you, Yosele," I told him. "I just need to write something on your forehead. All right?"

He didn't say no, then he let me scratch a word into the layer of mud smeared on his brow with the tip of my fingernail.

אמת

Emes.

Truth.

As in, *Defend the truth unto the death, for the truth will set you free.*

I can't remember who said that. But I'm pretty sure he wasn't Jewish.

"All right, this is it, Yosele. I'm going to run ahead, and you're going to follow me. Are you ready?"

"*Yes.*"

"Good. Let's go!"

I leapt to my feet and ran toward my "fellow Christians" as if the Devil himself were after me, leaping over the slanting stones as if nothing else in the world mattered except getting out of that cemetery as fast as possible.

"Run! Run! Dear God, save yourselves!" I shouted.

They looked my way and saw one of their own kind frantically bounding over the fallen headstones and waving his arms at them like a crazy man. Then they saw the creature chasing me, and the color ran out of their faces. They dropped the chunks of marble they were using to shatter the gravestones and took off toward Little Pinkasgasse.

I looked behind me. Yosele was ambling through the torn-up graveyard. If he were moving any faster, his costume might have come apart or somehow revealed itself as a man-made creation. But his very *slowness* somehow embodied the fearsome sight of a giant, soulless homunculus that is inexorably moving forward, impervious to pleas or reason. And he looked as if no human force on earth could stop him.

Smoke was pouring out of the windows of the Pinkas Shul as Jews fled in all directions, but one man turned to face the danger, alone. It was Markas Kral. He plunged headfirst into the smoke, and after a few tense moments, my brother shammes came running out swathed in blue-gray smoke, gagging for breath and hugging the Torah scroll to his chest as if it were an injured child.

Then a familiar voice filled my ears: "It is the just and splendid judgment of God that this place should be filled with the blood of unbelievers, and that His holy fires should cleanse the town of filth!"

Bad news sure travels quickly. My old friend Brother Volkmar was leading a group of true believers down the street past the burning houses to open the gate for the mob at the end of Pinkasgasse.

He warned the Jews fleeing the sound of his voice that someday a new king would arise in the west, who will be more warlike than all the others who came before him, and he will rule with an iron fist, and he will be surrounded by hard-hearted councilors who will make us all bow down to him and say that he is the Messiah.

He also predicted that the world would end sometime soon. He wasn't quite sure when, but we were all supposed to watch out for years containing the magical numbers seven and nine.

A real *n'vie sheker* that one. A false prophet.

I dodged a couple of Christians carrying armfuls of pewter and silverware, and made sure that Yosele wasn't too far behind me as I fought against the tide of refugees running from the danger. I kept on pushing all the way to Rabbi Gans's house, which was about to be engulfed by the flames from the house next door. I pounded on the front door.

A voice threatened me from behind the door: "Stand back or I'll shoot!"

"Rabbi Dovid! It's me! Reb Benyamin!"

There was a clanking of iron, and the door jerked open. Rabbi Gans pulled me inside and slammed and bolted the door. He wasn't holding anything more dangerous than a candle.

"We can't leave Yosele out there," I said.

"That's what you think," he said, peering out the window.

I leaned over his shoulder and saw that the roving bands of Christians were pointing and gesturing wildly, their jaws dropping as Yosele the Golem plodded stiffly toward them. I think it was the most beautiful sight I had seen all morning.

"Too bad you don't really have any gunpowder," I said.

"But I do. Surely you remember that my kinsman Joachim is a mining engineer?"

"Of course I do, but why on earth didn't you tell me about this sooner? Oh, never mind, let's get that whatchamacallit set up first."

"Ah yes, the magic lantern. I first found it described in a freebooter's copy of della Porta's *Magia Naturalis*," said Rabbi Gans, bringing the candle with us up the stairs to the second floor. "Of course I couldn't afford to buy all twenty volumes, even at flea market prices."

His manuscripts were spread across a table up here as well. A couple were unfinished works on mathematics, and another was a treatise on the Ten Tribes that I would have to look at more closely at another time.

"Are you still working on that chronicle of this week's events?"

"Yes, but I had to stop in the middle, which is unfortunate, since such historical chronicles are usually written by the winners."

"Well, maybe it's time for the losers to write a chapter."

The floor buckled slightly as Rabbi Gans led me to a table holding a black box the size of a child's coffin with a brass tube projecting out of one end. He opened the box and ignited a slew of candles that were impaled on spikes in front of a series of mirrored reflectors, then he closed the lid, which also had a mirror embedded in it. A bright glow emanated from the tube, spreading a buttery circle of light on the wall.

"Help me carry this over to the window."

The heavy lantern was fragile and unwieldy, and it cost us a good deal of sweat to balance it on the windowsill. From this high vantage point, I could just see over the ghetto wall as a fresh swath of Christians came marching up the street toward the Pinkas Gate, carrying enough pikes and halberds to level a forest.

If only the Jews could assemble like that, there would be no limit to what we could accomplish.

I even heard the raspy *zing zing zing* of knife blades on sharpening stones come sailing over the rooftops.

"Hold the slide while I position the lenses," said Gans, handing me a small pane of glass.

I held the pane up to the light and looked through it. Langweil had done himself proud, painting directly on the glass in vivid bloodred and green colors. It was an illustration of the passage from *Bamidbor* in which Korakh revolts against Moses and Aaron, and the earth splits open and swallows all of the rebellious tribesmen *and* their households as well.

In Langweil's nightmarish expression of it, the sky was split by a bolt of lightning that turned into a jagged rift in the earth as mountains toppled and panic-stricken Israelites plummeted headfirst into the eternal darkness of the abyss like so many faceless insects.

Gans was sweating and straining.

"What's wrong?" I asked.

"I guess I haven't used this in a while. I'm having a hard time focusing."

"You want me to try?"

"Are you familiar with the science of optics?"

"Not very."

"Then forget it."

Out in the street, Yosele kept lumbering toward us in his heavy boots, holding his arms out in front of him for balance. His unsteady gait made his appearance that much more convincing, and kept the Christians at bay.

But there were still a few men down there whose hearts must have been as cold as iron, or else their hatred was stronger than their fear, because they kept sowing mayhem even while facing this unnatural being who had been created by the manipulation of the hidden powers of the secret names of God. Nothing distracted them or swayed them as they went on their rampage, breaking open windows and tossing in burning sods, then kicking open doors and setting fire to the tapestries hanging in the hallways.

The mud on Yosele's forehead was starting to crack and peel, and even from this distance I could tell by the bewildered look on his face that he didn't understand why anyone would hate him or want to hurt him.

"Remember when Christians fought each other?" said Rabbi Gans, still struggling with the lenses.

"Yeah, those were the days."

"Got it! Hand me the slide!"

I did as he asked, and Rabbi Gans slid the glass into a slot and pointed the brass cylinder at the crooked houses across the street. But the colors were all blurry and diffuse. The image was out of focus.

"Damn!" said Gans, burning his hand on the cylinder as he tried to adjust the lenses.

Well, it's only physical pain, I thought. *How much could it hurt?*

I grabbed the cylinder and ignored the searing pain as I rotated the lens, just as I had seen Rabbi Gans doing. The colors became even more washed out and shapeless.

"The other way! The other way!" he said.

"All right!" I said. Only it came out sounding more like *Aaaargh!*

There was a heavy thud, and wood splintered.

Someone was kicking in the door downstairs. I looked down. Two mercenaries stood on the threshold, throwing their weight against the door. One had the curly black mustache and pointy beard of a Barbary corsair, the other was big enough to break a pig's back with his bare hands. The big one looked up and shook his Hussite thrasher at us.

I kept turning, despite the painful blistering, until the image became a little sharper, and Yosele stepped right into the beam of light so that his face turned red then green then red again, and the Christians pouring through the damaged Pinkas Gate slowed their pace for a few precious seconds.

The mercenary with the pointy beard shouted, "Time's up, Jews! Bring forth your evidence!"

"Turn it on them!" said Gans.

"No, the other way!"

"What? Are you nuts?"

"Just do it!" We struggled at cross purposes with the heavy lantern as the door gave way below.

We finally managed to point the lantern up the street so that the translucent image appeared on the jagged walls behind Yosele like a giant vision descending from the clouds. But the pale blobs of color were even more fuzzy and washed-out than before.

"I told you—!" said Gans.

The lantern was balanced awkwardly on the sill, with my right arm supporting most of its weight, so I snaked my other arm around inside my shirt-sleeve trying to get the coarse cloth to bunch up so I could grab some of it with my free hand.

"Damn these Christian clothes!" My long Jewish cloak would have been perfect for this job, but at the moment it felt like this short tunic was conspiring against me.

I finally gathered enough fabric to grab the cylinder without losing any more skin and turned the lens the *correct* way until the image came into closer focus, big and frightful against the distant walls. But the glass was so hot that the image started to bubble and melt, really making it look like Doomsday had come and our last moments were upon us.

A group of Jews was gathering on the corner of Pinkasgasse where it meets up with Broad Street, Belelesgasse, and Narrow Lane. And through the smoke, I saw the vague outline of weapons swaying in the breeze like wild barley.

"Is it supposed to get this hot?" I asked.

"Do you know how many candles I had to use to get this thing to shine in daylight?"

The two mercenaries stormed up the stairs, the big one wielding the thrasher and a battle-scarred sword that still looked sharp enough to cut both of us to ribbons.

"The game stops here, Jews," said the one with the curly mustache, and his hand went swishing under his cloak and came out holding a German wheel-lock pistol in one smooth motion.

In fact, it was one of the smoothest motions I'd ever seen.

CHAPTER 35

ERIKA WAS SWEEPING THE BACK hall when she noticed something sparkle on the floor amid the tracked-in dirt and dust from the street. It was a tiny strand of silver thread, too small to be of any real value, but it gave her an excuse to set down the broom and seek a moment of the master's time.

She scurried toward the master's counting room holding the fine thread between her thumb and forefinger. She made herself slow down so she could lift the hem of her apron with one hand and practice entering a room like a true lady. She straightened her back just as she had seen her mistress do, and took a few paces, but the steps felt stiff and awkward. No matter. Once she had a pair of real ladies' shoes, she was sure that gracefulness would follow.

But the master already had some visitors. So early in the morning on Easter Sunday? How strange.

Where was the master's wife? Probably out distributing bread and wine to the Jews.

She listened through the crack in the servant's door.

"—that scrawny female with the stringy hair?" said one of the visitors. "She's nothing but a rag mop with lips."

"True—but oh, what lips, *what lips*," said Kopecky. And they all laughed.

Erika peeked through the keyhole and saw the two horsemen, whose names were Big Klaus and Gottschalk, seated before the master's chair. Big Klaus was toying with a padlock, idly spinning it around with his fingers.

"So, my ferrets," said Kopecky. "What have you ferreted out for me?"

"This," said Gottschalk, reaching into a sack and pulling out an earthenware jar.

"What's *this*?"

"Smell it." Gottschalk pulled the cork out of the jar and passed it under the master's nose. The master wrinkled his nose and turned away.

"*Blecch*. Where'd you get it?"

"From across the river."

"Not from *my* place—!"

Erika heard footsteps. She straightened up and pretended to brush some lint off her skirt as the laundress passed by with a "caught-you-spying" look on her face. As soon as the laundress was out of sight, Erika pressed her ear to the door once again.

"Did anybody see you?" said Kopecky.

"Relax, it's all been taken care of," said Gottschalk. "Which reminds me—"

"Yes, yes, of course."

Erika heard the muffled jangling of a purse full of coins.

"Where's the rest of the money?"

"You'll get the rest after it's done," said Kopecky.

"How do we know you'll be here?"

"You have my word on it as a man of business."

Big Klaus laughed.

"So this erases your debts to the Jews *and* gets your business rivals expelled at the same time," said Gottschalk. "Just like the tailor who killed seven flies with one stroke."

"Serves 'em right for selling their meat during the holiest week of the year," said Big Klaus.

"How'd you ever convince that Janek fellow to go along with this, anyway?" said Gottschalk.

"I told him that he'd be able to use my distribution system to expand his markets."

"We should do 'em a favor and send 'em all to heaven," said Big Klaus.

"Shouldn't you be going, gentlemen?" said Kopecky.

"You just make sure you have the rest of our money when we get back."

The burly men showed themselves out with a heavy tread and much clanking of metal, then Kopecky turned to his desk to look over his account books. He skimmed through the pages, searching for some detail or other. Finally, he smacked his palm with his fist and let out an oath. Perhaps the cook had put too much mustard in his beef-and-calf's-foot pie, for it was well known that such foods were highly choleric.

Perhaps she should have waited for her master's humor to lighten, but she simply couldn't wait any longer.

She burst into the master's counting room unannounced.

"What do *you* want?" said Kopecky, irritably.

Oh, dear. He *was* too choleric (too much yellow bile), but she knew how to put him at his ease.

"I found this silver thread in the hall, Janoš darling. It looks like one of yours."

He looked at her is if she were speaking the language of the Turks.

"What did you say?"

She started to explain herself, but he cut her off:

"How dare you suggest such a thing? And on Easter Sunday, of all days! What kind of woman are you?"

But that wasn't what she wanted at all. She told him quite tenderly how it was the custom in Germany to enter into marriage by means of "consummation," and when his brow unfurrowed, she knew that he wasn't angry anymore, and that all she had to do was make him understand that they were now legally married, and that it would be a simple matter to annul his previous marriage to that Jew lover, and then everything would be all right. His smile was already brightening the room, then his jaw opened wide, and then something absolutely horrible happened: He laughed at her.

"Oh, I get it," he said, laughing so hard that tears were forming in the corners of his eyes. "Why, I don't know what to say."

He was laughing so hard he could barely breathe. "I'm speechless. You really are serious, aren't you?"

But soon he caught his breath and became quite stern, and he told her that it is God's will that men strive to acquire and maintain control over their wealth and property, and that in order to do this, one must invest wisely, and taste of many different wines; but while a finger or two of the cheap and ordinary wines may be good for a quick nip in the middle of the day, only the most valuable wines are lovingly stored in the master's cellar, and that this arrangement would remain in place for the rest of her days. Nothing could change the way things were, which was a nice way of saying that she wasn't fit to polish the hinges on the front door, much less cross its threshold as the lady of the house.

"So you just keep using the back door," he said, and went back to shuffling his papers.

After a minute passed and she hadn't budged, he turned back.

"What on earth is the matter with you? You stupid little girl! Did you actually believe that some handsome prince would whisk you away from the kitchen? Now get out of here!"

Erika left the room biting her lip to keep back the tears, because the awful truth was that she *did* believe that a handsome prince was going to whisk her away from all this drudgery. And now it wasn't going to happen.

By the time she slammed the back door and ran through the streets, the tears were flowing, but they were tears of rage. A man could only get away with ruining a girl without getting married or paying a fine if it was her word against his, but if there were *witnesses*, that changed everything.

Master Kopecky had just provided her with two witnesses, and she was going to make him pay.

She ran all the way to Cervenka's butcher shop, but her girlfriend wasn't there, just some idiot named Janoshik who was babbling to her friend's parents and saying that all he wanted was to get married, but that Anya had taken one look at him and Father Makofsky and had turned and fled *toward the ghetto*.

Erika dreaded the thought of going near that filthy place, but before she knew it, her feet were carrying her toward the *Judenstadt*. She passed a church where some well-dressed Jews had fled seeking sanctuary, and the city guards were dragging them down the steps in irons while a group of cutpurses and whores stood around laughing at the luckless Jews.

But she also saw the neighbors—*her neighbors!*—welcoming some of the refugees, who were sick with fright, and snatching them off the street moments before they were found out by the authorities. It disgusted her to see good German families taking such vermin into their homes and offering them protection. They were nothing less than traitors to the race, as far as she was concerned.

The *Reiters* had taken a roundabout route to the Pinkas Gate, but by the time she got there they had already found some way of squeezing past it and entering the ghetto, and the street was overflowing with different factions arguing over tactics and strategy.

"I say we burn down the whole ghetto!" said one of the Catholic defenders.

"Not before its riches have been secured and returned to the emperor and the Church," said another.

"So the plan is to loot first, *then* burn."

"Right."

"Why don't we attack Bethlehem Chapel instead?"

"What the hell for?"

"It's an easier target."

"That's because there's nothing to steal."

Erika felt herself being pulled in several directions at once as she got caught up in the maelstrom. The opposing streams repelled each other like oil and water, while a couple of Jews bobbled around between them like bits of driftwood.

One of the Papists grabbed the elderly Jew and cursed him for supporting the Protestant rebels, and was about to slay him on the spot when Sheriff Zizka arrived with a crew of his brothers, and swung his club at the Jew's attacker, smacking him so hard that the man's nose and mouth bled all over the front of his shirt.

"How can you protect our enemies when they're prepared to use black magic against us?" one of the assailants challenged him.

"They're entitled to the same legal protection as anyone else," said the sheriff.

By this time the gate had broken open, and the mob rushed in. Then suddenly everyone stopped in their tracks and stared open-mouthed at the hellish sight of a creature from the bowels of the earth standing in the middle of the street, surrounded by burning houses.

Erika heard the old Jew ask the sheriff, "Tell me, *pane Žižko*, why are you helping us?"

And she couldn't believe her ears when the sheriff answered, "Some of us remember when the Jews helped defend the city by digging a moat around the New Town, even though—"

"Even though you wouldn't allow us to swear an oath of loyalty to the homeland," said the old Jew.

Zizka nodded gravely.

"We also supplied you with food and weapons, and what did it get us?" said the Jew.

"It got us expelled from Bavaria," said the other Jew.

"Well, I say the hell with the Bavarians," said Zizka.

Awful screams and howls came from one of the burning houses, and strange lights danced before her eyes.

"What the hell's going on in there?" asked the sheriff.

The rabbi said some magic words in his Satanic language.

But only Erika knew the answer to the sheriff's question. She yelled the sheriff's name, and when she got his attention, she announced, her voice strong and unwavering, "There are two men in there, sent by my master, to plant a jar of cow's blood in the Jews' houses."

CHAPTER 36

THE BIG FELLOW YANKED OPEN the drawers and dumped out the contents, tossing papers right and left, until he found a brass optical scope and some kreuzers that he stuffed into his pocket, and the grand prize—a thick gold pocket watch on a chain. He tossed the watch to the man with the gun, who caught it one-handed and flipped it open.

"My, my. Will you look at the time," said the man with the mustache, glancing at the pocket watch.

His aim never faltered.

At least I knew who the leader was now. My eyes flitted to the other one, looking him over for any weapons besides what he was already carrying. The heavy leather sack hanging around his shoulders seemed to contain nothing but loot, but I couldn't be sure.

"What are you looking at, Jew?"

The other mercenary waved the long-handled pistol at me to regain my attention.

My nostrils tingled as the scent of burning wood and other chemical substances filtered up from below.

"We were just studying the workmanship of your gun," said Rabbi Gans, emphasizing the phrase as if every word held great significance. "It's a very finely wrought instrument, certainly a piece worthy of a nobleman or a burgher, not a lowly freelance soldier."

"You fancy yourself an expert on guns, old man?" The mercenary's eyes flashed as if he had just thought of something particularly vicious and amusing to do with us.

Thin gray tendrils of smoke were curling up through the floorboards.

"You fellows are going to be left holding the bag," he said with more glee than the situation really called for. "Klaus!"

The big man took the bag from his shoulder and laid it on the table.

I felt a tingling in my spine as I became aware of a light scratching in the walls, as if a million tiny insects had gotten into the woodwork. It gradually swelled to an angry crescendo as thousands of rats fled the burning houses. It almost felt like they were crawling over my skin.

"Ha! Just look at him turning yellow on us," said Big Klaus.

"He's barely worth the price of the ball and powder," said the other mercenary, raising the pistol and pointing it directly at my forehead.

"Wait!" I said.

The mercenary smiled coldly.

"O kind sir, grant us one last prayer of absolution before we die," I said.

"That would be the Christian thing to do," said Rabbi Gans, doing his best to sound like a pastoral minister.

The mounting flames were casting twisted shadows in the stairwell behind the two mercenaries.

"If we are to be martyrs," I went on, "then we need to spend our last moments contemplating the true and ineffable Name of God with such devotion that its glowing letters appear before our eyes. One who is so transported will feel the flames as cold."

This seemed to offer the promise of easy capitulation and some small amusement, so the mercenary agreed.

"O Lord, hear our prayer," I said. "Grant us the honor of being martyrs for the Sanctification of Your Name."

I started swaying like a candle in the breeze as the words poured out of me, keeping up the flow of formulaic syllables until I could get away with a short prayer in Hebrew that would translate roughly as, *Blessed art Thou, O Lord, our God, for giving me the scaling knife that is under my shirt.*

And Rabbi Gans swayed along with me and said many great and noble things in the language of our prayers before responding with the phrase, *Who hallows us with His Commandments, and Who commands us to know that mechanism of the wheel-lock pistol is notoriously unreliable at close range.*

"And let us say, Amen," I said.

"Amen."

Another shadow joined the ghosts of the dancing flames in the stairwell.

I continued: "For as Rabban Simeon ben Gamaliel says, the world is sustained by three things. One—"

"Justice."

"Two—"

"Truth."

"Three—"

"Peace!"

I lunged for the leader's gun as Rabbi Gans flung himself at Big Klaus and tried to hold him in a bear hug. I grabbed at the mercenary's forearm but he swung it away from me. Since he had no other weapon, he had to swing it back at me, only this time I got my hand around the barrel and pointed it at the ceiling. We wrestled for control of it, and I let him gain some ground, drawing his weight forward, so that just when he expected me to push harder, I gave way and let him fall toward me. Then I used his momentum to slip around and get him in an awkward one-armed neck hold while I grabbed the pistol stock with my scalded hand. I think I left some of my skin in the teeth of the wheel-lock device. It was painful as hell, and the pain came out of me in the terrible war cry of the tribe of Judah.

The floor was quaking beneath our feet, and the magic lantern fell to the floor with a crash. A number of candles rolled out and came to a stop in the middle of the pile of papers scattered around the floor. The papers caught fire and the flames spread quickly.

Rabbi Gans wasn't much of a challenge for Big Klaus, who tossed him off like a feather pillow. But the big bruiser's eyes widened when a giant of clay came stomping up the stairs and had to bend low to enter the room. Big Klaus stood frozen with fear as the Golem slowly straightened up and approached him, step by plodding step, inching ever closer.

My adversary jerked his elbow back and jabbed me in the gut again and again until I was forced to let go of him and pull away, but this also freed me up to get out the knife. He spun around and aimed at me, but I was already lunging at him with my knife. The pistol's mainspring must have been pretty heavy because he jerked the trigger a little too hard, raising the barrel just enough to save my life as the spark was struck and the powder exploded and blew a hole in the wall about two inches above my head. Hot powder residue flew into my face as I got in close and thrust the blade in under his arm.

Yosele didn't like the loud noise. He lifted Big Klaus off his feet and hurled him screaming through the window.

I released the mercenary, who staggered sideways a bit and slumped over the table, his fingers reaching for the leather sack.

"I wonder what's—"

The floor gave way in a shower of splinters and sparks.

We collapsed toward the center, then wood and earth slammed into me from below.

The next thing I knew, I was lying on some half-charred crossbeams, watching the flames slowly crawl up the front of my tunic. Actually, the fire was warm and kind of pleasant.

And it looked like the roof was getting closer. You might even say it was caving in. That was the term. Caving in.

Someone grabbed my shirt and hauled me to my knees and told me to get moving. It was Rabbi Gans, and somehow I snapped out of the daze I was in and followed him while swatting out the flames on my tunic.

Then a huge crossbeam came crashing down through the blackened timbers, and suddenly Yosele Golem was under it, stopping it at a sharp angle with his tremendously powerful arms.

As soon as Rabbi Gans pulled me through the narrow archway to safety, I turned around to help Yosele, but it was too late. Yosele had given us a few more seconds of life by holding the ceiling up, but now he was trapped, surrounded by flames. I tried to run back into the fire to save him, but Rabbi Gans held me back with all his strength.

I wanted to tell Yosele to let go and run, but he just stood there suspended between two worlds, since any move he made would lead to disaster.

Our eyes met. He was looking at me the way a startled deer stares at the hunter's bow, not fully understanding his predicament, and showing such wide-eyed childlike incomprehension of the forces beyond his control that a piece of my soul departed from me forever when the heat and weight became too much for him and he let it all come tumbling down on him.

I stood there like a dreamer amazed, unable to feel anything but the power of my vital soul draining out of me. For it is written that the Lord gave us a soul that was pure, and that if we do not return it to Him in the same state of purity, He will destroy it before our eyes.

I was vaguely aware of the body of Big Klaus lying facedown in the middle of the street, and somehow my hands found the will to grab hold of my collar and tear my shirt open. Then my legs buckled and I kneeled in the sandy soil and let the ashes swirl around me. The smoke was stinging my eyes, then the wind shifted and I caught a glimpse of Yosele's scarred, lifeless face amid the dying flames. The muddy *aleph* had been scraped off his forehead, leaving only the letters מת. *Mes*. Dead.

You're supposed to stay with the dying to hear their confession and say one last *Sh'ma* with them. Yosele had no sins on his head, so I said the *Sh'ma* for him. Perhaps his soul would transmigrate as Rabbi Loew teaches, and be born to a barren couple in the future.

From dust you came, and to dust you shall return, I prayed. *Goodbye, Yosele. May your memory be a blessing.*

I stood up and dusted off my knees, and felt a thousand eyes on me. The mass of Christians were standing strangely still about half a block away. Then Sheriff Zizka came trotting toward me, whether to arrest me or slay me or do something else, I knew not.

Zizka reached for his sword and unsheathed it. I bowed my head and prayed that somehow my death would redeem all Israel and wash away the sins of the people, then I prepared to fight the sheriff with nothing more than the bloody knife I had pulled from the ashes.

The opposing clans of Jews and Christians held their positions and stood watch, as if we were a pair of champions chosen to do battle with bronze-tipped weapons in front of our respective armies. But Zizka stopped about ten paces in front of me as a wounded man emerged from the smoking door frame of what had been Rabbi Gans's house. The mercenary was covered with soot, and his face was streaked with blood and sweat. He could barely stand, and he soon fell back against the charred wood, an oblong weight slipping from his hands.

The jar hit the ground and tipped over, and a couple of pints of thick red liquid slurped out into the hungry sands.

For a moment all was still, except for the faint gurgling. Zizka called for a doctor, but nobody moved. He repeated his call.

Finally, Rabbi Gans said, "All right, I'll take a look at him."

Big Klaus was still stunned from the fall. He had a few bruises and a broken collarbone, but he was in a lot better shape than he had a right to be. The other one was blackened and burnt, with a single chest wound where one of his ribs had stopped the blade from going through his heart. Rabbi Gans tended to them while Zizka shackled their hands behind their backs.

Only then did Zizka call for the victim's father to be brought forward. While the sheriff's men were combing the streets calling Janek's name, Rabbi Gans looked up and said, "There's something I need you to help me with."

He asked me to apply pressure while he cleaned and dressed the mercenary's wound, but I think he was just trying to keep me occupied and somehow bring me back into the land of the living.

The crowd made room for the city guards returning with Viktor Janek. The Praguers even showed some respect for Rabbi Loew, and let him through as well, along with another Jew. My eyes were still watery from all the smoke, but it looked like Jacob Federn. His clothes were filthy, and he shuffled along like an old beggar who's afraid they'll set the dogs on him. But he was alive and in one piece despite all that had befallen him.

One of the city guards handed Janek a loaded pistol. Then Janek stood facing the men who had murdered his daughter.

The first mercenary, who told us his name was Gottschalk, said in his defense that the gun had gone off by accident, and that Big Klaus was the one who had slit the girl's throat. He started to say something else, but Janek raised the pistol and convinced him to keep his mouth shut. It was too late for words, anyway.

The three of them faced each other for a long moment, then Janek uncocked the pistol and handed it back to Zizka. "I do not forgive you," he told the men. "But I will let you live. And may the Good Lord judge you in His own time."

Janek turned and walked away.

The mob started to break up. And like the inhabitants of an enchanted castle casting off a century of slumber, the Jews sprang into action, manning the hand pumps and breaking out the buckets. It's a good thing there was plenty of water in the wells. A rabbi with a Volhynian accent ordered a group of dedicated young men to pull down the weakened buildings with axes and hooks to keep the fire from spreading. Then somebody rolled out a barrel of wine, and soon we were all freely passing the water buckets from hand to hand. I got a few stares, but after Rabbi Gans wrapped a rag around my blistered hand, they let me take a few turns at the water pump.

We fell into a steady rhythm, and it wasn't long before a sound that seemed to come out of nowhere penetrated my senses. A lone voice was rising, and soon the others were joining in, taking up the lilting melody of the first of the *Hallel* Psalms, songs of praise that we feel in our bones, which we sing when a prisoner is set free, a sick man recovers from an illness, or the community is saved from disaster. And soon the words about the hills skipping like young sheep were carried on the breeze over the smoldering ruins.

"This is all my fault," I heard Federn say.

"You share some of the blame," Rabbi Loew agreed. "But you redeemed yourself by providing us with the clues we needed to bring an end to this grisly business."

"What clues did I provide?"

"If only all such questions could be so easily answered. I'm talking about that coded message you sent us through that Christian servant girl. It gave our *khaver* Benyamin the confidence he needed to conquer his fears and save the ghetto."

"What coded message?"

"The one based on the Book of Job."

"That? Well, I'm afraid I owe you a bit of an explanation."

After some prompting, Federn told the rabbi, "Janek didn't trust me, so he made me put the terms of our agreement in writing. But I didn't trust him either, so I just wrote down the first words that came into my head. I figured if he ever turned it over to the authorities, it would just be a bunch of meaningless nonsense."

Rabbi Loew said, "That's what you think, Reb Jacob, but the hand of God is evident even in this. You see, God was working through you in such a way that, although you believed you were selecting the words at random, they were in fact carefully chosen so that a close examination of their meaning would lead us directly to the solution we needed to protect the community."

Rabbi Loew was truly a miracle worker, because I could almost see the burden lift from Federn's shoulders.

The pumphouse men were singing about how the false idols of silver and gold have eyes but cannot see, and have ears but cannot hear, and as the buckets came round again, our verses were echoed by another group of singers approaching from the east.

"See?" said Rabbi Loew. "Look how even Rabbi Joseph and Rabbi Aaron are joining us in celebrating our delivery from danger."

I looked up. Could it be? Were the leaders of the Rabbinical Council actually bringing their followers together as a sign of unity?

Rabbi Loew wished Federn well, and the merchant of feathers drifted away, his step somehow lighter.

Rabbi Aaron stopped directly in front of Rabbi Loew.

"You see?" he told Rabbi Loew.

"Indeed I do."

"You see how no evil befell us thanks to our prayer and study?"

"I like to think our actions had something to do with it," I said.

Rabbi Aaron looked at me.

"And who are you?"

Rabbi Loew said, "Don't you recognize our *khaver* Benyamin?"

In all the confusion, I must have forgotten what I looked like to them, especially with the earring still stuck in my ear. But Rabbi Aaron made it quite clear what he thought.

"I see you've finally gone and joined forces with the Christians," he said. "If this outsider wants to be like the *goyim*, there's a whole wide world out there where he can do it."

He turned and addressed his followers. "You have seen what happens when we open our doors to foreign ways—fornication, heresy, and death. And the lesson is clear. It is time to return to our traditions and shun the ways of the Freethinkers."

His fellow rabbis agreed, their voices merging into one as they led their followers away. And all I wanted to do was disappear from this place and lose myself in the darkest reaches of Poland, the land of endless winter nights, where your spit freezes before it hits the ground.

"We need look no further for proof that man both deserves and does not deserve to have been created," said Rabbi Loew, watching the future leaders of the *Yidnshtot* recede into the smoke-filled streets. "I can only hope that you find the strength to forgive yourself."

"Why?" I said.

"Because a community is too heavy for one man to carry alone."

"Next you'll be telling me that a stitch in time saves nine."

"We need to make a fresh start," said Rabbi Loew. "Come, *mayn khaver*, let us travel together to Poznan."

"I'll be ready first thing in the morning."

"No, it will take me several days to pack up and get my affairs in order."

"Then I'll go ahead and wait for you there."

"No, it's not good to travel alone."

"Seems like I'm always traveling alone."

Rabbi Loew laid his hand on my shoulder in a fatherly way. "We will go together, and from now on you will travel as my companion and my equal. Believe it or not, I have learned a great deal from you, Rabbi Benyamin."

I heard what he said clearly enough, but it took a few moments to sink in.

"You have taught me something as well, Rabbi Benyamin," said Rabbi Gans, shaking my hand.

I nodded, and for a minute I felt as if I truly belonged here, with these two wise men by my side.

"So, when will you be ready to leave?" I asked.

"Soon. What's your hurry?"

"I want to get out before the Christians change their minds and attack us again."

"We'll leave soon enough," said Rabbi Loew. "And I happen to know some nice women in Poznan with an eye for a promising young scholar."

"I'm not that young anymore, Rabbi."

"None of us are," said Rabbi Gans.

The street was slowly filling with regular working people, some of them stumbling along like sleepwalkers, or tiptoeing as if they were testing the un-paved surface with the trepidation normally associated with tightrope walkers. But when they saw that the earth did not swallow them up, others followed, walking with more confidence, and soon the streets were filled with people stepping around me as if they couldn't wait to recover the last few hours that remained of the holy day and get back to their normal routine.

I even heard one Christian speak to a Jew who was carrying a bucketful of water, telling him, "So, I'll see you in the fish market on Tuesday, Mordecai," before turning to follow his fellow Christians out of the ghetto.

I stood there watching the smoking ruins, waiting until the embers were cool enough to recover Yosele's body. And I was still standing there when the timbers crumbled, sending up a shower of sparks and thick clouds of smoke, which made my eyes tear up again.

I covered my eyes for a moment. And when I finally blinked and wiped them clean, I saw Trine coming toward us through the haze, holding a bundle of clothing.

I didn't know what to say to her. Sometimes in my dreams I still see those dark eyes, following me wherever I go.

"I'm sorry," I said. "I tried to—"

She just handed me my cloak and turned away. There was nothing I could say to console her, so I just lowered my eyes and stared down at my cloak and the hateful yellow spot that marked me as the emperor's property. Then the sleeping dragon inside me opened its yellow eyes, loosed its hot breath of rage, and tugged at the chains that held it down, and acting against all propriety, I took out the knife and cut through a couple of inches of the threads forming the seam. Then I hooked my fingers through the yellow ring, tightened them into a fist, and ripped out the stitches of the Jew badge and threw the cursed thing in the mud.

And none dared approach me.

WE LAID YOSELE TO REST in a secret place inside the ghetto, within earshot of Zinger and his *klezmorim*, who were preparing for the Rožmberks' wedding. Soon they would be filling the streets with the gay sound of fiddles, hand bells, and hornpipes.

And later that evening, as the deep blue of twilight gave way to night, we delivered Freyde and Julie Federn to the ritual bath in the drafty cellar of the Klaus Shul, and Rabbi Loew's wife Perl personally oversaw the purification ceremony. The *mikveh*'s regular attendants wouldn't do it because they were afraid of upsetting the most powerful members of the Rabbinical Council.

Everyone went back to work the next day. The chisels rang out again, the tailors plied their needles, the butchers slaughtered animals and let the blood run out into the gutters.

The city rebuilt the gates of the ghetto, but they made the Jews pay half the damages. The emperor annulled the expulsion decree and ordered that the gates be marked with the image of the royal eagle and the words, "Protected by His Imperial Majesty," but the Jews still had to "lend" him 150,000 gold pieces in return for the privilege. And how many brigands can read, anyway?

Three days later, Emperor Rudolf quietly reversed the decree granting the Meisel Shul status as a sanctuary, but that's another story.

Tomáš Kromy was arrested for looting at least a dozen Jewish homes, but he blamed his actions on witchcraft, and the bishop granted him immunity from prosecution if he would cooperate with the investigation and help identify the heretics who had bewitched him and caused him to behave in such a manner, which he was only too happy to do.

No one ever charged his father Josef with anything, although he was just as responsible for his son's behavior as any witch.

The two mercenaries eventually led the authorities to Janoš Kopecky, who was charged with conspiracy to commit murder. When they called in his wife as a witness for the defense, she told the court, "A widow has rights that a wife does not have," and he received a sentence of death by public strangulation. But the emperor graciously reduced the sentence to a large monetary fine on the condition that the condemned man be newly baptized as a Catholic. Kopecky freely chose to redeem himself in this manner.

My colleagues offered me a permanent post as a shammes, since I was now a member of the Brotherhood. I thanked them, but said that I couldn't wait to go back to Poland and leave this intolerant empire behind.

Alone of all people, the country folk who shared the garret with me thanked me for all that I had done. The rest of the ghetto treated me as if I wasn't even there. They had cut me out of their world. Or rather, they had never let me in.

My father was a wandering Aramean, they say.

But I wasn't alone. Because many of my brethren are living among the nations of the world, traveling farther and farther east till they reach Siberia, and eventually crossing the ocean. And those who stay behind will mix in, hiding right under your noses and evading detection by changing their names from Mordecai to Angelo, from Hayyim to Juan, from Weissberg to Chiaromonte. They have published books under the names of de Rojas and da Ponte, been reborn as monks and bishops with names like de Santa Maria and Torrecremata, drawn up the astronomical tables used by Columbus and made maps for Amerigo Vespucci, and we will even learn to wash our linen on Sunday and call our children by Christian names like Matthew and Peter, hiding among you until the day we stand naked before God. (This is the hidden meaning of the verse, *and they knew that they were naked,* according to the *Zohar.*)

Rabbi Jaffe was elected the Chief Rabbi of Prague, and the next morning Rabbi Loew and I left the Land of Calamity behind, setting out on the long road north. Some days later, on our way through the mountains, we met a wise woman with green eyes and long brown hair who turned out to be a fellow outcast from Prague like ourselves, carrying all of her worldly possessions tied up in a bundle. She asked many clever questions about our faith and knowledge, and decided to join us in our travels, and we arrived in Poznan in time for Shvues.

And not a moment too soon, because not long after his kinsman's wedding, Vilém Rožmberk went to his reward. The old warrior was one of the last voices of tolerance among the Catholic gentry, and the uneasy coexistence between the Protestants and Catholics eventually collapsed, dragging the German Empire into thirty bloody years of all-out war.

At least one good thing came out of all this: the children on Würfelgasse went back to playing together. For it is written that the world itself rests on the breath of the children in our schools.

Of course, it is also written that the world is in the hands of fools.

Because a foolish idea can always come back to life, even after many centuries in the grave. And hatred always lies in a shallow grave.

After all, we had stopped the blood libel from becoming excessively murderous. But if the past was anything to go by, the word would soon be spreading and the Christian version of the tale would be told, first in songs and stories, and then in broadsides, pamphlets, and eventually in official documents, and in fifty or one hundred years their version would be the God's truth.

So we went looking for our version of the story in the ruins of Rabbi Gans's house.

We sifted through the remains, but came up with nothing but ashes.

GLOSSARY

aggadah—Talmudic legends.

alef-beys—the alphabet.

a likhtigen gan-eydn zol er hobn—May his light shine in Paradise.

babička—(Czech) grandmother.

badkhn—wedding jester, entertainer.

balkoyre—Torah reader.

Bamidbor—*In the Desert*, Hebrew name for the Book of Numbers. (*Bamidbar* in Modern Hebrew. Note: All Hebrew in this glossary reflects the sixteenth-century Ashkenazic pronunciation.)

Borukh atoh Adinoy eloyheynu meylekh ha-oylem—Blessed art thou, O God, Ruler of the Universe.

batlen—a man hired to remain in the synagogue all day in case he is needed to make up a *minyen*.

beys din—lit. "house of judgment"; a Jewish court of law.

Betlémská Kaple—(Czech) Bethlehem Chapel.

beys khayim—lit. "house of life"; a cemetery.

bimeh—platform in a synagogue between the congregation and the holy ark containing the Torah.

Blutschreiber—lit. "bloodwriter"; the official scribe in a criminal court.

bove mayses—stories from the *Bovo Book*, published by Elya Bokher in 1541; origin of the phrase *bubbe mayses*, "old wives' tales."

bulvan—dolt, blockhead; related to Moravian *balvan*, large rock (also dolt, blockhead).

chutzpah—nerve, guts, audacity (also used negatively, i.e., "gall").

converso—Spanish and Portuguese Jews who converted to Christianity in or after 1492, usually forcibly.

Defend the truth unto the death, for truth will set you free—a famous quote from Jan Hus, based on John 8:32.

emes—truth.

erev—eve.

eyrev-rav—lit. "mixture of multitudes"; source of the modern word "riffraff."

extra ecclesiam nulla salus—there is no salvation outside the Church.

farkakt—general negative modifier; befouled; crappy; the state of being up an excrement-filled creek.

fraylin—Miss.

froy—Mrs.

froyen-shpil—the woman's game.

Gemore—the Rabbis' commentary on the Mishnah that makes up the bulk of the Talmud. This Aramaic term sometimes replaced the Hebrew "Talmud" during the Middle Ages to avoid Christian censors. Both words mean "study."

Gvuroys Hashem—The Mighty Feats of The Name [of God].

golem—in Psalms 139:16, it refers to the "unshaped flesh" in the womb that has not yet taken on life and soul; in the *Seyfer Yetsireh*, it is a soulless figure of clay; according to eighteenth-century legends, Rabbi Loew made a *golem* to defend the ghetto from attack.

Goyim—Gentiles (hint: if you have to look this one up, you probably are one).

gutn Shabbes—good Shabbes.

Haggadah—lit. "telling"; the text, including the story of the Exodus from Egypt, read at the Passover Seder.

Jerusalem Talmud—also called the Palestinian Talmud, written in the Galilee region in the early fifth century C.E., one or two centuries before the larger Babylonian Talmud.

Judenschläger—Jew-bashers.

Kaddish—memorial prayer for the dead.

kashres—state of being kosher.

kehileh—town council.

kesef and mammon—silver and money; the difference is that "silver" (jewelry, ritual objects, etc.) may be handled on Shabbes, while handling "money" is prohibited.

ksubeh—marriage contract (Polish-Yiddish: *ksibeh*).

keynehore—contraction of *keyn ayin horeh*, "no Evil Eye."

keyser—emperor; king.

kharoyses—sweet mixture of nuts, apples, wine, etc. used at the Passover Seder.

khaver—close friend; comrade.

kheyder—school for elementary Jewish education.

khreyn—horseradish, used at the Passover Seder.

khumesh—printed text of the first five books of the Bible (as opposed to a hand-written Torah scroll).

kidesh—blessing recited over wine, the symbol of joy (*kiddush* in modern Hebrew).

kidesh Hashem—lit. "the sanctification of The Name [of God]"; fig. refers to choosing death rather than renouncing one's religious beliefs.

kleperl—large wooden club for knocking on doors.

klezmorim—pl. of *klezmer*, musician.

Koheles—"The Speaker," or preacher; Hebrew name for the Book of Ecclesiastes.

lamed-vovnik—one of the thirty-six righteous people in the world at any given time (the letters lamed-vov have a numeric value of thirty-six).

makher—lit. "maker"; big businessman.

Megillas Esther—the Book of Esther.

Meynekes Rivka—*Rebecca's Wet Nurse*, a guide book for midwives and young mothers by Rivka bas Meyer Tikotin (Tiktiner; d. 1605), published in Prague (1609) and Kraków (1618). No known copies of this work have survived.

Meor Enayim—"Light Unto the Eyes," or "Enlightenment to the Eyes" (Ghirondi, 1573–75).

meshuge/meshugene—crazy. (Polish-Yiddish: meshigene.)

Midrash—lit. "interpretation"; extensive body of exegesis and commentary on Biblical sources.

mikveh—ritual bath.

minkhe—afternoon prayer services.

minyen—a group of ten people (all men before the modern era), the number required to form a full community service. Psalm 82 says that God is present in a congregation (and by association, in a *minyen*), and a classic folk saying reminds us that "Nine rabbis can't make a *minyen*, but ten shoemakers can."

Mishnah—book of post-Biblical oral law written down in the second century C.E.

mishpokhe—family, clan.

mitsveh—lit. a Biblical commandment; also a good deed. There are 613 *mitsves* in the Hebrew Bible.

Moses ben Maimon—Maimonides, aka Rambam, rationalist philosopher (1135–1204). Born in Moslem Spain (Cordova), he wrote most of his works in Arabic using Hebrew letters.

Moyshe Rabbeynu—Moses our Teacher.

Nazirite—a person who vows not to drink wine or cut their hair, among other requirements, for a certain period of time, as described in Numbers 6:1–21.

ne, děkuji—(Czech) No, thank you.

nemt epes in moyl arayn—lit. "take something in your mouth"; fig. "eat something."

Niddah—a tractate of the Talmud dealing primarily with issues of when a woman is sexually unavailable due to ritual uncleanliness.

"No man should be held responsible . . ." The correct quote is ". . . for the words he utters in *grief*" (Bava Basra 16a).

noytsriyes—Nazarenes, i.e. Christians.

nudnik, tshaynik, pupik—bore; teapot; gizzard and/or belly-button.

olev ha-sholem—May s/he rest in peace.

omeyn—Amen.

On the Jews and Their Lies—*Von den Juden und ihren Lügen*, a late work by Martin Luther (1543), who had previously written a pamphlet relatively sympathetic to the Jews, *That Jesus Christ was Born a Jew* (1523), which advised people "to deal kindly with the Jews and to instruct them in Scriptures . . . and if some remain obstinate, what of it? Not everyone is a good Christian." What a difference twenty years makes.

Oral Law—another term for the Mishnah.

oysgelasene froyen—loose women.

Pesach—Passover.

Pirkey Avos—"The Ethics of the Fathers," a chapter in the Mishnah.

Purim—carnivalesque holiday celebrating the Jews' survival during exile in Persia.

Purimshpil—a comical or satirical play performed during Purim.

Reb—a simple title, equivalent to "Mr."

Reiter—rider, cavalryman.

ReMo—acronym for Rabbi Moyshe (Moses) Isserles (1520–1572).

Rambam—acronym for Rabbi Moyshe (Moses) ben Maimon (1135–1204), known for his rationalist approach to Scripture.

Ramban—acronym for Rabbi Moyshe (Moses) ben Nakhman (1194–1270), known for his mystical and Kabbalistic approach to Scripture.

reysh—Hebrew letter ר, for the sound "r."

Riboyne shel Oylem—Lord of the Universe.

royter—(adj.) red; *der royter* = the Red.

samekh/pey—Hebrew letters ס and פ, for the sounds "s" and "p."

Seder—the Passover meal, featuring symbolic foods and rituals, and a retelling of the story of the Exodus from Egypt.

seyfer Toyreh—Torah scroll.

Seyfer Yetsireh—*The Book of Creation*, a Kabbalistic work written cir. third to sixth century C.E. First published in Mantua in 1562.

schmuck—probably not from the German *schmuck* (jewel), as is often supposed, but from the Polish *smok* (dragon; "worm" in the archaic sense of snake, serpent).

Shabbes—Sabbath Day; Saturday.

shakhres—morning prayer services.

sh'khineh—the emanation of God's presence in the world, traditionally given a female shape or essence; similar in some ways to the Christian Holy Spirit.

Sh'ma—prayer of faith in one God, consisting of passages from Deuteronomy and Numbers.

Shmoys—*Names*, Hebrew name for the Book of Exodus.

shikseh—a Christian woman.

shmaltz—chicken fat.

shoykhet—ritual (kosher) slaughterer.

shrayber—writer; also used more derogatorily: scribbler.

shtetl—small city or town.

shulklaper—a person who goes around banging on doors and windows to announce that it's time to go to the synagogue services.

Staré Město—(Czech) Old Town.

tallis—prayer shawl.

talmid—student.

Talmud—expansion and commentary on the Mishnah, written down in the fifth to sixth centuries C.E. The longer Babylonian Talmud is better known and generally considered to be more authoritative than the Jerusalem (Palestinian) Talmud.

tateleh—father dear.

Tehillim—*Praises*, Hebrew name for The Book of Psalms.

tfiles—prayers.

toyu vo-boyhu—lit. "without form and void," the description of the earth in Genesis 1.2.; general chaos.

Torah—lit. the five books of Moses (the first five books of the Bible); used figuratively to refer to all Jewish religious study.

treyf—non-kosher.

tsadek—Hebrew letter צ for the sound "ts"; also, a righteous or wise man (pl. tsadikim).

tsures—trouble.

vey iz mir—lit. "woe is me"; often used with "Oy."

vi a toytn bankes—lit. "like cupping a dead man," i.e., applying suction cups to a corpse to improve circulation, etc.; a worthless or pointless activity.

yeshiva—school for advanced Jewish education.

Yidngas—Jewish street; Jewish neighborhood in a small town.

Yidnshtot—Jewish Town; Jewish neighborhood in a big city, specifically the name given to the Prague ghetto.

yikhes—stature; respect due to someone because of their stature, usually as a scholar.

zogerke—female speaker.

ACKNOWLEDGMENTS

I normally thank three people: my agent, my editor, and my wife for putting up with me.

But everything about this massive project has been at least five times harder than my previous work, and the acknowledgments are no exception. A *lot* of people helped bring this one to fruition. But the places of honor go to:

S.J. Rozan and Linda Landrigan

[Typesetter: please highlight these names with actual
working neon tubes (if practical).]

These fabulous women gave their time and expertise, reading early drafts and giving me crucial advice and confidence, as well as helping me find the main character's center. Their place in heaven is assured (with an unobstructed view, not too near the choir).

Special thanks are also due to Dr. Robert Goldenberg, Professor of History and Judaic Studies at SUNY Stony Brook, and to Dr. Robert Hoberman, Professor of Linguistics and Judaic and Middle Eastern Studies at SUNY Stony Brook, whose comments prevented me from making several errors. Of course, I also took fictional liberties with a few well-known historical details in order to fit them into the story: Rabbi Loew's famous visit to Rudolf II's castle reportedly took place in February, not March; the name

Our Lady of Terezín is a deliberate anachronism (the actual place name dates from the eighteenth century), as is the figure of Langweil (the real Antonín Langweil lived from 1791–1837, and he spent *eight years* building his model of Prague); also, the "Slonimer Rebbe" referred to in this story is not *the* Slonimer Rebbe, who is a much later figure (Rabbi Zvi Yosef Resnick, 1841–1912).

Other outside readers include my father Arnold, who spotted a couple of errors that only a scientist would spot, and my brother Steve, for his perspective and for his sociopolitical contributions, without which this book would have been a lot harder to write. Thanks to Laura Leis and Emily Krump at Morrow Books for their bright-eyed assistance with the midwifery of this book. Thanks also to Barbara D'Amato for her early support of this project.

Thanks to the members of the Faculty Association of Suffolk Community College/NYSUT-AFT Local 3038 and all my colleagues and superiors at SCCC for their support and for guiding me through the promotion and sabbatical application process, which was necessary for my sanity and went a long way toward making this book a reality, including Sarah Mackey Acunzo, Marie Hanna, Joseph Inners, Andrea Macari, Shaun McKay, Kevin Peterman, Rita Sakitt, Ellen Schuler Mauk, the infamous Prof. Dave Moriarty ("the Napoleon of crime"), Sandra Susman Palmer, Elaine Preston, Jane Shearer, Doreen Wald, and the staff in the Office of Instruction: Denise, Julie, Marie, and Marilyn. Thanks also to my student Tom Jordan, for letting me use one of his lines, Dana Loewy for the Prague connection, Daniel Vendrell for the Latin lesson, Konrad Bieber for the German books, and Patrick Kelso for providing the Jewish/ Christian calendar for the year 5352/1592.

Other notables include Michael and Mary Mart of the Good Times Bookstore for all the books over the years, including the hard-to-find large format facsimile of the *Prague Haggadah*; James M. Gannon, Deputy Chief of Investigations, Cold Case Unit, Morris County, NJ, for his interrogation techniques; Nancy K. Yost for her display of selflessness in recommending my current agent; Donald Maass for giving me some free advice; Prof. Sara Lipton for getting me started in the right direction; John Westermann for his early comments; Angel B. Peña for his support; Mick and Keith for "Backstreet Girl"; Eddie Sullivan and Matthew Hochman at IMS for handling the Macintosh computer troubles; and my own personal "rabbi," Dr. Carolyn Schwartz, for all her useful advice and counsel.

I would also like to thank the staff at the Museum of the City of Prague, who were so helpful with information about Langweil's model (except for one guy, who was kind of a prick, but that's how it is everywhere. Why should Prague be any different?); Aaron Kornblum of the Western Jewish History Center at the Judas L. Magnes Museum, for finding the information about Eva Kohen Bacharach; Zachary Baker of Stanford University; and Elise Fischer, Brad Sabin Hill, Yeshaya Metal, Vital Zajka, the late, great Dina Abramowicz, and the rest of the staff at the YIVO Institute in New York for providing access to rare books, articles, and documents.

Any novel with a plot and subject matter this ambitious requires a great deal of research. For general background, and to help re-create the spirit and consciousness of another age, I have fictionalized information—ideas, facts, and quotes—from scholarly, religious, and historical sources found mainly in the following works:

Israel Abrahams, *Jewish Life in the Middle Ages*; George Alter, *Two Renaissance Astronomers: David Gans, Joseph Delmedigo*; Bengt Ankarloo and Stuart Clark, *Witchcraft and Magic in Europe*; Karen Armstrong, *A History of God*; The Artscroll Mesorah Series, *Kaddish*; *Pesach*; *Shabbos*; *Shema Yisrael*; The Artscroll Tanakh Series, *Job*; *Jonah*; Hanan J. Ayalti, *Yiddish Proverbs*.

Salo Wittmayer Baron, *A Social and Religious History of the Jews*; Judith R. Baskin, *Women of the Word*; Katerina Becková, *Langweiluv Model Prahy (1826–1834)*; David Berger, "From Crusades to Blood Libels to Expulsions: Some New Approaches to Medieval Antisemitism"; Michael R. Best & Frank H. Brightman, *The Book of Secrets of Albertus Magnus*; Hayim Nahman Bialik & Yehoshua Hana Ravnitzky (William G. Braude, trans.), *The Book of Legends: Sefer Ha-Aggadah*; Abraham P. Bloch, *Day by Day in Jewish History*; R. Ben Zion Bokser, *From the World of the Cabbalah: The Philosophy of Rabbi Judah Loew of Prague*; Heinrich Bornkamm, *Luther and the Old Testament*; Lewis Browne, ed., *The Wisdom of Israel*.

Elisheva Carlebach, "Between History and Hope: Jewish Messianism in Ashkenaz and Sepharad," "Jewish-Christian Tension in Seventeenth-Century Prague: The Death of Simon Abeles," and "Discipline and Deviance: Life in the Pre-Modern Jewish Community"; Geoffrey Chaucer, "The Prioress' Tale"; Robert Chazan, *In the Year 1096*; John Robert Christianson, *On Tycho's Island*; Abraham Cohen, *Everyman's Talmud*; Mark R. Cohen, ed. and trans., *The Autobiography of a Seventeenth-Century Venetian Rabbi: Leon Modena's Life of Judah*; Bernard Dov Cooperman, ed., *Jewish Thought in the Sixteenth Century*; Petr Čornej and Jiři Pokorný, *A Brief History of the Czech Lands to 2000*.

Abraham David, ed., *A Hebrew Chronicle from Prague, c. 1615*; Peter Demetz, *Prague in Black and Gold*; Max I. Dimont, *Jews, God, and History*.

Mark U. Edwards Jr., *Luther's Last Battles*; Noah J. Efron, "Common Goods" in Diane Wolfthal, *Peace and Negotiation*; Yaffa Eliach, *There Once Was a World*; The Encyclopedia Britannica, 11th Ed.; The Encyclopedia Judaica; Frederick Engels, *The Peasant War in Germany*; R.J.W. Evans, *The Making of the Habsburg Monarchy 1550–1700* and *Rudolf II and His World*.

Avraham Yaakov Finkel, *The Great Torah Commentators*; ed. and trans., *Rambam: Maimonides' Introduction to the Mishnah*; Louis Finkelstein, ed., *The Jews: Their History, Culture, and Religion*; Solomon B. Freehof, ed., *A Treasury of Responsa*.

David Gans, *Tzemach David*; Moses Gaster, ed., *The Ma'aseh Book*; Nachum T. Gidal, *Jews in Germany*; Sylvie Anne Goldberg, *Crossing the Jabbok: Illness and Death in Ashkenazi Judaism in 16th- through 19th-century Prague*; David Goldstein, ed. and trans., *The Ashkenazi Haggadah*; Philip Goodman, *The Passover Anthology*; *Haggadah Shel Prague* (facsimile of the 1526 edition).

Barry W. Holtz, ed., *Back to the Sources*; R. Po-Chia Hsia, *The Myth of Ritual Murder* and *Trent 1475: Stories of a Ritual Murder Trial*; R. Po-Chia Hsia and Hartmut Lehmann, eds., *In and Out of the Ghetto*.

Louis Jacobs, ed., *Oxford Concise Companion to the Jewish Religion*; Alois Jirásek, *Old Czech Legends*.

Eli Katz, ed. and trans., *The Book of Fables*; Jacob Katz, *Tradition and Crisis*; Michael Katz & Gershon Schwartz, *Searching for Meaning in Midrash* and *Swimming in the Sea of Talmud*; David I. Kertzer and Marzio Barbagli, eds., *Family Life in Early Modern Times: 1500–1789*; Charles Kimball, *When Religion Becomes Evil*; Guido Kisch, "The Yellow Badge in History"; Scott-Martin Kosofsky, *The Book of Customs*; Thomas S. Kuhn, *The Copernican Revolution*; Shirley Kumove, *Words Like Arrows*; Benjamin Kuras, *As Golems Go*.

David S. Landes, *Revolution in Time*; Helen LeMay, lecture notes on the witchcraft craze of the sixteenth and seventeenth centuries; B. Barry Levy, *Planets, Potions and Parchments*; Isaac Lewin, *The Jewish Community in Poland*; John Lust, *The Herb Book*.

Jacob R. Marcus, *The Jew in the Medieval World: A Source Book*; Soňa Marešová, trans., *The Prague Golem: Jewish Stories of the Ghetto*; Christopher Marlowe, *The Jew of Malta*; Aaron Mauskopf, *The Religious Philosophy of the Maharal of Prague*; Otto Muneles, ed., *Prague Ghetto in the Renaissance Period*; the Museum of Torture in Prague (yes, there is such a place) and their guidebook, *Torture: Consideration about Tools*.

Jacob Neusner, trans., *The Mishnah*.

Iona Opie & Moira Tatem, *A Dictionary of Superstitions*.

Raphael Patai, *Gates to the Old City*; Eduard Petiška, *The Golem*; Eduard Petiška and Jan M. Dolan, *Beautiful Stories of Golden Prague*; Shlomo Pines, "Jewish Philosophy," in the *Encyclopedia of Philosophy*; *Pinkas Slonim*; Dennis Prager and Joseph Telushkin, "Why The Jews?"; Alexandr Putík, Eva Kosáková, & Dana Cabanová, *Jewish Customs and Traditions*; Alexandr Putík et al., *History of the Jews in Bohemia and Moravia*.

A. A. Roback, *The Story of Yiddish Literature*; Yaakov Rosenblatt, *Maharal: Emerging Patterns*; Leo Rosten, *Leo Rosten's Treasury of Jewish Quotations*; Cecil Roth, "The Feast of Purim and the Origins of the Blood Accusation," *History of the Jews*, and *The Jews in the Renaissance*; Ruth Rubin, *Voices of a People*; Ctibor Rybár, *Jewish Prague*.

Vladimír Sadek, "Rabbi Loew—Sa Vie, Héritage Pedagogique et sa Légende" and "Social Aspects in the Works of Prague Rabbi Löw"; Gershom Scholem, *Kabbalah, Major Trends in Jewish Mysticism*, and *Zohar: The Book of Splendor*; Jiřina Šedinová, "Old

Czech Legends in the Work of D. Gans"; Moses Shulvass, *Jewish Culture in Eastern Europe: The Classical Period*; Israel W. Slotki, trans., *Niddah*; Jaroslava Staňková, Jiři Štursa, Svatopluk Voděra, *Prague: Eleven Centuries of Architecture*; Adin Steinsaltz, *The Essential Talmud; The Talmud: A Reference Guide*; ed. and trans., *Ketubot*; Raphael Straus, "The 'Jewish Hat' as an Aspect of Social History."

Joseph Telushkin, *Jewish Literacy*; Frederic Thieberger, *The Great Rabbi Loew of Prague;* Joshua Trachtenberg, *Jewish Magic and Superstition* and *The Devil and the Jews*; Isadore Twersky, ed., *A Maimonides Reader.*

Milada Vilímková, *The Prague Ghetto*; Max Weinreich, *History of the Yiddish Language.*

Aryeh Wineman, *Ethical Tales from the Kabbalah* and *Mystic Tales from the Zohar*; Israel Zinberg, *A History of Jewish Literature*, vol. 6.

Thanks also to the moms, Victoria Peña and Judy Wishnia, for helping us out when the proverbial wolves were howling at the door.

AND NOW IT'S TIME to thank my agent, Leigh Feldman, for believing in me, for her enthusiasm and professionalism, and above all for helping me break out of the gulag; my editor, Jennifer Brehl, for her sharp eye and wit, for taking the time to nurture this book, and for saving me from my own excesses (these gals are a dream team, the best agent and editor anyone could ask for); and my wife, Mercy Peña, for putting up with long periods of economic sacrifice while I was working on this and, of course, for putting up with me in general.

And finally, thanks to God, who took a few minutes off one busy morning to *personally* take care of a few details that made this all possible (and who even gave me some good punctuation advice). All I asked for was a shot at this, and You gave it to me. Thanks, man. You rock. Totally.

Turn the page to find out what happened to Kassy the wise woman after she was banished from Prague, and before she met Benyamin and Rabbi Loew on the road to Poznan.

Burning Twilight

When rubles fall from heaven, there is no sack.
When there is a sack, rubles don't fall.

—Russian proverb

WE WILL MEET AGAIN UNDER THE STARS, the old woman had said. But by the time Kassy reached the village, it was too late. The old woman was gone.

Now she sat alone, hunched by the campfire, wrapped in a long black cloak, trying to keep warm until her supper was ready.

The wind blew the flames of the campfire low and ruffled the gamecock's feathers. The proud creature flapped its wings and pecked at the length of twine tethering its leg to a tree.

Although it kept her fed, Kassy worried that if the mountain folk kept paying her with live animals, she wouldn't be able to afford to buy another book as long as she lived.

But some sense of obligation to the spirit of her onetime guide and mentor had driven her to spend the past three days teaching the old woman's apprentice some of the secrets of their trade. The girl's name was Paulina, and thankfully she was a quick learner.

Kassy had been banished from the imperial city and expressly prohibited from entering any village or town of more than five hundred souls, and from practicing her herbal remedies in any one place for more than three days at a time, a sentence that doomed her to being a perpetual stranger in her own land.

Her practice had been destroyed. The bottles smashed. The books and papers burned. She had to start all over with nothing but the clothes on her back and a crude bundle of supplies that her friends had rescued from the flames.

And of course, no man wants a woman who's been publicly gagged and pilloried—especially if she's unrepentant about it and doesn't care who knows it.

By the morning of the third day, some of the villagers had taken to calling her Kassy the Wise, but others weren't so found of her wisdom. They came for her with that icy look in their eyes that said her time was up, and that nobody needed the services of a traveling female apothecary.

"Leave our village," they said, as the menfolk stood in the roadway, squinting into the afternoon sun, and made sure that Kassy ran the gauntlet of their stares and left the village by sundown.

Kassy watched the fading orange glow in the western sky. The last rays of the setting sun brought out the green in her eyes and highlighted the blond streaks in her long brown hair.

Once upon a time these mountains had been her home, and she knew them well. So she was not surprised when the sound of early springtime revels reached her from the nearby village, where they would soon be dancing around painted maypoles and making hasty love matches.

Her only companions on this cold evening were the arrogant gamecock and a battered copy of Paracelsus that had been readable when she had gotten it at the flea market a few months back in exchange for curing the bookseller's child of a high fever. But now the cover was gone, along with the last three sewn signatures, which meant that she was missing at least forty-eight pages. Still, she drew inspiration from the alchemist's most ambitious theories, even if they ended in mid-sentence, especially his unrealized dream of being able to refine plants and minerals to the point that their "active principles" could be applied more effectively, possibly by boiling their essences down to a thick syrup that would cure all manner of ailments and illnesses.

All things were possible, at least in our thoughts. Our bodies, the frail mortal shells that briefly house our eternal souls, were not in the least bit godlike. But our minds, illuminated by the divine secret of the knowledge of good and evil, were close to godlike. It said so in the book of Genesis.

The dusky path of exile had taken Kassy north and east, toward the Catholic lands. She was a Hussite, like the majority of Bohemians, but she had also learned something from the Jews of Prague. A book by one of their rabbis, now lost to the ashes, had proposed that each day that a person devotes to righteous acts translates into one more luminescent stitch in the celestial garment worn by their soul in the World-to-Come. Under such a system, Kassy figured that she might manage a loincloth at best if she didn't increase her righteous days, and quickly, too. It simply wouldn't do to be uncovered for all eternity in the Garden of Paradise.

The gamecock scratched around in the dirt, preening and searching for its mate.

By now the sky was darkening, and Kassy could just make out the angry red star in the Hyades that marked the heavenly bull's unblinking eye, and the bright cluster of stars a few degrees to its west.

Most people in the city could barely make out the six brightest stars in the Pleiades. Those with the sharpest eyes saw seven. But on a clear, moonless night like this, she could usually see at least nine, with the distinct impression of still more lying beyond them, a glorious cluster of stars drifting in a cloudy haze.

She drew her cloak close around her. It wasn't dark enough to see the stars clearly yet, but the curtain of night fell quickly in these mountains, which lay at the crossroads between the two mighty kingdoms of the Teutons and the Poles.

A ghostly sparkle caught the corner of her eye, and she turned reflexively. A pair of fiery marbles glowed in the dark just beyond the circle of firelight. The cock squawked and pecked at the disembodied spheres, but Kassy saw right away that it was only a cat straying from the village, her feline eyes catching the light in the way cats' eyes sometimes did that caused them to flash like two tiny mirrors floating in the darkness.

In spite of this knowledge, her heart had still jumped for an instant, and she understood how some of the backward mountain folk could easily be terrorized by the sight. What could possibly cause such an eerie effect? Everyone knew that cats could see well in the dark, but how did their eyes *glow* like that? What was the mechanism? She shivered, and lost the next thought before it even had a chance to form. She would have to look into the matter some other time, after she had finally settled somewhere and could begin attracting regular customers and restocking her laboratory.

The cock squawked and kicked up a minor dust storm, metamorphosing into a swirl of red-and-black feathers, but Kassy placed a burlap sack over its head, and it quieted down. Then she dipped a wooden stirrer into the pot simmering over the fire, fished out a tasty morsel of chicken, blew on it, and held it out with her long, delicate fingers. The cat's whiskers twitched, her muzzle a shiny black mask ringed with a mane of a bright orange fur. She was a genuine calico, a real mixture of everything. She padded toward Kassy's outstretched fingers, keeping low and wary. Kassy kept still as the cat crept closer. Its whiskers twitched, then twitched again, then it lunged, teeth flashing, and the bit of meat vanished from Kassy's fingers.

Kassy could hear the cat purring.

"Looks like I've made a new friend," she said to the pine needles and the stars above.

Suddenly the cat's ears pricked up, and she sprang off into the underbrush.

Leaves rustled as someone came running through the forest from the direction of the village. Kassy steeled herself for the worst, then a sturdy young woman pushed through the branches and stumbled into the clearing. It was Paulina, who had been drafted to be the midwife's new assistant. She stopped, breathing hard, her round face flushed and glistening, reflecting the glow from the fire.

"Miss Častava!" she said, using the Czech form of Kassy's name. "Thank God you're here. Mrs. Svoboda's baby doesn't want to come out and we need your help."

Kassy leapt to her feet, took the simmering pot off the fire and hung it from a branch. Then she gathered the ingredients for a groaning cake: dried woodruff, caraway seeds, and some flowering buds from the broad-leafed hemp plant.

The sky was still glowing with the faint purple of twilight, but the darkness was stealing up on them fast and rain clouds were gathering on the horizon.

No stargazing tonight, Kassy thought, as they hurried through the village square. A number of idlers watched Kassy's every move as she squeezed through the crowd gathered around a wagon watching a traveling company's Whitsunday pageant (though the holiday was still several weeks off), and stepped through the low doorway onto the dirt floor of the Svobodas' cottage.

Irina Svoboda lay on a birthing stool in the middle of the bare floor, sweating and straining and squeezing her husband's hand while Mrs. Lenka, the midwife, wiped her forehead with a damp rag.

The husband didn't even look up when Kassy came in with her bundle of herbs and got a quick summary from the midwife: Irina was in her seventh hour of labor, with minimal widening of the birth canal, and was suffering from terrible cramps and a low-grade fever.

Kassy sent Paulina out for a couple of fresh eggs, then kneeled by the hearth to prepare the cake. She mixed the flour with the woodruff and caraway, mashed the butter and a sprinkle of sugar together with the hemp in a separate bowl, then greased the pan with more butter—the butter was essential: it didn't work without the butter—and waited for the girl to come back with the eggs.

Outside in the square, the grim drama reached its climax as the Antichrist was unmasked as a Jew, who admitted under pain of death that for fifteen hundred years his people had kidnapped and murdered Christian children, poisoned Christian patients, and robbed Christian customers, all because of a perverse, soul-consuming hatred for the good people whose only offense was their heartfelt belief in the Son of God.

Paulina stoked the fire, and by the time Kassy put the cake in the pan, the performance had reached its satirical conclusion, as the tragic death-of-winter scenario was transformed into a bawdy springtime celebration of fertility in all its forms. Purged of sinful feelings by collectively witnessing the downfall of a common enemy, the townsfolk were free to vent their long-suppressed desires by joining the actors and prancing around the stage to the beat of drums and tambourines, singing, *The lawyer with his screed, The Jew with his greed, And what lies under a woman's dress; These three things make the world a mess!*

The lewd songs swelled with voices high and low, bumping and pressing against the somber mood inside the cottage, until Kassy could barely hear Irina calling her husband's name: "Ludye, Ludye . . ."

"Yes, my dear," said Ludyek. "Don't worry. Everything's going to be fine now that the lady apothecary's here," he said, giving Kassy a dark look that warned her not to make a liar out of him.

Kassy ignored him. She had worked closely with midwives like Mrs. Lenka before, so she did her part without having to be told what to do, massaging the travailing woman's neck and shoulders and laying warm towels around her belly while the midwife handled the delivery. Ludyek sat there holding his wife's hand, whispering soft words and snatches of prayers, as the midwife enlarged the opening around the shiny whorl of hair on the baby's head, and encouraged Irina to be strong and push some more. The skin beneath the baby's hair was slowly changing from red to purple.

Kassy brushed some loose hair out of her eyes, and was tucking the tiny gold cross on a silver chain back inside her blouse when Irina took Kassy's hand and said that she liked looking at the way the cross sparkled in the candlelight, so Kassy left it dangling there for her to fix her eyes on.

Soon she was feeding Irina bits of the cake along with soothing sips of cold water, while repeating a Latin prayer asking for God's protection. Kassy didn't believe in the healing power of the strange old words themselves, but many of her charges felt better because *they believed* in such powers. The mind's influence over the bodily humors had always fascinated her, and the effect was certainly worthy of further study.

The cake eventually brought Irina some relief, but by then Kassy was sweating under her clothes as she and the midwife worked against the dying light of the fire. Then without being asked, Paulina wiped the perspiration from Kassy's forehead and began rubbing the knot that had formed at the base of her neck with her free hand, and Kassy felt her shoulders relax a little. She thanked Paulina with her eyes.

Then the midwife finally got a grip on the baby's head and neck and pulled down and out.

A stream of new voices joined the whirlpool of passions rushing by the front window.

But even as the chaos swirled around them on all sides, a cool stillness fell like a shroud over the Svobodas' rooms.

Irina clutched Kassy's arm as Paulina wrapped the blue mass of flesh in sackcloth.

"At least wrap her in a clean towel," the midwife said softly.

Irina's face was as pale as wax. Her husband stared blankly ahead. Then he remembered where he was and tried to give Kassy a stone-cold stare, but all the hardness drained out of his face when his wife said, "Bless you all for trying to help," in a faint dry croak.

His eyes dropped to his hands, which were smeared with blood.

"I'll prepare you something—" Kassy could barely get the words out. "Something—to help build your strength back up."

She stayed to wash the mixing bowls and the pan she had used to make the cake while Paulina wiped off the birthing stool and swept the floor, and the midwife burned twice-blessed herbs in the four corners of the house.

Kassy carefully taught Paulina the Psalm for these occasions in plain Czech so that the simple folk would understand and take comfort from the words: *If I say that the darkness shall cover me, and the light be night about me, I must remember that the darkness and the light are alike to Thee, for Thou hast formed my innards; Thou hast knit me together in my mother's womb. I will praise thee, for I am wondrously made. Thine eyes did see my unformed flesh, and all my days are written in Thy book.*

The girl wanted to learn more, but Kassy told her to think about it long and hard, because there was precious little room in this world for women like herself.

Eventually, Kassy had to trudge back toward her campfire through the drizzling rain, ignoring the eyes of men and the filthy barefoot boys fondling bits of wood and stone to hurl at the effigy of a Jew that was being raised in the town square. The villagers listened open-mouthed as the local priest condemned the straw man of *okrucienstwo Zydowskie*, Jewish bestiality, then set the hateful thing on fire.

Kassy was fighting off the oppressive feeling that nothing would ever make the pain of this failure go away. But something else weighed heavily on her mind as well, the creeping sensation that the ways of the wise women were slowly disappearing, and she couldn't help wondering if she had been born in the wrong place at the wrong time, maybe even the wrong century altogether.

She found a little gift from her feline friend waiting for her on the ground beside the dying embers. A small gray mouse lay on the dirt, its legs stiff and lifeless. She was grateful that the cat had made a clean kill of it, because even mouse blood would have bothered her just then.

"Good girl," she said, kneeling to scratch behind the cat's ears and running her fingers through her thick orange-black fur. Then she picked up the mouse by the tail and tossed it into the woods.

She rewarded the cat with another bite of meat. Then she fanned the coals until the fire came back to life, laid a piece of wood on the newly glowing embers, and sat in front of the fire for a good long while, waiting for the dull flames to warm her up.

She closed her eyes, but she still saw the clotted clumps of scarlet and the shiny blue skin of the stillborn child like scenes from a magic lantern. The images made her shudder. Because the wise women who helped to coax difficult babies into this world labored under the constant suspicion that when no one was watching, they would go slinking off into the night with the blood-gorged remains of the afterbirth and umbilical cord to perform black magic with them, and God help you if they accused you of offering the child up to the Devil by killing it at the moment of delivery. She had watched helplessly as an old woman was stoned to death on the steps of the cathedral for just such a crime. She could still hear their voices:

"What are the charges against me?" the woman demanded.

"You should be able to figure them out for yourself," her accuser replied.

Kassy squeezed the cross around her neck. She could just picture herself trying to explain to an examining magistrate who didn't know a birth canal from a carpenter's bit that sometimes it just happens that way—a child is stillborn, and you are left with empty hands. There's no evil involved, it's just nature's way.

The cat brushed against her leg, looking for attention.

"Now what?" she said. "Don't tell me I need to think up a name for you."

She scratched the cat under the chin.

"But you must have one already. What is it? Calixta? Pyewacket? Nibbles?"

Then she heard it. She looked to the west. At first it looked like a cluster of stars gliding toward her through the forest. But the flickering shadows were all too human.

Villagers with torches.

They came after her with ropes to tie her hands and chains to weigh her down, for the rivers were deep and swift in this part of the wilderness.

Kassy grabbed her bundle and ran to the northeast, leaving the gamecock and all else behind.

The shadows grew longer, and a thick darkness spread over the land.

The lighter side of HISTORY

* Look for this seal on select historical fiction titles from Harper. Books bearing it contain special bonus materials, including timelines, interviews with the author, and insights into the real-life events that inspired the book, as well as recommendations for further reading.

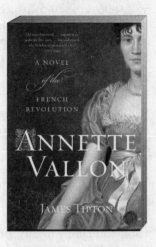

ANNETTE VALLON:
A Novel of the French Revolution
by James Tipton
978-0-06-082222-4 (paperback)
For fans of Tracy Chevalier and Sarah
Dunant comes this vibrant, alluring debut
novel of a compelling, independent woman
who would inspire one of the world's
greatest poets and survive a nation's bloody
transformation.

BOUND: A Novel
by Sally Gunning
978-0-06-124026-3 (paperback)
An indentured servant finds herself bound
by law, society, and her own heart in colonial Cape Cod.

CASSANDRA & JANE: A Jane Austen Novel
by Jill Pitkeathley
978-0-06-144639-9 (paperback)
The relationship between Jane Austen and her sister—explored through
the letters that might have been.

THE CONFESSION OF KATHERINE HOWARD
by Suzannah Dunn
978-0-06-201147-3 (paperback)
The gripping story of Katherine Howard, Henry VIII's fifth wife, and
the best friend she nearly took down with her.

A CROWNING MERCY: A Novel
by Bernard Cornwell and Susannah Kells
978-0-06-172438-1 (paperback)
A rebellious young Puritan woman embarks on a
daring journey to win love and a secret fortune.

DANCING WITH MR. DARCY:
Stories Inspired by Jane Austen and Chawton House Library
Edited by Sarah Waters
978-0-06-199906-2 (paperback)
An anthology of the winning entries in the
Jane Austen Short Story Award 2009.

DARCY'S STORY
by Janet Aylmer
978-0-06-114870-5 (paperback)
Read Mr. Darcy's side of the story—*Pride
and Prejudice* from a new perspective.

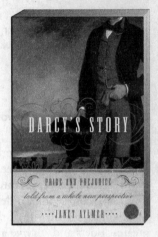

DEAREST COUSIN JANE:
A Jane Austen Novel
by Jill Pitkeathley
978-0-06-187598-4 (paperback)
An inventive reimagining of the intriguing
and scandalous life of Jane Austen's cousin.

THE FALLEN ANGELS: A Novel
by Bernard Cornwell and Susannah Kells
978-0-06-172545-6 (paperback)
In the sequel to *A Crowning Mercy*, Lady Campion Lazender's courage,
faith, and family loyalty are tested when she must complete a perilous
journey between two worlds.

A FATAL WALTZ: A Novel of Suspense
by Tasha Alexander
978-0-06-117423-0 (paperback)
Caught in a murder mystery, Emily must do the unthinkable to save her
fiancé: bargain with her ultimate nemesis, the Countess von Lange.

THE FIFTH SERVANT: A Novel
by Kenneth Wishnia
978-0-06-172538-8 (paperback)
In 16th century Prague, a young Christian girl is murdered on the eve
of Passover, and the city's entire Jewish population is threatened.

FIGURES IN SILK: A Novel
by Vanora Bennett
978-0-06-168985-7 (paperback)
The art of silk making, political intrigue, and a
sweeping love story all interwoven in the fate of two
sisters.

THE GENTLEMAN POET:
A Novel of Love, Danger, and Shakespeare's The Temptest
by Kathryn Johnson
978-0-06-196531-9 (paperback)
A wonderful story that tells the tale of how William Shakespeare may have come to his inspiration for *The Tempest*.

JULIA AND THE MASTER OF MORANCOURT: A Novel
by Janet Aylmer
978-0-06-167295-8 (paperback)
Amidst family tragedy, Julia travels all over England, desperate to marry the man she loves instead of the arranged suitor preferred by her mother.

KEPT: A Novel
by D. J. Taylor
978-0-06-114609-1 (paperback)
A gorgeously intricate, dazzling reinvention of Victorian life and passions that is also a riveting investigation into some of the darkest, most secret chambers of the human heart.

THE KING'S DAUGHTER: A Novel
by Christie Dickason
978-0-06-197627-8 (paperback)
A superb historical novel of the Jacobean court, in which Princess Elizabeth, daughter of James I, strives to avoid becoming her father's pawn in the royal marriage market.

THE MIRACLES OF PRATO: A Novel
by Laurie Albanese and Laura Morowitz
978-0-06-155835-1 (paperback)
The unforgettable story of a nearly impossible romance between a painter-monk (the renowned artist Fra Filippo Lippi) and the young nun who becomes his muse, his lover, and the mother of his children.

PORTRAIT OF AN UNKNOWN WOMAN: A Novel
by Vanora Bennett
978-0-06-125256-3 (paperback)
Meg, adopted daughter of Sir Thomas More, narrates the tale of a famous Holbein painting and the secrets it holds.

THE PRINCESS OF NOWHERE: A Novel
by Prince Lorenzo Borghese
978-0-06-172161-8 (paperback)
From a descendant of Napoleon Bonaparte's brother-in-law comes a historical novel about his famous ancestor, Princess Pauline Bonaparte Borghese.

THE QUEEN'S LOVER: A Novel
by Vanora Bennett
978-0-06-168987-1 (paperback)
In this sweeping historical love story, Catherine de Valois is a courageous woman who becomes the queen of two countries by making her own rules.

THE QUEEN'S SORROW: A Novel of Mary Tudor
by Suzannah Dunn
978-0-06-170427-7 (paperback)
Queen of England Mary Tudor's reign is brought low by abused power and a forbidden love.

REBECCA: The Classic Tale of Romantic Suspense
by Daphne du Maurier
978-0-380-73040-7 (paperback)
Follow the second Mrs. Maxim de Winter down the lonely drive to Manderley, where Rebecca once ruled.

REBECCA'S TALE: A Novel
by Sally Beauman
978-0-06-117467-4 (paperback)
Unlock the dark secrets and old worlds of Rebecca de Winter's life with investigator Colonel Julyan.

THE SIXTH WIFE: A Novel of Katherine Parr
by Suzannah Dunn
978-0-06-143156-2 (paperback)
Kate Parr survived four years of marriage to King Henry VIII, but a new love may undo a lifetime of caution.

WATERMARK: A Novel of the Middle Ages
by Vanitha Sankaran
978-0-06-184927-5 (paperback)
A compelling debut about the search for identiy, the power of self-expression, and value of the written word.